THE SUMMER QUEEN

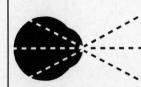

THE SUMMER QUEEN

A NOVEL OF ELEANOR OF AQUITAINE

ELIZABETH CHADWICK

THORNDIKE PRESS
A part of Gale, Cengage Learning

GALE
CENGAGE Learning·

Farmington Hills, Mich • San Francisco • New York • Waterville, Maine
Meriden, Conn • Mason, Ohio • Chicago

LIBRARY OF CONGRESS CATALOGING-IN-PUBLICATION DATA

Chadwick, Elizabeth, 1957–
    The summer queen : a novel of Eleanor of Aquitaine / by Elizabeth Chadwick. — Large print edition.
      pages cm. — (Thorndike Press large print historical fiction)
    Includes bibliographical references.
    ISBN 978-1-4104-8523-6 (hardcover) — ISBN 1-4104-8523-4 (hardcover)
    1. Eleanor, of Aquitaine, Queen, consort of Henry II, King of England, 1122?-1204—Fiction. 2. France—History—Louis VII, 1137-1180—Fiction. 3. Large type books. I. Title.
PR6053.H245S86 2015
823'.914—dc23   2015033688

Published in 2015 by arrangement with Sourcebooks, Inc.

Printed in Mexico
1 2 3 4 5 6 7 19 18 17 16 15

NOTE FOR READERS

I have called Eleanor "Alienor" in the body of the novel, rather than Eleanor, because Alienor is what she would have called herself and it is how her name appears in her charters and in the Anglo-Norman texts where she is mentioned. I felt it was fitting to give her that recognition.

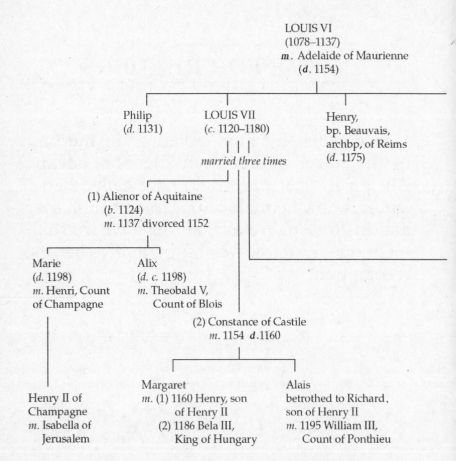

LOUIS VI
(1078–1137)
m. Adelaide of Maurienne
(*d*. 1154)

Philip
(*d*. 1131)

LOUIS VII
(*c*. 1120–1180)

| | |

married three times

Henry,
bp. Beauvais,
archbp, of Reims
(*d*. 1175)

(1) Alienor of Aquitaine
(*b*. 1124)
m. 1137 divorced 1152

Marie
(*d*. 1198)
m. Henri, Count
of Champagne

Alix
(*d. c*. 1198)
m. Theobald V,
Count of Blois

(2) Constance of Castile
m. 1154 *d*.1160

Henry II of
Champagne
m. Isabella of
Jerusalem

Margaret
m. (1) 1160 Henry, son
of Henry II
(2) 1186 Bela III,
King of Hungary

Alais
betrothed to Richard,
son of Henry II
m. 1195 William III,
Count of Ponthieu

The family

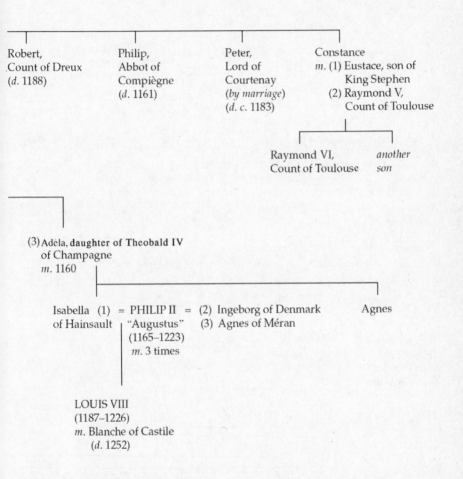

Robert,
Count of Dreux
(*d.* 1188)

Philip,
Abbot of
Compiègne
(*d.* 1161)

Peter,
Lord of
Courtenay
(*by marriage*)
(*d. c.* 1183)

Constance
m. (1) Eustace, son of
        King Stephen
    (2) Raymond V,
        Count of Toulouse

Raymond VI,   *another*
Count of Toulouse   *son*

(3) Adéla, daughter of Theobald IV
    of Champagne
    m. 1160

Isabella (1) = PHILIP II = (2) Ingeborg of Denmark   Agnes
of Hainsault   "Augustus"   (3) Agnes of Méran
               (1165–1223)
               m. 3 times

LOUIS VIII
(1187–1226)
m. Blanche of Castile
    (*d.* 1252)

of Louis VII of France

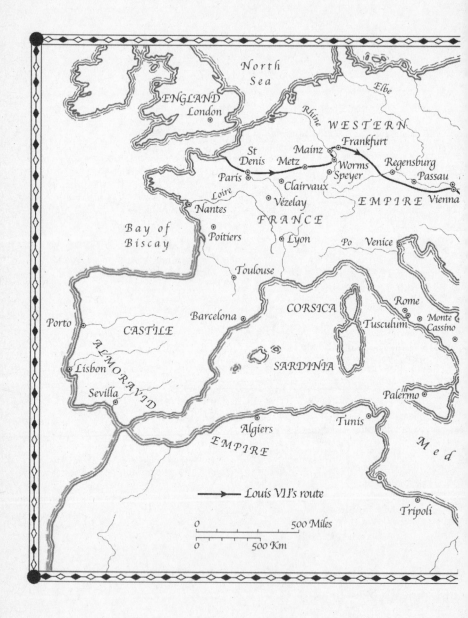

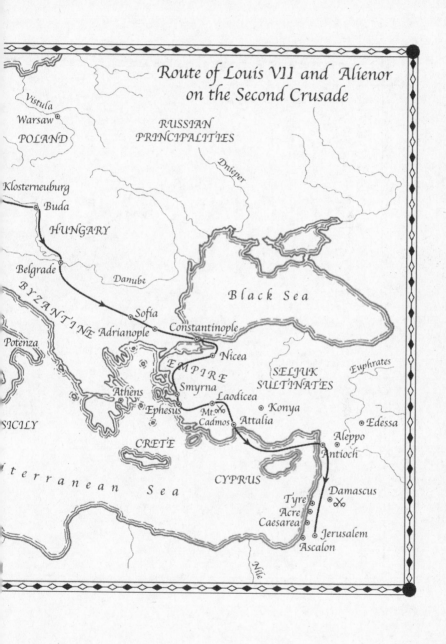

Route of Louis VII and Alienor
on the Second Crusade

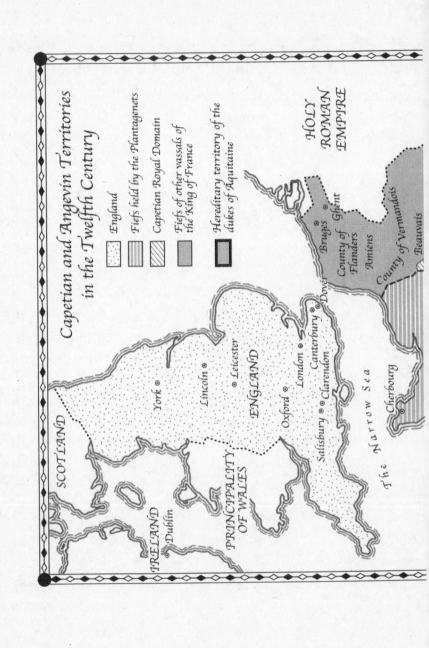

Capetian and Angevin Territories
in the Twelfth Century

England
Fiefs held by the Plantagenets
Capetian Royal Domain
Fiefs of other vassals of
the King of France
Hereditary territory of the
dukes of Aquitaine

SCOTLAND

IRELAND
Dublin

PRINCIPALITY
OF WALES

ENGLAND
York
Lincoln
Leicester
Oxford
London
Canterbury
Salisbury   Clarendon
Dover
Cherbourg

The Narrow Sea

HOLY
ROMAN
EMPIRE

County of Flanders
Ghent
Bruges
Amiens
Beauvais
County of Vermandois

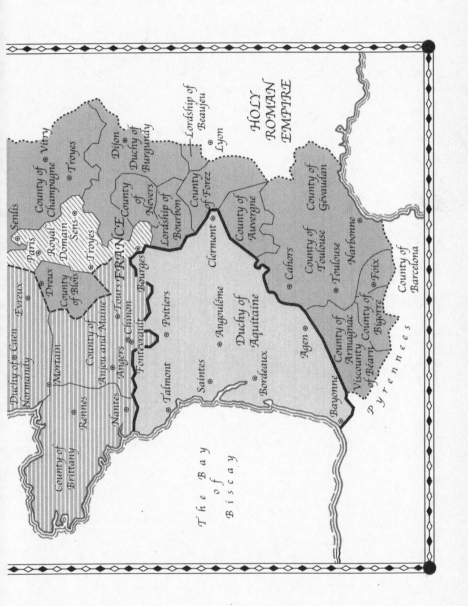

HOLY ROMAN EMPIRE

Lordship of Beaujeu

Lyon

County of Gévaudan

County of Vitry

County of Champagne

Troyes

Dijon

Duchy of Burgundy

County of Nevers

County of Forez

County of Auvergne

County of Toulouse

Narbonne

County of Barcelona

Senlis

Paris

Royal Domain

Sens

Troyes

FRANCE

Lordship of Bourbon

Clermont

Cahors

Toulouse

Foix

County of Foix

County of Narbonne

Dreux

Evreux

County of Blois

Tours

Bourges

Angoulême

Duchy of Aquitaine

Agen

County of Armagnac

Viscounty of Béarn

County of Bigorre

Bigorre

Pyrenees

Duchy of Caen Normandy

Mortain

County of Anjou and Maine

Angers

Chinon

Fontevrault

Poitiers

Saintes

Bordeaux

Bayonne

Rennes

County of Brittany

Nantes

Talmont

The Bay of Biscay

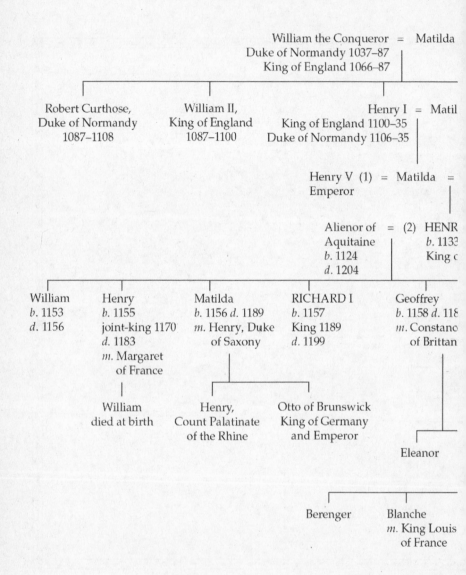

William the Conqueror = Matilda
Duke of Normandy 1037–87
King of England 1066–87

Robert Curthose, | William II, | Henry I = Matil
Duke of Normandy | King of England | King of England 1100–35
1087–1108 | 1087–1100 | Duke of Normandy 1106–35

Henry V (1) = Matilda =
Emperor

Alienor of = (2) HENR
Aquitaine b. 113
b. 1124 King o
d. 1204

William | Henry | Matilda | RICHARD I | Geoffrey
b. 1153 | b. 1155 | b. 1156 d. 1189 | b. 1157 | b. 1158 d. 118
d. 1156 | joint-king 1170 | m. Henry, Duke | King 1189 | m. Constanc
| d. 1183 | of Saxony | d. 1199 | of Brittan
| m. Margaret | | |
| of France | | |

William
died at birth

Henry, | Otto of Brunswick
Count Palatinate | King of Germany
of the Rhine | and Emperor

Eleanor

Berenger | Blanche
| m. King Louis
| of France

The Norman and Ange

of Flanders

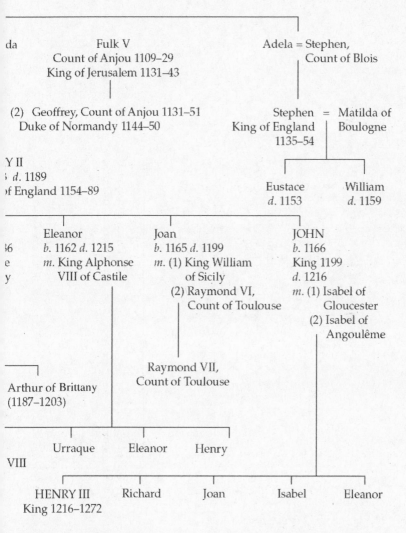

da   Fulk V
Count of Anjou 1109–29
King of Jerusalem 1131–43

(2) Geoffrey, Count of Anjou 1131–51
Duke of Normandy 1144–50

Y II
; d. 1189
of England 1154–89

Adela = Stephen,
Count of Blois

Stephen = Matilda of
King of England   Boulogne
1135–54

Eustace   William
d. 1153   d. 1159

Eleanor
b. 1162 d. 1215
m. King Alphonse
VIII of Castile

Joan
b. 1165 d. 1199
m. (1) King William
of Sicily
(2) Raymond VI,
Count of Toulouse

JOHN
b. 1166
King 1199
d. 1216
m. (1) Isabel of
Gloucester
(2) Isabel of
Angoulême

Raymond VII,
Count of Toulouse

Arthur of Brittany
(1187–1203)

VIII

Urraque   Eleanor   Henry

HENRY III   Richard   Joan   Isabel   Eleanor
King 1216–1272

vin kings of England

The Counts of Poitou, Dukes of Aquitaine

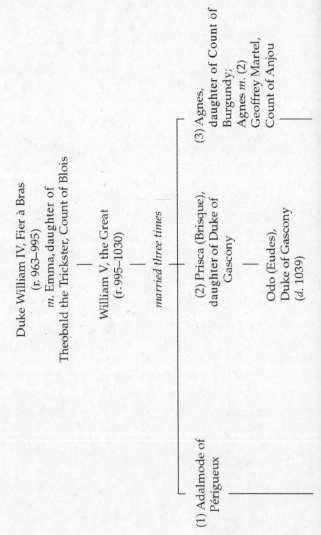

Duke William IV, Fier à Bras
(r. 963–995)
m. Emma, daughter of
Theobald the Trickster, Count of Blois

William V, the Great
(r. 995–1030)

married three times

(1) Adalmode of
Périgueux

(2) Prisca (Brisque),
daughter of Duke of
Gascony

Odo (Eudes),
Duke of Gascony
(*d.* 1039)

(3) Agnes,
daughter of Count of
Burgundy;
Agnes *m.* (2)
Geoffrey Martel,
Count of Anjou

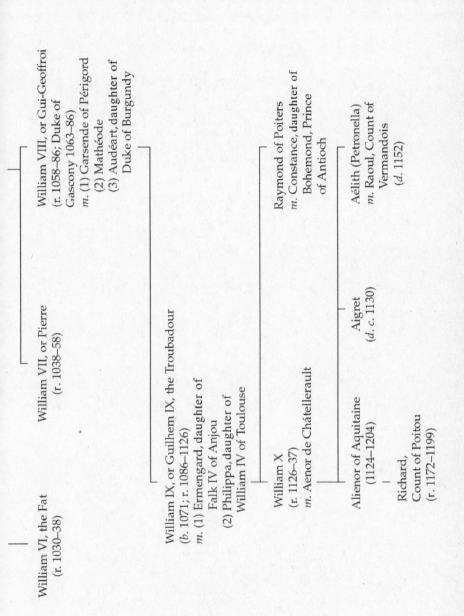

William VI, the Fat
(r. 1030–38)

William VII, or Pierre
(r. 1038–58)

William VIII, or Gui-Geoffroi
(r. 1058–86; Duke of
Gascony 1063–86)
m. (1) Garsende of Périgord
(2) Mathéode
(3) Audéart, daughter of
Duke of Burgundy

William IX, or Guilhem IX, the Troubadour
(b. 1071; r. 1086–1126)
m. (1) Ermengard, daughter of
Falk IV of Anjou
(2) Philippa, daughter of
William IV of Toulouse

Raymond of Poiters
m. Constance, daughter of
Bohemond, Prince
of Antioch

William X
(r. 1126–37)
m. Aenor de Châtellerault

Aigret
(d. c. 1130)

Aélith (Petronella)
m. Raoul, Count of
Vermandois
(d. 1152)

Alienor of Aquitaine
(1124–1204)

Richard,
Count of Poitou
(r. 1172–1199)

1

Palace of Poitiers, January 1137

Alienor woke at dawn. The tall candle that had been left to burn all night was almost a stub, and even through the closed shutters she could hear the cockerels on roosts, walls, and dung heaps, crowing the city of Poitiers awake. Mounded under the bedclothes, Petronella slumbered, dark hair spread on the pillow. Alienor crept from the bed, careful not to wake her little sister who was always grumpy when disturbed too early. Besides, Alienor wanted these moments to herself. This was no ordinary day, and once the noise and bustle began, it would not cease.

She donned the gown folded over her coffer, pushed her feet into soft kidskin shoes, and unlatched a small door in the shutters to lean out and inhale the new morning. A mild, moist breeze carried up to her the familiar scents of smoke, musty stone, and freshly baked bread. Braiding her hair with nimble fingers, she admired the alternating ribbons of charcoal, oyster, and gold striating the eastern skyline before drawing back with a pensive sigh.

Stealthily she lifted her cloak from its peg and tiptoed from the chamber. In the adjoining room, yawning, bleary-eyed maids were stirring from sleep. Alienor slipped past them like a sleek young vixen and, on light and silent feet, wound her way down the stairs of the great Maubergeonne Tower that housed the domestic quarters of the ducal palace.

A drowsy youth was setting out baskets of bread and jugs of wine on a trestle in the great hall. Alienor purloined a small loaf, warm from the oven, and went outside. Lanterns still shone in some huts and outbuildings. She heard the clatter of pots from the kitchens and a cook berating someone for spilling the milk. Familiar sounds that said all was well with the world, even on the cusp of change.

At the stables the grooms were preparing the horses for the journey. Ginnet, her dappled palfrey, and Morello, her sister's glossy black pony, still waited in their stalls, but the packhorses were harnessed and carts stood ready in the yard to carry the baggage the 150 miles south from Poitiers to Bordeaux where she and Petronella were to spend the spring and summer at the Ombrière Palace overlooking the River Garonne.

Alienor offered Ginnet a piece of new bread

on the flat of her hand and rubbed the mare's warm gray neck. "Papa doesn't have to go all the way to Compostela," she told the horse. "Why can't he stay at home with us and pray? I hate it when he goes away."

"Alienor."

She jumped and, hot with guilt, faced her father, seeing immediately from his expression that he had overheard her.

He was tall and long-limbed, his brown hair patched with gray at ears and temples. Deep creases fanned from his eye corners and gaunt hollows shadowed his well-defined cheekbones. "A pilgrimage is a serious commitment to God," he said gravely. "This is no foolish jaunt made on a whim."

"Yes, Papa." She knew the pilgrimage was important to him, indeed necessary for the good of his soul, but she still did not want him to go. He had been different of late, reserved and more obviously burdened, and she did not understand why.

He tilted her chin on his forefinger. "You are my heir, Alienor; you must behave as befits the daughter of the Duke of Aquitaine, not a sulky child."

Feeling indignant, she pulled away. She was thirteen, a year past the age of consent, and considered herself grown up, even while she still craved the security of her father's love and presence.

"I see you understand me." His brow

19

creased. "While I am gone, you are the ruler of Aquitaine. Our vassals have sworn to uphold you as my successor and you must honor their faith."

Alienor bit her lip. "I am afraid you will not come back . . ." Her voice shook. "That I shall not see you again."

"Oh, child! If God wills it, of course I shall come back." He kissed her forehead tenderly. "You have me for a little while yet. Where is Petronella?"

"Still abed, Papa. I left her to sleep."

A groom arrived to see to Ginnet and Morello. Alienor's father drew her into the courtyard where the pale gray of first light was yielding to warmer tints and colors. He gently tugged her thick braid of honey-gold hair. "Go now and wake her then. It will be a fine thing to say you have walked part of the way along the pilgrim route of Saint James."

"Yes, Papa." She gave him a long, steady look before walking away, her back straight and her step measured.

William sighed. His eldest daughter was swiftly becoming a woman. She had grown tall in the past year and developed light curves at breast and hip. She was exquisite; just looking at her intensified his pain. She was too young for what was coming. God help them all.

Petronella was awake when Alienor returned

20

to their chamber and was busily putting her favorite trinkets into a soft cloth bag ready for the journey. Floreta, their nurse and chaperone, had braided Petronella's lustrous brown hair with blue ribbons and tied it back from her face, revealing the downy curve of her cheek in profile.

"Where did you go?" Petronella demanded.

"Nowhere — just a walk. You were still asleep."

Petronella closed the drawstring on the bag and waggled the tassels at the ends of the ties. "Papa says he will bring us blessed crosses from the shrine of Saint James."

As if blessed crosses were any sort of compensation for their father's forthcoming absence, Alienor thought, but held her tongue. Petronella was eleven, but still so much the child. Despite their closeness, the two years between them was often a gulf. Alienor fulfilled the role of their deceased mother to Petronella as often as she did that of sister.

"And when he comes back after Easter, we'll have a big celebration, won't we?" Petronella's wide brown gaze sought reassurance. "Won't we?"

"Of course we will," Alienor said and hugged Petronella, taking comfort in their mutual embrace.

It was midmorning by the time the ducal

party set out for Bordeaux following a mass celebrated in the pilgrim church of Saint-Hilaire, its walls blazoned with the eagle device of the lords of Aquitaine.

Ragged scraps of pale blue patched the clouds and sudden swift spangles of sunlight flashed on horse harnesses and belt fittings. The entourage unraveled along the road like a fine thread, rainbow-woven with the silver of armor, the rich hues of expensive gowns, crimson, violet, and gold, and the contrasting muted blends of tawny and gray belonging to servants and carters. Everyone set out on foot, not just Duke William. This first day, all would walk the twenty miles to the overnight stop at Saint-Sauvant.

Alienor paced out, holding Petronella's hand on one side and lifting her gown on the other so that it would not trail in the dirt. Now and again, Petronella gave a hop and a skip. A jongleur started to sing to the accompaniment of a small harp and Alienor recognized the words of her grandfather, William, the ninth Duke of Aquitaine, who had reveled in a notorious reputation. Many of his songs were sexual in content, unsettling in their rawness and unfit for the bower, but this particular one was plangent and haunting and sent a shiver down Alienor's spine.

"I know not when I am asleep or awake
Unless someone tells me.

22

My heart is nearly bursting with a deep
  sorrow,
But I care not a fig about it,
By Saint Martial!"

Her father kept company with her and
Petronella for a while, but his stride was
longer than theirs, and gradually he drew
ahead, leaving them in the company of the
household women. Alienor watched him walk
away and fixed her gaze on his hand where it
gripped his pilgrim staff. The sapphire ring
of his ducal authority glittered at her like a
dark blue eye. She willed him to turn and
look at her, but his focus remained on the
road ahead. She felt as if he were deliberately
distancing himself, and that in a while he
would be gone completely, leaving only the
dusty imprint of his footsteps in which to set
her own.

She was not even cheered when her father's
seneschal, Geoffrey de Rancon, lord of Gençay and Taillebourg, joined her and Petronella. He was in his late twenties with rich
brown hair, deep-set eyes of dark hazel, and
a ready smile that made her feel bright inside.
She had known him since her birth because
he was one of her father's chief vassals and
military commanders. His wife had died two
years ago, but as yet he had not remarried.
Two daughters and a son from the match
meant that his need for heirs was not press-

ing. "Why so glum?" He peered around into her face. "You will darken the clouds scowling like that."

Petronella giggled and Geoffrey winked at her.

"Don't be foolish." Alienor lifted her chin and strode out.

Geoffrey matched her pace. "Then tell me what is wrong."

"Nothing," she said. "Nothing is wrong. Why should there be?"

He gave her a considering look. "Perhaps because your father is going to Compostela and leaving you in Bordeaux?"

Alienor's throat tightened. "Of course not," she snapped.

He shook his head. "You are right, I am foolish, but will you forgive me and let me walk with you a while?"

Alienor shrugged but eventually gave a grudging nod. Geoffrey clasped her hand in his and took Petronella's on his other side.

After a while, Alienor ceased frowning. Geoffrey was no substitute for her father, but his presence lifted her mood and she was able to go forward with renewed spirit.

2

Bordeaux, February 1137

Sitting before the fire in his chamber high up in the Ombrière Palace, William, the tenth Duke of Aquitaine, gazed at the documents awaiting his seal and rubbed his side.

"Sire, you are still set on this journey?"

He glanced across the hearth at the Archbishop of Bordeaux, who was warming himself before the fire, his tall spare body bulked out by fur-lined robes. Although their opinions sometimes clashed, he and Gofrid de Louroux were friends of long standing and William had appointed him tutor to his two daughters. "I am," he replied. "I want to make my peace with God while I still have time, and Compostela is close enough to reach, I think."

Gofrid gave him a troubled look. "It is getting worse, isn't it?"

William heaved an exhausted sigh. "I tell myself that many miracles are wrought at the shrine of Saint James and I shall pray for one, but in truth I am making this pilgrimage for the sake of my soul, not in expectation of a cure." He pinched the bridge of his nose. "Alienor is angry with me because she thinks I can just as easily save my soul in Bordeaux, but she does not understand that I would not be cleansed if I took that course. Here, I would be treated with leniency because I am the seigneur. On the road, on foot with my satchel and staff, I am but another pilgrim. We are all naked when we go before God, whatever our standing on earth, and that is what I must do."

"But what of your lands during your absence, sire?" Gofrid asked with concern. "Who will rule in your stead? Alienor is of marriageable age and although you have made men swear to uphold her, there will be a scramble by every baron in the land to have her to wife or else marry her to his son. Already they circle with intent, as you must have noticed. De Rancon for one. He has mourned his wife sincerely, I admit, but I suspect he has political reasons for not yet remarrying."

"I am not blind." William winced as pain stabbed his side. He poured a cup of spring water from the flagon at his elbow. He dared not drink wine these days; all he could keep down was dry bread and bland foods, when once he had been a man of voracious appetite. "This is my will." He pushed the sheaves of vellum over to de Louroux. "I well understand the danger to my girls and how easily the situation could spill into war, and I have done my best to remedy it."

He watched de Louroux read what was written and, as he had expected, saw him lift his brows.

"You are entrusting your daughters to the French," Gofrid said. "Is that not just as dangerous? Instead of wild dogs prowling outside the fold, you invite the lions inside?"

"Alienor too is a lioness," William replied. "It is in her blood to rise to the challenge. She has been educated to that end, and she has great ability, as you well know." He waved his hand. "The plan has its flaws, but it is safer than others that might seem promising at first glance. You have contacts with the French through the Church — and you are a wise man and eloquent. You have taught my daughters well; they trust you and are fond of you. In the event of my death, I commend their safety and welfare into your keeping. I know you will do what is best for them."

William waited while Gofrid read the will again, frowning. "There is no better solution. I have racked my brains until they have almost poured out of my skull. I am entrusting my daughters, and therefore Aquitaine, to Louis of France because I must. If I wed Alienor to de Rancon, honorable though he is, I will be condemning my lands to bloody civil war. It is one thing for men to obey my seneschal acting under my instruction, another to see him set above them as Duke Consort of Aquitaine."

"Indeed, sire," Gofrid conceded.

William's mouth twisted. "There is also Geoffrey of Anjou to consider. He would dearly love to unite his house with mine by betrothing his infant son to Alienor. He broached the subject last year when we were on campaign in Normandy, and I put him off by saying I would consider the matter when the boy was older. If I die, he may well attempt to seize the moment, and that too would be disastrous. In this life, we have to make sacrifices for the common good; Alienor understands that." He made a feeble attempt at a jest: "If grapes are to be trodden underfoot, then in Bordeaux we have always known how to make wine," but neither man smiled. The pain was making William feel sick. The long walk from Poitiers had taken its toll on his dwindling strength. Dear God, he was exhausted and there was still so much to do.

Gofrid continued to look troubled. "It may prevent your people from fighting among themselves, but I fear instead they will turn on the French as the common enemy."

"Not if their duchess is also a queen. I expect unrest from the usual areas, and there are always petty squabbles, but I do not believe there will be outright rebellion. I trust to your skills as a diplomat to hold the ship steady."

Gofrid plucked at his beard. "Is anyone else to see this?"

"No. I will send a trusted messenger to King Louis with a copy, but others need not know just yet. If the worst happens you must inform the French immediately and guard my girls until they arrive. For now I entrust you to keep these documents safe."

"It shall be done as you wish, sire." He gave William a worried look. "Shall I have your physician bring you a sleeping draft?"

"No." William's expression grew taut. "There will be time enough for sleep all too soon."

Gofrid left the chamber with a heavy heart. William was dying and probably did not have long. He might succeed in hiding the truth from others, but Gofrid knew him too well to be fooled. There was so much still to be accomplished and it grieved him that their business would now be like a half-finished embroidery. Whatever was woven in the other half would never match the work already completed and might even cause the former to unravel.

Gofrid's thoughts turned with compassion to Alienor and Petronella. Seven years ago they had lost their mother and their little brother to a deadly marsh fever. Now they stood to lose their beloved father too. They were so vulnerable. William had made their future certain in his will, and probably glorious, but Gofrid wished the girls were older and more tempered by experience. He did not want to see their bright natures become corrupted and tarnished by the grime of the world, but knew it was bound to happen.

Alienor removed her cloak and draped it over her father's chair. His scent and presence lingered in his chamber because he had left everything behind when he set out from the cathedral, clad in his penitent's robe of undyed wool, plain sandals on his feet and coarse bread in his satchel. She and Petronella had walked a few miles with him in procession, before returning to Bordeaux with the Archbishop. Petronella had chattered all the way, filling the void with her animated voice and swift gestures, but Alienor had ridden in silence and on arriving home had slipped away to be alone.

She moved around the room, touching this and that. The eagle motif carved into the back of his chair, the ivory box containing strips of parchment, and the little horn and silver pot holding his quill pens and styli. She paused beside his soft blue cloak with the squirrel lining. A single strand of hair glinted on the shoulder. She lifted a fold of the garment and pressed it to her face, taking it into herself as she had not taken in his final, scratchy embrace on the road because she had been so angry with him. She had ridden away on Ginnet and not looked back. Petronella had hugged him hard in her stead and departed with bright farewells enough for them both.

Alienor's eyes grew sore and hot and she blotted her tears on the cloak. It was only until Easter and then he would be home. He had been away many times before — only last year on battle campaign in Normandy with Geoffrey le Bel, Count of Anjou, and there had been far more danger in that than walking a pilgrim road.

She sat on the chair and, resting her hands on the arms, put herself in the position of lady of Aquitaine, dispensing judgment and wisdom. From early childhood she had been educated to think and to rule. The spinning and weaving lessons, the gentler feminine pursuits, had only been the background to the serious matter of learning and ideas. Her father loved to see her dressed in fine clothes and jewels — he approved of womanly pursuits and femininity — but he had also treated her as his surrogate son. She had ridden with him on progress through the wide lands of Aquitaine, from the foothills of the Pyrenees to the flat coastlands in the west, with their lucrative salt pans between Bordeaux and the bustling port of Niort. From the vines of Cognac and the forests of Poitou, to the hills, lush river valleys, and fine riding country of the Limousin. She had been at his side when he took the homage of his vassals, many of whom were turbulent, quarrelsome men, eager for their own gain, but acknowledging her father's suzerainty. She had absorbed her lessons by watching how he dealt with them. The language of power was exercised in more than just words. It was presence and thought; it was gesture and timing. He had illuminated her way and taught her to stand in her own light, but today she felt as if she had entered a land of shadows.

The door opened and the Archbishop walked into the room. He had exchanged his elaborate miter for a plain felt cap and his magnificent outer garments for an ordinary brown habit girded with a simple knotted belt. Tucked under his arm was a carved ivory box. "I thought I would find you here, daughter," he said.

Alienor felt a little resentful, but said nothing. She could hardly tell the Archbishop of Bordeaux to go away, and a small, forlorn part of her wanted to cling to him, even as she had wanted to cling to her father.

He set the box down on a table beside her chair and lifted the lid. "Your father asked me to give you this," he said. "Perhaps you remember it from when you were small." From a lining of soft white fleece, he produced a pear-shaped vase fashioned of clear rock crystal, the surface intricately worked in a honeycomb effect. "He said it was like you — precious and unique. When it gives off its light, it enhances all things that surround it."

Alienor swallowed. "I do remember it," she said, "but I have not seen it since I was small."

Unspoken between them lay the detail that this beautiful thing had been a gift from her father to her mother at their marriage, and at her death it had been put away in the cathedral treasury at Bordeaux and seldom brought out.

She cupped the vase in her hands and put it down gently on the trestle. The light from the window struck through the crystal, scattering rainbow-colored lozenges across the white cloth. Alienor gasped at the unexpected, shimmering display. Her eyes blurred on a prism of tears, and she choked back a sob.

"Ah, daughter, hush now." Gofrid came around the table to embrace her. "All will be well, I promise you. I am here; I will care for you."

They were the same words she always used to Petronella, whatever the truth of the matter; they were like a bandage on a wound. It might not heal the injury, but it made it easier to bear. She laid her head on his breast and allowed herself to cry, but eventually drew away and lifted her chin. The sun still dazzled on the vase and she put her hand in the light to see the colors dance on her wrist: vermilion, cerulean, and royal purple.

"Without the light the beauty remains hidden," Gofrid said. "But it is always there. Just like God's love, or a father's, or a mother's. Remember that, Alienor. You are loved, whether you see it or not."

In the third week following Easter Sunday the weather was bright and warm, and as the sun climbed in the soft spring morning, Alienor and Petronella took their sewing into the palace gardens with the ladies of the household. Musicians played softly in the background on harp and citole, singing of spring and renewal and unrequited longing. Water splashed in the marble fountains, making a drowsy sound in the fine golden warmth.

The ladies, emboldened because Floreta was absent about other duties, chattered to themselves, emulating the sparrows that bustled in the mulberry trees. Their foolish banter irritated Alienor. She did not want to become involved in gossip about who was making eyes at whom, and whether the baby the understeward's wife was expecting was her husband's or the result of an affair with a young hearth knight. When Alienor was a child, her maternal grandmother's household in Poitiers had seethed with such trivial but damaging rumors and she hated to hear them passed around like tawdry currency. Dangere-

use de Châtellerault had been her grandfather's mistress, not his wife; he had lived
openly with her, flouting all opinion save his
own, and there had been frequent accusations of moral laxity. Once gossip began,
there was no stopping it; a reputation could
be destroyed in moments by a few malicious
whispers.

"Enough," she snapped, exerting her authority. "I would listen to the music in peace."

The women exchanged glances but fell
silent. Alienor took a piece of candied pear
from a platter at her side and bit into the
sugary flesh. They were her favorite confection and she had taken to gorging on them.
Their intense sweetness was a consolation,
while knowing she could have them any time
she chose gave her a sense of control. Yet
there was discontent too, for what use was it
to have command over the petty gossip of
maids and the ordering of sweetmeats? Such
things were no more than gaudy flourishes
and there was no satisfaction in such empty
power.

A woman began showing Petronella how to
make dainty daisy flowers using a particular
embroidery stitch. Alienor abandoned her
own sewing and went to stroll around the
garden. A dull headache banded her temples,
not helped by the circlet at her brow. Her
monthly flux was due, and her stomach
ached. She had not been sleeping well, her

dreams haunted by nightmares that she could not remember on waking, but the feeling was always of being trapped.

She paused beside a young cherry tree and lightly brushed the green orbs of developing fruit with her hand. By the time her father returned, the fruit would be dark red, verging on black. Full and sweet and ripe.

"Daughter."

Only two people called her that. She turned to face Archbishop Gofrid and even before he spoke, she knew what he was going to say, because the look on his face, full of trouble and compassion, told it all.

"I have some bad news," he said.

"It is about my father, isn't it?"

"Child, you should sit down."

She faced him squarely. "He is not coming back, is he?"

He looked taken aback, but swiftly recovered his balance. "Child, I am sorry to say that he died on Good Friday within sight of Compostela and was buried there at the feet of Saint James." His voice had a hoarse catch. "He is with God now and free from his pain. He had been unwell for some time."

Grief shuddered through her like the surges of an underground tide. She had known from the outset that something was wrong, but no one had seen fit to tell her, least of all her father.

Gofrid gave her the sapphire ring he had

been holding in his hand. "He sent you this, so you would know, and he bade you to do your best as you have always done and to heed the advice of your guardians."

She looked at the ring and remembered it shining on her father's finger as he set out on his journey. She felt as if the bottom had dropped out of her world and everything that was stable had lurched downward in one piece. Raising her head, she gazed across the garden toward her sister who was laughing at something a maid had said. In a moment that laughter would cease and in its place would come grief and tears as Petronella's world shattered too, and that was almost harder to bear than her own shock and grief.

"What will happen to us?" She tried to sound pragmatic and mature, even though she could not control the wobble in her voice.

Gofrid closed her fist over the ring. "You will be looked after, do not worry. Your father left sound provision for you in his will." He moved to embrace her with compassion, but she stepped away and set her jaw.

"I am not a child."

Gofrid let his hands fall to his sides. "But you are still so very young," he replied. "Your sister . . ." He looked toward the group of women.

"I will tell Petronella," she said firmly. "No one else."

He made a gesture of acknowledgment,

although his expression was creased with concern. "As you wish, daughter."

Alienor returned to the women, Gofrid walking at her side. After the maids had curtsied to him, Alienor dismissed them and sat down beside her sister.

"Look what I have sewn!" Petronella held up the kerchief on which she had been working. One corner was carpeted with white daisies, golden knots at their centers. Petronella's brown eyes were alight. "I'm going to give this to Papa when he comes home!"

Alienor bit her lip. "Petra," she said, putting her arm around her. "Listen. I have something to tell you."

3

Castle of Béthizy, France, May 1137
Fetched from his prayers, Louis entered his father's sickroom in the top chamber of the castle. The wide-open shutters admitted a light breeze and revealed twin arches of blue spring sky. Bowls of incense burned on various tables around the room, but did little to dissipate the stench from his father's decaying, swollen body. Louis swallowed a retch as he knelt at the bedside and made his obeisance. He almost shuddered as his father's hand touched the top of his head in benediction.

"Stand up." Louis senior's voice was gravelly with secretions. "Let me look at you."

Louis strove to control his anxiety. His father's body might be a bloated ruin, but the ice-blue eyes still showed the mind and will of the keen hunter, soldier, and king trapped within the dying flesh. Louis always felt defensive in his father's presence. He was the second son, intended for a career in the

Church, but when his older brother had died in a riding accident, Louis had been brought from his studies at Saint-Denis and made heir to the kingdom. It was God's decision and Louis knew he must serve in whatever way God wanted, but it had not been his choice — and certainly not his parents'.

His mother stood by the curtains at the right of the bedside, her hands clasped in front of her and her lips pursed in the habitual expression that said she knew best and he knew nothing. To her left stood several of his father's closest advisers, including his mother's brothers William and Amadée. Also Theobald, Count of Blois. Louis's apprehension increased.

His father made a sound down his nose, like a horse trader not entirely satisfied with the beast on offer but knowing it would have to do. "I have a task that will make a man of you," he said.

"Sire?" Louis's throat was tight, and his voice emerged on a rising note that betrayed his tension.

"A matter of marriage vows. Suger will tell you; he has the breath in his lungs to do so, and he is fond of the sound of his own voice." His father beckoned, and the small, squirrel-eyed Abbot of Saint-Denis stepped forward from among the group, a scroll held in his thin fingers and a reproachful look on his face for the King's jibe.

Louis blinked. *Marriage vows?*

"Sire, we have great and important news for you." Suger's voice was mellifluous and his expression was open and candid. As well as being one of his father's closest confidants, Suger was Louis's tutor and mentor. Louis loved him as he did not love his father because Suger helped him to make sense of the world and understood his needs. "William of Aquitaine has died during a pilgrimage to Compostela, may God assoil him." Suger signed his breast. "Before he left, he sent his will to France, asking your father to care for his daughters in the event of his death. The eldest is thirteen and of marriageable age, and the younger one eleven."

Louis's father heaved himself into an approximation of upright against the mass of pillows and bolsters supporting his distended torso. "We must seize the opportunity," he wheezed. "Aquitaine and Poitou will increase our lands and prestige a hundredfold. We cannot allow them to fall into the hands of others. Geoffrey of Anjou for one would gladly snatch the duchy with a marriage between his son and the eldest girl, and that must not happen." The effort expended on speech left him purple in the face and fighting for breath and he waved at Suger to continue.

Suger cleared his throat. "Your father wishes you to take an army down to Bordeaux to secure the region and to marry the eldest girl. She is currently under guard at the Ombrière Palace and the Archbishop awaits your arrival."

Louis reeled, feeling as if he had been punched in the stomach. He knew one day he would have to marry and beget heirs, but he had always viewed it as a vaguely unpleasant duty in the distant future. Now he was being told he must wed a girl he had never met who came from lands where the people were known to be pleasure-seekers, lax in their moral habits.

"I will see to the girls' education in our ways," his mother said, securing her own authority in the proceedings. "They have been without maternal care for many years, and they will benefit from proper guidance and instruction."

His father's constable, Raoul de Vermandois, stepped forward. "Sire, I will begin preparations to leave immediately." He was another close adviser, and Louis's first cousin once removed into the bargain. A leather patch concealed the empty socket where he had lost an eye during a siege eight years ago. He was a reliable warhorse on the battlefield and an elegant and charismatic courtier, much appreciated by the ladies. The eye patch only added to his cachet where women were concerned.

"Make haste, Raoul," said the King. "Time

is of the essence." He raised a warning forefinger. "It is to be an escort of honor and largesse; the Poitevans value such things and we must keep their goodwill at all costs. Fly banners from your spears and wear ribbons around your helms. Make sure that for now you go bearing gifts, not blades."

"Sire, leave it to me." De Vermandois bowed from the room, his magnificent cloak sweeping behind him like a sail.

Louis knelt to receive his father's blessing again and somehow managed to leave the fetid chamber before doubling over to be violently sick. He did not want to take a wife. He knew nothing of girls except that their soft curves, their giggles, and their twittery voices repulsed him. His mother was not like that; she was a rod of iron, but she had never given him love. The only affection in his world had come from God, but God now seemed to be saying he should be married. Perhaps it was a punishment for his sins that he should have to do this thing, and therefore he should accept it gladly and give praise.

As servants rushed to clear up the mess he had made, Suger emerged from the chamber and was swiftly at his side. "Ah, Louis, Louis." The Abbé put a comforting arm across the youth's shoulders. "I know this is a shock, but it is God's will and you must surrender to it. He offers you magnificent opportunities, and a girl near to your own age to be your wife and helpmate. This is truly a moment to rejoice."

Louis composed himself under Suger's calming influence. If this was truly the will of God, then he must submit and do his best. "I do not even know her name," he said.

"I believe it is Alienor, sire."

Louis silently formed the syllables on his lips. Her name was like a foreign fruit he had never tasted before. He still felt like heaving.

4

Bordeaux, June 1137

Alienor felt Ginnet pulling on the rein as she rode beside Archbishop Gofrid. Like her mare, she was eager to race the wind. It was several days since she had been out and was always under heavy guard because she was such a valuable prize. This morning the Archbishop had taken responsibility for her welfare. His knights, although vigilant, stayed slightly off the pace so that he and Alienor had a private space in which to talk.

In the two months since her father's death, the warm southern spring had turned to blazing summer and the cherries had ripened to glossy black on the trees in the palace garden. Her father lay severed from life in his tomb at Compostela, and she dwelt in limbo, an heiress with the power to change destinies because of who she was, yet wielding no authority of her own beyond the bower, because what influence did a girl-child of thirteen have over the men brokering her future?

They reached open ground and Alienor heeled Ginnet's flanks, giving her free rein. Gofrid increased pace with her and dust rose like white smoke from the burn of hooves over the baked earth. She felt the warm wind in her face and inhaled the pungent scent of wild thyme as it was crushed under the mare's speed. Harsh summer light dazzled her eyes and, for an instant, her cares dissipated in the euphoria of the race, of being alive, her blood singing in her veins. Everything within her that had felt tight and constricted opened wide and filled her with vigorous emotion as hot and strong as the sun.

At last she swirled to a halt before a weathered Roman statue standing by the wayside and leaned over to pat Ginnet's sweat-darkened neck. Her father had taught her about the Romans. A thousand years ago they had been conquerors and settlers in Aquitaine, speakers of the Latin tongue that scholars used now and that she had learned together with the French spoken in Poitou and the north, so different from the *lenga romana* of Bordeaux.

The statue's right arm was raised as if in oratory and his white open stare considered the horizon. Stars of golden lichen embroidered his breastplate and the fringes of his cingulum. "No one knows who he is," Gofrid said. "His inscription is lost. Many have left their mark on this land but in their turn have been marked. The people here do not take kindly to being harnessed and ridden."

Alienor straightened in the saddle. The realization that she was Duchess of Aquitaine was stirring within her, like a sleeping dragon awakening and stretching sleek, sinuous muscles. "I do not fear them," she said.

The sharp sunlight deepened the frown between the Archbishop's eyes. "You should be cautious nevertheless. Better that than be taken unawares." He hesitated and then said: "Daughter, I have news for you, and I want you to listen carefully."

Alienor was suddenly alert. She should have known there was more to this ride out than the pleasure of exercise. "What sort of news?"

"Out of his love and concern for you and for his lands, your father left great plans for you in his will."

"What do you mean, 'great plans'? Why have you not spoken of this before?" Fear and anger began to churn inside her. "Why did my father not tell me?"

"Because everything has to grow before it comes to fruition," Gofrid replied gravely. "If your father had returned from Compostela, he would have told you himself. It was unwise to mention this until everything was in place, but now is the moment." He leaned across his horse to put his hand over hers. "Your father desired a match for you that would honor you and Aquitaine and lead you to greatness. He also wished to keep you safe and your lands peaceful. Before he left, he asked the King of France to safeguard your welfare, and he arranged a match for you with his eldest son, Louis. One day you will be Queen of France and, if God is good, mother to a line of kings whose empire will stretch from Paris to the Pyrenees."

The words fell on Alienor like a blow from a poleax and she could only stare at her tutor in shock.

"This is a great opportunity," Gofrid said, watching her closely. "You will fulfill the potential your father saw in you and your reward will be a crown. An alliance between France and Aquitaine will make both countries much stronger than they are alone."

"My father would never have done this without telling me." Underneath Alienor's numbness, a terrible sense of betrayal was blossoming.

"He was dying, child," Gofrid said sadly. "He had to make the best provision for you he could and it had to be kept secret until the time was ripe."

She lifted her chin. "I do not want to be married to a French prince. I want to marry a man of Aquitaine."

He squeezed her hand and she felt his

episcopal ring bite her flesh. "You must trust me and your father. We have done what is best. If you married a man of your own lands, it would lead to rivalry and a war that would tear Aquitaine apart. Louis will arrive within the next few weeks, and you will wed him in the cathedral. It will be done with every dignity and accolade, as your father wished, and your vassals will come to you and swear their allegiance. You cannot travel to Paris, because you are a great marriage prize and until you are wed men will attempt to seize you for their own ends."

Alienor shuddered. His words were burying her in a deep dark hole. Her lips formed words of refusal even though she did not speak.

"Daughter, did you not hear me? You will be a great queen."

"But no one has asked me. It has all been decided behind my back." Her throat tightened. "What if I do not choose to marry Louis of France? What if I . . . what if I want someone else?"

His gaze was compassionate but stern. "Such a thing cannot be. Put it from your mind. It is meet and fitting that a father decides with whom his daughter should match. Do you not trust his decision? Do you not trust me? This is right for you, and right for Aquitaine and Poitou. Louis is young, handsome, and educated. It will be an illustrious marriage, and it is your duty."

Alienor felt as if she were being forced into a box and the lid nailed down, shutting out light and life. No one had cared to tell her, as if she were no more than a valuable parcel to be passed from hand to hand. How was it going to benefit her to be lady of all she surveyed if it was going to be handed on a platter to the French? She felt hurt and betrayed that her tutor had known all this time and said nothing, that her father had been harboring this intent even as he bade her farewell forever. She might as well spend her life eating sugared fruits and listening to foolish gossip.

Reining Ginnet around, she dug in her heels and for a moment lost herself in the mare's furious burst of speed, but as the palfrey started to flag, she eased her down again, knowing that no matter how hard she raced, she could not outrun the fate sealed upon her by the deception of those she had trusted most of all.

Gofrid had not ridden after her, and she drew rein alone on the dusty road and stared into the distance like the anonymous Roman on his lichen-covered plinth. The Archbishop had spoken as if this match were the pinnacle of good fortune, but she could not see it in the same light. She had never envisioned being Queen of France; to be Duchess of Aquitaine was her sacred duty and all that mattered. When she had dreamed of marriage in her private moments, the man standing at her side had been Geoffrey de Rancon, lord of Taillebourg and Gençay, and she thought that Geoffrey had perhaps thought about her in a similar way, although he had never said so.

With an aching heart, she reined about again and returned to her tutor, and it seemed to her that as she rode, the last spangles of childhood fell in the dust behind her, glittered, and were gone.

On returning to the palace, Alienor went directly to the chamber she and Petronella shared to change her gown and make herself presentable for the main meal of the day, although she was not hungry and her stomach felt as if it were clamped to her spine. She leaned over the brass washbowl and splashed her face with cool, scented water, feeling it ease the tightness caused by the fierce heat of the sun.

Petronella sat on the bed, plucking the petals from a daisy and humming tunelessly under her breath. The death of their father had hit her hard. At first she had refused to accept he was not coming back and Alienor had borne the brunt of her anger and grief because there was no one else on whom Petronella could vent her misery. She was a little better now, but still prone to teary moments and dark moods were more petulant than usual.

Alienor drew the bed curtains to shut out the chamber ladies. They would know soon enough — perhaps already did in the way of court gossip — but she wanted to tell Petronella in private. Sitting down beside her, she brushed away the scattered petals. "I have news for you," she said.

Immediately Petronella tensed; last time Alienor had brought her news, it had been calamitous.

Keeping her voice low, Alienor said, "The Archbishop says I am to marry Louis, heir to France. He said Papa arranged it before he . . . before he went away."

Petronella gave her a blank stare and then flicked away the daisy stalk. "When?" she asked stonily.

"Soon." Alienor's mouth twisted on the word. "He is on his way here now."

Petronella said nothing and turned to one side, fussing with the knotted laces on her gown.

"Here, let me." Alienor stretched out her hand, but Petronella struck her away.

"I can do it myself!" she spat. "I don't need you!"

"Petra —"

"You're only going to go away and leave me, like everyone else. You don't care about me. No one does!"

Alienor felt as if Petronella had driven a knife into her body. "That's not true! I love you dearly. Do you think I would have chosen this for myself?" She met her sister's furious, frightened stare with one of her own. "Do you think I am not heartsick and scared? The one thing we have in this is each other. I will always care for you."

Petronella hesitated and, in one of her volatile changes of mood, flung herself into Alienor's arms, hugging her with ferocity and weeping. "I don't want you to go away."

"I won't." Alienor stroked Petronella's hair, tears spilling down her face.

"Swear it."

Alienor crossed herself. "I swear it on my soul. I won't let anything part us. Come now." Sniffing, wet-faced, she helped Petronella unpick the knot.

"What . . . what does Louis of France look like?"

Alienor shrugged and wiped her eyes. "I do not know. He was destined for the Church until his older brother died, so at least he will have some learning." She also knew that his father was called Louis the Fat and her vision kept filling with the sickening image of an overweight pasty youth. She heaved a pensive sigh. "It was Papa's wish and he must have had his reasons. We must do our duty and obey his will. We have no other choice."

5

Bordeaux, July 1137

In the stultifying heat of early July the arrangements for the arrival of the French bridegroom and his army continued apace. News came to Bordeaux that Louis had reached Limoges in time to celebrate the feast of Saint Martial on June 30. He had taken the homage of the Count of Toulouse and those barons of the Limousin who had come to tender their fealty as news of the impending wedding spread across Alienor's lands. Now, accompanied by Alienor's vassals, the French cavalcade had set out on the final stage of its journey.

From cellar to turret, Bordeaux prepared for Louis's arrival. Hostels were swept out and decorated with banners and garlands. Cartloads of supplies rolled into the city from the surrounding countryside, together with herds and flocks for the slaughter. Seamstresses toiled over yards of pale gold cloth of escarlet, sewing a wedding gown fit for their new duchess and a future queen of France. The train was hemmed with hundreds of pearls and the sleeves swept from wrist to ankle with decorative golden hooks to loop them back should they get in the way.

In the dawn of a baking July morning, Alienor attended church to confess and be shriven. On her return, her women robed her in a gown of ivory damask, the gold laces pulled tight to emphasize her slender waist. A jeweled cap covered the top of her head, but her burnished hair remained exposed, the thick strands woven with metallic ribbons. Her nails were pink with madder stain and had been buffed until they gleamed. Alienor felt as if she had been polished to a shine just like the silver-gilt cups intended for the marriage feast.

Through the open shutters the sky was a pure summer blue. Doves circled the red-tiled roof of the palace cote and the river sparkled like a treasure chest in the morning heat. Alienor gazed at the French tents on the far bank, arrayed like clusters of exotic mushrooms. Louis and his army had arrived shortly before dusk yesterday and had made camp as the sun sank over the limpid waters of the Garonne. The pale canvases of the ordinary troops marked the French periphery, while the center blazed with the bright silks and golden finials of the high nobility and the Church. She fixed her eyes on the largest pavilion of them all: lapis blue and powdered gold with the red oriflamme banner fluttering in the hot breeze outside its open flaps. She could see men coming and going but had no idea if one of them was her prospective husband.

All along the riverbank, small boats and barges plied their trade, rowing supplies of food and drink to the host on the far bank. A deputation of vessels sculled out toward the French encampment, the oars making white dashes in the water. Banners decorated the lead barge, which was draped with a canvas awning to shade its occupants from the sun, and she could see the figure of Archbishop Gofrid standing near the prow. They were on their way to greet the French delegation and bring Louis and his courtiers to the city for a formal first meeting of bride and groom.

Louis wouldn't be fat, she told herself, trying to be positive. This was all happening for the greater good. But her stomach was hollow because it did not feel as if it were for the greater good, and she was moving ever farther away from familiar shores.

Petronella joined her, jostling at the window. She was dancing on her tiptoes and the liveliest Alienor had seen her since their father's death. Her initial upset at the news of the wedding had been subsumed by the excitement of the preparations. She adored fine clothes, distractions, and entertainments, and this was satisfying all those appetites.

The Archbishop and her uncle disembarked on the opposite bank of the river and a servant hurried to the great blue-and-gold tent. Moments later a gathering of brightly clad courtiers emerged.

"Which one do you think is Louis? Which one?" Petronella craned her neck.

Alienor shook her head. "I do not know."

"That one — there in the blue!" Petronella stretched her arm and pointed.

Alienor could see various churchmen in glittering regalia and many nobles, but several were wearing blue and they were too far away for her to make a guess.

The awning shaded the party as the crew began to pull back across the water, but unlike her sister, Alienor felt as if she were watching an invasion rather than the joyful approach of a bride-groom and his retinue.

Louis felt sick with apprehension as the barge moored beneath the great walls of the Ombrière Palace. Envoys kept telling him how beautiful, gracious, and demure his bride-to-be was, but envoys often told lies. He was keeping a tight rein on himself and hoping his fear did not show on his face for others to see. His father had entrusted this responsibility to him and he had to deal with it like a man.

The intense heat made it difficult to

breathe. He could almost taste the sun-warmed canvas of the awning and feel it sticking at the back of his throat. Archbishop Gofrid of Bordeaux looked as if he were melting, sweat dribbling down his red face from the soaked brow band of his embroidery-crusted miter. He had greeted Louis with gravity and deference and had added a smile for Abbot Suger, who was an old friend and ally.

Louis's seneschal, Raoul de Vermandois, wiped the back of his neck with a checkered silk cloth. "I have never known a summer so hot," he said, mopping carefully around the leather patch over his left eye.

"You will find the palace cool and pleasant, my lords," the Archbishop said. "It was built long ago as a refuge from the summer heat."

Louis glanced at the towering walls. The palace of Shade; the palace of Shadows. There was more than one meaning here. "We will welcome it, Archbishop," he said. "We often traveled after dusk and by moonlight to avoid the heat on the way here."

"Indeed," Gofrid replied, "and we are glad for your haste in this matter."

Louis inclined his head. "My father understood the necessity."

"The Duchess looks forward to welcoming you."

"As I look forward to greeting her," Louis answered woodenly.

Raoul de Vermandois tossed a flash of silver coins into the water and they watched as youths dived for them, brown bodies glistening. "Your father said we should treat these people with courtesy and largesse," he said, grinning at Louis's raised brows.

Louis was not certain his father had meant quite so low down the pecking order, but Raoul was a man of cheerful and spontaneous gestures, and it could do no harm to throw money for the city youths to dive after, even if it was frivolous and less dignified than giving alms at the church door.

Once disembarked, they were greeted by various clergy and nobles before being escorted in slow procession under a shaded palanquin to the cathedral of Saint-André where Louis was to wed his young bride on the following day.

He entered under the decorated arch of the portico and stood in the holy presence of God. The cathedral interior was a cool and blessed haven from the burn of the midsummer sun. Drawing in the mingled scents of incense and candle wax, Louis sighed with relief. This was familiar territory. He walked down the nave with its decorated pillars, and when he reached the altar steps, he signed his breast and prostrated himself.

"Dear God, I am your servant. Grant me the strength to do Your will and not fail. Grant me Your grace and lead me along the paths of

righteousness."

This was where he and Alienor would celebrate their wedding. He still found it difficult to say her name, much less imagine her person. They said she was beautiful, but beauty was in the eye of the beholder. He wished he was home in Paris and safe behind the solid walls of Notre Dame or Saint-Denis.

At the sound of a fanfare, he turned his gaze down the nave. The columns made a tunnel of golden arches, leading his eye to the brightness of the open doorway. A girl came walking through the light toward him, accompanied by attendants, and for an instant his eyes were so dazzled that the entire group seemed to have a radiance not of this world. She was tall and slender; her deep-golden hair shimmered to her waist but the top of her head was decently covered by a virgin's jeweled cap. Her face was a pale, pure oval, not overtly feminine, but wrought with a blend of precise strength and delicacy that made Louis think of an angel.

She knelt to kiss the Archbishop's ring, and once he had raised her to her feet, she set her hand upon his arm and continued down the nave to Louis. "Sire," she said, kneeling again, and from that position lifted her eyes to his. They were the mutable color of the ocean, full of truth and intelligence, and Louis felt as if his heart had been set upon an anvil and struck into a different shape with a single blow.

"Demoiselle," he said. "I am pleased to meet you and to offer you the honor of marriage so that our great lands may be united." The words emerged by rote, because he had been rehearsing them with Suger in his tent for most of the previous evening, sweating in the canvas-intensified heat, the whine of mosquitoes in his ears. Saying them now, he regained a little of his equilibrium, although his heart was still bounding like a deer at full leap.

"As I am honored to meet you, sire," she replied, lowering her lashes, and then added with a little catch in her voice, "and to accept your offer of marriage as my father desired."

Louis realized she must have been practicing too and like him was anxious. He felt relieved, then protective and superior. She was more perfect than he had dared hope. God had answered his doubts and shown him that this was truly meant to be. Having a wife was a natural progression of manhood and kingship, because a king needed a consort. He raised her to her feet and kissed her lightly and swiftly on both cheeks, and then drew back, his chest tight.

She demurely introduced the girl beside her as her sister Petronella. This one was still a child, smaller and brown-haired with a heart-shaped face and a sensuous rosebud mouth. She curtsied to Louis and, after a single sharp look from bright brown eyes, lowered her gaze. Other than to think that she would make a fine reward for one of his French nobles, Louis dismissed her from his mind to attend to the matter in hand. Turning with Alienor to the altar, he pledged himself in formal betrothal, his hands trembling as he slipped a gold ring onto her right middle finger. And at that moment, he was certain that God had favored him with such bounty that he was overwhelmed.

A celebration feast had been prepared at the Ombrière Palace. Tables spread with white napery had been arranged in the garden cloister so that guests could sit in the open air, well shaded from the sun, and listen to musicians while they dined.

Alienor smiled and answered when addressed, but she was preoccupied and finding conversation difficult. A huge weight had landed on her with Louis's arrival and the knowledge that the changes in her life were now irrevocable. There were too many new people to weigh up, all so different in their speech and mannerisms to her own courtiers. They spoke the dialect of northern France, which she understood because it was the common language of Poitou, but the Parisian cadence was harsher on the ear. Their garments were of thicker, more somber cloth, and they seemed to lack the vibrancy of her people. But then they had been traveling hard in the blistering summer heat, so perhaps she should give them the benefit of the doubt.

Her fears that Louis would be fat and loutish were ungrounded. He was tall and narrow through the hips like a good gazehound. He had glorious, shoulder-length, silver-blond hair and wide blue eyes. His mouth was thin but well formed. She found his manner stilted and rule-bound, but that could be caused by the pressures of the day. He did not smile much — unlike his seneschal, Raoul de Vermandois, who never seemed to stop. De Vermandois was showing Petronella his sleight of hand by hiding a small glass ball under one of three cups and getting her to guess where the ball was. She was giggling at his antics, her eyes shining. The rest of the French party was more watchful and reserved, as if they all had planks stuck down the backs of their tunics. Theobald, Count of Blois Champagne, was eyeing de Vermandois with irritation, a muscle ticking in his jaw. Alienor wondered at the tension between the men. There was so much she did not know, so much she had to take in and assimilate.

At least, even if he was reserved, Louis did not appear to be an ogre, and she could probably find ways of influencing him. It might be more difficult to circumvent the older men, especially Suger and Louis's uncles Amadée de Maurienne and William de Montferrat, but she had been accustomed to getting her own way with her father, and there would be occasions when she would have Louis to herself with no one to interfere. She was of a similar age to him and that meant they had some common ground.

When everyone had eaten and drunk their fill, Louis formally presented Alienor with the wedding gifts he had brought from France. There were books with ivory cover panels, reliquaries, boxes of precious stones, silver chalices, glass cups from the workshops of Tyre, tapis rugs, bolts of fine fabric. Boxes and chests and sacks. Alienor's eyes ached at the largesse. Louis presented her with a pectoral cross studded with rubies as red as small drops of blood. "This belonged to my grandmother," he said as he fastened it around her neck and then stepped back, breathing swiftly.

"It is magnificent," Alienor replied, which was the truth, even if she did not particularly like the piece.

His expression had been anxious, but now he stood tall and proud. "You have given me the coronet of Aquitaine," he said. "It would be a poor thing indeed if I could not gift my bride with the wealth of France in return."

Alienor felt a frisson of resentment. Although she owed him homage as a vassal of France, Aquitaine belonged to her and always would, no matter that he was to be invested

64

with the ducal coronet after their wedding. At least the marriage contract stipulated that her lands were not to be absorbed into France but were to remain a separate duchy. "I have something for you also." She beckoned, and a chamberlain stepped forward with a carved ivory box. Alienor carefully lifted her vase from its fleece lining. The dimpled rock crystal was cool against her fingers as she turned and presented it formally to Louis.

"My grandfather brought this back with him from a holy war in Spain," she said. "It is of great antiquity."

The vase looked austere and simple when set against the opulent gifts that Louis had given her, but the backdrop only added to its impact. Holding the piece in his hands, Louis kissed her brow. "It is like you," he said, "clear and fine and unique." He set it down gently on the table, and immediately a shower of colored diamonds spangled the white cloth. Louis's face filled with astonished delight. Alienor smiled to see his response and thought that while he had given her all these rich and heavy things, her gift to him of captured light surpassed them all.

"May I?" Without waiting for consent, Abbé Suger picked up the vase in eager hands, his gaze frankly acquisitive. "Exquisite," he said. "I have never seen such fine workmanship." He ran his fingers over the carving in tactile delight. "See how clear it is, and yet it reflects all the colors of a cathedral window. Truly this is God's work."

Alienor suppressed the urge to snatch it from him. Suger was a close friend of Archbishop Gofrid and she ought to be delighted by his admiration.

"Abbé Suger is fascinated by such items," Louis said with a smile. "He has a fine collection at Saint-Denis, as you will see when we return to Paris."

Suger carefully replaced the vase on the trestle. "I do not make the collection for me," he said with a hint of rebuke, "but for the glorification of God through beauty."

"Indeed, Father." Louis flushed like a scolded boy.

After one sharp glance, Alienor looked down. She had noticed how often Louis glanced at Suger, seeking approval and support. This man could be friend or foe and he had Louis at his beck and call. She would need to tread very carefully indeed.

Later in the afternoon, as the sun cooled on the river and the Ombrière Palace drew on a mantle of deeper, slumberous shadows, Louis prepared to return to his camp across the river. He had become more relaxed as the day wore on, and he was smiling as he took his farewell of Alienor, setting his thumb over the ring he had given her and kissing her cheek. His lips were silky and warm, and his fledgling beard was soft against her skin. "I will visit again tomorrow," he said.

Something inside Alienor unclenched and opened. The notion of marrying him had begun to feel more solid — reality, rather than the cloudy haze of a dream. Louis seemed decent enough; he had been kind thus far and he was handsome. Matters could have been much worse.

Embarking to his camp across a sunset river of sheeted gold, Louis raised his hand in farewell and Alienor returned the gesture with a half smile on her lips.

"Well, daughter," said Archbishop Gofrid, coming to stand at her side, "have your fears been allayed?"

"Yes, Father," she replied, knowing it was what he wanted to hear.

"Louis is a fine, devout young man. I am much impressed by him. Abbé Suger has tutored him well."

Alienor nodded again. She was still trying to decide whether Suger was ally or foe, no matter that he was Gofrid's friend.

"I am pleased you gave him the vase."

"Nothing else would match what he had brought to me," she said. She wondered if her tutor had brought out the vase from the depths of the treasury with that intention. She firmed her lips. "I am glad Abbé Bernard of Clairvaux was not among their number."

Gofrid raised his brows.

Alienor grimaced. Twice the redoubtable Abbé Bernard had visited her father, on both occasions to harangue him about his support for the opposition during a papal schism. She had only been a small child on his first visit and vaguely remembered him patting her head. He had been as thin as a lance and had smelled musty, like old wall hangings. The second time, when she was twelve, Bernard and her father had argued violently in the church at La Couldre. It had been at the start of her father's illness, and Abbé Bernard, with his stabbing bony finger, blazing eyes, and eloquent speech threatening the fires of hell, had brought her father to his knees at the altar and claimed it was God's judgment on a sinner. Alienor had feared that Abbé Bernard might be among the French ecclesiasts and had been mightily relieved when he wasn't. "He humiliated my father," she said.

"Bernard of Clairvaux is a very holy man," Gofrid admonished gently. "Above all he seeks the clear path to God and if sometimes he is critical or zealous, then it is for the common good and for God to judge, not us. If you encounter him in Paris, I trust you to act with good and proper judgment as befits your position."

"Yes, Father," Alienor said neutrally, although she felt mutinous.

Gofrid pressed a light kiss to her brow. "I am proud of you, as your father would be if he were here."

Alienor swallowed, determined not to cry. If her father were here, she would not have to make this marriage. She would be cherished and safe and all would be well. If she thought too hard about it, she knew she would blame him for dying and leaving her this legacy in his will.

In Alienor's absence the wedding presents from Louis had been moved to her chamber and placed on a trestle for her to examine at leisure. Many items were only in her custody for a brief time; she would be expected to make gifts of them to the Church or bestow them upon families of importance and influence. There was a reliquary containing a sliver of bone from the leg of Saint James. The casing was of silver gilt, decorated with pearls and precious stones, and a little door of hinged rock crystal opened to reveal a gold box containing the precious fragment. There were two enameled candlesticks, two silver censers, and a box filled with tawny shards and lumps of aromatic frankincense.

For Alienor's personal use, there was a circlet adorned with gems, as well as brooches, rings, and pendants. Petronella had been given a chaplet fashioned from exquisite golden roses set with pearls and sapphires. She wore it now, pinned to her brown waves, while she played with some colored glass balls Raoul de Vermandois had given to her.

Alienor looked around; there were yet more boxes to be examined and she felt like a diner at a banquet with an excess of courses. There was too much richness, too much gold enclosing and smothering her. In haste she changed her elaborate gown for one of plain, cool linen and replaced her dainty embroidered shoes with her riding boots. "I am going to the stables to see Ginnet," she said.

"I'll come with you." Petronella put the glass balls away in her coffer. When Alienor suggested she should remove the golden chaplet, Petronella shook her head and pouted. "I want to keep it on," she said stubbornly. "I won't lose it."

Alienor gave her an exasperated glance but held her peace. Arguing with Petronella over such a trifle was too much trouble on top of everything else.

In the stables, Ginnet greeted Alienor with a soft whicker and eagerly sought the crust of bread her mistress had brought as a treat. Alienor stroked her, taking comfort in the sweet smell of straw and horse. "You're going to be all right," she whispered. "I'll take you with me to Paris; I won't leave you behind, I promise."

Petronella leaned against the stable door watching Alienor intently as if the words were meant for her. Alienor closed her eyes and pressed her forehead against the mare's smooth, warm neck. In a world where so much had changed so rapidly, she was taking what solace she could from the dear and non-judgmental familiar. She would rather bed down in the stable than return to her chamber and that glittering pile of wedding gifts.

As full dusk fell, Petronella plucked at Alienor's sleeve. "I want to walk in the garden," she said. "I want to see the fireflies."

Alienor allowed Petronella to lead her to the courtyard where they had feasted earlier. It was much cooler now, although the walls still gave off soft warmth. Servants had stacked the trestles against a wall and cleared away the white cloths and fine tableware. The fish in the courtyard pond made lazy splashes as they leaped for midges in the last reflection of light. The air was thick with an ancient smell of baked stone. Alienor's heart was heavy. On top of losing her father and being pushed into a marriage not of her choosing, she now had to leave her home and go to Paris in the company of strangers, one of them her own bridegroom.

She remembered childhood play here: darting around the columns, playing tag with Petronella. Colors, images, and echoes of laughter wove like a transparent ribbon through the reality of now and were gone.

Petronella gave her a sudden, fierce hug. "Do you think it will be all right?" she asked, burying her head against Alienor's shoulder. "You said it to Ginnet, but is it true? I'm scared."

"Of course it's true!" Alienor had to close her eyes as she hugged her sister, because this was unbearable. "Of course we are going to be all right!" She drew Petronella to sit on the old stone bench by the pond where they had so often sat in childhood, and together they watched the fireflies twinkle in and out like hopes in the darkness.

Louis gazed at the vase. He had placed it on the small devotional table in his tent beside his crucifix and his ivory statue of the Virgin. The simplicity and value of the gift filled him with wonder, as did the girl who had presented it to him. She was so utterly different from anything he had expected. Her name, which so recently had seemed like a strange, unpleasant taste when he spoke it, was now honey on his tongue. She filled him up, and yet he still felt hollow and did not know how this could be. When the light from the vase had spilled onto the tablecloth, he had taken it as a sign from God that the forthcoming marriage was divinely blessed. Their union was like this vessel, waiting to be filled with light so that it could shine forth with God's grace.

Kneeling before the table, he pressed his forehead against his clasped palms and thanked his maker with his heart and soul.

6

Bordeaux, July 1137

Alienor felt a constriction throughout her body as once more she entered the cathedral of Saint-André. This time she was preceded by two rows of choristers and a chaplain, bearing a processional cross on high. Usually marriages were conducted at the church door, but hers to Louis was to be celebrated within the cathedral itself before the altar, to emphasize its rightness before God.

Alienor took a deep breath and set her feet upon the narrow carpet of fresh green reeds, strewn with herbs and pink roses. The trail of flowers led her down the long nave toward the altar steps. Acolytes swung silver censers on jingling chains, and the perfume of frankincense rose and curled in pale smoke around the vaulted ceiling, mingling with the voices of the choir. Petronella and three other young women bore the weight of her pearl-encrusted train, and her maternal uncle Raoul de Faye paced at her side to represent her male kinfolk. Her skirts flared out and swished back with each step. Occasionally she felt the soft pressure of a crushed rose underfoot, and it seemed almost like a portent.

The congregation standing either side of her pathway to the altar knelt and bowed their heads as she walked past in slow procession. With their faces hidden, she could not tell their thoughts and see neither smile nor frown. Were they glad for this union of Aquitaine and France, or were they already plotting rebellion? Were they joyful for her, or filled with misgiving? She looked and then looked away and, lifting her chin, focused on the soft gleam of the altar, where Louis waited for her, flanked by Abbé Suger and the lords of his entourage. It was too late to do anything but go forward, or to think she had a choice.

Louis's blue silk tunic was embroidered with fleurs-de-lis and his swift breathing caused the fabric to shimmer with light. A coronet set with pearls and sapphires banded his brow and as Alienor joined him at the altar steps, the sun rayed down through the cathedral windows, illuminating her and Louis in slanting swords of transparent gold. He held out his hand, slender and pale, and gave her the faintest curve of his lips in greeting. She hesitated, and then put her own right hand into his keeping, and together they knelt and bent their heads.

Gofrid de Louroux, resplendent in embroidered and gem-studded episcopal robes, conducted the wedding service and the mass, each gesture and movement imbued with gravitas. Alienor and Louis gave their responses in firm neutral voices, but their clasped hands were mutually clammy with anxiety. The communion wine glowed like a dark ruby within the belly of the rock-crystal vessel that Alienor had presented to Louis at their betrothal. It surprised and unsettled her to see the vessel being used today. She felt as if she were being tied into this marriage and even helping her captors to secure the knots as she took the blood of the Redeemer into herself and promised to obey Louis in all things.

With the metallic taste of the wine on her tongue, she heard Archbishop Gofrid speak the final words of binding, pronounce the marriage, and seal her fate. One flesh. One blood. Louis kissed her on either cheek, and then on the mouth with closed dry lips. She accepted the gesture passively, feeling detached and a little numb, as if this moment belonged to someone else.

Married in the sight of God, they turned from the altar to walk back up the nave, and amid all the heads bowed in prayer and obeisance it was still impossible for Alienor to tell who was ally and who was foe.

The glorious singing of the choir accompanied her and Louis to the church doors in a swelling harmonious chant that was almost applause. At her side, she felt Louis stand taller and puff out his chest as if the music were filling him up and expanding him. A swift glance at his face showed her the tears glittering in his eyes and the beatific expression on his face. Alienor felt no such strength of emotion but by the time they reached the carved golden stone of the cathedral door, she had managed to hide behind a smile.

The air outside struck like a molten hammer after the cool interior of the church. Louis's coronet dazzled her eyes until they hurt. "Wife," he said, his complexion flushed with triumph and possession in his voice. "Everything is as God wills."

Alienor dropped her gaze to her new wedding ring, sparkling in the light, and said nothing because she did not trust herself to answer.

From Bordeaux the wedding party journeyed toward Poitiers via detours to fortresses and abbeys so that all could fete the young Duchess and her consort. On the third day they came to the great, reputedly impregnable castle of Taillebourg on the Charente River, belonging in heredity to the seneschals of Poitou. Taillebourg was the last crossing place before the river reached the ocean, and a steady stream of pilgrims passed through on their way to the shrine of Saint James at Compostela.

Their host was Geoffrey de Rancon, important vassal, family friend, and the man Alienor would have chosen to wed had she been permitted a choice. He had not been present at the marriage in Bordeaux for he had been dealing with matters on his lands, but he was pleased to welcome the bride and groom and to host their wedding night, which had been deferred until the third day, following long-held tradition.

Geoffrey knelt in welcome to Alienor and Louis in the castle courtyard and pledged his allegiance. Alienor gazed at the gleam of the sun on his rich brown hair. There was a dull ache in her heart, but her voice gave nothing away as she bade him rise. His own expression was courteous and neutral, his smile that of a courtier. Like her, this drastic change in circumstances had forced him to close the door on particular hopes and ambitions and seek a new focus.

Many lords who had been unable to attend the wedding in Bordeaux had come to Taillebourg to swear fealty to Alienor and Louis, and all had been arranged by Geoffrey to run as smoothly as oil from a jar. A formal feast had been prepared with Louis and Alienor as guests of honor and hosts to their subjects. Later, over an informal gathering, Louis was able to meet and talk with barons and members of the clergy whom he had not met before.

Amid the throng, Geoffrey paused to speak with Alienor. "I have arranged a hunt tomorrow," he said. "I hope the Prince will approve."

"He tells me he enjoys the chase providing it is not a holy day."

"You have made a very great match," he leaned forward to say softly. "One that any father would be proud to make for his daughter."

She looked across the room at Geoffrey's children, standing with their nurses. Burgundia was the eldest at seven, Geoffrey his namesake was six, and Bertha the youngest was four. "Would you have made it for one of yours?" she asked.

"I would do the best I could for them and for the name of Rancon. It would be too great an opportunity to pass up."

"But in your heart?"

He raised his brows. "Are we still talking of my daughters?"

She flushed and looked away.

"Whatever hopes I nurtured, I now see clearly were never going to come to fruition — even if your father had lived. He was a wiser man than me. It would not be beneficial for Aquitaine, and that is always our greatest duty . . . Alienor, look at me."

She met his eyes, although it cost her to do

so. She was horribly aware that they were under the gaze of the entire court and one beat too long, one moment of overheard conversation was all it would take to ignite a destructive scandal.

"I wish you and your husband well," he said. "Whatever you ask of me in loyal service, I shall perform as a faithful vassal. You may trust me, always and without reserve." He bowed and moved smoothly on to engage in urbane conversation with Raoul de Vermandois.

Alienor continued on her own trajectory, speaking a word here, giving a smile there, and a gesture of the hand to emphasize the gold lining of her sleeve and the shine of a topaz ring that had been among Louis's wedding gifts to her. She was the gracious and lovely young Duchess of Aquitaine and no one would ever see her wounds or know the turmoil she felt inside.

Alienor quietly entered the bridal chamber at the top of the tower. Night had fallen and the shutters were closed. Numerous candles and lamps had been lit and the room flickered with soft amber light and umber shadows. The escape she had made was brief. In a moment the women would arrive to prepare her for her wedding night.

Someone had hung her father's shield on the wall — Geoffrey, she suspected — both as a reminder of her bloodline and as a symbol of paternal sanction. She swallowed as she remembered picking it up as a little girl and running behind her father, pretending to be his squire, making him laugh as she strove not to drag its tip in the dust.

The great bed, which had traveled with them in their baggage train, was layered with fresh linen sheets, soft woolen blankets, and a silk coverlet embroidered with a design of eagles. Curtains of red wool formed deep swags, heavy with shadows. The bed had a long history reaching back beyond her parents and grandparents to earlier rulers of these lands, even to a son of Charlemagne who had been King of Aquitaine in the days when Aquitaine had kings. For centuries it had served its purpose as a platform for wedding nights, conceptions, births, and deaths. Tonight it would be a stage for the consummation of the bond between France and Aquitaine begun in the cathedral three days ago.

Alienor knew what to expect. The matrons in the household had explained her duties to her, and she was neither blind nor unknowing. She had seen animals mating and observed the intimate embraces of people in dark corners when bitter winter weather put outdoor trysting places beyond bounds. On more than one occasion she had heard her grandfather's explicit poetry and that in itself had been an education. Her fluxes had come regularly for over a year now: a sign that her body was producing seed and ready to mate. But having such awareness was not the same as personal experience, and she was apprehensive. Would Louis know what to do, having been raised as a monk until his brother died? Had someone explained everything to him?

Petronella opened the door and peered around it. "There you are! Everyone's looking for you!"

Alienor turned, feeling a flicker of resentment. "I wanted a moment just to be alone."

"Shall I tell them you're not here?"

Alienor shook her head. "That would only lead to more trouble." She forced a smile. "It will be all right, Petra; I told you so, didn't I?"

"But you don't look as if you think that. I wish you were still sleeping with me, not him."

Alienor wished it too. "There will be time in the future. You will always be a part of my chamber — always." She put her arms around Petronella, seeking comfort for both of them.

Petronella returned her embrace fiercely, and the sisters only parted when the ladies from the wedding party arrived to prepare Alienor for her bridal bed, scolding her for disappearing. Alienor imagined fending them off with her father's shield and projected an

82

air of pride and command to conceal how frightened and vulnerable she felt. Sipping from a cup of wine laced with spices, she let them remove her wedding clothes and dress her in a chemise of soft white linen, before combing her hair until it shimmered to her waist in golden ripples.

The sound of masculine voices lifted in praise to God heralded the arrival of the men. Alienor stood straight and faced the door like a warrior on a battlefield.

Archbishop Gofrid entered first, solemnly pacing, accompanied by Abbé Suger and twelve choristers, chanting a hymn of praise. Louis came next escorted by Theobald of Blois and Raoul de Vermandois, followed by the nobility of France and Aquitaine, bearing candles. There would be no bawdy revels tonight, but a dignified and solemn ceremony to witness the future King of France and the young Duchess placed side by side in the marriage bed.

Louis wore a long, white nightshirt similar to Alienor's chemise. In the candlelight, his eyes were wide and dark and his expression apprehensive. Gofrid instructed Alienor and Louis to stand together and join hands while he prayed over them, asking God to bless the marriage with fruitfulness and prosperity. While he was doing this, Louis's attendants set up a small portable altar at the bedside.

The bed itself was blessed with much

sprinkling of holy water, and then Louis was guided to the left side of the bed and Alienor to the right, the better to ensure the conception of a son. The sheets were cool and crisp against her legs. She stared at the embroidered coverlet, her hair swinging forward to screen her face. She was aware of Geoffrey among the group of witnesses in the chamber, but she did not look at him and had no idea if he was looking at her. Only let this moment be over. Only let it be morning.

At last the chamberlains ushered everyone from the room, the bishops and the choir being the last to leave in stately procession, singing. The latch fell, the chanting voices receded, and Alienor was alone with Louis.

Turning toward her, he propped himself on one elbow, one hand cupped behind his head, and gazed at her with unsettling intensity. She adjusted the pillows at her back and remained sitting up. He smoothed the sheet with his other hand, tracing the outline of one of the eagles. His fingers were long and fine; beautiful, in fact. The thought of him touching her made her shiver with fear — and a stirring of desire.

"I know what is expected of us," she said in a tight voice. "The women have explained to me my duty."

He reached out and touched her hair. "My duty has been explained also." His fingers brushed her face. "But this does not feel like

a duty. I thought it would, but it doesn't."
His brow furrowed. "Perhaps it should."

Alienor tensed as Louis leaned over her.
She had thought they would talk more, but it
seemed he was intent on his business and she
need not have worried that his early training
as a monk had left him ignorant.

"I won't hurt you," he said. "I am not a
beast; I am a prince of France." A note of
pride crept into his voice. He kissed her cheek
and temple with a butterfly gentleness that
was almost reverential. His touch was eager,
but he was not rough. "The Church has given
us sanction to do this, and it is a holy thing."

Alienor steadied herself. The marriage had
to be consummated. Proof would be sought
in the morning. The deed couldn't be that
terrible or else men and women would not
return to it so often or write songs and poetry
about it in vivid, carnal detail.

He kissed her on the mouth with his lips
closed and began tentatively to untie the laces
at the throat of her chemise. His hand was
trembling and his breath shook in his chest.
Alienor realized that he too was out of his
depth, and it gave her courage. She returned
his kiss and put her hands in his hair. His
skin was smooth and supple, and his breath
smelled of wine and cardamom seeds. Amid
clumsy, breathless kisses, they undressed each
other. Louis pulled the sheets over them
both, creating a barely lit tent within the

confines of the bed curtains, and he lay on her. His body was damp with sweat and as smooth as her own. His fair hair was silky under her fingers. She could have stayed like this all night, kissing and touching, wrapped in this mutual, tender embrace with everything still to discover. But Louis was keen to progress the matter and, after a moment, Alienor parted her legs for him.

It was the secret channel. The place where children were conceived from a blending of male and female seed, and from which they were pushed into the world nine months later. A source of sin and shame, but also of pleasure. The work of God; the work of the Devil. Her grandfather had been excommunicated for falling prey to his lust for that place within his mistress's body and refusing to give her up even though she was another man's wife. He had written paeans to the glories of fornication.

Louis fumbled and muttered something that sounded like an oath, but then she realized he was entreating God to be with him at this moment and help him do his duty. Alienor felt a sharp, stabbing pain as he pushed into her and she arched and gritted her teeth, striving not to cry out. He moved above her half a dozen times, and then, with a gasp and a final lunge, shuddered and was still.

After a moment he heaved a deep sigh and

withdrew from her. Alienor closed her legs as he lay down at her side. There was a long silence. Was that it? Was that all the deed consisted of? Was she supposed to speak? She had once come across a couple in an empty stable lazing in postcoital bliss and they had been talking and kissing in a warm and languorous way, but was that appropriate for her and Louis?

Eventually, he stroked her arm and, drawing away, donned his nightshirt. Leaving the bed, he knelt before the small altar and offered up a prayer of thanksgiving. Alienor was astonished at his action, but he looked so beautiful with the candlelight shining on his hair, and his features aglow with devotion, that she felt admiration too.

He turned to her. "Do you not come and pray too, wife?" he asked with a frown.

Alienor stretched. "If that is what you want me to do," she said.

His frown deepened. "It is what you should do for God, and without question. We should both thank Him and pray that He makes us fruitful."

Alienor thought they had already done that, but she humored him and, donning her shift, came to kneel at his side and make her own prayer. Louis's tense shoulders relaxed and his gaze grew tender. He stroked her hair again as if it fascinated him. And then he cleared his throat and turned back to his prayers.

When eventually they returned to the bed, Alienor's knees were on fire as well as the place between her thighs. She was shivering too. A small red blot had soaked into the center of the sheet. Louis looked at it with an expression of mingled satisfaction and distaste. "You have given proof of your purity," he said. "Abbé Suger and the Archbishop will bear witness tomorrow." He gestured her back into bed. Alienor climbed in and started to close the curtains.

"Leave them," he said swiftly. "I like to see the light; it helps me to sleep."

Alienor raised her eyebrows, thinking that Louis was just like Petronella. He needed the comfort and security of a candle. She gently touched his shoulder. "As you wish, sire," she said. "I understand."

He clasped her hand but said nothing.

Alienor closed her eyes. On her side of the bed the candlelight was so dim that it did not impinge. The blood spot was cold and damp under her thighs. She felt a little let down. The embracing, the kissing, and the twining had been delicious, but the strangeness and discomfort of the final act had left her feeling disappointed and more than a little sore.

Louis seemed to have found his pleasure. She wondered if God was pleased too and if she had conceived a child. That notion frightened her and she put it from her mind and turned over to face away from him, seeking her own space. Louis's breathing soon grew deep and slow as he fell asleep, but it was a long time before her own restless mind settled to slumber; there was too much to think about, not least how to deal with this stranger in the bed who had mingled his seed with hers so that they were now irrevocably bound as one flesh.

7

Palace of Poitiers, Summer 1137

Wearing a gown of red sarcenet, the coronet of Aquitaine held between her hands, Alienor sat alone by the pool in the palace gardens. A relentless sun had beaten down all day and now a bruised dusk was mantling the city.

No one had come looking for her yet, but they soon would. Not for her the freedom to do as she pleased. This last fortnight, she had either been immersed in public duties or traveling between them, constantly attended by servants, vassals, and family. Her every moment was accounted for as if her time were being apportioned like beads on an abacus counted out by a keen-eyed merchant. Even when she was kneeling in church or at her needlework, she was aware of being scrutinized by members of Louis's entourage and by Louis himself. He couldn't take his eyes off her and wanted her with him all of the time, as if she were a precious jewel stitched to his tunic.

She had grown accustomed to the night duty and it hurt less now; indeed it was pleasurable on the occasions when Louis lingered over the foreplay. She just wished he did not have to kneel and ask God's blessing every time, and then thank Him afterward and expect her to do the same. He did not share her bed on Fridays or Sundays because he said they should be kept pure for God, but she used those occasions to cuddle up with Petronella in the old way — except it wasn't the same anymore. Her marriage and bedding had severed her from girlhood. Petronella had demanded to know what it was like, sleeping with a man, and Alienor had put her off with vague remarks about it being part of the duty of a wife.

Alienor was still unsure what to make of Louis. Sometimes he was the aloof French prince, looking down from his tall horse, but he was like a child too, having to be told what to think and do by his courtiers, who vied for influence over him. Also like a child, he could be petulant, stubborn, and unreasonable. And then there was his stifling piety, born of his upbringing by the Church, coupled with his overweening need for structure and order. Unlike her, he was not good at adapting to suit his circumstances. Yet he could be sweet and charming. He was knowledgeable about nature, loved the trees and the sky, and enjoyed being on the road in merry company where he would shed his solemnity and find his smile, which was winsome and tender. She found him physically attractive too, with his lean, graceful physique, his shining fair hair, and his dark blue eyes.

Today he had been invested with the coronet of Aquitaine and the look of pride and satisfaction on his face as the diadem was placed on his brow had filled Alienor with resentment and misgiving rather than pride. It was as if he was taking it for granted that it should be his because God had willed it. Receiving her coronet at his side, she had been politically astute enough to show nothing on her face, but seeing him sitting in the ducal chair with that superior look in his eyes had brought to the fore all her feelings of grief and loneliness over her father's death, together with the certainty that Louis was never going to fill his shoes.

"There you are!" Floreta came hurrying down the garden path. "People are looking all over for you; it is almost dark."

"I was thinking of my father. I wish he was still here," Alienor said wistfully.

"We all wish that, mistress," Floreta said, her tone compassionate, but added, practical and brisk, "Yet we must make the best of what we have. He did his best to make sure you would be safe and secure."

Alienor sighed and stood up, dusting the back of her gown. The first stars had begun to twinkle over the battlements, but it was still no cooler. "I was also thinking of my mother," she said. "I miss her too."

"You were named for her." Floreta gave Alienor a hug. "She will always be with you. Assuredly she is watching over you from heaven."

Alienor turned with the nurse to go back to the palace. Heaven was all very well, but it was her mother's physical presence she craved. She wanted to feel her arms around her and to be tucked up in bed like a child. She wanted someone to lift the burdens from her shoulders and let her sleep without worry. Floreta for all her caring would never understand the true depth of her need. No one would.

Louis was enthusiastic in his lovemaking that night, keen to do his duty and continue the great success of the day following his investiture as Duke of Aquitaine. Alienor answered him fiercely, because it seemed to her that unless she replied with assertion she would lose her identity, and they finished in a sweating, gasping tangle, which left her feeling as if she had been dragged through the heart of a thunderstorm. Certainly Louis behaved as if he had been struck by lightning, and when they prayed afterward, he knelt at his little altar for a long time, his damp silver hair falling forward, hiding his face, and his hands clenched so tightly that his knuckles were bloodless.

"I was thinking we should visit the abbey at Saintes," Alienor said when eventually they returned to bed. "My aunt Agnes is the Abbess there. She is my father's sister and could not attend the wedding. I wish to make a grant to the abbey now I am Duchess in full."

Louis nodded drowsily. "That is a seemly notion."

"I desire to visit my mother's grave also and make her chapel into a proper abbey."

Again he murmured agreement.

Alienor kissed his shoulder. "Perhaps we could stay in Aquitaine a little longer."

She felt him tense. "Why?"

"Some of the vassals have not yet sworn allegiance. If we leave without their oaths, they may think they can do as they please. We need their allegiance, and the longer we stay, the more loyal people will be." She pressed small, seductive kisses to his collarbone and throat. "You could always send Suger and the others back to France and then you would be able to make your own decisions without them telling you what to do all the time."

He was silent, absorbing this, and then he said, "How long were you thinking?"

Alienor pursed her lips against his throat. As long as she could keep him here was the straight answer. "Just a little while," she coaxed. "Until it is cool enough to travel in comfort and the vassals are more settled."

He grunted and turned over, drawing away from her and pulling the sheet over his shoulder. "I will give the matter some thought," he said.

Alienor did not push further. It had to come as his idea and would be better digested after a night's sleep. She could work on him again over the next few days on their way to Saintes. The longer they remained in Aquitaine, the better pleased she would be.

During the night, Alienor was roused by a rapid banging on the door followed by the click of the latch and the sudden flare of a torch. She jerked to a sitting position, still struggling out of sleep, and cried out in alarm as Raoul de Vermandois clashed back the bed curtains. His gaze flicked over her tumbled hair and naked body with passing appreciation, and then shifted to the far side of the bed where Louis was sitting up and squinting against the blaze of the torch borne by Raoul's squire.

"What is it?" Louis demanded blearily.

"Sire, there is grave news from the court." Raoul dropped to one knee and bowed his head. "Your lord father took a turn for the worse five days ago at Béthizy and, at dusk, gave up his soul to God. You must return to France immediately."

Louis stared at him blankly. Alienor pressed

her hand to her mouth as she absorbed Raoul's words and everything expanded in a rush. Dear God, this meant that Louis was King of France and that she was Queen. Her plans to stay in Aquitaine were so much chaff in the wind. They would have to go to Paris now, not just to join the royal household, but to head it as its rulers.

Louis staggered from the bed to kneel at his altar, head bowed over his clasped hands. "Blessed Saint Peter, I beg you to intercede on my father's behalf so that he may be granted entry into heaven. God have mercy, God have mercy." He repeated the words in a continuous litany, rocking back and forth.

The seneschal eyed him with consternation. "Sire?"

Alienor rallied as she donned her chemise and turned to Raoul. His tunic was inside out and his thick white hair stood up in tufts as if he had come straight from his bed. "Has Abbé Suger been informed?"

A grimace crossed Raoul's face. "I have sent a servant to fetch him. He was dining with the Archbishop and staying with him until the morrow."

Swift to pick up nuances, Alienor had noticed the friction between Suger and Raoul de Vermandois during their progress. The men were not at ease with each other, although both would have vigorously denied there was any incompatibility. "My lord, we need to dress and compose ourselves."

Raoul's gaze on her sharpened, as if he was reassessing an item that was more interesting than he had first thought. He bowed. "I will send in your servants."

"No," she said. "I will summon them myself in a moment. My lord husband is over-wrought, and it would be imprudent for them to see him like this. It will give you time to sort out your tunic before the good Abbé arrives."

"My tunic?" He looked down, and then plucked at the exposed seams. His mouth twisted in a wry smile. "I will remedy the situation and see you are not disturbed until you are ready." He took his leave, his stride swift and authoritative. Alienor suspected it would give him great satisfaction to deny entry to the Abbot of Saint-Denis, if only for a few minutes.

Alienor went to kneel at Louis's side. She knew what it was like to lose a father, but her own prayer to God was swift and practical. The world was waiting outside their bed-chamber door and if they did not go out to face it, then it would come to them, and they would be at its mercy.

"Louis?" She put her arms around him. "Louis, I am sorry your father is dead, but let there be prayers and masses said for him in the proper places. You cannot do it all yourself here and now. We have to get up and dressed; they are waiting for us."

His chant faltered and ceased. He gave her a dazed look. "I knew he was sick and that his days were numbered, but I did not think his time was so short and that I would never see him again. What am I going to do?"

She made him sit on the bed and drink a cup of wine while she brought their clothes from the coffer where the servants had folded them the night before. "You are going to compose yourself and get dressed," she said. "De Vermandois has gone to organize the household, and Suger has been sent for."

He nodded, but she could tell he was not absorbing the information. She remembered feeling that initial numbness when her own father had died. Words had meant nothing. She held him against her and stroked his hair. It was like soothing Petronella, as if she were the mother and he was the child. He turned to her with a soft groan and pressed his face into her neck. She shushed him and he clung to her. But then he lifted his head and kissed her with his mouth open. She was startled but, recognizing his need, returned his kiss and opened herself to him.

When it was over, he lay beside her and panted like a shipwrecked sailor washed up on the shore. She stroked his back gently between the shoulder blades and murmured hush words, feeling a little tearful herself. They had shared something momentous. She had channeled his grief and panic away through her body and brought him to calm. "It will be all right," she said.

"I did not really know my father." Louis sat up and buried his head between his upraised knees. "He gave me to the Church when I was a child, and I was only taken out of the cloister when my brother died. He saw to my welfare and my education, but it was all at the hands of others. If I have a father, it is Abbé Suger."

Alienor absorbed the detail with interest but no surprise. "I thought I knew mine well," she reciprocated. "I had been his heir since I was six years old. But when he died, I discovered I barely knew him at all . . ." She fell silent before she said something she would later regret.

The sound of authoritative masculine voices rumbled in the antechamber. Suger had arrived, and she could also hear Archbishop Gofrid. She swiftly cajoled Louis into getting dressed.

"You must show everyone you are capable of fulfilling the role of king — even while you are mourning your father," she said as she slipped his shoes onto his feet. "You are God's chosen. Why should you fear?"

His focus returned as he stared at her, and some of the anxiety left his face. "Come out with me," he entreated her as she fastened his belt.

Alienor hastily donned her gown and bundled her hair into a gold-wire net. Her heart was pounding, but she raised her chin and, showing neither fear nor apprehension, set her hand upon his sleeve and drew him to the door. Under her palm she felt him trembling.

The antechamber was full of assembled courtiers who knelt as one in a rustle of cloth, Suger included. Looking at the serried ranks of heads, Alienor thought that they resembled cobblestones on a road awaiting the tread of their new king and queen.

8

Paris, September 1137

Adelaide of Maurienne, Dowager Queen of France, gestured brusquely with a pale, bony hand. "You will want to change your gown and take some refreshment after your long journey."

Alienor curtsied. "Thank you, madam." Her mother-in-law had spoken with emotionless practicality — the way she might address a groom about a horse that required tending after a hard ride. Adelaide's gray eyes were cold and judgmental. Her dress was gray too, matching the fur lining of her cloak. Austere and wintry. A short while ago she had formally greeted her new daughter-in-law in the spacious great hall of the palace complex with a stilted speech of welcome and a chilly kiss on the cheek. Now they stood in the chamber that had been allotted to Alienor, high up in the Great Tower.

The room was well appointed, with handsome wall hangings, sturdy furniture, and a big bed with heavy curtains smelling strongly of sheep. The shutters were closed, and since there were few candles, the effect was one of encroaching deep shadow. In full daylight, though, the double arched windows would give a view over the busy River Seine, much as the Ombrière Palace at Bordeaux looked out on the Garonne.

Under Adelaide's watchful gaze, servants brought washing water, wine, and platters of bread and cheese. Alienor's women started unpacking, shaking out gowns and chemises before draping them over clothing poles or storing them in the garderobes. Adelaide's nostrils flared at the sight of the colorful and detailed garments emerging from the baggage chests. "You will find us accustomed to plainer ways here," she said primly. "We are not a frivolous people, and my son has simple tastes."

Alienor tried to look demure, thinking that if Adelaide knew what her precious son had been doing throughout their progress of Aquitaine, she would have an apoplexy. Even for Louis, the Church was not the only influence in his life.

Petronella tossed her head. "I like bright colors," she said. "They remind me of home. Our papa loved them."

"Yes, he did." Alienor slipped her arm around Petronella's waist in support. "We shall have to set new fashions!" She smiled at

Adelaide, who did not smile back.

Several young women in Adelaide's retinue exchanged glances with each other, among them Louis's sister, Constance, who was of a similar age to Alienor, and Gisela, a young royal kinswoman with dusty-blond hair and green eyes. Someone stifled a giggle and, without looking around, Adelaide made a terse gesture commanding silence. "I can see you have much to learn," she said severely.

Alienor refused to be browbeaten. She would not allow her unfamiliarity with Paris and French ways to make her feel diminished. She would be proud and stand tall because she was the equal of anyone here. "Indeed I do, madam," she replied. "Our father taught us the importance of education." Because to outwit your rivals, first you had to know their ways and how to play their games.

"I am pleased to hear it," Adelaide said. "You would do well to listen to your elders. Let us hope he taught you the importance of manners too."

"She doesn't like us," Petronella said when Adelaide eventually left to attend to business elsewhere. "And I certainly don't like her!"

"You will be civil to her," Alienor warned, lowering her voice. "She is Louis's mother and owed respect. There are different customs here and we must learn them."

"I don't want to learn their ways." Petronella pursed her lips in fair imitation of Adelaide and folded her arms. "I don't like it here."

"That's because it is late and you are tired. Tomorrow, in daylight, when you have slept, it will be different."

"No it won't," Petronella said, just to be awkward.

Alienor suppressed a sigh. Tonight she did not have the wherewithal to humor Petronella because her own mood was low. Adelaide plainly disapproved of them and viewed their presence as a thorn in her side. Her power at court had grown stronger as her husband's health deteriorated, but to maintain that power, she now had to control and influence Louis. She clearly viewed Alienor as someone who would usurp her position if not put down from the outset.

Louis had been reticent about his mother but Alienor had gleaned the impression that the emotional ties between them were rigid and about dominance. There was no love, except in the way of a need for it on Louis's behalf, and a refusal to give it on Adelaide's. Alienor had already seen how easily Louis was manipulated by stronger personalities, and how stubborn he could be once persuaded to a certain decision. The factions at court fought over him like dogs over a fresh bone, and it was her duty to protect him and in doing so also protect herself and her sister.

If Louis needed the reassurance of lit candles at night, it was because of what had been done to him by others who should have cared for him and hadn't.

Alienor ran her hand over the smooth milky skin on Louis's back. He was asleep on his stomach, and he looked so handsome and vulnerable that he filled her heart. On their journey to Paris, he had been forced to divert to put down a rebellion in Orléans. Seasoned battle commanders Raoul de Vermandois and Theobald of Champagne had advised him, but he had taken overall responsibility and the rebellion had been successfully quashed. The victory had given him a new assertiveness and confidence that sat well on him.

She moved her hand lower, stroking the small of his back. He opened his eyes, stretched, and, with a sleepy smile, turned over and pulled her down for a kiss. "You are so beautiful," he said.

"So are you, my husband." He was erect from having just woken, and she took advantage, straddling him with a mischievous sparkle in her eyes.

His eyes widened at the sinful position and he gasped, but he did not push her off. A feeling of power tingled through her as she moved upon him and he thrust within her. In the two months since their marriage, she had grown accustomed to the procreation duty and had come to enjoy it and even find it needful. There was no sign of a pregnancy yet, but both she and Louis were certain it would happen. As Louis arched beneath her and gave her his seed, she clenched upon him, crying out in pleasure.

They lay together recovering, and she nuzzled his shoulder. She knew that beyond the chamber, the servants would be hurrying to report to Adelaide that the young King and Queen were still abed and fulfilling their duty to procreate, and it brought a sour smile to her lips. Adelaide would be on tenterhooks, hoping that she and Louis had conceived a child, and at the same time suspicious of the time they were spending together, time she could not influence.

Her mother-in-law continued to strive for dominance under the guise of teaching Alienor the etiquette of the French court and preparing her for the official crowning ceremony in December at Bourges, but she was like a snappy dog, always chivvying Alienor and criticizing her clothes, her manners, the way she walked, how much time she spent adorning her chamber, and her frivolity when she should be at prayer. Alienor was always civil to Adelaide's face and demure in her presence, but she was deeply resentful of the older woman's interference.

Louis sat up. "I should go," he said with reluctance. "Abbé Suger is expecting me, and

I have already missed first prayers."

"There are always people lying in wait," Alienor replied with a toss of her head. She set her palm against his back, claiming him for a moment longer. "Perhaps after we are crowned, we should consider returning to Poitiers."

He looked impatient. "We have officials there to keep us informed; there is too much to do here."

"Nevertheless, we should think about it," Alienor persisted. "We are Duke and Duchess as well as King and Queen, and our stay was curtailed because we had to return to Paris. We must not let my people think we have forgotten them."

He avoided her eyes. "I will ask Suger and see what he says."

"Why should it be up to Suger? He has a duty to advise you, but he treats you as if you are still his pupil, not the King of France. You can do as you please."

Louis said defensively, "I do take his advice, but I make my own decisions." He reached for his clothes and began putting them on.

"You could decide to go to Poitou after the coronation. It would not be too difficult, surely?" She tossed her head, making her hair shimmer over her naked body like cloth of gold.

Louis devoured her with a glance and his pale complexion flushed. "No," he conceded.

"I suppose it would not be too difficult."

"Thank you, husband." She gave him a demure, sweet smile. "I so much want to see Poitiers again." The image of the good and doting wife, she knelt at his feet to fasten his shoes.

"I do love you," Louis said, as if blurting out a shameful confession, before tearing himself away and hurrying from the room.

Alienor gazed after him and gnawed her lower lip. Obtaining what she wanted was a constant battle and had become more of a routine irritation than an interesting challenge.

Her women arrived to dress her. She chose a new gown of russet and gold damask with deep hanging sleeves and coiled her abundant hair into a net of gold thread set with tiny gemstone beads. Floreta held up a delicate ivory mirror for Alienor to study her reflection. What she saw pleased her, for while her beauty did not rule her life, it gave her an advantage she was prepared to exploit. Her face needed no enhancement, but she had Floreta add a subtle touch of alkanet to redden her lips and cheeks in defiance of her mother-in-law's scrubbed severity.

Her chamberlain announced that a set of painted coffers she had ordered had arrived, together with some new bed curtains and a pair of enameled candlesticks. Alienor's mood brightened further. She was gradually making her chamber into a little part of Aquitaine in the heart of Paris. Northern France was not without its great riches, but it did not possess the sun-drenched ambience of her homeland. The French palace was heavy with the weight of centuries, but no more so than Poitiers or Bordeaux. However, Adelaide's dull and somber tastes permeated everything, so that even this great tower, built by Louis's father, had the feel of a building much older and stultified with time.

Servants arrived with the new furnishings and Alienor began arranging them. She had one of the chests set at the foot of the bed and the other, depicting a group of dancers hand in hand, put against the wall. She had the existing bed hangings taken down and new ones of golden damask put up. The maids opened out a quilt of detailed whitework stitched with eagle motifs.

"More purchases, daughter?" Adelaide said from the doorway, her voice full of icy disapproval. "There is nothing wrong with what you had before."

"But they were not my choice, madam," Alienor replied. "I want to be reminded of Aquitaine."

"You are not in Aquitaine now, you are in Paris, and you are the wife of the King of France."

Alienor replied with a hint of defiance, "I am still Duchess of Aquitaine, my mother."

Adelaide narrowed her eyes and stalked farther into the room. She cast a disparaging look over the new chests and hangings. Her glance fell on the rumpled bed that the chamber ladies had yet to make, and her nostrils flared at the smell of recent congress. "Where is my son?"

"He has gone to see Abbé Suger," Alienor replied. "Would you care for some wine, my mother?"

"No, I would not," Adelaide snapped. "There are more important things in the world than drinking wine and frittering money on gaudy furnishings. If you have time for this, then you have too much free rein."

The air bristled with Adelaide's hostility and Alienor's resentment. "Then what would you have me do, madam?" Alienor asked.

"I would have you comport yourself with decorum. The sleeves on that dress are scandalous — almost touching the ground! And that veil and headdress do nothing to hide your hair!" Adelaide warmed to her theme, flinging out her arm in an angry gesture. "I would have your servants learn to speak the French of the north and not persist in this outlandish dialect that none of us can understand. You and your sister chatter away like a couple of finches."

"Caged finches," said Alienor. "It is our native tongue, and we speak the French of the north in public company. How can I be

Duchess of Aquitaine if I do not maintain the traditions of my homeland?"

"And how can you be Queen of France and a fitting consort for my son when you behave like a silly, frivolous girl? What kind of example are you setting to others?"

Alienor set her jaw. It was pointless arguing with this cantankerous harridan. These days, Louis was far more likely to listen to the "silly, frivolous girl" than his carping mother, but the constant criticism and sniping still wore her down and made her want to cry. "I am sorry you are vexed, Mother, but I am entitled to furnish my own chamber as I choose, and my people may talk as they desire, providing they are courteous to others."

Adelaide's abrupt departure left a brief but awkward silence. Alienor broke it by clapping her hands and calling brightly to her servants in the *lenga romana* of Bordeaux. If she was a finch, she intended to sing her heart out in defiance of everyone and everything.

Two days later, accompanied by her ladies, Alienor went to walk in the gardens. She loved this green and fragrant part of the castle complex with its abundance of plants, flowers, and lush turf. Sweet-smelling roses were still in bloom at summer's end, and everything stayed greener than in Aquitaine because the sun was less fierce. The gardeners were skilled and, even enclosed as it was, the pleasance was an escape into a different, fresher world that offered respite from the machinations and backbiting of the court.

Today, the September sun cast mellow, translucent light over the grass and the trees, the latter still clad in their summer green but beginning to crisp with gold at the edges. The dew sparkled on the grass and Alienor had a sudden desire to feel the crystal coldness under her bare feet. On an impulse, she slipped off her shoes and hose and stepped onto the cool, sparkling turf. Petronella was swift to follow her example, and the other ladies, after a hesitation, joined in, even Louis's sister Constance, who usually hung back from any kind of daring or giddy behavior.

Alienor took several dancing steps, turning and twirling. Louis never danced. He had not been raised to such skills and delights, whereas she had. When forced, he performed each move with rigid precision but did not find it pleasurable entertainment and could not understand why others thought it was.

Petronella had brought a ball out with her and the young women began tossing it to each other. Alienor hitched her dress through her belt. The suffocating feelings dissipated in the flurry of activity and she delighted in the vigor of the game and the feel of the cold, wet grass between her toes. The hem of her dress soaked up the dew and whipped around her bare ankles. She leaped, caught the ball against her midriff, and, laughing, flung it to Gisela, who had been assigned to her household.

A shout of warning from Floreta, accompanied by a frantic hand flap, made Alienor stop and look around. Several men in clerical garb carrying stools and cushions were advancing on them along one of the paths. They were being led by an emaciated monk, who was addressing them in a raised voice as they walked. "For what is more against faith than to be unwilling to believe what reason cannot attain? You might consider the words of the wise man who said that he who is hasty to believe is light in mind . . ." He ceased speaking and looked toward the women, an expression of surprised annoyance flitting across his face.

Alienor tensed. This was the great Bernard of Clairvaux, religious and spiritual crusader, intellectual, ascetic, and tutor. He was esteemed for his holiness, but was also a man of rigid principles, unswerving in his opposition to anyone who disagreed with his views on God and the Church. Four years ago, he had disputed with her father over papal politics, and she knew just how tenacious Bernard could be. What he was doing in the garden, she did not know, and he seemed to be thinking the same of her. She was suddenly very aware that her shoes and stockings were draped over the side of the fountain and was annoyed to be caught at such a disadvantage.

She made a small curtsy to him and he responded with the slightest inclination of his head, his dark eyes full of censure.

"Madam, the King told me that the gardens were available for me to discourse with my students this morning."

"The King made no mention to me, but by all means be welcome, Father," Alienor replied, adding with a spark of challenge: "Perhaps we could sit and listen for a while."

His lips thinned. "If you truly wish to learn, daughter, I am willing to teach, although to hear the words of God, one must first unstopper one's ears."

He went to sit down on a turf seat, prim as a dowager, and his students gathered around him, pretending to ignore the women while stealing furtive, outraged glances at them.

The Abbot of Cîteaux arranged his robes, resting a skeletal hand on one knee and raising the other, holding his tutor's rod in a light grip.

"Now," he said. "I spoke to you earlier of faith, and we shall return to that question in a moment, but I am suddenly reminded of a letter of advice I have been writing to a most holy virgin concerning earthly pleasures." He cast his gaze toward Alienor and her ladies.

"It is truly said that silk and purple and rouge and paint have their beauty. Everything of that kind that you apply to your body has its individual loveliness, but when the garment comes off, when the paint is removed, that beauty goes with it; it does not stay with the sinful flesh. I counsel you not to emulate those persons of evil disposition who seek external beauty when they have none of their own within their souls. They study to furnish themselves with the graces of fashion that they may appear beautiful in the eyes of fools. It is an unworthy thing to borrow attractiveness from the skins of animals and the work of worms. Can the jewelry of a queen compare to the flush of modesty on a true virgin's cheek?" His eyes bored into Alienor. "I see women of the world burdened — not adorned — with gold and silver. With gowns that have long trains that trail in the dust. But make no mistake; these mincing daughters of Belial will have nothing with which to clad their souls when they come to death, unless they repent of their ways!"

Anger and humiliation burned in Alienor's breast. How dare this walking cadaver insult her? His references and his contempt were not even thinly veiled. She was already judged and condemned without him knowing her. Her father had been forced to back down under Bernard's onslaught. She had wanted to stand proud for Aquitaine and show him

115

her mettle, but realized how pointless it was, because whatever the discussion, he would have the last word. Gathering her ladies, she retreated from the garden.

"Horrible old man!" Petronella shuddered. "What's a daughter of Belial?"

Alienor curled her lip. "A wicked woman, so the Bible says. But the good Abbot would see all women thus unless clad in coarse rags and begging on their knees for forgiveness for the sin of being born female. He sits in judgment of all, and yet he is not God, nor does he speak in place of God." Within her the core of rebellion hardened. She would dress as she chose, because clothes and appearance were part of a woman's armor in this world whether Bernard of Clairvaux approved or not. The soul was no better or worse for what its fleshly vessel wore.

Returning to the keep, they were met by Adelaide, who plainly knew about Bernard's presence in the gardens, for she was in the act of sending a chamberlain to order refreshments for the visitors. Her gaze widened with horror as she took in the state of the returnees. "Bare feet?" she gasped. "What are you doing? You are not peasants! This is disgraceful!"

"Oh no, my lady mother," Alienor replied innocently. "The good Abbé was very clear that we should all clothe ourselves as peasants and exercise humility."

"Abbé Bernard made you do this?" Adelaide's eyebrows disappeared into her wimple band.

"He made it known what was expected of us," she said and, having made a deep curtsy, swept on up the tower stairs to her chamber, raising her skirts above her bare feet and ankles to show them off.

Behind her, she heard Adelaide clucking like an old hen. Petronella was making strange noises in her throat as she strove to stifle her giggles, and the sound was so infectious that the other ladies joined in, although Constance's was a timid echo. By the time they reached their chamber, they were almost helpless and holding on to each other. But in the midst of laughter, wiping her eyes, Alienor felt very close to tears.

Hearing the giggles in the stairwell, Adelaide's throat tightened with anger and chagrin at the behavior of the young women, even her own daughter. The insolence of those pale, bare feet! The impropriety mortified her and filled her with unease bordering on fear. Had she still been Queen of France such conduct would not have been tolerated. The standards being set by this upstart foolish child from Aquitaine were lax beyond decent measure. She did not for one moment believe that the good Abbot of Clairvaux had commanded Alienor and her ladies to go barefoot — she would have the truth of that from Constance or Gisela. Something would have to be done. Adelaide rubbed her temples, feeling old and tired and beset.

"Madam?"

She straightened her spine and faced Matthew de Montmorency, one of the court stewards.

"Madam, I have spoken to the chamberlain, and he has sent out bread and wine to Abbé Bernard and his pupils." He gave her a knowing look. "I bade him serve the refreshment in plain vessels and without a cloth for the trestle board."

Adelaide gave a brusque nod. Bernard would appreciate the quality of the repast and, at the same time, be approving that it was humbly served. Matthew had judged it well, but then he always did. "Thank you, my lord," she said, exhaling on a sigh. "I am sorely tried these days and I appreciate your forethought."

"Whatever you need, you have only to ask, madam." De Montmorency bowed. Adelaide watched his firm stride and straight back as he walked away to attend to his duties and felt a lifting of her spirit. If only others possessed his sense of courteous propriety.

9

Bourges, Christmas 1137

The court assembled at the city of Bourges to celebrate the Christmas feast and to crown Louis and Alienor before a great gathering of vassals and courtiers. The city was full to bursting with nobles and their retinues and as always there was a large overspill of tents and shelters to lodge those who could not be accommodated within the castle or at the inns and hostels in the city.

Alienor intended wearing her wedding dress for the coronation ceremony, but it had to be altered because she had grown taller since her marriage and her figure had developed the fuller curves of womanhood.

Set free from yet another fitting by the seamstresses, she went arm in arm with Petronella to the great hall where an informal meal had been arranged on trestles for the senior barons and vassals. Tomorrow the seating would be official, but today the still-arriving guests could mingle as they chose.

"I wager you a gold ring that Louis's mother will find excuses to spend time with Matthew de Montmorency," Petronella whispered to Alienor as they prepared to enter the hall.

"I never wager when I'm certain to lose," Alienor replied. She too had noticed the flush in Adelaide's cheeks whenever the steward was near and had observed their frequent discussions — which always remained within the bounds of propriety. "I wish them well. Anything that distracts her attention from me is welcome."

A striding nobleman crossed the sisters' path and both parties had to stop abruptly to avoid a collision. He drew breath to remonstrate, but then his glance flicked over their rich garments and the attendant ladies, and he swept a bow instead.

"Madam, forgive me. Let all make way for the matchless beauty of the Queen of France."

Alienor had never seen a man so handsome. He was tall with thick, shining hair midway between red and gold. His skin was as pale as alabaster, and his eyes were a clear blue-green, made vivid by the contrasting darkness of the pupils. A closely trimmed auburn beard edged his jawline and gave emphasis to a firm masculine mouth. His nose was straight as an arrow and fine.

"Sire, I do not know your name," she said,

feeling flustered.

He bowed again. "I am Geoffrey, Count of Anjou. Your father rode on campaign with me in Normandy last year, God rest his soul. We had many mutual interests." His gaze was predatory and amused.

"You are welcome at court, sire." She tried not to show how much his direct stare perturbed her.

"That is good to know." His voice developed an edge. "There are times when such has not been the case, but I hope for harmony in keeping with the season." He bowed a final time and moved on, pausing once to dazzle a smile over his shoulder.

Petronella giggled behind her hand and nudged Alienor. "He's handsome!"

Alienor felt as if Geoffrey of Anjou had stripped her to her chemise in front of everyone, even though their exchange had been one of social formality. She was intensely aware of him in the room now and, because of that, was also aware of her own actions and how she might appear to others. "Behave, Petra," she hissed.

"Is he married?"

"Yes, to the Empress Matilda, daughter of old King Henry of England." Another memory came to her: of overhearing talk in her father's hall when Count Geoffrey had written to her father proposing a marriage between herself and Geoffrey's infant son.

Her father had refused with a snort of derision at Angevin audacity. But given different circumstances, Geoffrey could have been her father-in-law and her husband a boy not yet five years old.

Petronella gave her another dig in the side. "He's still staring at us."

"Well, don't look at him." Alienor grabbed Petronella by the hand and made her way through the gathering to join Archbishop Gofrid, knowing she would be safe with him while she recovered her composure. Even so, she could feel Geoffrey's gaze on her and dared not glance around to meet his knowing smile.

"Geoffrey of Anjou . . ." Louis paced the bedchamber like a restless dog. "I would not trust him as far as I could throw a lance, for all that he swears us his fealty and goodwill."

The informal feasting had finished late, and some carousing was still going on in the lodgings and amid the army of tents outside the castle walls. Dressed in her chemise, Alienor sat braiding her hair before the fire. Even the thought of Geoffrey made her feel restless and hot. It was like seeing a beautiful, spirited stallion arching his crest and swishing his tail in the stable yard. All that charisma, virility, and danger. What would it be like to master a beast like that — to ride it? "Why not?" she asked.

"Because he is fickle," Louis growled. "If it suits his purpose, he will renege on his oath of fidelity. He is hungry for influence and power. He wants Normandy every bit as much as that termagant wife of his wants England. Imagine if he did gain it? Where would he look next but to French territory?" He reached the end of the room and turned. "I heard he approached your father about a match between you and his son."

"Which my father refused."

"Yes, but it shows he will snatch at any opportunity that comes his way."

Alienor said nothing. Louis's own father had hardly been noble in his motives when he seized the moment.

"He thinks his looks and his influence will gain him whatever he desires, but he is a fool. That his father is King of Jerusalem means nothing to me."

"What does he want?" Louis must have been talking to Suger and Theobald of Blois to be this agitated. His own aversion would not be so strong. The Blois faction was the natural enemy of Anjou, and Geoffrey was fighting Theobald's brother Stephen for Normandy.

Louis snorted. "A marriage alliance," he said. "He was fishing for a betrothal between Constance and his son."

Alienor was briefly startled, but not surprised when she thought beyond the person of Louis's pale, fair-haired sister to the implications.

"I refused him," Louis said. "It is hardly in our interests to give a man like that a leg up to the saddle, and I would not entrust Constance to either him or that virago wife of his."

Alienor suspected Geoffrey of Anjou would find his way to the top anyway, and from what she had heard about the Empress Matilda, she was not unlike her own mother-in-law. "What did he say?"

Louis scowled. "That he understood, but hoped I would keep his offer in mind, since circumstances often change."

"Did you say you would?"

Louis flicked her an irritated look. "I made it clear the matter was not open to discussion. I have better things to do than to waste time on a red-haired Angevin upstart."

"But what if his wife becomes Queen of England?"

"God forbid," Louis snapped. "I doubt it will happen. Their cause is a lost one before they begin. Rather let Constance go to Stephen's heir and wed into the power already on the throne."

Alienor was thoughtful. That seemed a sensible decision, but there was something about Geoffrey that made her think Louis was underestimating him.

"I'll be glad to have him gone from court,"

Louis added. "He's a disruptive influence. I don't want you or any of the women to go near him, is that understood?"

"But it is my duty to speak with your vassals and be a good hostess," she protested.

"Well, speak to the old ones and to the bishops. Leave Geoffrey of Anjou alone — I mean it." He came to stand over her, hands on his hips. "Tongues are swift to wag. The Queen of France must be above reproach."

Alienor felt a spark of excitement at Louis's obvious jealousy. "Do you not trust me?" She rose to face him.

"I do not trust him — as I told you." Louis pulled her into his arms and kissed her. "Do I have your word on this?"

She kissed him back, and then smoothed away his frown with her fingertips. "I promise I will be very careful. Are you coming to bed?"

Over the ensuing days, Alienor made sure she was indeed careful, because the thought of being alone with Geoffrey of Anjou was far too unsettling. She talked to the older vassals and the bishops. She kept company with the wives and daughters. The nearest she came to being undone was when Geoffrey held her hand during a Christmas revel dance and, at the end, kissed the inside of her wrist, grazing her skin lightly with his teeth — the implication being that she was good enough to eat — before bowing and walking away. It was all play, but far from innocent on his part. The experience sent a jolt through her body, but also made her narrow her eyes. She had a great deal to learn, but learn it she would, and one day, her knowledge would be greater than his, and she would be the one to turn him inside out as lightly as breathing.

10

Alienor gasped and bit her lip as Louis withdrew from her and rolled onto his back, his chest heaving with exertion. He had been rough in his lovemaking and she felt mauled, but she was coming to realize that his passions in the bedchamber were frequently driven by events that happened outside of it. She had recently finished her monthly bleed and this was the first time they had lain together in eight days. He had stayed away from her during that time, preferring not to have contact while her menstrual blood made her unclean. Instead, he had occupied himself in prayer and contemplation.

They had been married for nine months and Alienor had still not conceived. Her flux had been late at Christmas but had proven to be nothing. Each month, when she bled, Adelaide would make pointed comments about fulfilling her duties and providing an heir for France. She herself had borne Louis's father six healthy sons and a daughter when she was Queen.

Alienor coiled a lock of Louis's silvery hair around her forefinger. "My father sometimes took me and Petronella to Le Puy to celebrate the feast of the Virgin," she said. "My grand-sire presented the abbey with a belt that had once belonged to the mother of Christ. She is said to confer the gift of fertility on couples who pray at her shrine. We should go there and ask her blessing."

He raised his brows and looked cautiously interested.

"Charlemagne himself visited Le Puy," she said. "You promised that after our coronation we would go to Aquitaine."

"I did," he agreed, "but I have been busy with other duties. However, you are right; I will tell Suger."

Alienor held her peace. At least Louis had said "I will tell" rather than "I will ask," and that was progress of a kind.

He sat up and gently rubbed her cheek before looking at his thumb.

"What?" she asked, thinking perhaps she had a smut on her face.

"My mother says that you dress inappropriately and paint your face and that I should be wary. But you listen to me and give me comfort. When has she ever once done that? I do not care if it is true or not."

Alienor looked down while she mastered

her anger and irritation. She and Adelaide continued to battle for influence over Louis. Her intimacy with him gave her the upper hand, but even so Adelaide was tenacious. "Do you think I should behave and dress like your mother?"

A small shudder rippled through him. "No," he said. "I do not want you to become like her."

Alienor made her tone sorrowful. "I know it is difficult for her to give up the power and position she has wielded for so long. I honor her, but I cannot be like her."

"You are right," he said abruptly. "We should go to Le Puy and pray together."

Alienor hugged him. "Thank you, husband! You will not regret it, I promise!" She leaped from the bed in her chemise and twirled around, her hair flying out in a golden veil, making Louis laugh. When Alienor was soft and doe-eyed like this, she made him feel as if he could accomplish anything, and he would have given her the world, so great was his love. Yet the depth of his feeling set up a strange friction deep inside him, especially when others expressed reservation. What if he was indeed being duped?

She sobered and became demure again. "We should go and tell Suger together and ask him what we should take as an offering." Because then Suger would be involved and could not disapprove, and if Suger approved, then it left Adelaide out in the cold.

Alienor and Louis prayed before the statue of the Virgin and child at the Shrine of Our Lady in the cathedral at Le Puy and made gifts of frankincense and myrrh, presented in a bejeweled golden casket. Alienor prayed over the golden belt of the Virgin and passed it three times around her waist for the Trinity, so that her womb might be fruitful.

Le Puy was crowded with pilgrims preparing to set out on the road to Compostela, for it was an important place of worship along the route. Alienor and Louis distributed alms to the throng and walked a little way with them. Alienor's eyes filled with tears as she was reminded of the day her father had set out from Poitiers, with herself and Petronella at his side. Taking her emotion for religious fervor, Louis was moved to love her even more and thought he would burst with pride and adoration.

Since the pilgrim hostels were overflowing, Alienor and Louis spent the night in the royal tent under a powdering of stars. With the Virgin's blessing upon them, they made love in the warm spring evening with holy sanction, and it was tender and perfect.

Alienor was sitting up in bed with Adelaide standing beside her when Louis hurried into her chamber. They had been back in Paris for almost three months, and life had returned to its usual routine, except that for the last four mornings Alienor had been sick on rising and today Adelaide had summoned the royal physician to examine her.

"Sire," said the man, diplomatically concealing under a cloth the urine bottle he had been examining. "I am happy to tell you that the young Queen is with child."

Louis stared at him with widening eyes. "Truly?" He turned to look at Alienor.

Despite feeling nauseous, she gave him a wide smile, brimming with triumph and joy.

"Then the Virgin answered our prayers at Le Puy!" Louis's pale face flushed with wonder and joy. "There will be an heir for France, my clever, beautiful wife!"

"It is early days yet." His mother raised a warning forefinger. "Alienor must rest quietly and do nothing that might harm the baby or herself."

Alienor hid a grimace. She knew perfectly well what Adelaide was up to and had no intention of retiring into seclusion for the rest of her pregnancy. She cast a shy glance at Louis. "I should like to go to church and give thanks to the Virgin for her great bounty."

He looked pleased but uncertain. "Is it wise to leave your bed?"

"Surely it can do nothing but good to go and pray?" Alienor turned to the physician, who hesitated, and then inclined his head.

"Madam, prayer is always efficacious."

Behind the closed bed curtains, Alienor had her women dress her in a gown of blue wool and covered her plaited hair with a veil of fine white linen edged with tiny pearls. When she emerged, intentionally looking like a madonna, Adelaide had gone.

Louis gazed at her with adoration. "I am so proud of you." He kissed both her hands and then her brow.

Side by side they prayed together at the altar in the ancient basilica of Notre Dame. Alienor still felt queasy, but it was bearable. She was carrying the heir to France, and Aquitaine, and that gave her an inner sense of power as a fertile woman and nurturer. On the outside, it was part of becoming a true queen and entering into her own light.

Emerging from the dark and candle glow of the old Merovingian church, Louis and Alienor found a messenger waiting for them. His clothes were dusty and he stank of hard-ridden horse and unwashed man. "Sire. Madam." He dropped to his knees and bent his head. "There is grave news from Poitiers."

"What is it?" Alienor demanded before Louis could speak. "Get up. Tell me."

The man stumbled to his feet. "Madam, the people have risen up and declared themselves a commune. They say they will throw off the rule of the Dukes of Aquitaine and of

France. They have occupied the palace and even now are strengthening the defenses." He reached into his travel-battered leather satchel and produced a creased letter.

Alienor grabbed it from him and broke the seal; as she read the contents, her hand went to her mouth. It was like looking over her shoulder and seeing her lands falling into a dark chasm. This deed could crack her inheritance apart and undermine all she had and all that she was; she would be nothing — unable to maintain her position and dignity at court. As Duchess of Aquitaine she could stand up to others, including Adelaide, with integrity. Without her lands she was prey for the wolves.

Louis took the note and as he read it, his lips tightened.

"We have to do something," she said. "If this should spread . . ." It was too terrible to think about. "We must quash it now; there can be no prevarication. I'll order my baggage packed."

Louis looked at her in surprise and alarm. "You cannot do that; you are with child. You know what the physician said." He took her arm. "I will deal with this. They are my subjects too, and an affront to you is also an affront to me."

"But you do not know them as I do." She struggled to free herself, but Louis tightened his grip until his fingers pinched.

"I know enough to deal with them." He puffed out his chest. "Do not trouble yourself. I will see to this. Your first duty is to our child."

It was easy for him to say, Alienor thought, but to her it brought back all the grief, fear, and anxiety she had felt after her father's death. First her family was stripped away, then she had to leave her home, and now revolt threatened the very notion of her own identity.

"Go and rest in your chamber, and I will set things in motion." Louis turned her with him toward the Great Tower.

She managed to shake free from his grip. "Today. You must make preparations immediately."

He heaved an exasperated sigh. "Yes, today, if you insist."

She wanted to be on a horse, galloping to Poitiers, and was frustrated that she could not do so. Had she not been with child . . . "I shall write letters to my vassals in Poitou and to the bishops." She rubbed her sore arm. "They will bring influence to bear." At least she could do that. And for the rest, she would have to trust Louis.

A month later, feeling dizzy and sick, Alienor stood in the abbey church of Saint-Denis, attending a mass to honor the saint's day. Courtiers packed the nave and everyone was wearing their finest clothes and had brought gifts to present at the altar step. Presiding over the service, Abbé Suger held aloft the vase that Alienor had given to Louis on their wedding day. The womblike base was opaque with wine as dark as blood. Suger had asked permission to use the vase as part of the service to honor the church's patron and also the King, who was Saint Denis's especial devotee. Even now, Louis was riding into Aquitaine under the protection of the abbey's sacred banner, the oriflamme.

Not every French noble had ridden with him. Theobald of Blois-Champagne had announced stiffly that he was not feudally obliged to go to Poitiers and had declined the muster, treating Louis and Alienor as if he were putting a pair of silly young pups in their places, and Louis had left for Poitiers in a sullen mood, bringing with him two hundred knights, a contingent of archers, and a train of carts piled with siege weapons, determined to make his mark as a king and commander. Alienor had noted Theobald's refusal. He would bear watching because, with his connections, he was capable of causing great disruption, and his family had rebelled before.

She began to wish she had not given Suger permission to use the vase as a receptacle, for the sight of the wine was turning her stomach. She felt stifled, as if people were stealing the air from her lungs. The walls were pressing in on her, and she had a fancy that the decomposing former kings of France were all staring at her through their stone tombs with disapproving eyes.

At her side, Petronella touched her arm with concern. "Sister?"

Alienor gripped her prayer beads and shook her head. She dared not open her mouth, lest she retch, and she could not leave the service, because then rumors would spread that she was impious and disrespectful, or even a heretic. She was the Queen of France, and she must do her duty whatever the cost. Closing her eyes, breathing slowly and deeply, she set herself to endure as time passed like the hot, slow drip of wax from a melting candle.

When the service eventually ended, the congregation left the church in solemn procession, following the great bejeweled cross held high on its gilded staff by Suger, who was clad in robes of scintillating white and silver. Alienor concentrated on putting one foot in front of the other. Just a little longer, just another step.

Outside the church, a man lunged from the crowd and hurled himself at her feet, kissing the hem of her gown. "Madam! Of your mercy, the people of Poitiers beg your intercession. I bear grave news!"

Guards seized him and, as he struggled in their hard, mail grip, Alienor recognized him as a groom from the palace of Poitiers: a man who had sometimes carried letters for her father. "I know this man. Release him," she commanded. "What news? Tell me!"

The guards flung the groom back at her feet and their spears remained poised.

"Madam, the King has taken Poitiers and punished the people with fines and imprisonments. He has ordered all the burghers and nobles in the city to give up their children. He says he will bring them back to France with him and scatter them throughout his castles as surety for their parents' good behavior." One eye on the looming guards, the man withdrew a handful of documents from his satchel, seals dangling from a multitude of colored cords. "The people invoke your mercy and beg you to intervene. They fear they will never see their sons and daughters again. Jesu, Madam, some are but babes in arms."

Alienor swallowed bile. "They try to cast me off, and now they seek my mercy?" Her lips twisted. "What did they think would happen?"

"Madam?" Suger arrived at her side in his glittering robes.

"The King has taken hostages in Poitiers." She showed him the letters, her stomach churning like a hot cauldron. "They deserve punishment for rebelling, but this will only fan the flames. I must go there; these people belong to me."

Suger took the letters and gave her a shrewd look. "Indeed, I share your apprehension, but it is not possible for you to go to Poitiers. If I may suggest . . ." He stopped speaking and looked at her in concern.

Cold sweat clammed Alienor's body. Petronella grasped her arm, her voice high-pitched with alarm. People crowded around, making it almost impossible to draw breath, and Alienor's knees buckled. She was vaguely aware of being carried back into the church and placed on a pile of cloaks. She could smell incense and hear the chanting of monks, and her vision filled with an image of the crystal vase raised on high, containing all that bleeding red.

They bore her back to Paris in a padded litter and sent for physicians, but by that time, her womb had started to cramp and soon afterward she lost the baby in a welter of blood and congealed matter. Adelaide tried to put Petronella from the room, but Petronella refused to leave, staying at Alienor's side and squeezing her hand, as the midwives dealt with the clotted mass and the corpse of a boy baby no bigger than the length of the midwife's hand. Adelaide was efficient but purse-lipped, making it clear by her body language that she blamed Alienor.

"Suger is going to Poitiers to speak with Louis," she said brusquely. "Louis will be so disappointed to receive this news as well as having to deal with your troublesome vassals."

"Then perhaps he should not have married me," Alienor replied, turning her face to the wall because she didn't want to speak to Adelaide, and she was so wretched and weak with blood loss that she lacked the strength to argue.

Raoul de Vermandois looked at Petronella as she emerged trembling and tear-streaked from Alienor's chamber. He had come in person to find out how the young Queen was faring rather than send a servant, who might be too easily put off or dismissed. "Child," he said softly, "whatever is the matter?"

Petronella shook her head. "Alienor has lost the baby," she said in a breaking voice. "It was horrible, and that old witch is so cruel to her."

"Queen Adelaide, you mean?"

Petronella looked up at him through glistening lashes. "I hate her."

He wagged his forefinger. "That is not a wise thing to say," he cautioned while absorbing the news that Alienor had miscarried. "She had your sister's welfare at heart."

"She has no heart," Petronella retorted, sniffing.

"Even if Queen Adelaide disagrees with your sister on some matters, she will do

everything she can to help her recover because it is in her interests to do so." Raoul set
his arm around Petronella's narrow shoulders. "You should be more careful. You can
tell me anything, and I shall not repeat it, but
others are not so trustworthy and could cause
trouble. Come, *doucette,* dry your tears." He
gently wiped her face with the soft linen
sleeve of his shirt and chucked her under the
chin until she gave him a watery smile.

"I should go back to my sister." Petronella
sniffed. "I didn't want her to wake and see
me weeping." Her chin wobbled again. "She
is all I have."

"Ah, child." Raoul circled her face with a
gentle forefinger. "You are not alone, never
think that. You may come to me with whatever
burdens you."

"Thank you, sire." Petronella lowered her
lashes.

Watching her return to the chamber, Raoul
felt an odd pang of tenderness. He had a
reputation at court for flirting with women.
Sometimes it went beyond banter and
glances, and he had several affairs tucked
under his belt — enough that his wife's uncle,
the prudish Theobald of Champagne, was
wont to curl his lip and call him a slut.
Perhaps he was a slut, but he meant no
malice; it was part of his nature, as much as
Theobald's sourness and Louis's obsession
with God. Petronella was too young to receive

that kind of attention from him. He felt avuncular and compassionate toward her, but at the same time his predatory instincts recognized her potential. In the not-too-distant future, she was going to blossom into a beautiful young woman, desirable for many reasons. Whoever took her to wife would be abundantly blessed.

11

Poitiers, Autumn 1138

Standing at a high window overlooking the palace courtyard, Louis eyed the gathered crowds with irritation. The wails of mothers and children filled his ears with a disagreeable clamor. The citizens of Poitiers and various vassals implicated in the rebellion had assembled to receive his judgment on them; as far as they were aware, Louis intended taking their dependents as his hostages. He was furious that they had sent messages to Paris begging Alienor's intervention and equally furious that Suger had felt it incumbent on him to rush down to Poitiers to interfere.

"I said it to put the fear of God in them," Louis growled over his shoulder to Suger. "Do you think I have the time and resources to send their offspring all over France? Let them stew a little longer in their fear, and then I shall announce that in return for their oaths never to rebel again, they may learn their lesson and go in peace. They will be grateful for my clemency, and that will bind them to me." He gave a ferocious glower. "You should have trusted me."

Suger pressed the tips of his fingers together. "Sire, we were told you fully intended to take hostages, and we knew it would cause great trouble and unrest."

"You will not let me take the reins, will you?" Louis snarled. "You are like everyone else. You want to restrain me as if I am still a child when, by God, I am not."

"Sire, that is not so," Suger said calmly. "But all great princes take advice. Your father knew this and no man was greater than he was, even if God is greatest of all."

Louis hated being compared to his father; he knew they did not think he measured up — that he was too young. "God chose me, and I have been anointed in His sight," he snapped and strode out to make the announcement official.

Louis did not have a carrying voice, and Wilhelm, Bishop of Poitiers, made the proclamation of lenience with Louis and Suger standing at his side. The crowds in the courtyard erupted with cheers and cries of relief and gratitude. Women sobbed and clutched their children to their breasts. Men embraced their wives and sons. Louis watched the jubilation without pleasure. Suger's arrival meant that everyone thought this was Suger's doing, not his, and it put him in the shade when he had been preparing to stand in the sun.

Taking the oaths and promises of the people whose children he had so magnanimously set free, Louis's bad temper weighed like a lead crown on his brow and began a dull headache. Once the courtyard was empty, he retired to his chamber intending to be alone, but Suger followed him and closed the door.

"I did not tell you before, my son, because I did not want to distract you from your business," the Abbot said, his manner quiet and intimate now, "but the Queen was unwell when I left."

Louis looked up with sudden alarm. "What do you mean 'unwell'?"

"She was taken with sickness and fainting after the mass at the feast of Saint Denis." Suger paused, then he drew a deep breath. "Sire, I regret to tell you that she has miscarried the child."

Louis met Suger's sorrowful gaze and recoiled. "No." He shook his head vigorously. "The Virgin blessed us!"

"I wish I did not have to give you this news. Truly, I am sorry."

"I do not believe you!"

"Nevertheless it is the truth. You know I would not tell you a falsehood."

A great chasm was opening up inside Louis — as if someone were prizing apart his rib cage with both hands and reaching inside to

144

rip out his heart. "Why?" he cried and leaned over, pressing his hands to his sides, striving to hold himself together. The world he had thought so perfect was dross. What the Holy Virgin Mary had granted at Le Puy she had taken away and Louis did not know the reason. If it had happened on the feast of Saint Denis at his own abbey, it must be a sign. He had done his best to obey God's will and be a good king, so it must be something Alienor had done. Yet she was so fine and beautiful, like pure crystal. He felt sick. All morning Suger had borne the news inside him like a man awaiting the right moment to open his bowels, knowing, and not speaking.

Suger spoke words of comfort and reason, but they were as nothing to Louis and he found himself almost loathing the little priest. "Get out!" he sobbed. "Get out!" He looked around for something to throw, but the nearest thing to hand was a wooden figure of the Virgin and, overwrought though he was, he stayed his hand, merely closing his fist around the little statue and shaking it at Suger. "It should not have happened!" he wept.

"Sire, you must not —" Suger stopped speaking and turned as a messenger arrived, bearing the news that Alienor's vassal, William de Lezay, castellan of Talmont, had reneged on his oath and seized for himself the white gyrfalcons reserved to the personal use of the Dukes of Aquitaine. The birds were a symbol of the dignity, authority, and virility of the ruling house and it was both a personal affront and a head-on challenge.

Louis stood up straight, breathing hard and swiftly as if he would use up all of the air in the room. The news ignited the red in his mind, turning it to a sheet of fire.

"If de Lezay will not come and swear his loyalty to us," he said hoarsely, "then we shall go to him. And before he dies he will crawl to me and rue the day he was born."

Resting in her chamber, Alienor watched Petronella teaching her fluffy white dog Blanchette to sit up and beg for tidbits. The bitch was a gift to her sister from Raoul de Vermandois.

"Isn't she clever?" Petronella called to Alienor as she dangled a shred of venison above the dog's quivering black nose. Blanchette danced on her hind legs for a moment before Petronella fed the scrap to her with words of lavish praise.

"The cleverest dog in Christendom." Alienor managed a smile for form's sake. It was a month since she had miscarried the baby. Her body was young and strong and she had made a swift physical recovery, but she was prone to bouts of weeping and dull sorrow. Although the child had been too young to have a soul, she felt his loss keenly, as well as her failure to fulfill her duty.

Her chaplains prayed with her daily and Bernard of Clairvaux had visited to offer his advice and condolences. Feeling antipathy toward the man but knowing how influential he was, she had taken care not to contradict him to his face, but there had been no thaw in their relationship and he continued to treat her as a flighty and shallow young woman in need of strict instruction.

The venison scraps all gone, Blanchette yawned and stretched out to sleep before the hearth. Disinclined to sew, Petronella offered to rub Alienor's feet in what was for her a rare altruistic gesture.

Alienor closed her eyes and relaxed as Petronella slipped off her soft kidskin shoes and began to work with firm, gentle strokes. Alienor was content to enjoy this healing, peaceful moment with her sister because opportunities like this were rare these days. When Louis was here, he was Alienor's constant business — his needs, his demands on her — and it had caused a distance to spring up between the girls.

Petronella sighed. "I wish we could stay like this forever," she said. "I wish this was Poitiers."

"So do I," Alienor murmured without opening her eyes.

"Do you think we will ever go back there?"

"Yes, of course we will." Alienor's dreamy, delicious feelings faded, although her eyes remained shut. "We couldn't go this time because it was a matter of urgency, and I was with child." She pushed away that particular darkness. "I promise we shall visit soon and stay at Poitiers and Bordeaux and go hunting at Talmont."

Petronella's eyes sparkled. "And wade in the sea and collect shells!"

"I will make them into a necklace and hang them around your neck!" Alienor laughed, imagining Adelaide's response to seeing her and Petronella splashing in the shallows with their gowns kilted between their legs like two fisher-girls. The thought of the castle on the promontory at Talmont, the golden beach and the sunlit glitter of the sea brought a lump to her throat. At Talmont, too, she had walked hand in hand with Geoffrey de Rancon at a court picnic, and strolled barefoot at the water's edge.

Her father had a hunting preserve at Talmont where he kept his precious white gyrfalcons, virile symbol of the Dukes of Aquitaine, and the fiercest birds of prey in Christendom. She could remember standing in the soft darkness of the mews, her wrist weighted down by one of them, its scimitar talons gripping the leather glove, its eyes like obsidian jewels. And then carrying the bird into the open and casting her aloft to fly in a jingle of silver bells and sharp white wings. That had been a delicious moment of power.

Petronella suddenly stopped rubbing and drew in her breath. "Alienor . . ."

She opened her eyes and struggled to adjust to the light after the smooth darkness behind her closed lids. Given her thoughts, she was shocked and astonished to see Louis advancing on her, a white gyrfalcon bating on his wrist, and for a moment thought he was an illusion. She leaped to her feet, her heart thumping. Blanchette, roused from her doze, began a shrill yapping that made the bird flap with increasing agitation.

Louis ducked away from the bating wings. "Get rid of the dog," he snapped.

Petronella grabbed Blanchette and, with a glare at Louis, stalked from the chamber.

Alienor stared at him. His garments were crumpled and dusty. He had lost weight and there was a sharpness about his features that had not been present before.

"I did not know you had returned. You sent me no message. What are you doing with one of my falcons?"

"I wanted to tell you myself." He untucked a hawking gauntlet from his belt and handed it to her. "Your vassal de Lezay declared against you and took your birds as an act of defiance. This one was in the chamber where I killed him. I have kept her by me ever since in token of how far I am prepared to go in your name. See, she still has the traitor's blood on her feathers."

149

Alienor's stomach tightened. There was a tense and dangerous glitter about Louis, as if he might whip out his sword and stab someone just because he could. Suddenly she was very glad that Petronella had left the room. "You killed de Lezay?" She pushed her fingers into the gauntlet.

"It was necessary," he said harshly. "They had offered an affront. I was lenient with the people of Poitiers, so I had to show severity at Talmont." He scowled at her. "There was no need for Suger to come to Poitiers. I was handling matters on my own, and his arrival undermined me. Everyone thinks I am weak, that I am not good enough and second-best, but I showed them; I showed them all." His face contorted. "De Lezay forswore his allegiance and dishonored us by taking the gyrfalcons, so do you know what I did?"

Alienor shook her head and eyed him warily.

"I cut off his hands and feet with my own sword as a lesson to others and had them nailed to the castle door. Let no one dare to take what is not theirs or to deceive me." His eyes were almost black because the pupils were so enormous and Alienor was afraid because she did not know what he might do next. Here was no pious, uncertain youth, but a wild and savage creature.

She held out her gauntleted wrist. "Let me have her," she said.

Louis transferred the hawk to Alienor's wrist, both of them dodging the beating wings. She felt the weight of the bird, the frantic strength of her. Gyrfalcons were the largest and most magnificent of their species. Their only predator was the golden eagle.

"Suau, mea reina. Suau," Alienor said softly in her own southern tongue. "Be quiet, my queen, be quiet." She stroked the falcon's soft white breast feathers and crooned to her. Slowly the wings ceased to flap and the legs to dance. She perched on Alienor's arm, gripping fiercely. There was a brown stain on top of her head where she could not reach to preen.

Louis watched Alienor, his chest heaving, and as she controlled the bird he too calmed from his crisis and the wildness left his eyes.

"You did what you had to do," she said.

He nodded stiffly. "Yes, what I had to do." He clenched his fists. "Suger told me you lost the child."

A pang of grief and guilt surged through her, but she kept her composure because of the bird on her wrist. "It was not to be."

"On the feast of Saint Denis, so I was told," he said almost accusingly. "God must have been displeased. We must have done something wrong for Him to take away that grace. I prayed and did penance in the cathedral at Poitiers."

"I have prayed too." The thought of the

151

dead child was a silent anguish. She felt the loss as a part of her own life-spark that had failed to kindle. Had she done something wrong? The thought haunted her.

He cleared his throat. "In Poitiers, I heard a priest say that our marriage would not be blessed by offspring because it was consanguineous."

Alienor gave him a bitter look. "Priests say many things out of their own thoughts as men and not directed by God. Did not the Church bind us in matrimony and advise we should be wed in the first place? Does that same Church now change its mind on a whim?" She spoke forcefully, and the gyrfalcon arched her wings and flapped. Alienor soothed her again and controlled her own anger.

"Yes." Louis looked relieved. "Of course you are right." He rubbed his forehead.

"I will have a falconer put a perch in here for her," Alienor said.

Louis exhaled and his shoulders slumped. She saw the exhaustion smudged beneath his eyes and gestured him to lie down on her bed. "Come," she said. "Sleep a while and your mind will be clearer."

He stumbled over to the bed, lay down, and fell asleep almost immediately. Alienor looked at his long limbs, his fair hair and handsome features, and then she looked at La Reina, and the brown stains on her white plumage, and shivered.

12

Paris, Spring 1140

Alienor had been busy all morning, attending mass with Louis, answering correspondence from Aquitaine, dealing with supplicants, before eventually finding a little time to spend with Petronella, who was being fitted for some new dresses.

Petronella's most spectacular new gown was for the celebration of the feast day of Saint Petronella on the last day of May. It was of a rose-colored silk that complemented her warm brown hair and turned her eyes the color of woodland honey. There had been remarks about how much Petronella resembled her grandmother, Dangereuse de Châtellerault, a fiery beauty, notorious for abandoning her husband and running off with her lover, William, the ninth Duke of Aquitaine. Not that anyone mentioned the scandal. The discussion centered on what a beauty Petronella was becoming.

The gown was sewn with hundreds of little

pearls, echoed in the double belt on the dress and in the rings on Petronella's fingers. More pearls wound through her braids and hemmed her veil. For Alienor this was more than just cladding her little sister in finery. It was a celebration of Petronella's womanhood and sent out a strong message that she was protected by wealth and power and therefore untouchable. Clothes were every bit as much a weapon and defense as a knight's sword and shield.

Petronella swished the full skirts of the gown back and forth, showing a glimpse of silk-clad ankles and dainty embroidered slippers.

"Our father would be so proud to see you," Alienor said.

"I wish he was here." The smile left Petronella's lips, only to reappear as her gaze lit on Raoul de Vermandois who was standing in the chamber doorway.

"Raoul, what do you think?" She skipped over to him and pirouetted.

He stared at her as if poleaxed. "I think I must be dreaming," he said. "You are a beautiful vision."

Petronella laughed and danced around him, light as thistledown. "I am flesh and blood. Feel!" she said and held out her hand.

He took her fingers and bowed over them. "Well then, a beautiful young lady," he amended with a bow. From behind his back, he produced a little dog collar woven with rose-colored braid and set with rows of pearls. "I heard rumors about a certain new dress," he said, "and I thought Blanchette should match her mistress."

Petronella clapped her hands and, with a cry of delight, flung her arms around his neck and kissed his cheek. Then, whirling away from him, she stooped to the little dog and replaced her collar of braided leather with the new one.

"Perfect," Raoul said. "Now you are perfect." With a courtly flourish to the women, he excused himself.

Alienor gazed in his wake, feeling warm in her heart for his consideration. Raoul was so much the surrogate father to Petronella, giving her the attention she sought and keeping the pestering young bloods at bay.

Leaving the women to their dressmaking, Alienor went to find Louis. He had been distant and difficult to reach lately and she had to work to maintain her influence. She had not conceived since her miscarriage, and on several occasions Louis had been unable to do his duty, a state of affairs that had sent him flying to church to beg forgiveness for whatever sin was inhibiting his virility. Even the times he did accomplish the deed, it bore no result, for her fluxes arrived regularly each month, and the predators circled, awaiting their moment.

Louis's chamber door was partially open and she could hear the raised voice of her mother-in-law. Alienor grimaced. Adelaide had become more difficult and inflexible since Louis had agreed to a marriage between his sister and the English King's heir, Eustace. Constance had gone to England in February to join her new household. Adelaide, having lost another ally and companion at court and her only daughter to boot, had been morose and querulous ever since.

Currently she was directing a tirade at Louis, her tone unpleasant and cutting. "You must not be swayed by those who would try to take you away from your true duty to rule France. When I think of all the sacrifices your father made for you . . . Your predecessors fought to put you on the throne and you carry all their striving, their dreams and hopes on your shoulders. Do not hold it lightly, and do not allow others to hold it for you. Do you hear me?" There was silence and Adelaide repeated the question in a strident voice. There was a solid bang as if she had struck something on a table.

"Yes, Mother," Louis replied in a neutral tone.

"I wonder if you do. I wonder if you understand that you rule this country for yourself, not at another's behest."

"And whose behest were you thinking of?" Louis demanded. "Are you going to name

157

me names? I do not rule at your behest either, Mother. I see you watching me in the council chamber and looking to meddle where you can, as you meddled in my father's policies. I see you watching Alienor and her sister and finding fault with them at every turn."

"Is it any wonder when they behave like hoydens and flout our ways? You may believe that butter would not melt in their mouths, but I know differently. I see them scheming like a pair of young vixens, but you do not notice because you are willfully blind! I am belittled. They never accord me proper respect, and money runs through their hands like water through a sieve. Have you seen the cost of the latest round of dresses for the younger one? The pearls alone would endow a convent! Do you know how much your wife spends on scented lamp oil?"

"That is what I mean about finding fault. There are worse things in the world. Alienor loves me, which is more than you have ever done."

"She plays you for a fool!"

"You take me for one," Louis retorted.

"In this, you are one, and it pains me to see you thus. But so be it. I wash my hands. Do not come weeping to me when your world comes to ruin."

Alienor took a step back as Adelaide stormed out of the room. "Spying at key-holes?" the older woman said with a curl of contempt. "That does not surprise me."

Alienor curtsied. "Madam," she said neutrally.

"You think you have won," Adelaide spat, "but you know nothing. I have toiled all my life in the service of France. I have been wife to one king and mother to another, and see where it has brought me. You will face the same downfall, my girl, because it all comes to naught in the end. I bequeath you my handful of dust. Take it and sow your own barren harvest. I am finished here."

Adelaide swept on past. Alienor drew a deep breath, gathered herself, and went in to Louis. "I came to find you," she said. "I did not realize you were busy."

His mouth twisted. "You heard what she said?"

Alienor nodded. "It must be difficult for her to relinquish power. I think it will indeed be better if she retires to her dower lands for a while." She came to place her hand on his shoulder. "I am sorry she feels that way about me and Petronella. In truth, we have never disrespected her. She has not been herself ever since your sister went to England."

"Nothing is ever good enough for my mother." His eyes were dark with pain. He fixed her with a hard stare. "Is she right, Alienor? Do you play me for a fool?"

"You know I do not."

"I don't know anything anymore." Seizing

her around the waist, he pulled her into his embrace and began kissing her with clumsy desperation. Alienor gasped at the roughness of his assault, but he paid no heed and, pulling her to the bed, took her, both of them fully clothed and in open daylight, with him bucking and sobbing as he worked in and out of her body. It was as if he was using her to expunge all his frustration in a frantic splurge of lust — casting off all his bad feelings by releasing them inside her and setting the world to rights once more.

When it was over, he left her lying on the bed and went away by himself to pray. Alienor rolled onto her side; she wrapped her arms around herself for comfort and stared at the wall, feeling sore and used.

Louis looked around the chamber that had belonged to his mother. She had been gone from court for almost two months. Alienor had had the walls replastered and painted with a frieze of delicate scrollwork in red and green and had hung colorful embroideries around the walls. They were rich and detailed without being heavy. The window seats sported cushions with white backgrounds embroidered in gold, and there were vases of flowers on coffers and tables. The perfume of roses and lilies was heady and sensual.

"You have been busy," Louis said.

"Do you like it?"

He gave a cautious nod. "It is very different. It is no longer my mother's room."

"Indeed not. It needed light and air."

Louis wandered to the embrasure and looked out at the clear blue sky.

Alienor eyed him. Adelaide and Matthew de Montmorency had announced their intention to marry. It had come as no surprise to anyone at court, but Louis was still trying to assimilate the fact that his mother had chosen to take for her second husband a man of no significant rank. It was as if all that had mattered before had suddenly become unimportant — or perhaps the emphasis had been put on other things.

"I am going to make Montmorency a constable of France," said Louis, picking up a cushion and gazing at the embroidery. "I think it is for the best."

Alienor nodded agreement. That would satisfy honor and ensure Adelaide was not disparaged in the eyes of her family. "She must have great affection for him," she said.

Louis grunted. "He will do her bidding, that is why. She would never choose the cloister for herself, and Montmorency will keep her occupied."

Alienor thought it all to the good. While Adelaide was busy with her new husband, she wouldn't be poking her nose into the business of the court. Let them stay away as long as they chose.

She joined him at the window. "Have you thought any more about the situation at Bourges?"

"What situation?"

Alienor mustered her patience. "About Archbishop Alberic. He is increasingly frail, and if he dies a new archbishop will have to be elected."

Louis gave an impatient shrug. "They will elect whomever I choose. It is my prerogative."

"Even so, would it not be prudent to introduce them to your candidate while Alberic still lives? I know you have your eye on Cadurc in your chancellery."

His nostrils flared. "I will see to it all in good time. I told you, they will elect whomever I put forward."

She noticed the mulish set to his jaw and mentally sighed. For a man who lived by rigid rules and structures, Louis had a propensity for making the simplest things awkward beyond belief. If she pressed him, he would only become more stubborn and querulous. The right of a king was absolute, and that was that.

13

Paris, Spring 1141

"Toulouse," Alienor said to Louis. "My paternal grandmother Philippa was heiress to Toulouse, but was usurped by those with less claim and greater strength. Had my father been alive, he would have fought to restore it to our family."

It was late at night and she and Louis were sitting in bed drinking wine and talking by the light of a scented oil lamp. The signs were auspicious for making a child. It wasn't a holy day, or a proscribed day; Alienor did not have her flux. Everyone was anxious for news of success but she knew that such expectation built fear of failure within Louis. He said that fornication was a sin, and that either he or Alienor must be doing something against God's wishes that was preventing them from being successful in conceiving. She could sense his tension now.

"My father was born in Toulouse," she said. "But I have never seen it."

"Why speak of this now?"

She set her wine to one side and leaned over him. "Because it is business that has already waited too long. I must visit Aquitaine also — that too has been neglected."

"Are you not content in Paris?"

Alienor did not give him the reply that came first to mind: that Paris was a cold exile from the warm southern lands of her childhood. Since Adelaide had left, she had been able to extend her chambers, refurbishing to her own taste as she went, and she liked them well enough. Paris with its crowded streets and vibrant intellectual life was always stimulating, but it was not home and did not belong to her. "France is the land of my marriage," she replied gracefully. "Aquitaine is that of my birth and entitlement and it is my duty to show myself in person." She painted the tip of her braid back and forth over his lips. "Think of riding out at the head of an army to conquer Toulouse. Think of the prestige such an undertaking would confer on you. You would be exerting your authority and righting a wrong."

Louis felt a frisson of desire as he envisioned leading his troops: the jingle of harness; the smooth motion of a powerful horse under him. He imagined Alienor beside him with La Reina perched on her wrist. He thought of camping out under the stars with meadow scents blowing on the summer wind.

He imagined adding Toulouse to his conquests and proving to everyone, not least his wife, what a great king and warrior he was.

She adorned his collarbone and throat with small nipping kisses and followed with the tip of her tongue. "Say yes, Louis," she whispered, her breath in his ear. "Say yes. For me. Do it for me . . . do it for France."

He closed his eyes and savored the erotic charge of her words and the butterfly touch of her mouth. He was achingly hard. With a groan, he rolled her over, pushed apart her legs, and thrust forward. "Very well," he gasped. "I will do it. I will show you what France can do!" He surged strongly within her, fired up by the notion of performing great and virile deeds at the behest of his wife even while he conquered her beneath him.

With the warm southern sun on her face, Alienor felt as if she had returned from exile. Apart from her brief visit to Le Puy, she had not seen Aquitaine in four years, and it was like standing in sweet rain after a long drought. Everything that had been wound up tight inside began unfurling and she felt replenished. She found her laugh again, and her bloom.

In Poitiers, she danced through the chambers of the palace, the skirts of her gown flying out in a circle. "Home!" She grabbed Petronella and hugged her. "We're home!"

And knew if she could have her way in all things, she would live here forever and only visit Paris out of duty.

Her vassals gathered to join Louis for the campaign against Toulouse, among them Geoffrey de Rancon, who brought the men of Taillebourg, Vivant, and Gençay to the muster. Alienor's heart quickened as he knelt before her and Louis. She still experienced that jolt in his presence; time and distance had altered nothing.

He was courteous toward Louis and full of the business of organizing the army for the march on Toulouse. Their discussion was cordial and professional — there was even an element of friendship that some of the northern barons regarded with suspicious and hostile eyes.

When he had an opportunity to talk to Alienor, he treated her in the same courteous manner, but there was an underlying tension, as if they stood on the course of a vibrant underground river of which only they were aware.

"The King has done me the honor of asking me to be his standard-bearer," Geoffrey told her with pride.

"He knows it is good policy to involve my vassals," she replied. "And it is only fitting that a man of your ability should benefit and flourish."

"There are some who do not approve of a

southern upstart being in so prominent a position," he said wryly, "but success always breeds envy. I am glad of the opportunity to serve you and the King."

That first night in the hall, the company was entertained by the famed noble troubadour, Jaufre Rudel, son of the castellan of Blaye, and after he had sung the obligatory battle songs and ballads, he struck a minor chord on his citole and performed another piece of heartbreaking love and yearning.

> Well I believe he is my true Lord,
> Through whom I shall see that love
> Far away. But for one piece of good
> Fortune I have two misfortunes, for
> She is so far away. Ah, would that I
> Were a pilgrim there, so that my staff
> And cloak could be mirrored by her
> Beautiful eyes!

Alienor's throat tightened. She cast a swift look at Geoffrey, and for the briefest instant he met her gaze and the river under their feet surged in spate.

Once she had played chase with him in the gardens here, laughing as she avoided his efforts to catch her. She had gone hunting in his company; they had sung songs and danced together. She had practiced the delicious art of flirtation with him, knowing she was safe and he would do nothing to harm her. He had been the joy of her childhood and the object of her longing as her body became a woman's. It was all in the past, but the attraction and the memories remained. She longed to use them to build a bridge across the chasm, but for both their sakes she could not. She would not flirt with him ever again, because it would have true meaning when all other flirtations were frippery.

Fired up and eager to take Toulouse, Louis left Poitiers the next morning with his own French contingent and those of Alienor's vassals who had come to the muster. Others who had been summoned had been ordered to meet him en route. Wearing the coronet of Aquitaine on her brow, Alienor embraced him and, when he had mounted his horse, handed up his shield. "God be with you," she said. From the corner of her eye, she was aware of Geoffrey carrying Louis's fleur-de-lis banner and flying beside it the eagle of Aquitaine. He was looking straight ahead, his jaw set. "With all of you," she added.

"I will return to you with the gift of Toulouse, should it please God," Louis replied.

Alienor stepped back and mounted her father's great chair, which had been brought out from the hall and placed on a raised platform covered by a silk canopy. Taking a leather gauntlet from her falconer, she settled La Reina on her right wrist. In her left hand she held a jeweled rod surmounted with the image of a dove. Presiding in state as Duchess of Aquitaine, she watched the cavalcade ride out, brave and bold and glittering. Louis was in his element and Alienor thought he had never looked more handsome and assured than he did now. Her heart swelled with pride both for him and for the man who bowed to her from the saddle before leading out the banners.

14

Poitiers, Summer 1141

Louis returned to Poitiers from his campaign much as he had left it, with banners flying, harness flashing in the sun, and the news that he had made a truce with Alfonso Jordan, Count of Toulouse, whereby the latter retained the city in exchange for his oath of allegiance to the French Crown. Louis's attempts to storm the city had failed, as had his efforts to successfully besiege it. The most he had been able to salvage was the oath and the truce. "I needed more men," he told Alienor in their chamber as a servant knelt to remove his shoes and wash his feet. "I had neither sufficient troops nor equipment."

"The Count of Champagne must bear much of the blame," said Raoul de Vermandois, who was present in his capacity of adviser and senior family member. "Twice now he has denied you service. If we had had his contingent with us, we could have taken Toulouse, I am certain of it." He took a drink from the cup of wine Petronella handed to him.

Alienor looked from him to Louis. "Theobald of Champagne refused your summons?" He had been one of those expected to join Louis at Toulouse but plainly he had not done so.

Louis curled his lip. "He sent a messenger saying he would not come because making war on Toulouse was outside of his obligations to me and he had no quarrel with its Count."

Alienor dismissed the servant and took over the foot washing herself, the better to listen with her head bowed, and the fewer ears to hear what was being said. Theobald of Champagne certainly seemed bent on going his own way. He had undermined Louis's authority while bolstering his own, and since he was wealthy, influential, and had royal blood in his veins, he was dangerous. Partly because of him, Toulouse remained untaken. All they had was a truce and an oath that in effect meant nothing.

"I will not forgive his perfidy," Louis growled. "When we return to France I shall deal with him."

"But you will not forget Toulouse?"

Louis gave her an impatient look. "No," he said curtly.

His tone was not encouraging and Alienor dropped the subject because there would be a better time and she wanted to persuade Louis to stay in Aquitaine for a little while. She could not bear the thought of returning to Paris just yet. "There is still much we can do while we are here, to our better profit concerning the people and the Church," she said.

Louis gave a noncommittal grunt.

Raoul cleared his throat. "I have business to attend to, if you will give me your leave, sire."

Louis waved his hand in dismissal. Alienor looked meaningfully at Petronella, who raised her eyebrows and, for a lingering moment, acted as if she did not understand, but then curtsied and left the chamber in Raoul's wake, taking the serving women with her.

Alienor gently dried Louis's feet on a soft linen towel. "I have been planning a progress during your absence, just in case you did not summon me to a victory feast in Toulouse."

Louis tensed. "You expected me to fail?"

"My father said it was always wise to have another plan lest the first one did not succeed — like having a change of clothes in case it rains." She set the towel aside and sat in his lap.

"And what exactly have you mapped out?" He slipped his arm around her waist.

"I thought we could go first to Saint-Jean-d'Angély and pray at the relics of the Baptist. And then to Niort to hold court. I would also like to give royal status to the church where my mother is buried at Nieuil, and then we could ride to Talmont for some hunting." She stroked his face. "What do you think?"

He frowned with distaste. "Talmont?"

"We should reinforce our rule there in peace after what happened before."

"I suppose you are right," he agreed, although he was still frowning, "but we should not linger."

She did not reply for she had learned when to push Louis and when to leave alone. She had his agreement. That was all she needed for now.

Throughout her vast lands Alienor held court with Louis at her side. They received the homage of petitioners and vassals, witnessed and signed charters together, always with the caveat that anything to which Louis put his name was with the "assent and petition of Queen Alienor."

Most poignant for Alienor was visiting the tombs of her mother Aenor and little brother Aigret at Saint-Vincent. Alienor and Petronella laid chaplets of flowers on the simple slabs carved with crosses and took part in a solemn mass to honor them. The church, as Alienor desired, was granted the status of a royal abbey.

Alienor returned to their graves in the early evening and took a moment to contemplate in solitude. Her ladies stood well back, heads bowed, giving her space to pray. Her memories of her mother had softened and faded with time. She had only been six years old when Aenor died, and all she remembered was a faint lavender scent and her mother's brown hair, so long that Alienor scarcely had to reach up to touch the thick braids. That and the quiet air of sadness, as if she had fixed that mood upon herself before the world could do it for her. Her brother she recalled even less; she had barely more than the impression of a small boy running around the bower with a toy sword in his hand, yelling and causing mayhem and being encouraged because he was the male heir. Quick with life, burning bright, burning with fever. Dead before he had barely lived. Now they both had a fitting memorial to house their mortal remains and constant tending for their immortal souls. She had done her duty by them. Amen. She signed her breast and turned to leave.

"Madam?"

Geoffrey de Rancon had arrived on silent feet and stood between her and her ladies.

Her heart skipped. "Is there something wrong?"

"No, madam, but I saw you come this way while I was checking the guards. If you want me to leave . . ."

She shook her head and then gestured at

the tombs. "I barely remember them, yet their loss is always inside me. What would my future have been had they lived?"

His cloak brushed her sleeve. "I learned not to think that way after I lost Burgondie and the child in her womb," he said. "It does no good. All you can do is live each day in their honor."

Her throat tightened and ached. He had missed the point, perhaps deliberately so. Had her brother not died, she would not have had to marry Louis, and had her mother lived, she might have borne more sons. It made all the difference.

"Your mother was a gracious lady, may she rest here in peace, and your brother with her. It is fitting that she should have her own place of honor."

"Yes," she said. "I wanted to do this for them."

This was the closest moment they had shared since his return from the abortive campaign to Toulouse. She saw him on most days, but always in the company of others and connected with his official position. They were careful to avoid being alone together, and their conversation was never overfamiliar. That was for the sake of observers, but the underground river still flowed. She did not believe for one moment that he had just happened to see her come this way.

Geoffrey cleared his throat. "Madam, I

want to ask your permission to return to Taillebourg. My lands need attention and I have not seen my children in three months."

Alienor felt his words like a cut on her heart. "Would you stay if I bid you to?"

"I will do whatever you wish, madam, but I know what I would consider wisdom."

"Wisdom," she said with a bitter smile. The dusk was encroaching, filling the abbey with shadows beyond the light. "Indeed, without wisdom where would we be? You have my leave."

"Madam," he said. Under cover of the cloak, he briefly squeezed her hand, and then he was gone, walking briskly toward the door. Her fingers tingling from his grip, Alienor joined her ladies.

The court had been at Talmont for three days and was preparing to ride out on a hunting picnic when news arrived that the life of Alberic, Archbishop of Bourges, had finally guttered out.

"God rest his soul." Alienor crossed herself and looked at Louis. "I assume you will put Cadurc forward as his successor."

"Of course," Louis said. "Cadurc has served me diligently and deserves promotion. He is the best man for the task."

"And useful to have someone beholden to the Crown," she said and put it from her mind as a routine matter to be dealt with later

176

in council. For now the day was waiting to be enjoyed.

Petronella reclined on a silk cushion in the shade of a sweet chestnut tree. Dappled sunlight shone through the heavy leaves and branches, weighted with clusters of green spiky cases that in another month would split open upon bright brown nuts to be roasted on the fire, or made into delicious sweet-meats. Petronella loved the chestnut season and hoped the court would still be in Poitou by then.

The company had been hunting all morn-ing in the forests of Talmont and had paused to eat and socialize at a prearranged spot where servants had set up charcoal cooking fires and put out blankets and cushions in the shade. Everyone was taking their ease, drinking wine that had been cooled in a nearby stream and eating delicacies: fresh fish caught in the bay beyond the castle walls, spicy tarts, fine cheeses, and dates stuffed with almond paste. The hawks, including Alienor's gyrfalcon La Reina, perched on stands in the shade, resting with heads tucked under their wings.

Musicians played in the background, pick-ing out tunes on lute and harp, singing songs that alternated between rousing military af-fairs, robust hunting sagas, and plangent love songs filled with unrequited longing. One such entertainer, a young troubadour with golden ringlets and dazzling blue eyes, had been casting looks at Petronella, and she had been flirting back at him, playing the thoroughly interested but unattainable highborn lady. It was bold behavior, but Petronella did not care; she was enjoying herself. Alienor was too wrapped up in her own concerns to give her the attention she craved. The young knights of the household were not immune to her flirting, and the musician's eyes were deeply appreciative. Perhaps she would sneak him a token later — a small piece of embroidery, or a gold bead from her dress. If she felt particularly bold, she would let Raoul de Vermandois catch her at it, because it would secure his attention too, and that would be exciting. She dozed, lulled by the breeze swishing through the leaves, and the whisper of the troubadour's fingers over the lute strings.

"Here is sweetness, for a lady who is sweeter than honey itself," a man's voice whispered, and something syrupy and sticky touched her mouth. Petronella's eyes flew open and she gave a soft gasp. Raoul was leaning over her and dripping honey onto her lips from a small pot in his hand.

Licking it off, she sat up and swatted at him playfully. "Do you always accost sleeping ladies in such a way?"

Raoul chuckled and raised one eyebrow.

"Usually the ladies I accost are not asleep," he replied. "But if they are, they very soon wake up." He flicked the tip of her nose with his forefinger. "I was offering you this while there is still some left. Those greedy gorgers were prepared to devour the lot. Of course, if you would rather not, then all the more for them." He indicated the other members of the party, who were finishing off their repast with fruits dipped in honey.

Petronella took the pot from him, scooped up a fingerful, and sucked the honey off it. Then she repeated the move but this time popped her finger in his mouth. Raoul made a sound of amusement in his throat and proceeded to lick away the honey using his tongue with a delicate finesse that sent a shiver down Petronella's spine and made her forget all about the young knights and the troubadour. No one could see what he was doing, because her finger was concealed inside his mouth.

"All clean," he said, drawing her hand away from his lips.

Petronella looked at him coquettishly. "Do you want more?" she asked.

"Ah, now that is a leading question." He laughed softly. "You cannot keep playing with fire and not suffer the consequences, you know that." He gave her an assessing look. "It does not seem a moment since you were a wide-eyed little girl in Bordeaux, staring

very suspiciously at all these strange Frenchmen — especially me." He pointed to his eye
patch.

"I am still suspicious of Frenchmen," Petronella retorted, "and I still think them
strange."

"Why should you be suspicious of me?
Have I not always had your well-being at
heart?"

"I do not know, sire. Perhaps you court
your own benefit."

"Certainly that is true in your case. How
could you not be beneficial for me?" He ran
his right forefinger lightly down her cheek.
"You remind this old warhorse what it is like
to be young and alive."

The troubadour began another song. Petronella shifted position so that she was leaning
against Raoul's shoulder and chest rather
than her cushions. "You are not old to me,"
she said. "The young knights and squires are
like children, but you are a man . . . And I
am not a little girl."

He said nothing, and she twisted her head.
"I'm not!"

"Oh indeed," he said with rueful amusement. "You are a beautiful young woman,
and I am as a bee drunk on nectar."

"How did you lose your eye?" She reached
up and lightly traced the outline of the leather
patch.

He shrugged. "It was at a siege. I was struck

in the face by a shard of flying stone, and that was that."

"Does it hurt?"

"Sometimes. I was sick with a fever for a while after, and in great pain, but I coped because what other choice did I have? I was never a man for looking in mirrors. I know the value of fine clothes and appearance, but a battle scar like this is honorable and does not prevent me from doing my work, or taking part at court. And these days I am not a young hothead to charge into the thick of the fray at the first trumpet, so it matters not that I have less vision with which to fight."

Petronella enjoyed the way he was talking to her as one adult to another, and she liked the feel of his strong body supporting hers. He lit her up inside. He had always been able to make her laugh and banish her cares. At first she had thought of him as a surrogate father, but now she was very aware of him as an attractive and powerful man. He had a wife, but she was far away and of no consequence; indeed, it only added spice to the mix.

She covered one eye with her hand and tried to imagine what he must be seeing. Raoul watched her with a smile, but added with a slight edge: "Now imagine that you cannot take your hand away, and that is what you will see forever."

Petronella was immediately contrite. "I am

sorry; I was not making little of it."

"I know, *doucette,* but some things in my life you cannot begin to imagine or understand."

"I could try if you taught me."

"Perhaps." He left her to go and mingle with others. Petronella watched him, a sinking feeling in her stomach as she wondered if her remark had caused him to walk away. He did not return to her, but socialized with various groups, speaking a word here, touching a shoulder there, laughing at a jest, making a quip of his own. He was thoroughly at ease and knew exactly how to talk to everyone. His face might be seamed and scarred with decades of experience, but he moved with grace and his body was lean and hard.

A young knight settled at her side, and she deliberately flirted with him while still watching Raoul from the corner of her eye. He glanced her way now and again, looking amused, but continued his rounds and was still not disposed to return to her.

When the court prepared to return to the castle, Petronella went to her mare, but as the groom prepared to boost her into the saddle, she stepped back, frowning. "She's going lame on her front foreleg," she said, pointing. "I don't think I ought to ride her."

The groom ran his hand down the mare's shoulder and leg. He picked up a hoof and examined the underside. "She seems sound enough to me, mistress."

"I am telling you, she is lame," Petronella said impatiently. "Do you argue with me?"

"No, mistress." He clamped his jaw and looked down at his feet.

"What is it?" Already mounted, Alienor arrived, La Reina perched on her wrist.

"Stella's lame," Petronella said. "I'll have to ride pillion with someone."

Alienor raised her eyebrows. "I can see straight through your ruse," she said. "Even if it is not plain on your face, Aimery de Niort is giving the game away." She glanced toward the young knight who was holding his own horse at the ready, his expression expectant and smug.

"The lady Petronella can share my saddle." Raoul shouldered forward. "Barbary has a good broad back; he will bear two of us with ease."

Alienor gave him a grateful look. "Thank you." That would keep Petronella out of mischief. Crestfallen, de Niort turned away.

Petronella lowered her head but sent Raoul a coy upward glance, her hands clasped behind her back like a naughty child.

Raoul shook his head. "I hope Stella makes a swift recovery."

"I am sure it is not a serious injury, and I know I will be safe with you, because you're such a good rider."

Raoul's mouth twitched. "I've had a lot of

practice," he replied.

A groom held the iron-gray steady while Raoul cupped his hands to make a step for Petronella to launch herself onto Barbary's wide rump. Raoul then mounted in front of her and shortened the reins. Petronella slipped her arms around his waist, enjoying the feel of his strong muscles under her hands. She imagined how his skin might feel without the barrier of clothes. As close as she was, she wanted to be even closer. To be inside him . . . and have him inside of her.

15

Talmont, Summer 1141

Alienor felt the familiar cramp low down in her belly, and the sudden hot trickle of blood between her thighs told her that yet again she had failed to conceive. She called Floreta to fetch the soft cloths she used for those times of the month and pretended not to see the pity in the woman's eyes.

She would have to tell Louis that yet again there was not going to be a child. But then his visits to her bed were so haphazard and dependent on whether it was a permitted time that the odds of her conceiving were poor. How could there be a baby if there was no seed to make one?

The cramps were painful, but Alienor was not one to linger in bed and instead took some sewing over to the window, where the best light would fall on the fabric. As she picked up her needle, Louis burst into the room. His face was flushed and his eyes glittering with tears of fury. "They have denied me," he snarled. "How dare they!"

"Who has denied you?" Alienor put her sewing down and looked at him in alarm.

"The monks of the cathedral chapter of Bourges." He shook the letter clenched in his fist. "They have rejected Cadurc and elected their own archbishop. Some upstart called Pierre de la Châtre. How dare they meddle with the will and right of an anointed king — God's chosen! Is this the gratitude I receive for being a loyal son of the Church?" His breath sawed in and out of his lungs.

Alienor drew him to the embrasure and, making him sit, poured him a cup of wine. "Calm yourself," she said. "Their candidate is not yet consecrated."

"And neither shall he be!" Louis snatched the wine and drank. "I will not have these vile ruffians contradicting me. There is no precedent for what they are doing. The right is mine. No matter what happens, I swear by Saint Denis that they shall not prevail."

"I knew this would happen," she said, and then tightened her lips. Done was done. She had told him to visit Bourges and make his intentions clear, but he had chosen to believe that his authority would be obeyed from a distance.

"I shall write to the Pope telling him to forbid the election, and I shall deny de la Châtre entry into Bourges."

"Pope Innocent supports free elections of

prelates," she said. "He may choose to uphold their candidate."

"I do not care what he does. I am not having this monk I do not know for my archbishop. I shall uphold my right to choose my own clergy in my own kingdom to the last breath in my body!" Louis screwed the parchment into a ball and hurled it across the room.

"You should write to the Pope in conciliatory terms," she warned.

"I shall write to him as I see fit. I am not the one causing strife here." He jerked to his feet.

"I have my flux," she said, choosing to deal with the bad news all at one blow.

"Why is everything so difficult?" He exhaled a sound filled with massive frustration. "What have I ever done wrong that everyone and everything conspires against me? I try to live my life as an exemplar and this is my reward: a disobedient clergy and a barren wife!" He flung from the room, kicking over a stool on his way out.

Alienor leaned her aching head against the cool stone of the embrasure wall. The situation at Bourges need never have arisen had Louis cultivated the monks there as she had advised. Now there would be conflict and awkwardness, and Louis would stamp around in a temper, poisoning the atmosphere for everyone. Though supposedly a grown man and an anointed king, he was so childish and naive that she despaired of him.

It was late. Petronella was tipsy having drunk too much wine at the dinner feast. Next week the court was returning to Poitiers and then to Paris and the idyll was almost over. She had danced in her thin kidskin shoes until her feet were sore. Raoul claimed not to like dancing, but even so he was graceful on his feet and had been swift to step in and cut off the young bloods vying for her favors. She had laughed at the jesters until her sides ached, had joined in the songs, clapping her hands and raising her voice in harmony. Now all that was finished and people were retiring for the night, Alienor to her chamber and Louis to his prayers.

Raoul sat at the dais table with her amid the crumbs and the candles burning low. He poured more wine into his cup and just a splash into hers. Around them the servants were tidying away the trestles, stacking them against the side of the hall, but conspicuously leaving the high table alone.

"So," said Raoul, "what shall we toast, you and I?"

"I do not know, sire," she said with a flirtatious smile. "You are more experienced at raising toasts than I am."

"Then to fine wine and the beautiful women of Aquitaine." He raised his cup.

She frowned at him. "Beautiful women?"

"To just one woman," he amended. "To the Queen's most perfect sister."

"Say my name," she said.

"Petronella."

The timbre of his voice made her shiver. She raised her own cup. "To fine wine and strong men," she said. "And to the King's most imperfect cousin." She swallowed with a long ripple of her throat.

"Say my name," he responded.

"I have said it time and again at night with only my pillow to hear." She ran her index finger around the rim of her cup. "But if your head were on my pillow, you could hear for yourself."

He lowered his voice and glanced around at the servants. "That would be a very hazardous thing to do."

She sent him a look filled with challenge. She desired this man and she would have him, just as her grandmother, the aptly named Dangereuse, had had her grandfather. The risk only added spice. They would be together under everyone's nose, and no one would be the wiser, not even her sister, who thought she knew everything. "Yes, it would," she said. "It is very late and you should escort me to my chamber."

A deliberate look passed between them, and Petronella's loins liquefied. She was on fire with excitement and apprehension. A tiny part of her could not believe she was doing this. Another part wondered if Raoul would follow her lead, or draw back. If they crossed the line, they could not go back. When she stood up, her legs almost gave way.

Raoul moved to catch her. To the servants, it looked as if the King's constable was assisting the Queen's sister, who had been injudicious with the wine, and no one thought any more of it.

Instead of taking Petronella to her chamber, Raoul drew her to the gardens. Petronella leaned against him, bumping her hip against his and giggling. The night breeze was like warm, feathered fingers scented with roses and the salt tang of the ocean. Petronella thought she could hear the roar of the waves, or perhaps it was just the surge of blood in her veins. Above them the full moon was a swollen silver disc in a sky of luminous dark blue.

Raoul took her to an arbor seat half concealed by roses and columbine and drew her into his lap. Petronella curled her arms around his neck and angled her head, inviting Raoul to kiss her. He lowered his lips to hers, parted them, and showed her what to do.

Desire wound through her blood like strong wine. She pressed herself against him, giving herself up to the delicious sensations he was creating with his mouth and fingers. But then he stopped. His hand was under her skirts, against the soft skin of her bare thigh, where he had been lightly stroking her in a way she could hardly bear. "Go on," she gasped, pushing her hips forward, rocking on him. "Go on!"

"If I do," he said, "you know there is no turning back. We are bound to whatever fate deals us from this."

Petronella felt swollen with lust, but hollow too, desperate for his love and attention — for his hard male body. That was all that mattered. She would deal with the consequences later. "No one need know if we are careful!" she gasped.

Raoul knew all about being careful. He had had decades of practice during the various affairs he had conducted. He had a slight conscience about Petronella, but it wasn't enough to subjugate his lust or his drive as a sexual predator. She was beautiful, desirable, wild, but innocent and full of a hunger he well recognized, because it was a part of himself.

He lifted her to straddle him. "Gently," he said. "Go gently, my heart. A little, and then a little more."

Petronella closed her eyes and bit her lip. There was pain, but it was bearable, and there was pleasure, which wasn't because it was so exquisite that it was like pain. She knew Louis and Alienor would never experience anything like this. This was hers alone, and that made it all the more wonderful. It was very wrong, but how could it be wrong when it felt so right? And then she didn't think at all and let the moment carry her, each of them inside the other as she had imagined. As she shuddered in her crisis, she bit the collar of his tunic to prevent herself from crying out. Raoul gripped her, gave three more strong thrusts, and lifted her up on the next surge to spill himself outside her body.

As she collapsed on him, Raoul threw back his head, gasping. His heart slammed against his rib cage. He hadn't felt this raw excitement since he was a green youth with his first woman.

Petronella giggled breathlessly. "I want to do it again," she said with shining eyes.

He looked dubious, but chuckled. "Not tonight, *doucette.* People will be wondering where we are. A stroll for some fresh air should not take until dawn, and we are probably already at the limit. Besides, I need time to recover even if you do not."

"But tomorrow . . . ?" She leaned forward and kissed him, proving how fast a learner she was.

He cupped his hand at the back of her head and returned the kiss with slow thoroughness. "We'll see what can be arranged."

He had a napkin with him from the feast,

and he used it to wipe away the evidence of their lovemaking from her thighs and between her legs.

"Give it to me," Petronella said. "I will put it on the fire."

He handed it to her and assisted her to her feet. She shook out her gown before turning to kiss him again, loving the feel of his stubble against her tender skin and the firmness of his hands at her waist.

"Come," he said. "Time to be a demure young lady in the eyes of the court."

Petronella gave a mock yawn. "The fresh air has done me good; I think I shall sleep well tonight, very well indeed."

Raoul saw her as far as the stairs to her chamber door. Having glanced around to make sure no one was looking, he kissed her again and, with a final salute, melted away into the night.

Petronella sighed softly and, still marveling, entered her chamber. Floreta was waiting for her in a state of high anxiety. "Where have you been?" she cried. "I have been beside myself!"

Petronella twirled around in the center of the room. "I went for a walk. There's a lovely moon."

"Alone?" Floreta looked horrified.

"Don't fuss," Petronella said. "This is Talmont. Everyone knows me. I'm not a prisoner."

"What's that in your hand?" Floreta pointed to the napkin, her eyes full of suspicion.

"Nothing," Petronella said swiftly. "I felt sick and didn't want to spoil my gown." She made a gesture of dismissal. "My head is spinning. Go to your bed and leave me to mine. I can see to myself."

Floreta hesitated, but eventually gave in, curtsied, and left the chamber. Petronella cast the towel onto the foot of the bed. The fire wasn't lit so she couldn't burn the evidence tonight. Besides, in a strange way she did not want to, because it was proof of her wedding night and the same as any bridal sheet. Raoul might be married, but that didn't matter. She would have him whatever it took. He was hers now.

Removing her gown and shoes, she climbed into bed and blew out the lamp, then she lay awake, reliving what had just happened and savoring the memory. Before she fell asleep, she retrieved the towel from the foot of the bed and tucked it under her pillow.

Having been to mass and broken her fast, Alienor went to talk to Petronella about the imminent return to Poitiers. As usual, her sister was still abed, although awake and sitting up; her hair was a tangled nest and her eyes were still hazy with sleep. Floreta had only just arrived with a bowl of warm water for morning ablutions, together with bread and a jug of buttermilk.

Alienor shook her head with exasperation. "You are like a night-blooming flower," she said. "All wilted in the morning, and not perking up until dusk approaches."

Petronella gave her a strange, sly look. There was a hint of a smile on her lips. "My petals open when others' close," she agreed and stretched. A faint aroma filled the air between them that Alienor knew, but could not place. Petronella left the bed to wash her face and hands.

Alienor's gaze lit upon what looked like a towel poking out from beneath Petronella's pillow. It wouldn't have caught her attention, except that it was bloodstained. Her stomach lurched with shock. "What's this?" she demanded.

Petronella turned around and lunged for the towel but Alienor snatched it away.

"It's nothing," Petronella said, her complexion scarlet. "I had a nosebleed last night, that's all."

Alienor opened up the cloth and noticed there were other stains too, and the cloth itself was slightly damp. She raised it to her nose, and the smell of a man's spilled seed was unmistakable. She turned to the wide-eyed Floreta. "Leave us," she commanded, "and not a word to anyone."

Floreta draped Petronella's clothes over the foot of the bed and left the room with a worried look over her shoulder. Alienor waited until she heard the latch click, and then fixed her sister with a furious stare. "What do you think you are doing, you fool? This could ruin us both. Who is it? Tell me!"

Petronella folded her arms under her breasts. "No one," she said.

"Do not lie to me! Tell me who it is!"

Petronella lifted her chin and stared back at Alienor, her brown eyes made almost golden by the pink flush on her skin. "I will tell you nothing, because there is nothing to tell." Turning her back, she tore a piece off the loaf Floreta had brought and popped it in her mouth.

Goaded by rage and hurt, Alienor seized Petronella's arm and spun her around so they were face-to-face. "You silly child, I am trying to protect you! Do you know what danger you are courting?"

"You are only trying to protect yourself. You know nothing! You don't care about me!" Petronella shook her off, her chest heaving.

"I care about you more than you will ever realize. Someone has taken advantage of you. I will find out, and when I do, it will go hard for him."

Petronella did not answer. She broke off another piece of bread and ate it, her stare filled with insolent challenge.

Feeling sick at heart, Alienor turned to the door, the cloth in her hand, but immediately stopped. She dared not make a fuss outside this chamber because it would bring Petronella into total disrepute with the court, and with her sister's shame would come her own. She had been so careful with Geoffrey de Rancon, had avoided and abjured what could so easily have become a burning scandal, but now Petronella, by this foolish, giddy act, had endangered them both. She hurled the cloth at her. "Dispose of this foul thing," she spat. "You have disgraced and betrayed me, and our household. Think on that if you have any conscience outside your own selfish desire for pleasure and dalliance." Her voice developed a ragged tremble. "I trusted you . . . You do not know what you have done."

Still Petronella did not speak. Alienor left the room and pulled the door closed with a hard hand on the latch. Floreta stood outside, wringing her hands and looking agitated.

"What do you know of this matter?" Alienor demanded. "Answer me!"

Floreta shook her head. "Nothing, madam, I swear! I prepared my lady's chamber as usual. When she was late, I began to worry, but then she arrived with that towel in her hand and said she had it because she felt unwell and feared she might vomit. She told me she had gone to take some air."

More than air, Alienor thought grimly. "She arrived alone? There was no one with her?"

"No, madam."

Alienor fixed Floreta with a hard stare. "Say nothing to anyone. If this gets out, there will be terrible repercussions, and they will fall on everyone."

"You have my word, madam, on my soul." Floreta crossed herself.

"I will find out who is responsible for this. Make sure Petronella keeps to her room today. I do not want to see her out among the court. If anyone asks, she is sick. Report to me if she says anything you think I need to hear."

Floreta returned to the chamber, and Alienor went to pray, not only to ask God for His help, but to ponder what to do. She wondered if she could escape this morass without telling Louis, because if he found out, it would trigger one of his rages. She gripped her prayer beads, feeling an enormous sense of guilt. She ought to have watched Petronella more closely. Her sister had always been needy and vulnerable and had plainly sought in the wrong places for the attention she craved. Alienor had strong suspicions as to the culprit. Aimery de Niort had been making his intentions known for some time. But he was a mere hearth knight and totally unsuitable as a marriage partner for Petronella.

Dear God, what if there was a child from this? That was less easy to disguise than lost virginity. If Petronella was with child, she would have to enter a convent, at least for the duration of the pregnancy. It was of no consequence if a man sired bastards, but for a woman of their status it was a disgrace that reflected on her entire family. Their grandmother Dangereuse de Châtellerault had lived in open adultery with her lover, Alienor's grandfather, but it had caused a huge scandal that she and Petronella carried like a stigma. As the granddaughters of a lecher and a whore they always had to be better than good, knowing that people were constantly watching for the evidence of their tainted blood to show.

She bowed her head against her clasped palms, feeling as if everything had shattered into little pieces around her, but if she was very clever, surely she could fashion the shards back into the delicate shell they had once been? No one but her need ever see the cracks.

Alienor regarded with disgust the shocked young man who had just been flung at her feet by two of her trusted knights. Seized when he returned from exercising his horse, Aimery de Niort was still clad in his riding gear, with spurs on his heels and a cloak at his shoulder clasped by a jeweled brooch.

"Stay on your knees," she commanded. "You will not rise from them in my presence."

"Madam, what have I done to offend you?"

The young knight's eyes were full of bewilderment.

"You well know," Alienor replied, noting with anger how handsome he was. "Did you think I would not find out what you had done?"

"Madam, I have done nothing!" He shook his head. "I know not of what you speak."

"Do you not?" Alienor considered having him flogged. She took the fear in his expression as guilt. "Then shall I mention my sister to you, the lady Petronella?"

He reddened and she saw him swallow.

"I see you understand," she said. "I could have you whipped and strung up for what you have done."

"Madam, I have done nothing." His voice strained and cracked. "I but asked the lady Petronella for a keepsake. Whatever it is you accuse me of, I am innocent."

"I have heard such protestations before," she said icily.

"If you wish, I shall swear my innocence on the bones of my ancestors. Whatever you have heard it is a lie!"

His expression was so dazed and disbelieving that for a moment Alienor's conviction wavered. Perhaps he was a good liar too. The main thing was to be rid of him. "You are dismissed from my service. Take your horse and your life and go." She flicked her fingers and the knights manhandled him from the room, still protesting his innocence.

Alienor closed her eyes. If she thought about matters too hard she would weep.

Raoul de Vermandois put his head around the door. "You sent for me, madam?"

She beckoned him to enter. "Yes, I did. I want to ask your advice, and a favor of you."

He looked at her warily, his shoulders tense. "Whatever it is, I shall be glad to help."

She gestured him to the bench at her side. Although she had summoned him, she was not sure if she could tell him.

"It's about Petronella," she said.

Raoul's face was expressionless. "Madam?"

Alienor bit her lip. "My sister looks upon you as she once looked upon our father," she said. "She likes you and you are kind to her."

Raoul cleared his throat and folded his arms, but said nothing.

"I am worried about her. She has been dallying with the squires and young knights — you must know because you have intervened at times. She does not think of the consequences — or if she does, she does not care. She must be reined in, but not so harshly that people talk. I would like you to keep watch on her as we journey back to Paris, and on any young suitors who step out of line."

Raoul looked away. "I am not worthy of your trust," he muttered.

"She will listen to you when she will certainly not listen to me or to Louis."

"Madam, I . . ."

She laid her hand on his sleeve. "I know she is difficult, but please, as a favor to me."

He rumpled his thick silver hair and let out a resigned sigh. "As you wish, madam."

"Thank you." Alienor sighed with relief. "I do not want Louis to know about this. It would be to no good purpose — you know what he is like. I value your discretion in this matter, my lord."

Raoul inclined his head. "He shall not find out from me, I promise you."

As he bowed from the room, Alienor breathed the tension away and closed her eyes. She fervently hoped she had contained the situation.

Her next move was to have Petronella brought to her chamber where she could be watched. "We need to pack for the return to Poitiers and Paris," she said. "There is much to do. Aimery de Niort has left court and will not be returning. We shall not speak of the other matter again — understood?"

Petronella gave her a startled look, then without a word she went to sit in the window embrasure.

Alienor followed her. "Petra . . ." She wanted to take her in her arms and at the same time she wanted to slap her. "I wish you would talk to me. We used to be so close."

"I wasn't the one who went away," Petronella said. "All you care about is what people will think. You're not bothered about me, you're just afraid of the scandal and your position and what Louis will say."

"That is not true!"

"Yes it is! I'm just the annoying little sister who gets in the way. You said you would look after me, but you haven't." Petronella rounded on her, eyes flashing. "All you want to do is be the Queen. I don't matter."

"You're wrong. You're so very wrong. Of course you matter to me." A wave of guilt washed over Alienor because she recognized both the truth in Petronella's words and the injustice of them too.

"No I don't!" Petronella jumped to her feet and pushed past Alienor. "And I don't care, because you don't matter to me anymore! You don't keep your word. I hate you!" The last words rose to a shriek. Petronella stamped over to a baggage chest and began flinging the contents around. The chamber ladies lowered their eyes and went about their duties as if nothing was wrong.

Alienor swallowed nausea. Petronella was exactly like their grandmother Dangereuse, who had been so volatile that as children they had never known from one moment to the next how she was going to react. All ordinary emotion was intensified to passion and Petronella seemed to be developing the same worrying traits as she became a woman. She would just have to keep her occupied and try to diffuse some of that raw intensity before it did any more damage. But she loved her, and the rejection was pain.

For the next several days Alienor was on tenterhooks, but as the danger faded that Petronella's indiscretion might become a larger scandal, she started to relax. The court was preoccupied with packing for long days on the road and Louis was too busy praying and fulminating over the matter of the Archbishop of Bourges to pay attention to other undercurrents.

Alienor was relieved that Petronella seemed to have taken the warning to heart. Having gone to church and been shriven, she had since been behaving in a subdued and demure fashion. However, she was still refusing to speak to Alienor, and the quarrel lay between the sisters like an open wound that had been bandaged but was still bleeding.

Raoul was as good as his word and was attentive to Petronella in a formal, courteous way when she emerged from the bower to socialize. He partnered her in the dances, sat with her to eat, and rode at her side as the court made use of the final days to go hunting with the hawks and dogs.

Raoul's polite reserve upset and angered Petronella. He bowed and smiled at her with the blandness of a courtier and pretended not to notice the way she looked at him. She could not bear to think that the one occasion in the garden had been all it was — another little conquest — and that the tawdry gossip about his affairs with women where he used them and moved on was all true. She set out to bait him in an effort to make him respond and to warn him that she would not be ignored. On passing him in a corridor with other people around them, she brushed against him intimately and flashed him a bold glance. She was successful: he responded with a look composed of desire and reprimand. He was not as indifferent as he pretended. Later, she sat beside him for the main meal of the day and, under cover of the tablecloth, curled her foot around his.

Raoul withdrew rapidly as if she had burned him and gave her a slight shake of his head, which she chose to ignore.

The servants brought food from the kitchens and began setting out the dishes at the high table, including tender venison and marinated fruits on skewers with piquant dipping sauces. There was a golden cameline sauce made with cinnamon, a purple one of blackberries, and another that was warm with the taste of ginger.

Raoul served Petronella with two skewers, one of meat, one of fruits.

"They look like a row of courtiers," she

giggled. "Here's Thierry de Galeran, and next to him the fat one is William de Montferrat. And this one looks just like Louis. See, it's the same color as his gown. Shall I eat him up? Hold the skewer for me."

Raoul held the length of whittled ash as Petronella closed her teeth around a chunk of golden marinated pear and pulled it off, her action sensual, almost provocative. She chewed and swallowed. "Wouldn't it be good if we could be rid of all our enemies like that?" she said.

"I hope you do not mean that the King is your enemy?"

Petronella shrugged. "I meant all enemies in general. Come, I will hold yours for you now. Who are you going to eat? That one looks a bit like Theobald of Champagne, no?"

Raoul shook his head but he was chuckling. "You are a very naughty girl."

Petronella gave him a measured look, smoky and dark. "No more naughty than you are," she said and licked her lips.

"Hush." He glanced around. "This is neither the time nor the place for such behavior." He wanted to grab her and silence her, but his fear was all knotted up in desire, and he imagined that silencing as a hard kiss, her body drawn tightly against his. He glanced around to see if anyone had noticed their whispered discussion and saw one of Louis's chaplains observing them with neutrality that might at any moment become censure.

"Then tell me what is the time and place," she retorted, breathing swiftly. "You keep me company, but you ignore me, and I am left to wonder."

"*Doucette,* you do not know what you do."

She tilted her head. "The other day you seemed to think I did know what I did."

Raoul swallowed, feeling increasingly at a loss. "If you do not behave yourself, we shall be discovered here and now. Do you really want to face the consequences of that?" He grimaced at her. "We have to find a way to manage this. Now, let me help you to a piece of this fine salmon, my lady." He reached to a silver dish in front of them, his courtier's mask fixed firmly in place.

"Perhaps, my lord de Vermandois, you are discovering you have bitten off more than you can chew," she said with a narrow smile.

He slowly shook his head and knew that she was his nemesis.

"Aimery de Niort," Louis said to Alienor.

Alienor ceased putting away her rings in her jewel coffer, and her heart leaped with fear. "What of him?"

"His older brother has asked me for redress. He says you dismissed Aimery without cause and treated him dishonorably when he had never done a dishonor to you. Are you going to tell me what this is about?"

Alienor fiddled with a ring set with small red stones like pomegranate seeds. "He was showing too much interest in Petronella and I had to intervene."

Louis arched his brows. "Dismissing him sounds like more than just intervention."

"It was necessary, trust me."

He gave her a brooding look. "Petronella must have encouraged him."

"I have taken her to task and rebuked her for the folly of indiscretion, but even so it takes a spark to light kindling. I have dealt with the matter and there will be no more of it."

Louis made an irritated sound. "It is past time she had a husband," he said. "I will look into it the moment we return to Paris."

"She is my heir until we have a child, and it is my prerogative to find her a suitable consort," Alienor replied to the point. "But you are right. She should be wed as soon as a fitting one can be found."

16

Poitiers, Late Summer 1141

Cloaked and hooded, Petronella glanced furtively around, gave three taps on the door, and then slipped into the room at the top of the tower. Raoul was waiting for her, seated before the hearth where a small brazier gave off pleasantly scented smoke. His traveling bed stood in a corner of the room, the coverlet and fresh linen sheets turned back invitingly. When Petronella entered, he rose and went to her, took her face in his hands, and kissed her on the mouth. She returned the kiss as if she were dying of thirst and made small whimpering sounds in her throat. He lifted her in his arms and took her to the bed, dropping her on the mattress; she lay back, hitching her gown up, desperate for him. Panting, he freed himself from his braies and joined her, grabbing her hips and thrusting into her like a young man in his first season of rut.

Their need for each other was so frantic

that it was over in moments, leaving them gasping and unsatisfied beyond the sheer physical sensation of release. Raoul thought his heart was going to burst through his chest. Filled with tenderness, still alive with lust, he leaned over Petronella and kissed her eyelids, her nose, and her mouth. Her eyes were soft and dark with wanting. She looked delectable. He began to undress her slowly, taking his time now, and she followed his lead, smiling, nipping and licking him, tasting his skin.

Their second lovemaking was a more leisurely affair, and when they had both taken their pleasure, they lay curled together in each other's arms. Petronella closed her eyes and savored the feel of his hands gently running through her hair, drawing it back from her temples. He was all she wanted. Her father, her lover, a man of standing and prowess who shared her needs and her drives. It was impossible to think of herself as separate from him.

"What is going to happen to us?" she asked. "I want to be with you always. I don't care about politics. I don't care about being the sister of the Queen. If we have to go into exile, I will gladly follow you barefoot in my shift."

"I would not ask that of you," he said with graceful tact, while being unnerved at the thought of such a fate. Barefoot and impoverished was only romantic as a figure of speech, not in reality.

"I would do it." Leaving the bed, she went to the trestle and took a bunch of sweet, dark grapes from the fruit bowl there. Her long dark hair hung down below her waist. Eyeing her figure with appreciation, he reached for his shirt.

She returned to him and leaned over, a grape between her teeth to feed him, mouth to mouth. "A papal legate once told my grandsire to give up my grandmother, who was his mistress, and my grandsire replied that luxurious curls would grow on the legate's bald head before he ever did that. Would you do that for me? Would you face down Church and State just to have me at your side?"

Raoul's chest tightened as he saw the vulnerability in her eyes and the way she trembled like a young deer. "Ah, darling," he said, cupping her cheek. "Don't fret. We'll think of something when we get to Paris."

She fed him another grape. "You promise?"

"I promise." He patted her buttocks. "Come, put on your clothes."

"Only if you dress me," she said with a wicked sparkle.

Raoul grinned and picked up one of her silk leg hose. "That, my love, will be a pleasure — mayhap not as keen a one as undressing you, but still pleasure enough."

Taking her ankle in his hand, he rubbed his thumb over it, and then leaned over to kiss her toes and lick between them, making her squeal.

Their business finished, Alienor and Louis went to walk in the gardens as dusk encroached. A chill breeze had sprung up and both of them wore soft woolen cloaks trimmed with fur. Side by side, they paused at the pond to gaze into the twilight-colored water. Alienor remembered a time when they had made love here, their bodies entwined like a pair of sleek fauns. It seemed so long ago now, so distant. In the space of a few short years they had become very different people from the girl and youth who had lain here, discovering and worshipping each other's bodies. She dared not ask if he remembered that time, because she dreaded the answer he might give. There was a feeling of sadness in the gloaming, as if more than just the evening was drawing to a close. These were their last hours in Poitiers, and when they departed, she did not know when next they would return.

"I should go to my prayers," Louis said with a glance at the sky and she felt him start to draw away from her.

"You can as easily see God here as in a church," she said. "Do you not wonder at the marvels of His creation? What does man have to compare with this?" She indicated the dark band of royal-purple cloud, scored with an underribbon of deepest red. "Even Abbé Suger would have to agree. This is better than any stained window he could ever devise."

"That is true," he acknowledged, taking her hand in his — a rare gesture these days, coming of its own accord. She moved into his touch and stroked his hair. It was his finest feature, thick and silver-blond, and she loved the way it swung against the column of his throat.

"Louis . . ." she said softly and thought that there might be a way back after all.

"Sire?" The moment vanished like the last vermilion streak of sunset as they broke apart and faced his chaplain, Odo of Deuil.

"What is it?" Louis snapped. "Why do you interrupt us?"

Looking uncomfortable, the priest cleared his throat. "Sire, madam, I am sorry to be the bearer of ill news, but once it becomes common knowledge, there will be no containing it."

"What ill news? No containing what?" Louis demanded. "Don't speak in riddles, man. Out with it!"

Father Odo said, with a glance at Alienor, "Sire, it is a matter that touches on the lady Petronella and her relationship to a man of the court."

Louis threw up his hands in exasperation.

"Gossip again! I am sick of all the petty tittle tattle."

Alienor's heart froze. Dear God, what had Petronella done now? She had thought her sister safe with her women and the crisis averted. "Which man?" she demanded.

"Madam . . . it is the constable, the sire de Vermandois."

Louis exhaled hard, his eyes steely with anger. "This is typical court gossip. The Queen and I are well aware of the matter concerning my sister and the lord of Vermandois."

A look of utter shock crossed the clergyman's face. "Sire, madam, with due respect, I do not believe you are."

Alienor narrowed her eyes.

"Very well," Louis said, rubbing his forehead, "but let this be an end to it. We have more important matters to deal with than this foolishness."

"Sire, Raoul de Vermandois is entertaining the Queen's sister in his chamber in a licentious manner. My scribe overheard them planning their tryst earlier and watched to see where they went. It is all true, I swear it. De Vermandois's squire is keeping watch in the stairwell even now."

Alienor felt sick. De Deuil's scribe would not just have happened to see Raoul and Petronella together. Plainly the court spies had been very busy.

Louis was white. "Show me," he said.

De Deuil gave a stiff bow and, folding his arms inside his habit, led them out of the garden. More clerics were waiting there in deputation, and Alienor began to feel very afraid as Louis summoned guards to accompany them. Something terrible was about to happen and she could do nothing to prevent it.

Odo de Deuil led the way into the palace and climbed the twisting stairs of the Maubergeonne Tower to the private chambers. They heard the footsteps of the squire in the stairwell dashing up to warn his lord. Louis's guards pushed past the chaplain and ran up after the young man, seizing him and clubbing him to the ground outside a heavy wooden door as he yelled a warning. Panting from his climb, Father Odo gripped the wrought iron latch ring, twisted it, and pushed the door wide open.

A brazier burned in the hearth. An empty padded bench stood before it with a wine jug and cups on a table close by. Farther into the room was a bed and Petronella was in it, clad in her shift with the laces untied and her breasts exposed. Raoul de Vermandois, wearing shirt and hose but no tunic, stood over her, preparing to defend her with his drawn sword.

Louis made a choking sound. Alienor stared in horrified shock, because there was no mistaking the evidence, and she was responsible for having allowed the fox into the chicken coop. Petronella had stifled a scream at the intrusion, but now gazed at everyone in brazen defiance, making no effort to cover herself.

"Drop your sword," Louis snarled. "Would you show steel to your king?"

Raoul swallowed and, throwing the weapon aside, fell to his knees. "Sire, I can explain . . ."

A shudder ran through Louis. "You are very good at explaining," he said icily, "and I have always been foolish enough to listen to you and trust you, while all the time you have been betraying me and God. I do not want to hear what you have to say, because my eyes see very well what duplicity you have wrought. This is treason. What I must decide now is what to do with you." He turned to Alienor, his voice thick with rage. "Madam, deal with your sister." He pointed a finger at the soldiers. "Until further notice, my lord of Vermandois is under house arrest and will speak to no one but his confessor. See to it." Turning on his heel, he strode from the room.

Alienor glared at Raoul. "I trusted you," she said with loathing. "I asked you to protect Petronella, and instead you have desecrated her. May you rot in hell forever." She stepped to one side so that she could look at her sister who had still not covered herself. "I trusted you too."

Petronella's expression was hard with defiance. "I love him." Her voice was fierce. "You don't know anything about love."

"Oh, but I do," Alienor replied bitterly. "Because I love you, and you have just broken my heart."

Petronella's chin wobbled and she made a small, desperate sound in her throat. Raoul turned to her and gently draped her cloak around her shoulders. "You cannot stay here, my love," he said. "They will not allow it, and, one way or another, this must be sorted out. Go with the Queen. All will be well, trust me." He looked at Alienor. "Do not blame her, madam. It is my fault."

Alienor could not bring herself to answer him because she was choked with rage and shame, much of it on her own account. She should have seen this coming; she should have realized. "Come," she said brusquely to Petronella. "If you do not of your own will, the guards will force you."

Petronella was trembling, but she drew courage around her like the cloak and, leaving the bed, walked from the room and past the assembled gathering of clergy with her head carried high. Alienor followed her, and she too ignored the clergy. They were vultures, who had only been awaiting the opportunity to feast at the kill.

■ ■ ■ ■

"Do you know what you have done?" Alienor demanded of Petronella once her chamber door had closed behind them. "How are we ever going to mend this scandal? I could shake you until your teeth rattle!"

"I love him," Petronella said again and folded her arms inside the cloak, hugging herself. Her voice cracked. "And he loves me."

"You only think you love him," Alienor said harshly. "You are a child, and he has seduced you."

Petronella's voice grew shrill. "It isn't like that, it isn't! And I'm not a child!"

"Then stop acting like one! How long has this been going on under everyone's nose? How long have you been practicing this deceit? That night at Talmont — that cloth. You had been with him, hadn't you?"

"What if I had?" Petronella lifted her chin. "It was the best night of my life. He cares about me. You don't. You only care about your own reputation as Queen."

Each statement of Petronella's struck Alienor like a blow. "Irrespective of my reputation as Queen, Raoul de Vermandois was in a position of trust; he violated that trust and broke his honor and yours. He is old enough to be your grandsire, let alone your father.

You allowed Aimery de Niort to be your scapegoat and to be punished for something he did not do." Alienor's voice burned with disgust. "What do you think our father would have said if he knew about this? Do you think he would approve?"

"He went away and left us! If you are talking of ancestors, then our grandparents did not stop to worry what anyone would think. They lived and made love as they chose!"

"And others have paid for it ever since — including you for following their example."

"Better I should be like them than that my juices should dry up for want of use."

Alienor's hand cracking against Petronella's cheek was a shocking punctuation to the exchange. The feel of the blow tingled through Alienor's palm as the mark turned from white to red on Petronella's face. Shaking, Petronella stared at her with eyes full of hatred, misery, and furious bravado. In that moment, Alienor saw a wounded creature run to bay and doing its utmost to take its slaughterers down with it. "Have we come to this as sisters?" Alienor whispered. "To be enemies? Surely we have enough of those already without ripping each other apart."

The battle light died from Petronella's eyes. She gave a wrenching sob, then another and another, as if small pieces were being torn from her body.

"Petra . . ." Alienor could not bear to see

her sister in such pain. She drew her into her arms and held her tightly, tears running down her own face as Petronella sobbed. Her sister was so damaged, so vulnerable. Gelding was too merciful a punishment for Raoul de Vermandois.

Once the worst of the storm had passed, Alienor drew Petronella to the hearth, gave her a napkin to wipe her tears, and poured them both wine. "What were you thinking?" she asked. "It was bound to surface sooner or later. You could not keep something as great as this a secret."

"We were living in the moment." Petronella sniffed. "The future didn't matter."

"The future always matters."

Petronella raised her right hand and held it out to Alienor, palm open. "Why can't you just let us be? Raoul and I can go away somewhere together. You can settle us in Aquitaine. There are people who will look after us. No one will know."

Alienor felt heartsick and frustrated. "Of course people will know. You are living on dreams. Just because you forget the world does not mean that the world forgets you. You and Raoul de Vermandois cannot just disappear into the countryside like a pair of peasants."

Petronella said mutinously, "You are Queen of France; you can arrange things. You have your life and your husband. Why should I not have mine?"

Alienor stared at Petronella in disbelief. "Raoul is not free to marry. He is wed to the niece of Theobald of Champagne. He has a child. What you have done is to commit fornication and adultery."

"He does not love his wife; he never goes home to her."

"Being with Raoul is not the way to happiness."

"How do you know the way to happiness?" Petronella demanded. "Can you look me in the eyes and tell me you are happy with Louis?"

"My situation is not yours, and what is between me and Louis is not the issue."

"Hah!" Petronella rose from the bench and paced the room, rubbing her arms. "Do what you will, but I shall never change my mind."

It was all such a mess, Alienor thought. She had believed at the outset that she was containing a minor scandal, a girl's peccadillo, but this was enormous and beyond concealment. She supposed she could send Petronella to the nunnery at Saintes, but it would be like throwing a wildcat into a dovecote. If only she had seen what was going on under her nose, but it was too late now. The damage was done.

17

Paris, Autumn 1141

The court, much subdued, arrived in Paris after a week of steady travel on hard autumn roads. Raoul was kept under guard, permitted to ride his own horse but shunned by Louis. They had had strong words on that first night at Poitiers, or rather Louis had bellowed and Raoul had stayed silent in shame, and since then they had not spoken. Taking their lead from Louis, the rest of the court spurned Raoul, so that although he rode among them, he might as well have been invisible — and this a man who was the heart and soul of long journeys with his stories and humor. Petronella was kept under close guard, traveling in a litter well away from Raoul's part of the progress.

On their arrival in Paris, Raoul was escorted to a chamber and put under house arrest while Petronella was brought to Alienor's apartments under close supervision and given no opportunity to have any sort of contact with her lover. Her manner remained stubborn and unrepentant, but Alienor heard her weeping behind the closed bed curtains and, despite her vow to remain unmoved, her heart ached for her fragile sister.

"Louis, may I have a word alone?" Alienor said.

He raised his head from the document he was reading. "About what?"

"The matter in hand."

He hesitated, and then ordered everyone to leave the room.

Going to the window, Alienor gestured to the cushioned embrasure seats. "Will you sit with me?" A flagon stood close by and she poured wine into two goblets.

He sighed and tossed the scroll onto the trestle. "What is it?" He folded his arms and made no move to join her.

She sipped her wine. They had brought it back with them and it tasted of Bordeaux. "I have been thinking what to do about Petronella and Raoul. They cannot stay under lock and key for the rest of their lives."

Louis shrugged. "Tell me why I should loosen the reins? They have sinned grievously against God and they have betrayed us both. If you have come to make excuses for them, then your journey is wasted."

His priggish reply irritated her. "Whatever blame we apportion, it does not solve the problem. I agree that they should do penance, but I also think they should be allowed to return to some kind of life. You need Raoul in council, and Petronella cannot live out her days at the top of the Great Tower."

Louis examined his fingernails. Eventually he heaved a sigh and, leaving his chair, joined her at the window. "If Raoul and your sister will shrive themselves and spend time in repentance and contemplation of their sin, I will see what can be done."

"Thank you." Alienor lowered her eyes, knowing it best to yield a little to sweeten his mood. She suspected Petronella would not be in the least repentant, but if she could pretend remorse, then perhaps there was a way through. After a moment she said thoughtfully, "It would be much simpler if we were ordinary folk not watched by all. Petronella and Raoul could be wed and no harm done."

Louis frowned at her. "Raoul has a wife. He is not free to marry."

"He conveniently forgot that fact when he seduced my sister," she said acidly. "He may have a wife, but he has long lived apart from her."

"She is the niece of Theobald of Champagne."

"Yes, and Theobald has defied you twice and treated you as if you are of no consequence. If they married, Petronella would be safe with her chosen man and you would not have to send Raoul away. The criticism would have to be quelled, but eventually people would have no choice but to accept the match."

Louis gnawed his thumb knuckle.

"All you would have to do is arrange an annulment for Raoul so he and Petronella could wed," she said, her tone soft and persuasive. "It solves our dilemma."

Louis's frown deepened. "That may be so," he said slowly, "but we shall have to find bishops willing to annul the marriage."

"I have thought of that. The Bishop of Noyon is Raoul's cousin, and Laon and Senlis will also be willing to assist." Bishops who could be bribed, in other words, or who had an interest. The knowledge hung between them like a bad odor, but she was determined to do everything in her power to make this right for Petronella. There would be opposition, but once Louis had decided, she could count on him to see this through. His motivation might have more to do with slighting Theobald of Champagne than securing Petronella's future, but that did not matter.

"Very well, I shall write to them," he said curtly, "but we should say nothing until plans are finalized. It will do your sister and Raoul no harm to spend time repenting without knowledge of this."

"As you wish."

"You had this all planned before you came to me, didn't you?"

She looked up at him and put her hands on his chest. "Only a little," she said. "I had been worrying about it, that is all, and I wanted to talk to you. I knew you would know what to do."

With a gleam in his eyes he set his hands to her waist and kissed her. The notion of slighting Theobald of Champagne through his niece filled him with a sense of power and royal righteousness that translated into a sudden strong sexual urge. And besides, he needed to put his wife in her place.

Alienor responded willingly to his excitement, because she had gotten him to do her will; she had solved the problem of Petronella and Raoul, and perhaps this time she would conceive.

Cold rain had turned the crowded streets of Paris into a vile, sulfurous-smelling sludge. No one could go about their business without miring their shoes and clothes. Even if puddles were skirted and leaped over, the noisome splatter from the press of general traffic was unavoidable.

At the palace, the shutters were open to admit the daylight, but they also brought in the stink from the city coupled with that of musty stone, damp from a cold, wet autumn.

Wrapped in a warm mantle lined with the

pelts of Russian squirrels, Alienor sat before a brazier in her chamber holding a document with several seals dangling from cords at the base; despite the dismal day and the stench, she was smiling.

The door opened and Petronella entered, followed by her customary escort of ladies, all of them sober matrons. Petronella flung her cloak across a chest and tore off her head-dress to expose her long brown braids. "That is the end!" Her eyes flashed. "I am shriven whiter than a newborn lamb. I have been washing the feet of the poor all morning after they have trudged through that stinking mire. I have given them bread and alms and touched their sores." She screwed up her face. "I have inhaled their stench and let it out again on the breath of prayer. I have bowed my head and begged for forgiveness." She cast a defiant look at Alienor. "I didn't beg forgiveness for loving Raoul; I begged it because I am sick of people turning away from me. I am who I was before, but every-one hates me now."

"No one hates you." Alienor tried not to sound impatient. "Come sit here by me."

Petronella sighed and flounced over to Alienor. She picked up the piece of sewing she had been working on before she went to church. It was a tunic hem half-embroidered with green silk acanthus scrolls.

"Look," Alienor said. "I do not know if this

will make a difference to you, but Louis and I have been making inquiries into the likelihood of an annulment for Raoul and we think it may be possible."

Petronella let her sewing fall to her lap. "An annulment?" she said with widening eyes.

"I did not want to tell you before, not until it seemed certain, and besides you have had your penance to do, but we have found three bishops who have agreed to dissolve Raoul's marriage." She tapped the piece of parchment in her hand. "If matters go well, you and Raoul can be wed as soon as we can arrange matters."

Petronella clutched her breast as if holding her heart inside her body and gasped. When Alienor leaned toward her in concern, she shook her head and laughed exultantly. "I knew you would not let me down! When all is said and done we are the same blood. This is a miracle. I begged and prayed for one all the time I was on my knees in church and washing the feet of the poor!" She flung her arms around Alienor and kissed her. "Thank you, sister, thank you!"

Alienor returned the embrace, tears pricking her own eyes because a sister's love was unconditional, whatever Petronella did.

"I promise to be good from now on. I will be the best wife in the world!" Petronella vowed. "We can be sisters just as we were before all this happened!"

But Alienor knew they could never go back: she was wise enough to see that too much had changed, too much had been said and done; yet it was so good to feel Petronella's arms around her, and to know that at least some of the ties between them, frayed though they were, remained fast.

"What about Raoul?" asked Petronella. "Does he know?"

"Louis will tell him. We were waiting for this news from the bishops." Alienor raised a warning forefinger. "I tell you now there will be great opposition. Theobald of Champagne will not accept it because he will take it as a personal insult to his bloodline. He and Louis are already on bad terms over the matter of Toulouse, and this will only sour their relationship further. I suspect he will call on clergy of his own to refute what we put forward."

"They won't succeed," Petronella said with a vehement shake of her head. She hugged Alienor again. "I promise I will never ask for anything else in my life now that I have this! It means everything to me!"

Alienor's smile did not reach her eyes because having something that meant everything was a double-edged sword. It meant you had so much more to lose.

Raoul entered Louis's chamber with trepidation. A swift glance showed him that the servants had all been dismissed. Abbé Suger, Louis's brother Robert de Dreux, and his uncles William de Montferrat and Amadée de Maurienne, however, were in close attendance.

"Sire." Raoul knelt and bowed his head. This was the first time he had seen Louis in several days. He was still being kept under close watch, although no longer strict house arrest. He had felt the weight of disapproval at court; instead of being welcomed into the royal inner circles he had been forced to the outer edge and knew how vulnerable he was. Men who were out of favor were easily picked off.

Louis ordered him to rise. "You are here to answer on the matter of your conduct with the Queen's sister," he said icily.

Raoul bowed his head. "Sire, my life is in your hands. I do not expect to receive clemency. I will do whatever I must do to make amends."

Louis looked contemptuous. "Indeed you shall. You have ever had a glib tongue, but let us hope this time your words and deeds are a match for each other."

Raoul cleared his throat. "Sire."

"This is family business, as well as a matter of state," Louis said. "Whatever I decide will have repercussions far beyond this chamber. To set this right, you must marry the Queen's sister."

Raoul stared at Louis in dumbstruck silence.

"I have found three bishops, including your cousin, willing to declare your marriage to Leonora null and void, which leaves you free to wed the lady Petronella." Louis's mouth twisted. "I could wish it otherwise, but this seems the best decision."

Raoul swallowed. "I do not know what to say, sire."

"That has to be a unique experience for you," Robert de Dreux said nastily.

Louis shot his brother a warning look. "The wedding will take place as soon as the bishops have pronounced the annulment, and as swiftly as the nuptials can be arranged. While this is being done, you will go with Abbé Suger to Saint-Denis, where you will dwell in penitence until the day of your marriage."

Raoul's stomach clenched. He did not want to enter Saint-Denis lest he didn't come out again, but what other choice did he have? His life was forfeit anyway and Louis could easily have had him killed long before now. The older men were looking at him with ill-concealed scorn. "Sire, you are gracious," he said.

"I am not," Louis retorted. "I am acting out of expedience and necessity. There is no grace about this scandalous matter at all."

Raoul left Louis's chamber in a daze, but slowly began to realize and rationalize what the annulment meant. He and Leonora barely saw each other from year to year and when they did they seldom spoke. She would probably be pleased to be rid of him. The only reason for her to fight would be the diminishing of her status. He felt a slight qualm about that, but it couldn't be helped.

He thought of Petronella instead, He truly did love her, and beyond the physical attraction, it did no harm that she was Alienor's sister and, while Alienor remained childless, Petronella was heiress to Aquitaine. Should he make her pregnant, their offspring would stand in line to succeed to the duchy. In truth, despite the rough road he had recently been forced to travel and the difficulties still to come, things might just work out rather well.

Petronella and Raoul were married quietly at Christmastide in the chapel of Saint Nicholas in the royal palace, the nuptials absorbed into the general Nativity celebrations. Petronella wore a gown of deep red wool trimmed with ermine. Raoul was plainly besotted by his nubile young bride, as well he might be. What the bride saw in a one-eyed man beyond his fiftieth year was not quite as obvious to the court, but she seemed just as infatuated as he was.

Following the wedding, the couple retired to Raoul's estates north of Paris to spend time alone as newlyweds and wait for the dust to settle on the scandal. However, trouble rapidly fermented. Theobald of Champagne was furious at the insult to his niece and called Raoul a fornicator, adulterer, and debaucher of young girls. Bernard of Clairvaux allied with him and together they lobbied the Pope. Theobald slighted Louis by giving succor to Pierre de la Châtre, elected but spurned Archbishop of Bourges, providing him with a safe refuge at his court.

Louis promptly threatened to cut off de la Châtre's head and stick it on a pole on the Petit-Pont in Paris, with Theobald's rammed beside it for good measure. He made a public vow before the altar at Saint-Denis that while he was king, de la Châtre would never set foot over the threshold of Bourges Cathedral. Pope Innocent immediately retaliated and put all of France under an interdict. Louis replied with a furious letter declaring he had always supported the Church, that he revered the Pope, and that the rebellious clergy at Bourges in collusion with Theobald were the real malign influences at work.

The silence that followed was akin to the still before a storm. Louis existed in a state of strung tension, his temper to the fore, and the court jumped at every footfall.

Alienor was in her chamber sorting through her casket of rings. She had several she intended giving as gifts to people who had served her well. A particular one glinted at her from the bottom of the coffer and she slipped it onto her finger. It had once belonged to her grandmother Philippa and was set with several rubies resembling pomegranate seeds. The stones were supposed to represent the women of her bloodline and the ring had been passed down through each generation.

Alienor held out her hand to study the ring on her finger and wondered if she would ever pass it on to her own child. Louis continued to lie with her in his intermittent way, but without success. The red stones might equally stand for her wasted blood as each month the result of his infrequent attentions failed to take root in her womb.

Her thoughts were interrupted by a frantic knocking on her chamber door. Gisela opened it to a flushed and panting squire. "Madam, you are summoned to the King's presence immediately!"

She stood up. "What's wrong?"

"A letter has arrived from the Pope. The King is asking for you."

Alienor could tell from the young man's expression that the news was bad. Bidding Gisela accompany her, she followed him to Louis's chamber.

Louis was sitting at his lectern, clutching a parchment scroll and looking grim. When Alienor entered the room, he fixed her with a furious glare. "Theobald of Champagne has hosted a council in Troyes, behind my back, with the Papal Legate in attendance. See what he has done now!" He thrust the parchment toward her.

As Alienor read the scroll, her heart sank. The Pope had upheld Theobald of Champagne's protest on behalf of his niece. He had declared Raoul and Petronella's marriage invalid and suspended the bishops who had agreed to the annulment of Raoul's first match. Furthermore, Innocent had ordered Raoul and Petronella to separate on pain of excommunication and had expressed astonishment that Louis should condone such a union.

"I will not be dictated to by meddling prelates," Louis snarled. "Their words do not belong to God, and I will brook no more interference from Theobald of Champagne or the Pope!"

"You must do something about it," Alienor said, wondering whom they could influence in Rome to lobby the Pope on their behalf.

"I intend to. I shall root out this wasps' nest in Champagne. If an insect stings you, then you squash it underfoot."

Later, in their chamber, Louis took her with all the vigor his fury lent him, uncaring that he hurt her, expending his temper on her body as if it was all her fault. Alienor endured the pummeling because she knew once he was spent, his rage would dissipate and she would be able to deal with him. He was like a child having a tantrum. Finished, he adjusted his clothes and, without a word, strode from the room. She knew he was going to pray: to spend the night on his knees doing penance and exhorting God to strike down his enemies.

Sore from his aggression, glad he was gone, Alienor hugged her pillow and tried to think of solutions to the dilemma of the papal opposition, but there seemed no way out. Innocent was a stubborn old mule, and when he did listen, it was to pernicious troublemakers such as Bernard of Clairvaux, who was Theobald's advocate. Eventually, she rose, lit a candle, and knelt to pray, but while the ritual helped her to sleep, it delivered no answers.

18

Champagne, Summer 1142

Louis took a mouthful of wine, swilled it around his mouth, and leaned over his destrier's withers to spit it out. If he had swallowed it, he would have been sick. He had been unwell with belly gripes for several days, but not so much that he was unable to ride, and his invasion and destruction of Champagne had continued apace. He had crossed borders both geographical and moral. Ever since the monks of Bourges had elected their own archbishop against his wishes, his frustration and fury had been gathering inside him, adding to the morass already festering there. All the bewilderment of a small boy taken from his nurse and given to the Church to be raised with the rigid discipline of the rod. All the hurt caused by the disapproval of his cold and rigid mother, who thought him second-best and not good enough. All the rage at the perfidy and lies of people he trusted. His skull felt as if it were full of dark red fleece. He had frightening dreams of demons grasping his feet and pulling him down into the abyss while he scrambled for purchase at the chasm's smooth edge. Even sleeping with candles burning did not afford him enough light and he had taken to having a chaplain and a Templar knight keep vigil at his bedside all night.

Between the daily marches through Champagne, Louis spent his time on his knees praying to God, but his mind remained a fog and the only way God showed himself was by granting him victory after victory as he progressed along the valley of the Marne. His army encountered no resistance and they plundered and looted as they rode, trampling the vines, burning the fields, leaving a trail of destruction in their wake. Each town Louis took and ravaged was a triumphant blow upon the backs of Count Theobald and the monks of Bourges. He felt as if he were striking back for the honor of his family and all the old slights visited on his house by the Counts of Champagne. He had ridden so far from the path that he had lost his bearings, his only compass that of knowing he was a king with a divine right to rule, and everyone must bow their heads to his yoke.

Ahead of his army lay the town of Vitry, close upon the River Saulx. The inhabitants had fashioned makeshift barriers out of tree stumps and overturned carts and had shored up the walls with rubble as best they could, but they were helpless in the face of the attack that Louis ordered his mercenaries to launch on them.

The assault was fierce and vicious. Fire blossomed along the rooflines and took hold in barns, swiftly spreading from house to house, fanned by a hot summer wind. Louis reined in his stallion on a high vantage point and watched his troops wreak destruction. Battle cries and the clash and scrape of weapons rose amid gouts of smoke and twists of flame. A dull ache throbbed at his temples and the leaden sensation in his belly made him feel as if all the foulness inside him was going to spew out in a glistening dark mass. He imagined that his mail shirt was a burden of sin, weighting his body.

His brother Robert joined him, sitting easily in the saddle but holding his destrier on a tight rein. The sun glittered on his hauberk and helm, reflecting polished stars of fire. "The way the wind is veering, there will be naught left of the town come morning."

"Theobald of Champagne has brought it on himself," Louis replied grimly.

Robert shrugged. "But I do wonder what we are bringing down on ourselves by this."

A grim silence stretched between the brothers. Abruptly Louis reined away from Robert and rode back to the tent that his attendants had set up to provide respite and shade while

Vitry was devoured.

The canvas dissipated some of the sun's punishing strength. Louis dismissed everyone and knelt to pray at his small personal altar. The cold gold and marble concealing various saintly relics gave him a momentary respite from the pounding red darkness inside his mind. Bernard of Clairvaux had warned him that God could stop the breath of kings and he was intensely conscious of each inhalation and of the weight of his hauberk, his coat of sins. He counted his prayer beads through his fingers, trying to find calm in the cool, smooth agates, while he recited the Lord's Prayer.

The tent flaps flurried open and Robert ducked inside. "The church is on fire," he said. "Most of the townspeople are inside, including the women and children."

Louis stared at him and as comprehension dawned, so did the horror. While the monks of Bourges deserved all that came their way, the wider Church was still the house of God. Even if he was laying waste to Theobald's lands, it was with the expectation that the people would have opportunity to flee or seek refuge. "I gave no such order." He jerked to his feet.

"It was wind-borne from the houses."

"Well, give the people space to flee." Louis had removed his sword belt to pray, but now he buckled it on again. "Tell the men to stand back."

"It is too late for that, brother."

Feeling sick, Louis followed Robert from the tent back to the vantage point. The church was indeed ablaze: the roof, the walls, everything. The wind had veered and the flames surged toward heaven like the ravenous tongues of a thousand demons. No one could survive such a conflagration.

"Douse it," Louis commanded. Emotion twitched across his face like raindrops in a pool. "Organize buckets from the river." He fancied he could feel his mail shirt becoming as hot as a griddle and see the flame light dancing on weapons, leaving an indelible stain.

Robert eyed him askance. "It will be like a child trying to quench a bonfire by pissing on it. We won't be able to get near."

"Just do it!"

Robert turned away and began snapping orders. Louis called for his horse, and the moment his squire brought the sweating gray from the lines, he grabbed the reins and swung into the saddle. His men scrambled to follow as he galloped down the path and entered the town. Around him the dwellings were ablaze and drifts of choking smoke obscured his vision. He rode through arches of fire. Ragged whips of flame swept out at him, as if striving to drag him in and devour him. His stallion balked and began to plunge until it was all Louis could do to stay in the saddle and he was forced to pull back. The wellheads and buckets had been destroyed by fire and, even with access to the river, the church and its occupants were doomed.

Louis returned to camp with his head thrown back and tears streaming down his reddened cheeks. His eyebrows were singed, a raw stinging burn shone on the back of his hand like a stigma, and his mind was a red conflagration.

He spent the night kneeling at his altar and refused to let anyone tend his injuries. In the pale light of dawn with smoke rising from the ashes and mist curling off the river, he visited the smoldering ruins of the church: a pyre for more than a thousand men, women, and children. Although the fire had died, the charred timbers were still too hot to touch. From the corner of his eye, although he tried not to look, he could see twisted, blackened shapes sticking up like the limbs of bogwood trees rising out of a swamp. The stench of burned flesh, timber, and stone made him gag. Falling to his knees in the hot cinders, he wept, and in between sobs raised his voice to God in remorse and fear. His rage toward Theobald of Champagne and the monks of Bourges only intensified, however, because this desecration was entirely their fault.

19

Paris, Summer 1142

Alienor glanced around the chamber prepared for Louis's triumphant return from Champagne. Water had been heated and the tub made ready for a bath. The best sheets had been aired and laid on the bed. Curtains of gold brocade hung from the canopy poles and tawny nuggets of frankincense burned in the braziers. Servants had set out dishes of food on trestles covered with fine white napery. There were crisply roasted songbirds, cheese tarts, almond balls dampened with honey, pastries and fritters, fragrant white bread and bowls of blood-red cherries.

During Louis's absence, she had received sporadic messages of a general nature. The campaign was progressing well. They had encountered little opposition from Count Theobald and, despite all the latter's posturing, Champagne's underbelly was soft and the defenses had not stood against the French. Naturally the Church had condemned Louis's actions. Letters had flown between Bernard of Clairvaux and the papal court on Theobald's behalf and Louis had been ordered to cease his attacks on Champagne on peril of his soul. He had obeyed in person and turned back, but his troops had remained in Champagne and continued their ravages. As far as Alienor knew, Louis was doing what he must to bring Theobald of Champagne to heel, and doing it well. She was anticipating a victorious return and had dressed carefully for the occasion. Her gown was embroidered with golden fleurs-de-lis, her hair was twisted into elaborate braids, and she wore a coronet set with pearls and rock crystals.

When her chamberlain announced Louis's arrival, Alienor's heart began to pound. Part of her was desperate to see him: his tall, athletic body and glorious silvery hair. She imagined flinging herself into his arms and welcoming him with kisses. Perhaps they could start afresh; pretend they were meeting for the first time as man and woman instead of boy and girl. Her ladies in tow, she left the chamber and processed to the great hall to welcome her husband home.

Louis and his retainers entered the chamber on a flourish of trumpets. Alienor looked for him but there was no sparkle of flaxen hair, no flicker of gold silk, no sense of his presence. All that met her eye in the space where she expected to see him was a bedraggled, travel-stained monk with stooped shoulders. For a moment she thought he was one of the minions of Bernard of Clairvaux, but then the monk raised his head and looked at her and she realized with a jolt of absolute shock that she was looking at her husband. Dear God, dear God, what had happened to him? He was an old man! Drawing on all her reserves, she curtsied to him and bowed her head. He shuffled forward to raise her up and kiss her lips, and it was like being touched by death. His hands were clammy, his breath so fetid that she almost retched. He stank of sweat and sickness. A monk's tonsure glistened on his skull and around the shaved area his hair was greasy and flat, all its silver beauty gone. Shorn almost to his scalp, it looked gray not blond.

Alienor was aware of all the servants and attendants staring at him. She caught the eye of Robert de Dreux, who gave an infinitesimal shake of his head. Rallying, she touched Louis's sleeve, managing not to flinch as a flea jumped onto the back of her hand. "Sire," she said, "I can see you are tired. Will you come to your chamber and let me tend you there?"

Louis hesitated, but then allowed himself to be led from the hall on stumbling feet. Arriving at his room in the Great Tower, he stared at the food laid out, and his throat jerked. He flicked a single glance at the tub and steaming cauldrons of hot water and shook his head. "If I eat I shall be sick," he said, "and the state of my body does not matter."

"Of course it matters! You must eat after your journey and wash for your ease and comfort."

"I must do neither." Louis sat down in a chair and put his face in his hands.

Alienor knelt to remove his boots and recoiled at the stench from his feet. They were filthy beyond belief, black between the toes and the skin peeling off. His toenails were long and rimed with dirt. She almost gagged. In her peripheral vision, she was aware of Raoul de Vermandois and Robert de Dreux exchanging glances. "Bring me a bowl of warm rose water and a cloth," she snapped to a staring maid.

"I have told you, I do not need tending," Louis said stiffly.

"But it is a sacred task to wash a wayfarer's feet," Alienor replied. "Would you have me shirk that duty?"

He made a fatigued gesture of capitulation. When the maid returned with the water, Alienor steeled herself to the vile task of cleaning his feet. She wondered what had happened to him. He had set out as a great prince at the head of his army, proudly flaunting his banners, determined to grind Theobald of Champagne underfoot, and had returned looking like a wild holy man who had been starving and mortifying himself to the point of madness.

He continued to refuse all offers of food and wine until she brought him some plain spring water in a chalcedony cup. "It will purify your blood," she said.

He raised the cup to his lips with trembling hands and sipped while she knelt to finish her task. She rose and touched his brow to see if he was feverish, but he pushed her away. Immediately he was contrite. "I need to rest," he said. "That is all."

"You cannot do so like this. At least change into clothes more suited to the chamber than the stable."

"I care not," Louis replied, but allowed the maids to remove his soiled garments.

Once more Alienor was horrified. If his outer robes were dirty and dusty then his shirt and braies were rancid. Insect bite marks pocked his body and stinking black grime threaded every fold and crevice of his skin. He had lost muscle and bulk and was as bony as an old man. She wondered when he had last eaten a decent meal and felt a mixture of revulsion, compassion, and deep anxiety. "I will care for you now," she soothed, wiping the rosewater cloth over his emaciated body.

He shook his head. "It is a waste of time."

He refused to wear the fine linen shirt she

had ready for him, insisting instead on a coarse chemise from the ones her women had been stitching to give to the poor. At least it was clean, and Alienor yielded to his whim. She eventually persuaded him to lie down on the bed. As well as keeping the light, he insisted on having chaplains sit either side of him to pray for his soul.

Alienor left the room in a state of anxiety. It was one thing to deal with enemies when you had a powerful husband to protect you, but if Louis lost that power, the implications for herself were terrifying.

"What has happened to him?" she demanded of Raoul de Vermandois and Robert de Dreux. "Why is he like this? Tell me!"

Raoul rubbed a tired forefinger across his eye patch. "He had not been himself for some time, but Vitry was what tipped him over the edge. He has barely eaten or slept since, and as you see he has to have his chaplains with him all the time."

"What happened at Vitry? There has been nothing in the letters I have received."

Robert said, "The church burned down with the townspeople inside it — over a thousand men, women, and children." He looked away and swallowed. "I never wish to witness or smell such a thing again. I fear it has turned my brother's mind. He blames Theobald of Champagne and the monks of Bourges, but still he sees his own hand upon the torch."

"You should have warned me before he arrived," she said. "I could have been better prepared."

"We thought he would recover and come to terms with it," Raoul replied. "Indeed, he may do so now he is back in Paris." He gave her a piercing look. "He called out in the night for you . . . and for his mother."

Alienor bit her lip. She had not been prepared for this — could never have imagined it happening — but she would have to bring Louis around. If she did not, others would seize the moment and she had precious few allies at the French court.

20

Castle of Arras, October 1143

At Raoul's home in Arras, Alienor sat in a window embrasure with Petronella. Outside the leaves were turning russet and gold. Petronella was spending her confinement here, having conceived in the months following Raoul's return from Champagne.

"There is no room for the child to kick now," Petronella said ruefully. "It surely cannot be long, or I will burst asunder!" She laid her hand on her swollen belly. "I can barely walk as it is."

"You look well," Alienor said. Her sister's skin was blooming, her hair as lustrous as brunette silk.

Petronella preened a little. "Raoul says that too."

"Now that Pope Innocent has died, we might be able to resolve the matter of the Archbishopric of Bourges and your marriage. Pope Celestine is prepared to be more conciliatory. He has already said he will lift the interdict on France."

Petronella jutted her chin. "It does not matter what the Pope says. I know I am married to Raoul." She picked up her sewing. "How is Louis?"

Alienor made a face. "Better than when he returned from Champagne, but so changed. He dresses like a monk and he talks like one too." She waved her hand impatiently. "It's 'God wants this' and 'God wants that.' You could not begin to imagine how much God wants! Sometimes I do not see him for days on end, and when I do it is impossible to talk to him. You and Raoul, you are at ease with each other, you laugh and kiss; yet you are under interdict and vilified by Rome and the Church. When I reach out to Louis, he draws away as if I am unclean. You are round with child, but how am I to bear an heir for France when I sleep alone? Since his return from Vitry, he has not lain with me once."

"You should give him a love philter," Petronella suggested. "Slip some grains of Paradise into his wine."

"I have tried that, but it made no difference."

"Then perhaps you should dress as a nun, or a monk . . . or a Templar. Have you already tried that too?"

Alienor wagged her finger at her sister. "Enough. That is going too far."

"Is it?" Petronella gave her a long look and

rose to her feet, pressing her hands to the small of her back. "I would do those things if that was what it took. Who knows, you both might enjoy it."

Alienor bit her lip. Petronella was incorrigible, and yet there was a worrying truth in her sister's words. The delayed remark about the Templar was telling. Louis had been taking fiscal advice from a Templar knight called Thierry de Galeran who had also been one of his father's advisers. He was a eunuch but had been made so after manhood and still exuded an aura of power and virility. Louis was unduly influenced by him, especially since Thierry had become one of the guardians at his bedside dedicated to banishing the fear of demons that plagued his nights. Once she had come to see Louis early in the morning and Thierry had been there clad only in his shirt and braies as he washed his face and hands in Louis's basin. She suspected that he and Louis shared the same bed, platonically or otherwise, but suspicion was not proof, and she could not bring herself to take that final step and find out.

Alienor gazed at the washed and swaddled baby girl lying in the crook of her arm. She was to be baptized with the Vermandois family name of Isabelle. Her skin was softer than petals, the hair on the tiny skull had the glint of a gold coin, and she was utterly beautiful.

Petronella had had a swift and easy delivery and was already sitting up in her clean, fresh bed, drinking wine fortified with strengthening herbs and enjoying the attention following on from the drama.

"Madam, your husband is asking to see you and the child," announced a chamber lady who had just taken a message at the door.

"Give her to me," Petronella said to Alienor, setting her cup aside and gesturing for the baby. Alienor carefully transferred the small bundle into Petronella's arms and, with a pang of envy, watched her sister arrange herself like a madonna. "Tell my lord that I am pleased to receive him," Petronella called to the maid.

Raoul entered the chamber and tiptoed to the bed, an incongruous sight for he was such a large man. He kissed his wife tenderly. His gaze then flicked to her engorged breasts with appreciation, and she laughed softly. "These aren't for you just yet," she said.

"I'll look forward to the day when they are then." He folded aside the blanket to look at the new arrival. "Ahhh, she is almost as beautiful as her clever mother."

Alienor left Raoul and Petronella and went to look out of the window. She felt wistful and teary because she would never have such an intimate and tender bond with Louis. He would be horrified at the thought of coming anywhere near the birthing chamber, let alone taking her hand and sitting with her so soon after childbirth, especially of a girl, because it would sully his purity and he would view the baby's sex as failure. The teasing, the frank sensuality, the genuine love shining between her sister and Raoul made her throat ache. Petronella, despite all the opposition she faced, was rich indeed, and standing here now in this chamber, a party to their joy in each other and their daughter, Alienor felt bereft and impoverished.

"A baby girl," Alienor said to Louis. "They have named her Isabelle."

Louis grunted. "That is all to the good since Raoul has a son from his first marriage. At least there won't be a fight over inheritance."

"But she may yet bear a son. She quickened swiftly with the first."

"That bridge can be crossed later. We have a year's grace at least."

Alienor poured Louis a cup of wine and brought it to him. Today he was wearing a long tunic of plain wool, dyed a rich midnight blue, with a large gold and sapphire cross around his neck. Although he had kept his tonsure, his hair had grown back around the shaved area and was silvery bright. He had mercifully recovered some balance since his return from Champagne and the grubby hermit now resembled an aesthetic prince of the Church. The effect was not unattractive and, despite their difficulties, Alienor still felt affection for him. Besides, being with Petronella and Raoul had spurred her on to try to conceive. It was politically essential for herself, for France, and for her husband.

"I missed you while I was gone," she said, putting her hand on his sleeve.

"And I missed you," he replied with a wary note in his voice.

"Will you come to me later?"

He hesitated, and she could see him working through all the possible excuses not to do so. She swallowed her anger and impatience. Petronella would not have to ask it of Raoul even once.

"We have to beget an heir," she said. "We have been wed for more than six years. I cannot give a child to France unless you give me the means. Surely it cannot be so difficult a thing to contemplate."

Louis stepped away from her and, drinking the wine, went to look out at the river. She allowed him to stand alone for a while before joining him. "Let me rub your shoulders," she said in a soothing voice. "I can see how tense you are, and we have not talked in a while."

He sighed and allowed her to lead him to the bed. She fetched a small vial of scented oil from a wall niche and bade him remove his gown and shirt. His skin was pale and smooth, cool as marble. She set about the task with slow sweeps of her palm. "Will this new Pope sanction Raoul's annulment, do you think?"

"I do not know," he said into his folded arms. "He has lifted the interdict, but there are factions who continue to press him to hold firm. There is a meeting tomorrow at Saint-Denis with Suger and Bernard of Clairvaux to discuss matters."

"And what of de la Châtre and Bourges?"

She felt him tense under her hands. "There is no news on that. I swore my oath, and they know where I stand."

She continued to knead and smooth and said casually, "If you accepted de la Châtre, it would take the wind out of their sails and we could go forward."

"You would have me go back on my sworn word?" He twisted to look up at her, his eyes bright with anger. "You would have me glide through all this like a false serpent? I have so sworn and that is the end of it."

Alienor thought he was being foolish and stubborn, but she was trying to gentle his mood. "Of course you must do what you think fit," she soothed. She kissed his ear and his neck and worked her way down his back, under his shirt.

He turned over and with a groan put his arms around her and began to kiss her. She kissed him back and loosened her braids, shaking them out in a tumble of golden twists. Her loins were heavy with a dull ache. She knew she would conceive from this. She could feel the seed within her body, ripe and waiting. Louis rubbed his face against hers, and she felt the prickle of his beard. He pressed himself against her and unfastened the laces at the sides of her dress to put his hands inside. They rolled on the bed, pulling clothing out of the way, gasping between kisses. Alienor tugged off her gown and swiftly followed it with her chemise so that she was naked except for her stockings, tied with blue silk garters. Louis, still in hose and braies, ran his eyes over her; he licked his lips. His pale complexion was flushed with lust. She lay back, parting her thighs for him.

"Louis, come to me," she said. "Make us a child."

He fell upon her, his hips bucking and thrusting. She reached down to free him and guide him home, felt him firm and hard as she stroked him. He groaned at her touch, but as she opened to him, he suddenly became flaccid and soft in her hand.

"Louis?"

He pushed her aside and rolled away. When she reached for him, he struck at her. "Let me be with your whore's tricks!" He stuffed his failure back into his braies and, almost weeping, threw on his tunic and strode from the room.

Alienor sat up and covered her face with her hands. She could smell him on her fingers. What was she going to do? How could she reach him? If this state of affairs continued her position as queen would become untenable. And, as much as she loved Petronella, she wanted her own offspring to rule Aquitaine after her, not those sired by Raoul de Vermandois. Wearily she sought her chemise and gown. Perhaps Petronella's jesting was right. Perhaps she ought to dress as a nun . . . or a Templar.

"God does not love me, but I have ever striven to obey him," Louis said to Suger, his voice echoing between the carved pillars of the new ambulatory in the abbey church of Saint-Denis. Behind him the light from the magnificent stained glass arches strewed the tiled floor with jeweled luminescence. He sat down on a bench and rubbed his hands over his tonsure.

Suger had come from contemplation in his cell to attend on Louis, who had arrived on a lathered horse in a state of agitation. "Why do you say you do not have God's love, my son? Is it because of this meeting tomorrow? Is that what bothers you?"

Louis shook his head. "No," he said bleakly. "That will just be more talk of the kind I have heard many times over." He swallowed, struggling to say the words. "It is because . . .

because I cannot procreate with the Queen. I am cursed and robbed of my purpose as a king and a man." He raised a tormented gaze to Suger. "I swore a public oath that de la Châtre would never cross the threshold of Bourges Cathedral as its archbishop. Do you think that oath is the reason for my failure? The Queen suggested I should rescind my vow, but how can I do that when I made it before God?"

Suger frowned at him. "What prevents you from procreating with the Queen?"

Louis flushed. "I cannot . . . cannot perform the deed," he muttered. "When I go to her, it is with every intention of begetting a child, but my body refuses to obey my will — sometimes in the final moment. It is God's punishment."

Suger laid a firm hand on Louis's shoulder. "Then you must ask for God's help and mercy, and so must the Queen. He will show you the way if only you ask Him with an open heart."

"I have asked." Louis's voice grew querulous. "I have prayed and made offerings, but He has not answered." He leaned forward, clasping his hands. "Perhaps it is her fault," he said, his mouth twisting. "Perhaps she has done something to anger God. After all, she was the one who miscarried our child."

"That is, for her conscience, not yours," Suger said neutrally. "For yourself, I tell you to lay yourself open to God's will with true humility and intent and accept His chastisement if it be necessary. I will do what I can for you — as I always have." He transferred his hand to Louis's disheveled tonsure in a tender gesture. "However, perhaps the Queen is right. If you show your humility by agreeing to let Pierre de la Châtre take his place as Archbishop of Bourges, it will ease the pressures on you and on France, and that in turn will lead to greater harmony in your life. I will pray for you and ask God to look with favor upon you and the Queen." He added after a moment, "It will do no harm for you and the Queen to show humility and respect to Abbé Bernard. He is a terrible enemy but a powerful ally, and it is in your interests to wean him away from Theobald of Champagne."

Louis began to feel a little better. "You are right," he said. "I will think on your advice." He raised his gaze to the glorious windows. Their shining clarity gave him tenuous hope and inspiration. Suger always knew what was for the best.

Alienor held the rock-crystal vase between her hands. Although she cupped it securely, she still imagined dropping it and watching it shatter on the tiled floor like ice smashed on a frozen pond.

Louis had suggested they should present it

to Suger as a dedication gift to the new church of Saint-Denis. He was fired up with enthusiasm, and it was as if last night's tearful rage had never happened.

"It will be a fitting place to keep it," he said.

"And Suger has long coveted it."

"It was not his notion, but mine." Louis sent her a sharp look. "I saw the light shining through the windows and I wondered what I could give that would be fitting for a dedication. I thought this might cause God to shine His light on us and give us a child."

The overcast daylight painted the vase in varying shades of white and pale gray, revealing none of the subtle, heavenly fire. Alienor had the feeling that it would never do so again in her hands. Remembering that she was loved was difficult indeed. She had always known Suger would eventually claim it, but what did it matter? Whatever it took to render Louis capable of performing his duty, she would embrace. If the vase could accomplish such a miracle, it was worth the price. "As you wish," she said. "Whatever you deem necessary." She gave it to him, just as she had done in Bordeaux, with equal care, but the feeling was different now — flat rather than optimistic.

Louis took it carefully and for a moment their fingers overlapped. Then he withdrew. "I am going to break my oath and allow Pierre de la Châtre to assume his position as

Archbishop of Bourges," he said.

She looked at him.

His mouth turned down at the corners. "It is a great shame for a king to break his word, but I have no choice. I have done all I can, but it is like beating my fists against a solid castle wall until my hands are worn down to the bleeding bones."

"In exchange for that, at the very least, we should have the ban lifted on Raoul and Petronella's marriage," she said quickly.

"That will be open to negotiation," he replied in a way that told her not to expect a positive outcome. "I expect you to do your part in this too." Holding the vase as carefully as he might hold an infant, he left the chamber.

Alienor sighed, and then drew herself upright. She would not shirk what had to be done. And Louis might have finished beating his fists against walls, but there were other subtler means of taking castles down.

21

Paris, June 1144

The dedication of the refurbished and extended basilica church of Saint-Denis, burial place of the kings of France, took place on June 11 and drew crowds of worshippers from all across France. The small town of Saint-Denis had grown fields of tents overnight. Every lodging house bulged at the seams, and every guesthouse within a twenty-mile radius was packed with visiting travelers. Everyone was eager to see the remodeled church, its glittering interior said to resemble a bejeweled reliquary built to house the presence of God. Even the mortar was flecked with gemstones.

Alienor had slept in the abbey lodging house, while Louis had spent his own night in vigil with Suger, the monks of the abbey, and various ecclesiastics, including thirteen bishops and five archbishops.

Alienor had shared the guest room with her mother-in-law, who had traveled from her dower lands for the ceremony. The women had been civil but cold with each other. They had not shared company since the Christmas feast, and that at least made tolerance possible. Adelaide eyed Alienor's ruby silk dress with a slight curl of her lip as if she found it garish and distasteful, but she kept her thoughts to herself. Nor did she mention Petronella and Raoul, although the very absence of the subject was like a dark hole in the middle of the conversations they did have. Petronella and Raoul were absent because they were excommunicate and not permitted to enter a church.

In the hazy morning, still cool and dusky blue, the women left the guest quarters and processed to the church with its new doors of gilded bronze, inscribed in lettering of copper-gilt. *The noble work is bright, but, being nobly bright, the work should brighten the minds, allowing them to travel through the lights to the true light, where Christ is the true door.* Alienor read the words and then raised her eyes to the lintel where was written: *Receive, stern Judge, the prayers of your Suger. Let me be mercifully numbered among your sheep.*

Suger's stamp was everywhere, if not in actual name as it was on the doors, then in all the glittering gold and jewels and color-stained light flooding through the lucent glass windows. The gold altar front was studded with a fortune in amethysts, rubies, sapphires, and emeralds. Adorning the choir a magnificent cross stood twenty feet tall, ornamented with gold and gems, crafted by famed Mosan goldsmiths. The darkness shone. Alienor felt as if she were at the heart of a jewel, or indeed a reliquary, and was glad she had worn her gown of red silk with all its adornments, for it made her feel as if she were a part of this glowing, luminous tableau.

Borne aloft by Louis, who was dressed in the simple robes of a penitent, the silver reliquary containing the sacred bones of Saint Denis were processed around the exterior of the abbey in drifts of fragrant smoke. Suger and the attendant clergy sprinkled the outer walls with holy water contained in silver aspergilla and then returned to the congregation, who also received a judicious sprinkling. Louis placed the reliquary on the gem-studded altar and prostrated himself, body stretched out in the shape of a cross. His skin was bone white and shadows of fatigue hollowed his face, but his eyes were filled with light and his lips were parted with rapture. The glorious sound of the choir rose with the frankincense and dissolved into the colored radiance from the windows.

Alienor was surprised to be moved by the experience, because she had expected it to be just another of Suger's ceremonies. Instead she felt the presence and breath of God. Tears filled her eyes, blurring her vision to a liquid prism. Beside her, Adelaide quietly dabbed her own eyes with her sleeve while her husband patted her arm. Louis filed out with the monks at the end of the ceremony, looking dazed — almost drunk.

By noon, the dedication was finished but the celebrations continued into the hot summer afternoon. The poor were provided with alms of bread and wine. Vendors sold refreshment from stalls set up outside the abbey. Some pilgrims had brought their own food and found patches of shade in which to sit and eat. People queued to look at the incredible array of relics and decoration that Suger had lavished on the abbey and to read the pictorial stories in the marvelous windows.

Alone, because Louis was still with the monks, Alienor paused by a lectern of an eagle, wings outspread. She had paid to have it regilded because its pinions had been rubbed bare by the constant touch of pilgrims and worshippers, and after all it was her symbol as Duchess of Aquitaine.

A monk came softly to her side and murmured the summons she had been anticipating. A small feeling of dread unfurled in her stomach. Bidding her ladies and household knights stay behind, she accompanied the monk to an upstairs chamber of the abbey guesthouse. As he knocked on the door and set his hand on the latch, she drew a deep breath and steeled herself.

Within, waiting for her, was Bernard of Clairvaux, clad in a grayish-white habit of unwashed wool. He looked more undernourished than ever, with a fever flush reddening his cheekbones. Although his expression was composed, she could sense that his tension mirrored her own. They were here to negotiate, but neither of them desired to be in the other's presence.

She wondered what he thought of Saint-Denis, for his own vision of the worship of God was a practice of plain simplicity, in which wealth and precious objects were to be shunned. He had rebuked Suger before now for his interest in material goods, and yet he had attended the consecration. Perhaps it made him feel superior, or perhaps he wanted to observe in order to write one of his damning sermons.

She curtsied to him and he bowed to her, but it was like two opponents entering the arena. "Father, I am pleased to have this opportunity to speak to you," she said. "Perhaps we can reach a better understanding with each other today than we have had before."

"Indeed, my daughter," he replied. "That is also my wish."

Her red silk gown rustled over the tiled floor as she moved farther into the room and sat down on a cushioned bench. She saw his nostrils flare and his lip curl. He often spoke disparagingly of women who enhanced their appearance with the fur of animals and the work of worms, but then his own robe was but the woven fleece of a sheep. She thought him afraid of the sexual power women wielded, so very different from that of an ascetic male.

She folded her hands in her lap and sat with her spine erect. "I am here in the role of peacemaker to ask you to use your influence and petition Pope Celestine to lift the excommunication and marriage ban on my sister Petronella and her husband," she said. "In return for which, my husband will accept Pierre de la Châtre as Archbishop of Bourges and make a peace treaty with the Count of Champagne."

He stared at her without speaking, but the silence was eloquent.

"Do you have no compassion?" she demanded. "No thought for their souls and that of their baby daughter?"

"I have compassion for the cast-off wife of Raoul de Vermandois," he replied implacably. "Your sister and her paramour are suffering the consequences of their lust. They have made their bed with covers of dishonor, but God sees all and shall neither be mocked nor bargained with."

Alienor was irritated. People always made bargains with God. That was what most prayers were about. "Raoul's wife has not

268

fulfilled her role to him in many years," she said. "The marriage was dead a long time ago, in all but the unraveling."

"Nevertheless, it was made before God and cannot be unmade, and never for such a bargain." His black gaze bored into hers. "If the King desires to do right by the Archbishop of Bourges, then he must do so without condition, and the only way your sister and the lord of Vermandois may return to Holy Mother Church is by repenting of their lust and giving each other up." He raised one bony hand in the gesture of a tutor. "It is not for me to say what conversations you have with your sister, but you must consider the correctness of your own behavior when you are with her and make it clear that you do not condone impropriety under any circumstances."

"I will support my sister in every way I can," Alienor said stiffly. "I have never acted with impropriety."

His look became sorrowful. "In that case you should be encouraging her to submit to holy writ. I do not wish you harm, but I am deeply concerned for your spiritual welfare, daughter. If you wish to help your sister and your husband, then you must cease meddling in these affairs of state and toil to bring your husband into a state of grace with the Church."

Alienor gave him a cold look. "That is why

I came to you: to talk of a solution that would end this fighting. My sister is my heir, and her daughter stands next to her in line. I have to be concerned about her welfare, because it is Aquitaine's welfare too — and France's, because Raoul de Vermandois is close kin to my husband."

"Then perhaps you should apply yourself to asking God to provide you with an heir for France," he said. "That is surely your first duty."

"Do you think I have not tried? How can I provide an heir for France without my husband's assistance? Surely it is his duty too? But God punishes us by rendering him incapable when he does come to me, and often he does not visit at all. He would rather spend time in prayer, or in the company of men like Thierry de Galeran." She looked down at her tightly clasped hands. "What am I supposed to do? I cannot conjure a conception out of thin air."

There was a long silence. She drew breath to speak again, but he held out his thin, pale hand to her, bidding her be still, his gaze fixed and powerful. There was a slight curve to his lips, almost but not quite a smile, and although superficially it was compassionate, underneath it held satisfaction because she had exposed her vulnerability to him.

"God has ways of bringing His flock back to him," he said. "Only do what is right and

He will accept you back into His fold." He gestured at her silk gown. "If you wish to conceive a child, then you must leave off all of these fripperies, these wicked ways that have come to be so important to you. You must forsake them and hold tight to Christ your savior." He took the wooden cross on a cord from around his own neck and pressed it into her hands. "Just as Christ died on the Cross to the physical world and rose again, so let your soul die to the world of physical delights and rise again stronger than before. God will admonish you and test you again and again until He is certain that you are one of His. You must carry His Cross and be worthy of it, for it is no easy task to bear the burden of a country upon your back, as your husband well knows, and you must be ready for it and worthy of it. You must scourge your life and make it as God would wish, and only when you are fruitful in the ways of the spirit shall you be fruitful in your womb. In order to make new life, you must leave behind your old life of sin and do God's work fervently. Do you understand me in this?"

Alienor felt like a cornered deer faced by the hunter's drawn bow. "Yes, Father, I do understand."

"You must change your ways," he reiterated. "And if you do this, I shall pray to God our Heavenly Father that he grants you and the King the great gift and mercy of a child for France."

She bowed her head over the plain wooden cross in her hand; the leather thong was greasy and dark from the contact with the back of Abbé Bernard's neck. Despite her revulsion, she felt a strange moment of humility. After all the wealth that had surrounded her today, this object brought her feet back down to the ground. More importantly, it made her see her way forward with Louis.

"Good, my child," he said. "I suggest you spend three days and nights in fasting and prayer to purge yourself of any deleterious spirits. And then, doing as I have told you, go to your husband, and all will be well."

He bade her kneel with him to pray. Alienor closed her eyes as the tiled floor struck cold against her knees through the fine stuff of her garments. She pressed her palms together and tried not to breathe in the sour smell of his body. If prayer and humility would bring her closer to her desire, then she would do what she must.

Newly returned from her three days of fasting and contemplation, Alienor went to her chamber window and looked out on a dazzling blue arch of sky. She felt light-headed, but her thoughts were lucid and focused. The sky was clear and plain, so unlike Suger's jeweled use of light in Saint-Denis, and yet its simplicity was the true wonder of God and nothing plain was ever really simple. In that at least, if nothing else, Bernard of Clairvaux was right.

Turning from the window, she studied her bed with its soft sheets and rich golden hangings embellished with scrollwork embroidery in warm fire orange. She loved them, but she could now see her problem. "Strip the bed," she commanded her women. "Bring me plain sheets and bolster cases, the kind the monks use at Saint-Denis."

Her ladies eyed her askance. "Do it," she commanded. Her gaze fell on the beautiful brass bowl at the bedside that was used for her ablutions. It had a flower design worked over its surface that matched the hangings and she loved it. Steeling herself, she bade someone fetch an unembellished one. Everything had to be made simple. She had the niches stripped of their ornaments, her caskets and coffers tidied away into her painted chest, and the chest itself covered with a gray blanket. She placed a book of the lives of the saints on top of it and put crosses in the embrasures.

When she had finished, the room was stark, but possessed a certain austere beauty. Her ladies were even more wide-eyed when she ordered them to change their fine gowns for others of sober wool and to cover their heads with full wimples of thick white linen.

"It is to please the King," she told them. "That is all you need to know. It is important to put him at ease when he visits, and to do that, the surroundings must suit."

Alienor opted for a gown of blue wool with modest sleeves and the same wimple as her women. She hung Abbé Bernard's wooden cross around her neck and removed all rings but her wedding band. And then she took up some sewing — a chemise to be given in charity to the poor — and stitched the hem while she waited. It was one of Louis's "duty" evenings, and since she did not have her flux, he had no excuse for keeping away.

He walked into her chamber in his usual rigid manner, like a man forced to wear a garment with seams that irritated, but then he stopped and looked around quizzically. Alienor watched him sniff the air like a deer tasting the dawn. She left her sewing and went to greet him with a demure curtsy. He dismissed the attendants he had brought with him, including the Templar Thierry de Galeran, who flicked her a narrow, speculative look as if measuring an opponent before he bowed and departed.

"Changes?" Louis said with a raised eyebrow.

"I hope you approve of them, sire."

He made a noncommittal sound and went to examine a cross standing in an embrasure.

She waited for him to return to her and

give her his cloak. He washed his hands and face using the plain ewer and dried them on the coarse linen towel neatly folded at the side of the bowl. Sitting down on the edge of the bed, he patted the rough woolen coverlet. "Yes, this is better," he said. "Perhaps at last you are beginning to understand."

Alienor bit her tongue on a sharp retort, determined to play the role of submissive, prayerful wife to the hilt if that was what it took to succeed in begetting an heir for France and Aquitaine. "Everything became clear to me at Saint-Denis," she said demurely. "I realized that a change was needed and that I had to be the one to make it because you had already done so." All of which was true. She had married a young man, never realizing he would become this warped semblance of a monk.

Louis pointed imperiously to her side of the bed, indicating she should lie down in it. Anger coiled within her, but force of will held her to her purpose. She was sad too. She wanted him as he had once been, with his tender, shy smile, his tumble of long fair hair, and all his boyish enthusiasm and desire. But that person no longer existed.

The sheets were scratchy and uncomfortable and she had to suppress a grimace. Louis, however, seemed to relish the feel of them against his skin, as if their very coarseness made them more real. She turned toward him and put her hand across his chest. "Louis . . ." His eyes were closed and she felt him recoil. "Is lying with me really so terrible?" she asked.

He swallowed. "No," he said, "but we must guard our honor and do this thing not out of fleshly lust, but because it is the will of God."

"Of course," she said as if surprised. "It is my intention to follow God's will. I do not kiss you out of lust, but out of a desire to do His bidding and be fruitful." Slowly, as if a sudden move might startle him, she sat up and removed the wimple.

He touched her tightly braided hair. "All I have allowed myself to feel are harsh things," he said in a hoarse voice. "Punishment things, because I am not worthy of more. The soft and beautiful things are sent to lure us. You must see that?"

Alienor was tempted to say that the beautiful things were God's creation too. Where else had Eden come from? But that would only agitate him further. "I see that we are being tested, just as the Abbot of Clairvaux said we would be," she replied. "And I see that we are punished in all manner of ways, but procreating is the will of God and we must do our duty."

He groaned and rolled on top of her, pushing up her chemise and gown. Alienor lay inert and forced herself not to be a participant. Usually she would have raised her knees and parted her thighs; she would have twined her arms and legs around him and moved her hips in counterpoint to his; but now she did nothing. He kept his eyes tightly closed, as if even to look at her was unbearable. She heard him muttering a prayer between clenched teeth. He tugged her legs apart and she felt him fumbling. "God wills it," he gasped. "God wills it. God wills it!" And then he was inside her and thrusting wildly, calling on God to watch him doing his duty, his voice rising to a shout that was a mingling of triumph, guilt, and despair as he spilled his seed.

He lay inert on her for a moment and then withdrew to gain his breath. She closed her legs and pressed them together. She was sore from the intrusion without any preparation, but she had achieved her goal — as had Louis. A glance at him showed that his eyes were still closed, but his features had relaxed. He left the bed and went to kneel at the cross she had placed at the foot of it, and there thanked God for his great mercy and benevolence in restoring grace to him. Joining him, Alienor thanked God too and silently prayed for a swift result.

22

Paris, Autumn 1144

Alienor arrived at the abbey church of Saint-Denis feeling tense and sick. The prayers and the strategies had worked and she was certain she was with child. She had wanted to be sure of her condition before she told Louis, but now that the time had arrived, she was apprehensive.

Abbé Suger greeted her with a bright gleam in his eye. "I think you will approve of this," he said and took her to a locked cupboard containing the vessels used in the mass. Standing on the middle shelf in pride of place was her rock-crystal vase, but she barely recognized it, for Suger had had the neck and base adorned with filigreed gold, precious gems, and pearls. There was an inscription around the base, detailing the history of its giving.

"How beautiful," she said, because it was, even if no longer hers. Bernard of Clairvaux would have approved of its plain state — pure

278

and unembellished. Now it was entirely Suger's thing. He hardly needed an inscription to set his mark on it. "And so in keeping with the rest of the church."

"I am glad you approve. I wished to do full justice to your gift."

"Indeed you have." Alienor was almost fond of Suger. He was a consummate politician, prepared like her to deal in practicalities. "I have a favor to ask of you."

Suger looked wary. "If I can help, I assuredly will."

She studied the quatrefoil pattern of the floor tiles. "All our prayers have borne fruit," she said. "I am with child." She placed her hand on her belly, which showed a slight curve under her belt.

Suger's face lit up. "That is wonderful news! Praise God that He has heard our entreaties!"

Alienor bit her lip. "I have not yet told the King. I did not want to raise his hopes after so many years and our other loss. I do not know how he will react to this. I would be grateful if you would prepare him to hear the news."

"Leave it with me." Suger set his hand over hers in reassurance. "I cannot see that the King will be anything but overjoyed by this news."

Alienor smiled, but her feelings remained ambiguous. These days she did not know how

Louis would react from one moment to the next.

Louis gazed at Suger with barely concealed anxiety. He had recently come from prayer and had been in a relaxed frame of mind until the Abbé said he wanted a private word. He was bracing himself for yet more tidings of court and ecclesiastical machinations. The matter of Bourges had been concluded and de la Châtre was smugly ensconced in his archbishopric, but something else was bound to have cropped up.

"The Queen asked me to convey the news to you that God has heard your prayers and supplications and seen fit to bless your marriage. Your lady is fruitful and will bear a child in the spring," Suger said.

Louis's stare widened with astonishment. The news was so enormous it was like colliding with a giant. At last. After all the years of prayer and struggle and doubt. Finally they had been successful by following God's rule. If of course she bore a living child this time. "Are you certain of this?"

Suger nodded. "As certain as the Queen is herself," he said. "She wanted me to tell you since it was through the advice and intervention of the Church that it has come about, and also to prepare you for when you meet."

Louis felt excitement fermenting within him. A child! A son for France at last!

"The Queen has retired to the guesthouse," Suger said, smiling.

"I shall go to her in a moment," Louis said, for first he would return to the church to fall to his knees and give thanks. Perhaps he ought to take Alienor a gift? His first thought was that she would appreciate a fine brooch or ring, but he swiftly dismissed the notion. He must not encourage such embellishment because it was not godly and they had only begotten this child by getting rid of such tawdry items from their congress. Better to make a donation to the Church to glorify God rather than beautify his wife.

Alienor's maids had just lit the lamps in the guest chamber when Louis arrived, his pale face flushed, his eyes sparkling with tears and his demeanor alive with a glow that Alienor had not seen for a long, long time.

"Is it true?" he demanded. "What Suger tells me, is it true?" He seized her hands in his.

"Indeed it is," she replied, smiling but still wary.

He leaned forward and kissed her face, although not her lips. "You have done well. You have pleased God, and now may it please Him to give us a healthy son." He knelt to her and pressed his head and one palm against the swell of her belly. Alienor looked down at his tonsure and tried to feel affection for him. A thread still existed but it was so thin and frayed.

He stood up. "You must rest and not overexert yourself. I am trusting you to bear a strong living son this time. You must have your women with you at all times, and you must employ midwives immediately. Indeed," he said, with a frown, "you should not have ridden here today lest it harm the child."

Alienor felt the prison door closing on her already. He would put her in a cage in order to protect his blessed heir. "I knew I would be safe," she replied, "because our prayers for a child were made at Saint-Denis."

"Perhaps, but you must not take such risks again where our son is concerned."

"Be assured I shall take heed of all wise counsel," she said.

"Make sure you do. I do not want you to lose this one as you did the last."

Alienor clenched her fists at her sides. Perhaps going into confinement would not be such a bad thing after all.

Eventually he left, and Alienor slumped down with a feeling of wrung out relief. There was so little left of their marriage now, just the rags and tatters of a once-bright cloth. She knew how dependent she was on his approval. For now she had it, but he was not consistent. She never knew from one moment to the next how he was going to behave toward her and therefore she constantly had to adjust her balance. It was exhausting.

23

Paris, Spring 1145

Alienor gasped and pushed, summoning all her strength to bear down, and then fell back, panting, as the contraction subsided. Her labor had begun the previous evening; it was full morning now and early April sunshine flooded through the window arches, reminding her of Aquitaine.

"Not long now," Petronella soothed, wiping Alienor's brow with a cloth dipped in rose water. "I know you think you'll burst but you won't, I promise you."

"You sound very sure of that," Alienor panted. Her hair had been unbound so that it would not bind the child in her womb and was spread on the pillow in a heavy golden fan.

"I am. I am smaller than you, and I managed." Petronella's expression was smug. Having been through the ordeal of childbirth once, and with her second pregnancy beginning to ripen her breasts and belly, she was feeling well qualified to give advice.

"But Isabelle was a small baby," Alienor said.

"Well then, yours is bound to suit your size. Raoul's much taller than Louis."

Another contraction surged. Alienor grimaced and gripped the eagle stone in her fist. It was an egg-shaped rock that contained another stone inside it and was supposed to ease the pains of childbirth. In a rare act of compassion, her mother-in-law had presented it to her, saying it had helped her during her own labors. If its powers were working, Alienor dreaded to think what labor was like without one. Once again she pushed for all she was worth. The midwives bustled around her, encouraging, watching carefully, oiling her perineum so that it would be less likely to tear.

The head was born and then with a gush and a slither the shoulders and the rest of the body. A baby's wail filled the space around the bed, growing stronger with each breath, but the silence of the attendants in the room told Alienor everything she needed to know.

"Oh, how beautiful!" Petronella was the first to recover. "Alienor, you have a daughter, a perfect little girl!" She bent to kiss Alienor's cheek. "And a playmate cousin for Isabelle!"

Alienor looked beyond Petronella. A shaft of sunlight illuminated the squawking baby still attached to her by the umbilical cord, and it was a holy thing. Then a midwife snicked the cord with a small, sharp knife and removed the child from the sun shaft to bathe her in a brass bowl of warm water — the decorated one that had not been used since the night before her conception.

Adelaide, who had been witness to the birth, watched the women bathing the infant. "Girls are always useful for forming marriage alliances," she said. "I had one daughter myself in between seven sons. It is better to bear the boys first to secure the lineage, but at least a healthy living child is cause for thanksgiving and reason to believe you will do better next time."

Alienor let the words flow over her, imagining she was protected inside an impervious glass bubble where nothing could do her harm.

The senior midwife brought the baby to her, now wrapped in a soft blanket. She was tiny and perfect and so very alive, with all of her limbs in motion and her little face screwed up. Alienor took her in her arms and her heart blossomed. She would not think about Louis's reaction or anyone else's. Not in this moment, because there would never be another one like it. The baby's skin was so soft, and each finger was tipped with a miniature pink fingernail.

"How is she to be named?" Petronella asked.

Had the baby been male, he would have been christened Philippe, for his paternal grandsire. "Marie," Alienor said. "For the Holy Virgin Mary, to thank her for her grace."

Louis was dining with the court in the magnificent hall built by his ancestor Robert II. He knew Alienor was in labor, but had tried to push the awareness to one side. Both Abbé Suger and Bernard of Clairvaux had sent special prayers and supplications to God for a living heir for France. He had done all in his power to safeguard a good outcome and to ensure Alienor fulfilled the same obligation. He had even sent her into confinement a fortnight early in order to give his son additional peace and quiet before his birth. His main anxiety was for the child. If Alienor died bearing him, he could always find another wife, but the boy was of supreme importance: as well as being his heir, the child would also be heir to Aquitaine.

An usher made his way down the hall and around the back of the high table. Louis wiped his lips on his napkin with fastidious care and beckoned the man over. The servant stooped to whisper in Louis's ear. Bidding everyone continue with their meal, Louis left his seat and followed the man from the hall to a small antechamber where his mother was waiting for him.

"Well," Louis snapped with impatient

anxiety as she curtsied and rose again. "What news? Is my son safely born?"

"The child is indeed safely born," she said. "Alive and well."

"Praise be to God! Let all the churches in France ring out the news! I shall —" He looked down at the hand she had laid on his sleeve. The grip was as strong as steel, reminding him of the times she had slapped him and brought him to order as a small child. "What is it?" He thought that perhaps Alienor had indeed died in the bearing.

Her eyes on him were as flat as stones. "The child is a girl," his mother said. "You have a lusty baby daughter."

His breath emerged in a harsh gasp; he felt as if he had been punched. "A daughter? Are you sure?"

She raised her eyebrows. "I was a witness; I am sure." She removed her hand from his sleeve. "Your wife weathered the birth well. As soon as she is churched, you can set about getting a son on her."

Louis swallowed. The idea of bedding with Alienor and going through the whole process again sickened him. Could a woman ever be clean again after she had given birth, especially to a daughter? "First she delivers me blood and now she delivers me a girl," he said. "How am I to deal with this?"

"Through prayer." His mother's tone was impatient. "And through perseverance. A king needs daughters as well as sons. Rejoice in the birth of this one and pray for a better outcome next time."

Louis said nothing. He felt let down by God and the Church and especially by his wife. What else did he have to do to beget a son? All of his prayers, all of the promises made by Suger and Bernard of Clairvaux had come down to this. A girl.

"You will need to acknowledge your daughter and attend to her baptism," Adelaide said. "Your wife desires to name her Marie in honor of the Virgin, should it meet with your approval."

Louis had not even considered girls' names because he had been so certain that Alienor would bear a son. "As she wishes," he said.

When his mother had gone, Louis put his face in his hands. He could not return to the feast, knowing they would all be looking at him, awaiting an announcement, although in the way of things, the word would already be filtering through the hall. He could not face the sidelong looks, the smirks. He knew the lore about men who begot girls: that they were ruled by their wives and that their seed was weak. He didn't even want to see the child, but knew he must, and arrange her baptism, because it was his duty.

The first bells began to toll, telling him that the news had already escaped the confines of the palace. Saint-Barthélemy, Saint-Michel,

Saint-Pierre, Saint-Éloi. Louis had always loved the sound of their bells, ringing out the canonical hours, bringing order and structure into daily life and reminding all of God's presence and purpose. But now, as they greeted the arrival of a princess, the noise jangled inside his skull, mocking him and fueling his rage.

24

The November day outside the palace was bright but bitterly cold. The River Seine bore a blue reflection of the sky but beneath that surface the water was brown and sluggish from recent heavy rain. The oiled linen in the window embrasures let in grainy light, but drafts too. Candles flickered in most of the niches and every charcoal brazier was in use to keep the damp chill at bay.

Alienor sometimes felt as if she were dwelling in a cage. She had been out of her confinement since May, but much of the time she could not tell the difference, except that she had Louis to deal with and all of his foolishness.

This morning, however, there were several diversions to contemplate, courtesy of her uncle Raymond, Prince of Antioch, and his wife, Constance, who was Louis's second cousin. The couple, having heard of the birth of the Princess Marie, had sent a cornucopia of gifts to their close and beloved kin in France. Alienor's chamber overflowed with riches from the East. Bolts of precious silks shimmered like the still backwaters of the Garonne on a hot day. There were books with carved ivory panels set with gemstones, bags of frankincense, and tablets of scented white soap. A gold and rock-crystal reliquary containing a fragment of the Virgin Mary's cloak. Damascened swords and a mail shirt so fine that it draped like a cobweb. For the baby, there was a silver cup set with amethysts . . . And then there was the letter, full of felicitation and graceful words, but between the lines, snared with the subtle asking price for all these rare and precious gifts.

Alienor paused by the cradle to look at her sleeping daughter. Marie lay on her back, her tiny fists curled up like flower buds and her chest rising and falling in swift, shallow breaths. Alienor felt a tender sorrow whenever she looked at her. The birth of a daughter had disappointed all of France, but she had not disappointed herself, and that was what mattered.

Louis entered the room. He flicked a glance at the cradle but did not venture over for a look and quickly turned to the pile of gifts of which he had been told by Alienor's steward. "Generous indeed," he said, but with a slight curl of distaste at the luxury, although that changed when Alienor gave him the reliquary containing the scrap of the Virgin's cloak. His face lit up and his breathing quickened.

"My uncle says he sends it to you for safekeeping because he knows you will treasure it."

Louis ran his thumb over the smooth rock crystal. "For safekeeping?"

She held out the letter to him. "He says his situation is becoming increasingly perilous since the fall of Edessa and that he is involved in constant skirmishes with the Saracens."

Louis took the letter over to the window to let the light filtering through the oiled linen fall on the parchment.

Alienor stroked Marie's soft pink cheek. She had been close to giving birth when the news had reached Paris that the Turks had taken the Frankish Christian principality of Edessa and under their leader Zengi, Prince of Aleppo, now threatened Antioch, governed by her uncle Raymond, the County of Tripoli, and the Kingdom of Jerusalem itself.

The letter reiterated the dangers faced by the remaining states. Representatives were being sent to Rome to discuss what might be done to support those in Outremer, and Raymond hoped Alienor and Louis could bring their weight to bear, given that their kin were so closely involved.

Louis pursed his lips. Last year at Saint-Denis he had made a vow to go on pilgrimage to the Holy Sepulchre to do penance for what had happened at Vitry, to expiate his broken vow over Bourges, and to fulfill a promise to pray for the soul of his dead older brother at the tomb of the Holy Sepulchre. The first news of the fall of Edessa had deeply agitated him. Although the initial upset had diminished, it still needled him. "It is our duty to help," he said, looking at the reliquary. "We cannot allow the infidel to overrun our holy places. We should offer them all the support we can muster."

"In what way?"

He turned from the window. "I shall issue a summons to arms when the court assembles for Christmas at Bourges. I shall fulfill my vow of pilgrimage and free Edessa from the infidel at the same time." He spoke as if it were a simple matter, no more complicated than organizing a day's hunt.

His words jolted her for a moment, but underneath she was unsurprised, because such a venture would be perfect for him. He would be the humble penitent and pilgrim, but he would also be the conquering hero, imbued with all the glamour of the devout king riding at the head of an army to save Christendom.

A spark of hope kindled in her breast. During his absence someone would have to take the reins. She could accomplish so much if only she were able to use her power instead of being constantly stifled and pinned down.

Moreover, he would be gone for perhaps two years, and so much could happen in that time. "It is indeed a great undertaking," she said, her voice made vibrant by the possibilities.

Louis gave her a wary, slightly puzzled look, and she swiftly turned away to fuss the baby again. "Is it wrong to say I am proud of my husband?"

His expression softened. "Pride is a sin," he said, "but I am pleased you think well of my idea."

"We must make the Christmas court a great occasion," she said, and when Louis began to frown added, "with due seriousness and praise to God, of course, but men who are well feted will be more open to suggestion. Besides, since the festival is to be held at Bourges, all will see that you are God's anointed King."

"Very well," he said, as if offering her a gracious concession, and came to the cradle to chuck his daughter under the chin, and that too was an honor, for usually he took no interest in the child.

Alienor wore her crown at Bourges and presided with Louis over a gathering of all the nobles and bishops of France. They had been feasted, entertained, and then addressed by Louis and the Bishop of Langres concerning the matter of relief for Edessa and ultimately the Kingdom of Jerusalem.

"Make no mistake!" Louis cried, his face suffused with passion and his eyes glittering like sapphires. "If we do not go, then Tripoli will fall, then Antioch, and even Jerusalem itself. We cannot let this happen in the very place where Christ's footsteps as a mortal man imprinted the dust. I tell you all, it is your God-given duty to ride with me and bring succor to our beleaguered kin!"

It was a fine speech and the Bishop of Langres followed it with more burning oratory designed to put fire in men's bellies. Louis's household knights banged their fists on the tables and stirred the cheering to greater heights, as did the men of Aquitaine and Poitou, but following the initial surge, there was less enthusiasm. Men were dubious about being away from their dealings at home for so long a time, living in tents and fighting infidels. Although reaction to the speeches was politely enthusiastic, privately many barons held back from commitment. Abbé Suger openly declared that France needed Louis more than the Holy Land did and the expedition, while well intentioned, was ill conceived.

Louis was furious. In the privacy of his chamber he wept and kicked the furniture and stormed about like a thwarted child. "Why do they not see it?" he raged. "Why will they not follow me? Have I not given them everything?"

Alienor watched him rant and felt irritated. She too had been disappointed by the response, but again not surprised. It was like driving cattle. You had to constantly prod them to keep them moving and nip their heels when they came to an obstacle in the road. "Give them time to grow used to the idea," she said. "Many will change their minds when spring begins to heat their blood. We have yet to hear a ruling from the Pope. You have sown the seed today on the feast of the Christ child's birth. Now give them time to ponder the idea and approach them again at the time of His crucifixion and rising."

Louis unclenched his fists and breathed out hard. "When I think of how they have refused me . . ."

"If you spend that time in lobbying and making preparations, it is not wasted," she said. "As to Suger, he is growing old. He would rather not have you away from France, but that is his weakness, not yours."

"My mind is made up; I shall go whatever the objections." Louis's face wore the stubborn look she knew so well.

Alienor was thoughtful as she joined her ladies. They were dancing to music and had inveigled some of the younger household knights to join them. Raoul was in their midst, laughing and flirting as usual. Petronella was not with him at court, being in confinement at Arras, soon to bear their second child.

Catching Alienor's eye, he excused himself and joined her.

"You make bold in your wife's absence, sire," she remarked.

Raoul shrugged. "It is only dancing."

"And what the eye does not see, the heart does not grieve over?"

"I would never do anything to grieve Petronella."

"I am pleased to hear it, because if you did, I would have to cut out your heart and the part of you that has offended."

"Your sister is full capable of doing that herself," he said wryly, and then folded his arms. "Did you desire to speak with me other than to warn me off other women?"

She gave him a taut smile. "I want you to exert your talents in other directions of persuasion. I would like you to put your mind to swaying the opinion of men who are reluctant to commit to Louis's project to rescue Edessa."

He eyed her with sharp amusement. "Even if I am one of them?"

"I doubt that," she said. "You are shrewd and ambitious enough to know the benefits. Given your years, you may prefer to remain in France with all the advantages that might entail."

He continued to look amused, but wary

too. "You are keen to have this project succeed. I understand your desire to help your uncle. You say to me that what the eye does not see, the heart does not grieve over, but perhaps it is true for you also. Does it not concern you that your husband will be absent for two years at the least and facing great danger?"

"Indeed it concerns me, which is why I desire him to have strength of numbers and support and supplies," she replied. "He will go whatever the outcome, but I would rather he had the backing of all factions, because how else will he be able to aid my uncle and do all that is necessary?"

"And just how might it work to my advantage?"

"I think you know very well, my lord. The King will need trustworthy men to assist in governing France during his absence."

"To 'assist' whom?" he asked.

Alienor smiled and extended her hand. "Come, dance with me and we will talk."

Raoul laughed softly. "I think I am in more danger now than I was a moment ago," he said as he led her into the circle.

A week after the Christmas court dispersed, news arrived from Rome that the Pope had called for France and all the Christian nations to mobilize an army and go to the aid of Edessa. Louis was furious at the timing.

"If the news had arrived last week, I would have had papal sanction," he snarled.

Alienor looked up from the letter she had been dictating to one of her vassals. "It will still add to your strength for the summons at Easter. Christmas was a great gathering, but the Easter one will be greater still; and if you take the Cross, you will bring others with you. Now that Rome is involved, many will reconsider. Ask the Pope to send Bernard of Clairvaux to preach at Easter. His oratory is renowned." Even though she heartily disliked Abbé Bernard, she respected his ability to whip a crowd into a frenzy.

"Monks are banned from preaching outside their own monasteries," Louis said, but his expression had brightened.

Alienor sniffed. "Since when has that ever bothered Bernard of Clairvaux? He may preach humility, he may talk mightily of the sin of pride in others, but the fact is that he loves the sound of his own voice in full flow — and so do others."

"You should not say such things about a man so holy," Louis admonished.

"He is certainly holier than thou," she retorted. "But that is not the point. When the court convenes at Vézelay at Easter, you must ensure you have the tools to stir men's souls. I shall write to my aunt Agnes at Saintes and to the nuns of Fontevraud and ask them to sew crosses to be given out by all those taking the road to Outremer."

"That is a fine idea." Louis came over to her and placed his hands on the back of her shoulders. The gesture was almost tender.

Alienor made an effort not to draw away. If she was having fine ideas, it was because the more support she could garner for her uncle Raymond in Antioch, the better, and with Louis safely gone for at least two years, France would be hers.

Alienor watched Petronella gently bathing her infant son in a brass bowl before the hearth and tried not to feel envious. Here was her sister, excommunicated and shunned by the Church, but still able to produce a healthy male child, whereas she and Louis still only had Marie. She had gotten him to lie with her twice in January, but her bleed had come as usual, and after that, throughout Lent he would not share her bed because it was against Church law. He had spent much of his time either at Notre Dame or Saint-Denis in prayer or in organizing for the Easter gathering and crown wearing at Vézelay, to be held a fortnight from now once the court reached there from Paris.

"I am glad you are here," Alienor said. "I missed you."

Petronella lifted the baby out of his bath and wrapped him in a warmed towel. He fussed and protested, sucking on his little fist.

Petronella kissed his brow and handed him over to the waiting wet nurse. "I am glad too," she said. "I don't like Raoul being at court without me." Her tone was querulous. "There is nothing to do in confinement except wait and sew and pace the room, while he can do what he likes." She pouted. "You didn't come this time either."

"I couldn't," Alienor replied. "I had matters to attend to at court."

"So apparently did Raoul."

Alienor suppressed a sigh of irritation. "He is a royal constable, and Louis had need of him and will continue to do so when it comes to mustering for the Holy Land, and then for governing afterward. His life is the court. You know that."

Petronella was not mollified. "Has he been faithful to me?"

"How would I know such a thing?" Alienor demanded, not adding that Raoul had succeeded in hiding his fornication with Petronella when they were right under her nose. "I do know he loves you and cares for you. When he heard the news that you had borne a son, he was the proudest man at court."

"But he did not come to Arras to see us," she said. "And he was not here to greet us in Paris."

"Because Louis needed him at Vézelay. You will see him soon." Alienor clung to patience. Petronella was acting as if this were a great issue, when so much more was at stake. Whether Raoul was faithful or not was a trifling matter. She had made her bed; let her lie in it. "He will have a full role to play when Louis is gone, and he needs to prepare for that; as his wife, you should be preparing with him."

"As his concubine, you mean," Petronella said bitterly. "Bernard of Clairvaux made very sure of that."

"I have not given up on the matter. You shall have your marriage contract, I promise."

Petronella tightened her lips into a prim rosebud. Alienor gave up. There was no reasoning with her when one of her dark moods was upon her. Once reunited with Raoul, in Vézelay things would be different. She would shine for him, and the responsibility for handling her would be his. Yet Alienor still felt a duty of care to her sister, because she knew Petronella would never take responsibility for herself.

Louis had spent the first part of his day in prayer in the Merovingian Basilica of Notre Dame before returning to the palace to dine in the great hall. It was still Lent and the food consisted of fish and bread, and the only seasoning was gray salt.

Alienor was in a quiet mood, as was her sister, and Louis noted it first with approval, and then with growing suspicion, wondering what they might be plotting. He knew Alienor's way of winding people around her little finger. He had been a victim of her seduction in the past, but he was on his guard now and knew all about her glances, her smiles and little tricks. The way she moved her arm, exposing a glimpse of wrist as she adjusted her sleeve; the emphasis of the manicured fingers adorned by a single rare and beautiful ring. He saw the way she entrapped men and was disturbed and infuriated. During the time Marie was conceived, she had changed her ways and become sober and godly, but of late, she had returned to her earlier patterns of behavior and dress. Considering that he was about to take the Cross, he found it perturbing and distasteful. What might she do during his absence?

"I am wondering what to do about the Queen," he said later in his chamber to Abbé Suger and his Templar adviser Thierry de Galeran, who was dealing with fiscal matters connected with the pilgrimage.

Suger folded his hands inside his sleeves. "In what way do you mean?" he asked warily.

"While I am gone. I am wondering what provision I should make for her. I am worried she will foment discord and seek power for herself."

Suger gave a slow nod. "That is a valid concern, sire."

"I would have appointed the Count of Nevers as your coregent and he would have stood up to her, but he is to enter the Carthusian order and will not change his mind. That means I must give more responsibility to Raoul de Vermandois and I do not trust him to stand firm with the Queen, even if in all other ways he is fit to govern. He is too easily swayed by the scent of a woman."

"He is also an excommunicate," Thierry said darkly.

"That is a matter for his soul, not his administrative abilities," Louis snapped. "He is too long in the tooth to go on crusade, and he needs to be gainfully occupied while I am gone." He gnawed his lip. "I have a notion to bring the Queen with me where I can keep an eye on her. She won't be able to stir up trouble at home and she will be a figurehead for the men of Poitou and Aquitaine to follow — although naturally the command will be with me as her husband."

Suger shook his head. "It is not a good idea to bring the Queen on such an undertaking," he said. "It will encourage other men to bring their wives, and perhaps even their families, and it will make the army unwieldy and slow, especially the whole train of servants and the amount of baggage required. The men will be distracted from their fight for Christ if there are women in the camp."

"They will cause immorality," Thierry

agreed. "Women always do."

Louis rubbed his chin. That was indeed a consideration. He was well aware that Suger did not want him to go, but his mind was set. The decisions now were those of policy: leave Alienor behind under close watch, or bring her with him where he could keep an eye on her. Perhaps the journey to Jerusalem and the pilgrimage would bring her back to God's way again? "I need her with me in order to secure the full support of the Aquitaine contingent," he said. "If I do not, they will do as they please and either not come at all, or turn back midway, and who knows what havoc they will all wreak in my absence."

Alienor was preparing for bed when Louis came to her chamber. She was so unaccustomed to his late-night visits these days that it took her a moment to gather herself and offer him a cup of wine. "This is an unaccustomed pleasure," she said, directing Gisela to pour Louis a drink.

He sat down on her bed. The curtains had been loosened from their loops and the sheets were turned down.

"Are you intending to stay?"

He hesitated, and she was even more surprised when he nodded. "Yes," he said, "for a while."

She dismissed her ladies and sat down beside him.

"I want to talk to you," he said.

"About what?" She tried to sound interested rather than wary.

"The pilgrimage to rescue Edessa," he said. "I want you to come with me."

Alienor's expression froze. Louis took her hand and squeezed it hard enough to cause pain. "The men of Aquitaine will follow with greater commitment if you are present, and I know you will welcome the opportunity to speak with your uncle Raymond since he is your father's only living brother."

She was aware of him watching her narrowly, calculating her response. "What of France and Aquitaine? One of us should remain here to oversee matters."

"Suger is full capable of governing. There is the Count of Nevers too, and even if he takes the cowl as he says he intends to, my lord of Vermandois is well able to deal with the secular side of matters."

Alienor's stomach sank. "What of Marie? It is not right to leave her motherless for two years."

Louis waved his hand. "She has nurses and women to care for her. A small child does not notice who its mother is. By the time she is capable of reason, we will be home." His expression hardened. "You shall accompany me. If we pray at the tomb of the Holy Sepulchre, you may yet bear me a son. I want you with me."

She wondered how far Louis had seen through her intentions and set out to thwart her plans. He plainly was not doing this out of love. If she refused, he would find ways to either keep her restricted and powerless in France, or bring her along in far closer confinement than if she agreed. He had outflanked her.

"As you wish," she said, lowering her eyes. The way he was squeezing her hand was agonizing, but she refused to gasp or wince. "I will take the Cross with you at Vézelay."

"Good." He raised her hand to his lips and kissed her bloodless fingers before relaxing his grip. "We shall speak more tomorrow."

When he had gone, Alienor got into bed, but she left the lamp burning and, rubbing her bruised hand, began to rethink her strategy.

Swords of sunlight cleft the clouds and illuminated the pilgrim church of the Madeleine crowning the hill of Vézelay. For those arriving on Easter Sunday 1146, it was as if the fingertips of God were reaching down to touch the abbey in benediction.

The town had long since burst at the seams and tents had sprung up in the surrounding fields. All of the hostels and houses were full. People slept at the roadside, their heads pillowed on their belongings. Cook stalls were doing a brisk trade. The bakers could not keep up with the demand for bread, and there was keen competition for the firewood to fuel their ovens. The thoroughfares to the abbey were choked with people, eager to be part of the Easter rites. Even with the new narthex, the abbey church could not contain the sheer numbers, and outdoor pulpits had been raised so that those outside could listen to the word of God in the same way that the crowds had first listened to Christ.

Alienor and Louis were shriven before the altar, which was surrounded by iron railings wrought from the fetters and chains of prisoners who had offered them on the occasion of being set free. Alienor prayed fervently to be rid of her own invisible fetters.

Following the service, they processed outside, the soldiers forcing a path through the pilgrims packing the nave and narthex, until they came to a pulpit standing upon open ground a little way from the church. Two thrones stood behind it adorned with silk drapes and cushions, the banners of France and Aquitaine planted either side. Louis and Alienor wore robes of plain undyed wool, although a large and elaborate gold cross set with numerous gemstones glimmered on Alienor's breast.

Behind and around the thrones were gathered the nobility of France and Aquitaine. A cold wind ruffled the hilltop, but the sun continued to cut through the clouds and was even warm in the sheltered places.

A procession of white-clad monks approached the pulpit, led by the cadaverous Bernard of Clairvaux. His tonsure gleamed silver-gray in the light, and there was a translucent quality about him, as if he were not of this world. He fixed his burning gaze on Louis and Alienor, and then mounted the steps to the pulpit. Facing his audience of pilgrims and crusaders, he unrolled the parchment scroll in his hand and displayed the papal bull calling on all Christians to rescue the holy places of God from the infidel. His voice, despite his frail appearance, was powerful, and his emotive, moving oratory held the audience spellbound. A chill formed at the nape of Alienor's neck and rippled down her spine. She glanced at Louis and saw tears glittering in his eyes.

Bernard struck the edge of the pulpit. "Let all who are prisoners this day go free! In the spirit of Saint Mary Magdalene at Vézelay, let all who wear fetters for their sins cast them off and take this cross of Christ and bear it to Jerusalem!" Bernard spread his arms wide. "All shall be granted absolution. Only take up your swords for God and let your hearts be pure! Take the oath, take it now, take it for Christ who died on the Cross for your sins and rises again triumphant this very day!"

Louis prostrated himself at the foot of the pulpit, openly weeping. Bernard of Clairvaux presented him with a cross of white wool to stitch to his cloak and, lifting him to his feet, embraced him. Then Alienor knelt to receive her cross. She was trembling, a little with fear, but mostly with the emotion of the moment, which marked a new phase in her life.

Abbé Bernard presented her with the scrap of wool, ensuring that their fingers did not touch. His gaze fell on the magnificent cross on her breast and Alienor unfastened the chain and handed it to him. "A gift for the campaign," she said.

"Thank you, my daughter," he replied and, as if it were burning his flesh, swiftly handed it to one of his attendants to place in an offerings chest. From inside her gown, Alienor hooked out the plain wooden cross that Bernard had given her at Saint-Denis.

People crowded forward to receive their crosses from the monks who had brought sackfuls to hand out, stitched in convents and monasteries the length and breadth of France, and for a while all was frantic activity. Louis and Alienor doled out crosses to eager, outstretched hands until there were none left. The crowd dispersed to tents and lodgings or took the opportunity to pray in the church to seal their new vows. On her return to the guesthouse, Alienor saw many people sitting cross-legged on the grass, busy with needle and thread, sewing crosses onto cloaks and tunics. Someone was banging on

311

a drum and singing a song in rousing tones.

"Qui ore irat od Lovis
Ja mar d'enfern avrat paur
Cars s'arma en iert en Pareis
Od les angles de Nostre Segnor."

Alienor suppressed the urge to mock the words. *Whoever goes with Louis need not fear because his soul will go to Paradise and dwell with the angels and Our Lord.* A worthy sentiment indeed, but if they went to Paradise, she suspected it might just be because Louis had gone and gotten them all killed. What she must do now was survive until she reached Antioch and the sanctuary and protection of her uncle Raymond.

25

Poitou, Autumn 1146

It was so good to be back in Poitiers, if only for a short time. Alienor felt as if her body had been bound in coils of rope, wound so tightly that she could barely breathe. Now, suddenly, the end had been pulled, twirling her around, unraveling her until she was dizzy with exhilaration.

Golden sunshine flickered through the trees, burnishing the leaves of chestnut and oak with the first tints of autumn. The sky was a clear, fierce blue, and the weather perfect for the progress she and Louis were making through her lands to muster support for the crusade. Louis concentrated his efforts on churches and abbeys. Alienor spoke to her vassals, urging them to provide support for the relief of Edessa and Raymond of Poitiers, the only surviving adult male in the direct line of the Dukes of Aquitaine.

Petronella traveled with her in her household, all trace of her darker moods banished by being home under the warm southern sun. Her laughter rang out and she romped like a child, captivating Raoul all over again. It was not uncommon to come across them kissing in corners like a pair of lustful adolescents. Going for a walk one night, unable to sleep, Alienor came across them making love in the moonlit garden. Petronella's legs were clasped around Raoul's waist as they urged each other on with words better suited to a dock-side brothel. It had been a shock to witness: raw, powerful, yet strangely beautiful. Alienor had tiptoed away without being seen, feeling wistful, even sad. Raoul and Petronella's relationship might be volatile and imperfect, but it was real.

They came to Taillebourg, and there she received the homage of the vassals of the Charente. Geoffrey de Rancon knelt at her feet to pledge his oath and swore that he would lead the men of Aquitaine with honor and defend her with his life on the journey to Antioch.

She raised him up and gave him the kiss of peace, inhaling the warm scent of his skin. "Then I shall be protected indeed." To know she and Geoffrey were going to be in close proximity to each other for many months gave her a frisson of pleasure mingled with apprehension.

Having traveled as far as Bordeaux on their

progress to raise funds and recruit for the crusade, Alienor and Louis returned to Poitiers. Geoffrey of Anjou arrived to pay his respects and Alienor felt a gleam of interest when he requested an audience with her. The last time she had seen the Count of Anjou had been at her coronation when she was a bride and little more than a child. The way he had looked at her had filled her with frightened excitement. These days she no longer lacked knowledge or confidence. She had become one of his kind and knew exactly how to deal with him.

On the previous occasion, he had come to pay his homage as a vassal to the young King of France. The daring red fox of Anjou, circling the edges of the court, ready to snatch at any morsels of opportunity that came his way. Now his military doggedness and prowess had rewarded him with the rule of all Normandy, and his power and prestige had risen to a level that could not be nudged aside.

"Do you think he is here to take the Cross?" Petronella asked, eyeing him avidly.

"I doubt it," Alienor said with hard amusement. "His wife is fighting for her right to England and he is part of that fight. He has only just won Normandy and he is far too shrewd a player to abandon his gains."

Petronella's smile dimpled out. "I'm sure he will have a diverting answer."

"I am sure too," Alienor said with a gleam of anticipation. She was keen to match wits with him and see the differences that time had wrought. Summoning her ladies, she began making preparations for the exchange.

"You are setting yourself up to be eaten alive," Petronella warned her.

"On the contrary, I am donning my armor," Alienor replied, watching her ladies cascade rose petals into a large bowl of warm water. "A thousand petals to take the place of a sword. These are a woman's weapons."

Petronella licked her lips. "What will Louis say?"

Alienor tossed her head. "I have gone beyond caring what Louis will say. Let him speak as he chooses. He needs me and he needs my wealth and my vassals for this great enterprise of his."

She perfumed her wrists and throat with the scent of roses and nutmeg. She had her women cover her hair with a veil of transparent silk gauze crowned with a coronet of pearls. Her dress was of cream silk damask, adorned by a gold belt stitched with more pearls. She slipped a ring on each hand: one a hoop of embellished gold, the other set with a large topaz, and that was all. Rather than hide behind her jewels, she wanted Geoffrey of Anjou to see the power and confidence of the woman wearing them.

Her guest was waiting for her in the great

hall, standing before the hearth, and she saw him before he saw her. He was stooping to fondle the ears of Raoul's silky gray gazehound. There was no sign of Louis, but she did not expect him yet. He had gone to pray at the cathedral, and once on his knees, he lost all sense of time. Nor would the announcement of the arrival of the Count of Anjou cause him to make haste, because time for God was more important than time for anything else.

Taking a deep breath, Alienor bade an usher bring the Count before her. The servant gave Geoffrey his message and the latter looked up and across at Alienor. This time, as their eyes met, she was ready for him and her regard was cool and steady. He did not back down, but neither did she, and she saw his glimmer of amused surprise. He still thought he was in control.

"Madam," he said as he reached her and bent his knee.

"My lord Count," she replied. "This is an unexpected pleasure."

"I find they are often the best kind." He raised his head, giving her the full effect of his gaze.

"Well, let us hope so in this instance." She gave him a mischievous look. "I wondered, considering your ties with the Kingdom of Jerusalem, if you had come to pledge yourself to the rescue of Edessa?"

"Madam, it is a vow I have often considered taking," Geoffrey replied smoothly, "but today I am here on other business that requires me to speak with the King."

"All that you say to my husband can be said to me," Alienor responded in a honeyed voice that nevertheless held an underlying sharpness. "Especially in Poitiers, where I am duchess."

"Indeed, madam, but it is a matter that concerns both of you."

"Well then." She extended her arm to him formally. "Come and take some wine and sit with me until the King returns from his devotions."

"Madam, I would be delighted to do so." He gave her one of those looks that had so devastated her when she was a girl. Now she acknowledged it with pleasure, like a cat lapping cream.

She took him outside to the garden and had the servants spread a trestle under the rich blue sky. She sent for her ladies and musicians. The former arrived in a flurry of butterfly color, among them Petronella with her children, and leading by the hand little Marie, now almost eighteen months old and toddling. Her hair was a mass of silky gold ringlets and her eyes were deep blue like her father's. Petronella curtsied to Geoffrey and sent him a flirtatious look. Geoffrey responded in kind, and Petronella giggled behind her hand until she caught Alienor's eye and sobered. Geoffrey's gaze turned to the children and lingered on the toddler.

The musicians arrived, wine was poured, and the pleasantries observed. Alienor lifted Marie onto her lap. Knowing she would be parted from her daughter for at least two years was so difficult that she kept trying to distance herself from the child. At times she succeeded, but then a glance, a giggle, a wave would wring her heart and her love for Marie would overwhelm her again, almost unbearable because of the terrible burden of impending loss. She wanted to give her everything, but at the same time realized how much was being taken away.

"Like her mother she will leave a trail of broken hearts," Geoffrey said gallantly.

Alienor wondered if he had ever flirted with his wife, the indomitable Empress Matilda, like this. By all accounts their marriage was more of a battlefield than their political struggles. "And like her mother, doubtless her own heart will be broken more times than she can count before life is done with her and she learns to guard it," she said. At least she would be too young to remember the parting caused by the crusade. But Alienor would, and the only way not to break her own heart was to put it away and pretend she did not have one.

Geoffrey leaned toward her. "As soon as

my son Henry is of age, I shall make him Duke of Normandy," he said. "And in the fullness of time he will be King of England, do not doubt it."

So now they came to the reason for him being here. Alienor handed Marie to her nurse. "But I do have cause to doubt," she replied. "Louis's sister is wed to King Stephen's heir, so why should Louis or I support your endeavor?"

Geoffrey fixed her with a direct stare. "Because the Pope favors our cause and will block Eustace's succession. Because Normandy is mine, and I am sure you would rather there was peace between France, Normandy, and Anjou while you are absent. If France does not meddle in my affairs, then I shall not meddle in hers except to lend aid to Abbé Suger."

Alienor ran her middle finger slowly around the rim of her goblet. "That will depend on what meddling entails."

"I have a proposition for you."

"How interesting." She raised her eyebrows. "Do you mean for me alone, or is my husband a part of this too?"

"I am sure there are many propositions I could make to you alone," Geoffrey replied with a wicked smile, "but the one I had immediately in mind was of national rather than personal importance. Perhaps where England is concerned, you might want to think about putting your eggs in more than one basket?"

"Meaning?"

"Meaning that Stephen's son Eustace is wed to a French princess, but might it not be useful to wed my son to another one? That way, whichever of them becomes England's King, you cannot lose — although of course I know the crown will go to my boy."

Alienor ceased circling the goblet rim. "You are ambitious, my lord."

"That is no bad thing, especially when one is pragmatic about matters. When your daughter is old enough for marriage, Henry will still be a young man. There is no great age gap between them. Marie will be Queen of England."

Alienor thought him presumptuous, but it was typical of the sort of plan he would hatch. Perhaps it was an idea worth considering too. "You are gambling that your son will win the crown and that I shall not bear Louis sons to inherit Aquitaine."

Geoffrey smiled. "You might say my dice are loaded. Henry is a young man of great ability and I have every confidence in recommending him to you, not just because of what he will inherit in terms of land, but in the potential he has within him."

A flurry at the garden entrance heralded Louis's arrival from his prayers. "I hope I may have your support in this proposal," Geoffrey said in a low voice as he prepared to go make his obeisance.

"I shall consider what you have said," Alienor replied courteously, giving him a gracious and enigmatic smile that told him she was the one in control now. She thought the notion had potential, but she was not going to show her hand so easily.

Alienor went to prayers with Louis that evening in the chapel of Saint Michael and afterward returned with him to his chamber. She glanced briefly at the crucifix on the wall facing Louis's bed and the bloodstained Christ hanging there in suffering. Louis's God was everywhere, and he was not a loving one.

"Have you received the proposal from Geoffrey of Anjou concerning the match between Marie and his eldest son?" she asked.

Louis gave her a narrow, almost suspicious look and sat down, then he indicated that she should remove his boots, as was the duty of an obedient wife. "Who told you about the matter?"

Alienor knelt to perform the task while judging the tone she should take. Louis's moods were so difficult to negotiate. At prayer he was meek and calm, almost vapid, but that could change in an instant. She could sense his hostility. "Count Geoffrey told me," she replied. "It seems a good match in many ways."

Louis glowered. "He had a duty to tell me first — that is my prerogative as head of State and head of the household. I am his liege lord, and I will not have him tattling to women and going behind my back in this dishonorable way."

Alienor removed his second boot. "I thought only of what would be best for our daughter," she said. "I gave him no answer."

He looked away. "But you discussed it without my authority and without my leave."

"It is a queen's duty to be a peacemaker," she said. "And to assist in such business."

"Your first duty is to me," he said tautly. "I will not have you dealing without my say-so. My mother warned me you were not to be trusted and that you would go your own way. She was right."

"And of course your mother is the fount of all wisdom," Alienor retorted. "Did she not have a say in the rule of France when she was wed to your father?"

"Yes, she had a say, and most of it was meddling and false." His face contorted. "I shall not make that mistake with you."

Alienor met his stare. "I am not like her. The Count of Anjou said nothing to me that I would not say to you and I made no commitments, but I think it a good match."

Louis narrowed his eyes. "Do you indeed? Perhaps you are seduced by the Angevin's glamour, but I am not. He went to you first and behind my back, and that does not make him suitable as a father by marriage for our daughter, or to aspire to be closer kin."

"He did not go behind your back."

"He did not tell me he had already aired the proposition to you. I count that as going behind my back. However, I did not refuse him. I told him it was too early to make a decision but if he remained loyal while we were gone, I might consider it on our return. That will keep him within bounds. He has acquired too high an opinion of himself and he needs cutting down to size."

Alienor agreed with him, but she hated the way he treated her as if she too needed cutting down to size. "And when we return and he asks again?"

Louis shrugged. "Even should I wish to consent, I cannot. Abbé Suger informs me that the match is consanguineous. They share common ancestry."

"But closer blood ties have been wed. Our own for example." Alienor raised her brows. "Abbé Suger did not object to that as I recall, yet we are related within the prohibited degree."

"I will hear no more," Louis snapped. "You will not dispute with me. If you better knew your place, we would have sons by now."

"If you better knew yours, I could give them to you. How can I bear children when you do not sow the seed? Perhaps we should indeed seek an annulment."

Louis's color darkened. "That is enough! You take my words and you twist them until they become snakes. Since you ask me to sow seed, I will do so." He began undressing and gestured her to lie down on the bed.

Alienor swallowed, feeling sick. She had not bargained for this. She knew it was just another way of him putting her in her place and a part of his inadequacy that he could only do the deed these days if driven by fervent religious passion or rage. She started to shake her head.

"Do as I say!" He grabbed her arm and shoved her down. At first she fought him, but he bent her arm behind her back and hurt her so much that she gave in.

At least it was swift. Louis had been told by his advisers that the longer a man remained within a woman's body, the more vitality she took from him to heat her own cold humors and that intercourse could seriously weaken a male constitution. Within seconds he was shuddering through his crisis, his voice locking in his throat and releasing in a series of small stutters.

"There," he panted as he withdrew from her. "I have given you the means; now go and pray on your knees and make me a child."

Alienor managed to leave the room with a straight back and her head carried high, but once outside, she doubled over and retched.

When she reached her own chamber, she did fall on her knees and pray. With Louis's seed sticky on her thighs, she asked God to forgive her sins and grant her the blessing of a child, and then, she prostrated herself and vowed on the bones of Saint Radegund that she would win free of this marriage whatever the cost.

26

Hungary, Summer 1147

It began raining again as the cart in front of
Alienor shuddered to a halt, its wheels
bogged down in the soupy mud churned up
by the passage of the endless train of French
soldiers and pilgrims. German crusaders had
preceded them like a swarm of locusts, strip-
ping the ready supplies, alienating the native
populations, and turning the roads into pig
wallows.

Soldiers and pilgrims hastened to lend their
shoulders to the back of the cart while others
threw down logs and hurdles into the mire to
add purchase. As they heaved and pushed,
one man fell; when he staggered to his feet
again he was dripping like a primordial
demon. Another lost his shoe in the slurry
and had to grope with his hands like a beggar
hunting through a bowl of pottage for meat.

Geoffrey de Rancon handed Alienor a
mantle of robust waxed leather and a cowled
hood of the same. "Good Christ, madam,"

he muttered, "we'll not reach the border before sunset at this rate."

Grimacing, Alienor struggled into the garment. It had not properly dried out from the last occasion she had used it, and the smell of beeswax and leather was permeated by that of damp and smoke. By the time they made camp tonight, she would stink like a charcoal burner, but it was preferable to being soaked to the skin and covered in glutinous mud like most of these poor wretches.

After much heaving, cursing, and struggling, the cart eventually sucked out of the ooze and rolled on its tortuous way, but more carts were following, and the same fate awaited them. Alienor had no idea where Louis was, save somewhere ahead, and in truth she did not care, as long as he was out of her sight.

They had been on the road for six weeks, having set off from Saint-Denis at the end of May. On a burning hot day, in the presence of Pope Eugenius, Louis had received the oriflamme banner from the hands of Abbé Suger as part of an elaborate ceremony to bid Godspeed and success to the French army as it embarked on the long march to Jerusalem via the bone-bleached battlefields of Edessa, Antioch, and Tripoli. Alienor had sweltered in the many layers of her formal attire. Adelaide too, and for a moment the women had been in accord as they stood side by side, struggling to cope with the heat.

Louis had retired to dine in the cool of the abbey with His Holiness and various clerics. Everyone else had to wait outside, and Alienor added inconsideration and disparagement to her grievances.

At least she did not have to travel with Louis. The army was divided into sections and she rode either with the noncombatants and the baggage in the center, or else with the men of Aquitaine under the leadership of Geoffrey de Rancon. The latter suited her very well indeed, for among her own she was respected.

Alienor tried not to dwell on the farewells she had made on the steps of Saint-Denis, but still the visions came. The hard hug from Petronella and the tears welling in her sister's eyes had reminded Alienor of their father leaving for Compostela.

"What will I do without you?" Petronella had sobbed.

"Survive," Alienor had replied, her throat swollen with emotion and her eyes full of tears. "Survive, my sister, and care for Marie until I return."

"As if she were my own daughter." Petronella wept.

The children had not been present among the gathering at Saint-Denis. Alienor had kissed Marie farewell earlier in the guesthouse. She had told her daughter she would bring her jewels from Constantinople, silks and frankincense from far lands, and a candle from the Holy Sepulchre in Jerusalem to light her way on God's path. And then she had gone from the room, closed the door on her child, and buried her emotions deep.

Thunder rumbled in the distance and Alienor shuddered. Ten days ago on the road from Passau to Klosterneuburg a cart had been struck by lightning and the driver and horses killed instantly.

"Let us hope the worst holds off until we have crossed the Drava," muttered her constable, Saldebreuil de Sanzay, glancing at the sky from under the rim of his helm. "The last thing we need is a flood."

Alienor agreed with him and sent up a silent prayer. Of late she had developed an active interest in the weather. When it rained, roads swiftly turned into quagmires and traversing rivers became a matter of life and death. Crossing the Rhine and the Danube had been moderately simple due to decent barges on the one and a fine bridge on the other. Alienor thought they should have taken the sea route via Sicily, but Louis had refused because of the enmity between Roger of Sicily and Konrad, Emperor of Germany. Louis had not wanted to risk upsetting the Germans so instead they were following the land route to Constantinople. Thus far they had traveled through Metz, Worms, Wurzburg, Ratisbon, Passau, and Klosterneuburg, heading for the crossing of a tributary of the Danube lying across their path into Bulgaria.

Shortly after noon, they arrived at the site where the Germans had camped a week previously as they prepared to cross the Drava. The ground was muddy and water-logged. The surrounding area had been stripped of resources; the horses had eaten all the immediately available grass and Louis's army had to make do with what they had brought with them. Since half of that was in bogged-down carts stretching back down the road, neither man nor beast was going to eat or be comfortable for some time.

The few ships, barges, and rafts at the bank were insufficient to carry the horses. Two rafts proved large enough to take a couple of carts at each crossing and twenty people, but the going was painfully slow. The horses had to be swum across, and although the bank was shallow upon entering the river, the opposite side was steeper and the state of the bank worsened as each animal churned up the mud when lunging to gain solid ground.

Alienor watched with trepidation as her groom took her dappled gelding. The current was not particularly swift, but the river was muddy and turbid and her mind filled with images of an aquatic monster dragging horse and rider under. She had read stories in bestiaries about such creatures. Crocodiles for certain. Were there crocodiles in Hungary?

The river's milky-brown surface dimpled with raindrops as Alienor accepted Geoffrey de Rancon's hand and boarded the barge to cross to the far bank. Her groom, wearing only shirt and braies, waded into the river with the cob, grasping its mane at the withers, speaking constantly to the horse in reassurance as they went out of their depth and began to swim, the man being towed along by the animal's strength. The gray was placid and strong and they reached the far bank without difficulty, but others were taken by the current and ended up far downstream. Some animals were skittish, refusing the water. One horse panicked in the shallows and kicked the side of the barge. Gisela screamed and Alienor gripped Geoffrey's sleeve to steady herself. Cursing, the horse's rider whipped his mount back to the boggy river's edge before reining around and spurring back into the water in a surge of muddy spray. Geoffrey swiftly turned his back to the deluge, pulling Alienor into his body so that his heavy woolen cloak took the brunt of the drenching.

"Thank you," Alienor said with a swift glance at him.

He briefly tightened his grip before he stepped back and bowed. "I but fulfilled my duty to protect my liege lady."

"Then I am glad you were swift to do so."

Her heart was uplifted and warmed as she turned to her women. "Come," she encouraged, "let us pray and sing. All will be well. God will look after us."

"Then why is He making it rain?" Gisela sniffled. Her fine blond hair showed beneath the end of her wimple in draggled rats' tails.

"That is not for us to question," Alienor replied sharply. "We cannot know His plan." Her only hope was that God's mysterious ways would bring her safely to Antioch and the haven of her uncle Raymond's court.

The army continued its muddy crossing of the Drava. Once disembarked, Alienor made a point of thanking her groom and checking on the gray.

"He's a good horse, madam. No more than one pace in him, but he's game. We both are."

"I know that." She smiled and gave him a coin, which he tucked into the waistband roll of his sodden braies.

The German army had stripped the grazing on this side of the river too, and the only available supplies were for sale at exorbitant prices from the few locals who dared to enter the camp with their wares.

Alienor's servants found a place to pitch her tent on a shelf of ground slightly higher than the river. It was hardly salubrious but at least it afforded shelter. Many of the poorer pilgrims had nothing but a single waxed linen sheet held up with sticks to protect them from the elements. Alienor's tent canvas stank of mustiness, smoke, and mold. The servants covered the floor with a thick layer of straw. That too was damp, but better than standing in mud. Alienor grimaced. This was no way to live — little better than a pigsty. Sleeping under the stars on a balmy summer's evening in your own territory was one thing, but doing so night after night in the pouring rain far from home with scant supplies was a very different prospect.

Supper was stale bread and ammoniac goat's cheese washed down with sour wine on the verge of being vinegar. As dusk fell, Geoffrey de Rancon returned from overseeing the crossing. It was still raining and the heavy edges of his cloak dripped water onto the straw. "Just a few stragglers left," he said. "We lost another cart and will have to redistribute the load. We can use the horses as pack beasts."

"As you see fit," she said.

"Supplies are low, but providing we husband them, we should have enough to reach the border." His gaze was troubled. "I had to hang two men for thieving from the rations cart and selling on the goods. It's constant; they are like rats in a granary."

Alienor said with contempt, "When the sainted Abbot of Clairvaux released all prisoners who vowed to expiate their sins on crusade, did he truly believe they would re-form?"

Geoffrey looked wry. "I think he lived in that hope."

"And left us to deal with the consequences of his idealism. Talking of resources, we must ensure what we have gathered from the wealth of Aquitaine goes to supply the men of Aquitaine."

Geoffrey's hazel eyes were shrewd with understanding. "Madam, it is already being done and shall continue."

"Good. I want the soldiers beholden to me to be in their best condition when we reach Antioch." She gestured to Gisela. "A towel for the sire de Rancon."

Geoffrey took the proffered cloth and rubbed his dripping hair. "I heard a rumor that the King was short of funds."

Alienor widened her eyes in sarcasm. "Surely not with the wise and judicious Thierry de Galeran in control of his money chest? How can that have happened?"

"I am sure de Galeran will have a plausible explanation," Geoffrey said neutrally. "He always does." As he returned the towel to Gisela they again exchanged glances of perfect understanding. Thierry de Galeran was a Templar knight and effectively Louis's chancellor on the journey because he was in charge of the money chests in Louis's entou-rage. Alienor disliked him intensely for the influence he had over Louis and the way he treated her as if she were a serpent in female clothing.

"Well then, Louis must apply to Suger for more funds in his next message home. Let me know how much silver our own contingent has and how many horses, sacks of grain, and the like. You don't have to count every one, a good estimate will suffice."

"Madam, I will go and set it in motion now." He bowed and left the tent.

The rain ceased and a three-quarter moon shone between tatters of cloud. Soldiers clustered around the fires they had built out of whatever firewood they had come across along the way. The wood was damp and belched smoke but eventually caught. Resin hissed and knots in the branches spat out showers of sparks. Alienor wrapped herself in a dry cloak and, sending for her musicians, left her tent to join her household knights at their fire.

The damp had played havoc with the stringed instruments, but the pipes and whistles were still in good tune and the tabors beat out the rhythm as the singing began. *"High are the mountains and the valleys deep in shadow, and the waters swift . . ."*

Alienor folded her cloak around her and leaned toward the flames. Joining her, Geoffrey pressed a cup of wine into her hand.

"It's decent," he said. "I bought it from one

of the merchants hanging around the out-
skirts of the camp."

She smiled at him. "That must have cost
you dear."

"Anything for my queen," he said with a
toast of his cup.

She took a cautious sip and discovered he
was right. It was indeed drinkable . . . and if
she drank enough it might make this journey
bearable for another day, and it would be one
day closer to Antioch.

Geoffrey studied the sky. "Let's hope it
stays clear now," he said. "We need the drier
ground."

Alienor nodded and continued to savor the
wine. "I wonder what an astrologer would
say if he read the sky now. What would he see
for all of us? Are our fates truly dictated by
the position of the stars at our birth?"

"Did your father never have your horoscope
cast?" Geoffrey asked curiously.

"He did." She grimaced. "The portents said
I would make a magnificent marriage, bear
many sons, and live to a ripe old age. The
astrologer also cast a glittering future for my
brother, but it's one he never lived to see."

"But you have made a magnificent marriage
and may yet bear sons."

The glance she sent him was skeptical.
Sometimes things written in the stars did not
happen or happened differently to expectation. She had envisioned a great marriage for

herself, but it had not been to Louis of France. "What does it matter?" she said. "This is but a little life and we will be back with God before we know it." She gave him her cup to refill and their fingers briefly touched.

The music hesitated, then caught again and continued. Alienor looked up and in the firelight saw the Templar knight Thierry de Galeran watching them. She was immediately on edge. During their journey, de Galeran had constantly tried to ingratiate himself with her, but she knew it was about poking his nose into her business rather than having a better working relationship. He was always striving to find out her plans and discover what resources she had. She would not have him meddling in her affairs and pretending friendship.

He bowed to her, his gesture supple and easy, reminding her of the sinuous winding of a snake. Like a snake, too, his eyes were unblinking.

"What brings you to my fire, Messire de Galeran?" she asked.

"Madam, the King has asked me to check around the camp on his behalf and see that all is well. I have also brought some news from him."

For "news" she knew he meant "instructions." "Does the King send his underlings to me to conduct his business? Does he not check the camp for himself?" She eyed him coldly, knowing full well he would return to Louis with the tale that he had found the Queen sitting casually around the campfire sharing songs and wine with her knights.

"Madam, he has retired to his prayers and delegated both matters to me, which I am pleased to do. I have a soldier's eye and the business is fiscal."

Alienor sent a quick glance to Geoffrey. It was exactly as she had thought. "Then the sooner you tell me what it is, the sooner it is dealt with." She sent a servant to fetch de Galeran a cup of wine from the sour barrel, but the Templar declined with a raised hand.

"Thank you, madam, but I need none now. What I do not drink is conserved for another time." He adjusted his cloak, sweeping it back to reveal the hilt of his sword. "Supplies are running low. The King decrees that we must conserve what we have. He is sending to Paris for more silver and bids you command the same of the lords of Aquitaine. He also desires you to send him any spare horses you have in your contingent."

Alienor swallowed her immediate response that she would give him nothing. "I do not see why he needs all these things when we have been traveling the same road. Does he think I have no need of them? Perhaps he should look after his horses and husband his own supplies with more care and then he would not have to come seeking mine."

She could not tell if the barb hit home because Thierry de Galeran never allowed emotion to show on his face. Whatever was cast at him either bounced off or was absorbed without reaction. "What reply shall I take back to him, madam?"

"Tell him to do me the courtesy of asking me personally instead of sending me his eunuch," she said. "In the meantime I shall make an inventory and tell him what I can spare."

"Madam." De Galeran swept her another supple bow and departed the camp. Alienor glanced at Geoffrey, whose own expression was also blank.

"What?" she snapped and felt more than just the warmth from the fire heat her face.

"Madam, it is not my place to say, but perhaps you should be more circumspect with de Galeran. He is a Templar and a bad enemy to make."

"No," she said with hauteur, "it is not your place to say. He tries to infiltrate my camp. He is always talking to the knights — jesting with them on the road, worming answers out of them, and then reporting back to the King. I will not stand for it. Let him stay away from me if he does not wish to be insulted, and let the King do me the courtesy of speaking to me personally if he desires these things." She gave him a hard look. "You had best be swift about that inventory."

De Rancon's eyes were darkly reproachful in the firelight. "You will have it by dawn prayers, madam," he said.

"Good." She turned back to the music and held out her cup for him to refill, which he did with the polished ease of a courtier. Alienor sighed. "Ah, you are right," she said softly, "but you know my thoughts on de Galeran. Louis should not have sent him, but what else did I expect?"

He acknowledged her reply with a wry gesture. "I should go and begin counting," he said, rising.

She caught his wrist. "I know I said swiftly, but please, at least finish your wine at the fire."

Geoffrey hesitated and then sat down. The musicians struck up a new tune, delicate and plangent. He and Alienor listened in silence, and when the last note had faded into the sky, Geoffrey stood up, bowed, and took his leave. Alienor left the fire and retired to bed, aching as if the notes had been plucked on her bare heartstrings.

Morning dawned with misty sunshine, although the terrain was still waterlogged and everything damp and mud-caked. Breaking her fast on hard bread smeared with honey, Alienor knew she would remember the cloying, earthy smell for the rest of her days.

Geoffrey, all practical business this morning, brought her tallies of what they had and what they would need in order to reach Belgrade. "That is assuming that no more horses die and that our remaining carts hold up for the journey," he said grimly.

"So if this is the minimum, should we keep a surplus?"

"We have to balance keeping a surplus against the cost of supplying and moving that surplus, but I would say yes."

She thanked him and placed the tallies in the small coffer where she kept her ready coins. "Then we shall do so. I trust your judgment."

He gave her a troubled half smile. "That is a lot to live up to."

"Indeed, because I give it to the rare few."

He stared at her and swallowed. "I am made of very coarse stuff compared to the lady of my heart."

"I do not believe she would think so," Alienor said softly.

Outside the tent they heard a flurry of hoofbeats and a cry saluting the King's arrival. Alienor drew back and Geoffrey bowed to her and left to attend to his duties.

Through the open tent flaps, Alienor watched Louis dismount from his palfrey with vigorous ill temper. The frown lines between his brows had become habitual since Vitry and just now they were deep grooves.

"Madam, I received your message last night," he said without preamble as he pushed his way into her tent. "You will not speak to Thierry de Galeran in such a way again. It is unworthy of a queen."

"It would please me greatly not to speak to Thierry de Galeran ever again," she retorted. "I will not have your spies in my household. If you desire things from me, at least have the courtesy to come and ask me yourself."

His lips thinned. "It was a routine matter. I am told you were drinking around the camp-fire with the soldiers. That is unseemly behavior for the Queen of France."

"I was speaking with my commanders. There was nothing unseemly about it at all. You sent de Galeran with a message that you wanted to take my horses and my supplies. When we set out, you accused me of being extravagant; you said I had brought too much of everything, but now you are the one without coin or supplies, so what does that say about our respective wisdom in this mat-ter?"

Louis glowered. "Have a care, madam. You are my wife and under my discipline. Unless you want to be confined under house arrest, you will be reasonable."

Loathing him, Alienor wondered how she could ever have found him attractive or even likeable. What she saw now was a querulous man, old before his time, full of righteous anger, his guilt and self-loathing twisting within him, so that all the ills in the world became the sins of the nearest scapegoat. The sympathy she had felt for him had been used up. She had once thought to draw him out of the morass and change him, but he was too deeply embedded, and all he had done was pull her down. "Reasonable," she said. "Oh indeed, sire, you lead by example. You will be pleased to know my lord de Rancon is assembling the horses and supplies you have requested, and I have also authorized more resources from Poitou and Aquitaine." She presented him with a sealed parchment.

Louis took it from her by his fingertips and without a word strode from her tent. She knew he would be unhappy with what she had given him, but hoped she had judged it well enough that it would not be worth his while making trouble. For now she had no choice but to endure, but the closer she came to Antioch, the stronger she felt.

27

Bulgaria, Summer 1147

Alienor turned her head aside as she rode past the rotting body of yet another horse at the roadside. A German one this time — a knight's solid destrier, unable to cope with the burning August heat through which they journeyed toward Constantinople. She gagged at the stench rising from the maggot-riddled flesh and pressed her wimple across her face. Shallow graves of pilgrims and soldiers who had died along the route mounded the roadside. Some of the bodies had been dug up by scavengers and the dismembered remains scattered abroad. At first Alienor had been sickened but now she was mostly inured, except that sometimes the smell, heavy and fetid like the butchers' quarter in Paris at the end of a sweltering summer's day, made her queasy.

Her cob was flagging in the heat, sweat dripping from its belly, leaving a trail of droplets. For the moment there was water available to replenish that loss, but once across the Arm of Saint George and into Anatolia, that resource would become scarce and the horses would be many hundreds of miles farther along the road and less robust than they were now.

Louis's money had arrived from France on swift pack ponies, their speed not slowed by the noncombatant morass of pilgrims that so hampered the main army. The news from France was one of routine and steady government. Abbé Suger and Raoul de Vermandois were holding the country stable and any minor troubles were being easily resolved. Petronella had written a brief note to say that Marie was running around now and wearing proper little dresses instead of baby smocks. *I tell her about you every day,* Petronella had written. *She will not forget her mama.* Alienor had put the letter aside and not read it a second time. Whatever Petronella told Marie, the child's notion of who her mama was would not be Alienor — would never be Alienor.

Other letters had arrived too, from the Empress Irene, consort of Emperor Manuel Komnenos, asking Alienor what she could do to provide comfort for her when she arrived in Constantinople and welcoming her as one royal lady to another. Alienor was looking forward to meeting the Empress of the Greeks, who was of a similar age to herself and of German birth. Her real name was Bertha, but she had changed it to Irene on her marriage to Komnenos. Alienor was also interested in seeing Constantinople. The immense wealth of gold, mosaics, and holy relics contained within the city was the stuff of legend.

Louis was less sanguine because of the many constraints being piled upon them by the Greeks, who controlled the route through Bulgaria and had rigid ideas about what the French and German armies were here to do. Louis was infuriated by the demand that he and his barons must do homage to Emperor Manuel for any former imperial lands they took from the infidel. Why should he give allegiance for such gains when they were won by his hand?

The governor of the town of Sofia, a cousin of Emperor Manuel's, had joined the French army and was helping to supply it along the way, but he had a difficult task. Fights broke out over the exchange rate of five French silver pennies to a single coin of Greek copper. Frequently the Greeks closed up their towns when they saw the French approaching and would only provide food by lowering it over the walls in baskets. There was never enough to go around and as a result, tempers frayed and skirmishes were commonplace. People broke ranks to go on foraging raids. Some returned with heavy sacks over their shoulders and blood on their hands. Others never returned at all.

As the heat of the day increased Alienor began to feel unwell. She had broken her fast on cold grains mixed with raisins and spices and the taste lingered at the back of her throat. Her stomach somersaulted and cramping pain gripped her lower back. She forced herself forward. Another ten strides of her cob and another ten. Just as far as that bush. Just as far as that clump of trees. Just as far as . . . "Stop!" she cried and gestured frantically to her women. They helped her down from her horse and one of her women, Mamile, hastily had the necessary private canvas screen lifted off the packhorse and directed the other ladies to form it around her mistress.

Alienor heaved and retched. Her bowels cramped. Dear God, dear God. What if she had contracted the bloody flux? They still had days to go until they reached Constantinople and decent physicians, rest, and care. She had seen people die along the way, one moment robust, the next expiring in stench and agony.

When it was over, she felt limp and drained and still desperately nauseous.

"Madam, shall I find a cart for you to ride in?"

Alienor shook her head at Mamile. "I will be all right by and by. Do not make a fuss.

Bring my horse."

By the time they made camp, Alienor had been forced to retire behind the screen three more times. She refused food and took to her bed, but the vomiting and purging continued intermittently through the night.

Toward dawn, Alienor fell into a fitful doze only to be woken by shouts and yells outside the tent, some in French, some in a harsh, foreign tongue. Then the clash of weapons and sounds of hard fighting. She struggled out of the bedclothes and grabbed her cloak. Mamile hastened over to her, a lantern shaking in her hand and her eyes wide. "Madam, we are under attack."

"Who . . . ?"

"I don't know . . ." The women stared toward the tent flaps as the noise of battle intensified. Alienor's other ladies clustered around, skittish as horses hearing the howl of wolves.

"Help me to dress," Alienor commanded. She swallowed a heave as the women did her bidding. When they were finished, she picked up the sheathed hunting knife she kept at her bedside. Gisela whimpered. Outside someone screamed and screamed again until the sound abruptly choked and cut off. The sound of battle diminished and the shouts reverted to French.

Alienor approached the tent flaps.

"Madam, no!" Mamile cried, but Alienor

stepped outside, her knife at the ready.

Dawn was flushing the eastern horizon and in the strengthening light the camp resembled a kicked ants' nest. Soldiers were out of their shelters, many still in their undergarments, spears in hands and faces puffy with sleep. Men were throwing jugs of water over a burning tent. Nearby a serjeant wrenched a lance out of a corpse's chest. There was a dead horse and a dead infidel warrior trapped under it, his scarlet turban winding away from his body like a ribbon of blood. Geoffrey was striding about issuing brisk orders.

Seeing Alienor standing at her tent entrance, he hastened over to her, slotting his sword back into his scabbard.

"What's happening?" she asked faintly.

"Nomad Cusman raiders." Geoffrey was breathing hard. "They were trying to steal our horses and supplies. They killed two sentries and torched some of our tents. Three of ours are dead and another has an arrow through his leg, but we gave them the worst of it." He grimaced. "They're the same ones who have been attacking the German lines, so our guides say, in retaliation for pillaging and raids on their herds and livelihoods."

"You are unharmed?" She looked him over quickly.

He gave a short nod. "They didn't get near. We'll have to be ever more vigilant because the raids will only worsen the farther we go.

Once we cross the Arm of Saint George, we'll be subject to far greater hostility than this. I will double the guard, but I do not think they will be back for the moment." His gaze sharpened as he took in the knife in her hand. "It would not have come to that. I would have defended you with my life."

"And then what?" she said. "It is always best to be prepared."

He looked wry. "Are you feeling better?"

"A little," she said. It wasn't true.

He studied her for a long moment. "Rest today if you can," he said, then he bowed and left, shouting orders to strike camp.

Alienor's head was pounding and her mouth was dry. The thought of food made her feel sick and she made do with a few swallows of milk from one of the goats they had brought with them. She was dizzy when she mounted the cob, but the thought of bumping along in one of the carts was unbearable, and she felt more in control on a horse.

Following the Cusman attack, they traveled in anxiety, looking around with wide eyes, but the land shimmered in a late summer heat haze and they saw no one for the twenty miles they covered that day. The local population had moved themselves and their herds away from the depredations of the advancing French. All they encountered were more unburied German corpses, their positions marked by the wild dogs and kites that temporarily abandoned their scavenging as the troops plodded past. No one was keen to go foraging today. Alienor managed to eat some dry bread at noon, but it lay in her stomach like lead and gave her no sustenance. They passed a small town that bartered them a few sacks of flour, crocks of lamb fat, and eggs, again let down from ropes over the walls and only a spit in the ocean of what they needed.

Alienor clung to her saddle and thought of Aquitaine. The soft breezes in the palace garden at Poitiers; the sweeping rush of the ocean at Talmont. The spread wings of a white gyrfalcon. La Reina. Angel wings. *Holy Mary, I am coming to you. Holy Mary, hear me now for the love of God and Christ Jesus your son.*

Mercifully they found a good camping place by a small stream an hour before sunset and her servants pitched her tent. Alienor almost tumbled from the cob's back, feeling weak and wretched. Perhaps she was going to die out here and become another set of bones bleaching under this burning foreign sun.

She lay down in her tent, but the bread she had eaten had only been biding its time, and she had to make another sudden dive for the brass ablution bowl.

"Madam, the sire de Rancon is here," a

squire announced from outside the tent.

"Tell him to wait," she gasped.

When she had finished retching, she ordered Mamile to remove the bowl. The smell remained though and she had to clench her teeth and swallow hard. Outside, she heard Mamile speak to Geoffrey. Moments later, without her permission, he entered the tent followed by an olive-skinned young woman neatly dressed in a plain dark robe and white wimple, a large satchel carried on a strap between her shoulder and hip.

Dear God, he had brought her a nun, Alienor thought as the woman curtsied.

"This is Marchisa," Geoffrey said. "She is skilled in healing women's complaints; she comes highly recommended and she will help you."

Alienor felt too wretched to argue or concern herself with details. She limply waved the young woman to rise. She could have been anything between twenty and thirty with beautiful dark eyes set under well-defined black brows. Although her behavior was demure, the curve of her lips revealed humor and spirit.

"Madam, the lord tells me you are sick." Her voice musical and fluent. She pressed her hand to Alienor's forehead. "Ah, you are burning," she said and turned around to Geoffrey. "The Queen needs to be with her women."

"I will leave you then." He lingered until Marchisa gave him a stronger look. "Make her better," he said and ducked out of the tent flaps.

Marchisa returned her attention to Alienor. "Your blood must be cooled," she said. "Permit me." With delicate fingers she removed Alienor's veil and gold net undercap. She directed the other women to fill a large brass bowl with tepid water. Producing a pouch from her satchel, she sprinkled into it a powder smelling of rose and spices with a clean note of ginger. She gently combed Alienor's hair, knotted it, and pinned it up on her head, and then, dipping a cloth in the scented water, bathed Alienor's hot face and throat.

"So many suffer on the road," she said as she worked. "You eat and drink things you should not; you wear the wrong clothes; you breathe bad humors." She clucked her tongue against the roof of her mouth. "You must take off your gown." She set aside the bowl to unfasten the lacing on Alienor's dress and help her remove it. "Come now, come now."

Alienor obeyed listlessly. It was almost too much effort to raise and lower her limbs. The coolness was a relief but it also accentuated the discomfort in her stomach, which felt worse in contrast. Marchisa continued to wipe her down and helped her through another bout of shuddering sickness. When it was over she made Alienor rinse her mouth with a decoction of licorice and ginger in boiled spring water. She had Alienor's sour bedclothes stripped and her pallet remade with clean linen.

"The sire de Rancon is a good man," Marchisa said. "He is deeply concerned for you."

Alienor made a small sound of acknowledgment. All she wanted to do was sleep. Marchisa helped her into a clean chemise and saw her tucked into the newly made bed. She anointed her temples with a fresh-smelling unguent. "Now," she said. "You will sleep for a while, and then drink a little and sleep again, and then we shall see." Alienor closed her eyes and felt the healer woman's hand at her brow, cool-palmed and soothing. She dreamed again of Aquitaine, of Bordeaux and Belin, of the roar of the ocean at Talmont. Of Poitiers and the deep green forests of the Limousin uplands. She flew above them on outspread wings like a white gyrfalcon, and her feathers were as cold as snow. The bird's hunting cry pierced the frozen blue air, and she woke with a sudden gasp. For a moment she lay blinking, uncertain where she was, for the pure, cold blue had vanished and the air she breathed now was dark and scented with spices. She could see the young woman grinding herbs by the soft glow of an oil lamp. As Alienor strove to sit up, she put down the pestle and mortar and came to her side.

"You have slept well, madam, and the fever is diminished," she said, having felt Alienor's cheek and neck with cool hands. "Will you take a drink now?"

Alienor felt light and dizzy, as if all the marrow had been drawn from her bones, leaving them hollow like a bird's. "I dreamed of flying," she said and took the cup the young woman handed her, once again tasting the ginger and licorice mixture. "Marchisa," she said. "I remember your name."

"That is so, madam." She curtsied.

"And how do you come to be in my tent, other than by the grace of the sire de Rancon? Where did he find you? What is your story?"

"My name is Marchisa de Gençay. I am traveling with my brother to Jerusalem to pray for the souls of our parents."

Marchisa folded her hands in her lap. "As a young man my grandsire went on a pilgrimage and settled on land in the principality of Antioch, where he married my grandmother, a native Christian. She bore him a daughter, and in her turn that daughter married my father, who was on a pilgrimage to Jerusalem. He brought her home to Gençay with him and they lived out their lives there. Now they are both dead and my brother and I are traveling to pray at the tomb of the Holy Sepulchre."

Alienor sipped the ginger and licorice tisane. "And how are you known to my lord de Rancon?"

"My brother Elias is a serjeant in his service; the seigneur de Rancon heard that I had some skill with nursing the sick and he thought I might be able to help you."

"You have no husband then? I thought perhaps you were a nun."

Marchisa looked down. "I am a widow, madam, and content to remain so. My husband died several years ago. We had no children and I returned home to care for my parents until they too died."

Alienor absorbed the tale with sympathy but without pity, because she could tell from the set of Marchisa's jaw that pity was the last thing her pride would accept. She was tired again and she needed to sleep, but a notion was forming in her mind.

By dawn, Alienor was much improved. She drank more of Marchisa's soothing tisane and ate some bread and honey without bringing it back up.

"I am in your debt for Marchisa; thank you for sending her," she said to Geoffrey when he visited while the army made preparations to set out on the road.

"She speaks Greek and Arabic too." His tone was enthusiastic, like an eager suitor presenting his lady love with a courtship gift.

"You look much better."

"I am on the mend," she agreed. "Thank you."

"I am pleased to be of service, madam."

There had been no word from Louis, no concern for her well-being, although he must know how sick she had been, but Geoffrey had been there immediately. She turned to Marchisa, who had been silent throughout the exchange. "I am in your debt," she said. "I would take you into my household."

"I shall be glad to serve you, madam," Marchisa replied with a graceful dip of her head that reminded Alienor of a self-contained small cat. "But first I must fulfill my duty to my parents and pray at the tomb of the Sepulchre."

"Since I will be praying there too, it is settled," Alienor replied. "Go and fetch your things to my tent."

Marchisa curtsied and left. Geoffrey took Alienor's hands and his lips touched her knuckles. They exchanged a wordless glance, and then he bowed and followed Marchisa outside.

For three more nights, as she recovered, Alienor had the eagle dream. It was always a jolt to awaken and find herself in the dark confines of her tent rather than soaring above the world, but each time the dream came, she felt stronger and more sure of herself.

Louis had still not visited to see how she fared, although he sent messages via Geoffrey, who visited Louis's daily councils and reported back to her.

"The King is delighted you are recovering and glad that his daily prayers for your well-being have been successful," Geoffrey said with the neutrality of a polished courtier.

Alienor raised her brows. "How gracious of him. What else?"

He gave her a questioning look. "About you?"

She shook her head. "I doubt there is anything I want to hear on that score from his lips. I meant what news of Constantinople?"

Geoffrey's mouth turned down at the corners. "The King has still heard nothing from the lords he sent as heralds. The Emperor's envoys say all is well and our men are preparing for our arrival, but we have no news of our own. They could be dead for all we know."

"We should consider this carefully." Alienor paced the tent. "If we are to deal with the Greeks successfully, we must be as cunning as they are and know their ways. We must learn from them everything we can."

Geoffrey rubbed his hands over his face. "I dream of Gençay and Taillebourg. The harvest will recently be in and the woods full of mushrooms. My son will have grown again, and Burgundia will have made me a grand-father by now."

"You are not old enough to have grand-children!" she scoffed.

Wry humor deepened the lines at his eye corners. "Sometimes I feel that I surely am," he replied.

She put her hand lightly on his sleeve and he clasped it briefly in his own before releasing her and going to the tent flaps. Outside, one of Louis's senior squires was dismounting from his palfrey. He bowed to Geoffrey, knelt to Alienor, and said, "The King sends word that Everard of Breteuil has returned."

Alienor exchanged looks with Geoffrey. De Breteuil was one of the barons Louis had sent into Constantinople. His return meant news.

Geoffrey called for his horse.

"I shall attend," Alienor said.

He eyed her dubiously. "Are you well enough? If you prefer to remain here, I can report to you later."

Alienor's eyes flashed. "I shall appear in my own capacity and hear matters as they are discussed here and now." She swept her shoulders into the cloak Marchisa was holding up behind her and fastened the clasp with decisive fingers. "Do not seek to put me off."

"Madam, I would not dare." He delayed mounting his horse to help her into the saddle of her gray cob and plucked her eagle banner from the ground in front of her tent to bear as her herald. "It is always an honor."

She firmed her lips. Her anger continued to simmer. She was a match for all of them but had to fight every inch of the way to be recognized and accorded her due, sometimes even with Geoffrey, who was one of the best.

The army had spread out over a mile: an assemblage of ragged tents, flimsy shelters, horse pickets, and cooking fires. In the pilgrim camp, women stirred grains and vegetables in cooking pots or ate meager portions of flat bread and goat's cheese. One sat suckling a newborn baby, conceived when its parents had had a roof over their heads and the security of mundane daily labor. If it survived the journey, which was unlikely, it would be forever a blessed child, born on the road to the Sepulchre. Some women were showing pregnancies that had been conceived along the road. Many pilgrims had sworn oaths of celibacy but had given in to temptation, while others had preferred to remain unsworn and sow their wild oats in the face of death. Alienor was glad Louis had taken such a vow, for she could not bear the thought of lying with him.

Riding into Louis's camp, she saw the looks of consternation from his knights and felt a glimmer of satisfaction. The falcon of her dream was flying over her and she felt strong and lucid.

Louis was stamping about the tent, hands

clasped behind his back, jaw tight with irritation. His commanders and advisers stood in a huddle, their expressions grim. At their center stood the newly returned baron Everard de Breteuil, a cup in his hand. An angry graze branded his left temple and gray hollows shadowed his cheekbones. Louis's chaplain Odo of Deuil sat at a lectern, writing furiously between the lines pricked out on a sheet of parchment.

Louis looked up at Geoffrey's arrival. "You took your time," he grumbled. His gaze fell on Alienor and his nostrils flared as he drew a sharp breath.

"I have come to hear your news, sire, since it must surely affect us all," Alienor said, preempting him. "It will save you coming to tell me yourself." She went to sit on a low curved chair in front of the screen that concealed Louis's bed, making it clear she was here to stay. "What has happened?"

Louis's brother Robert de Dreux answered. "We were meant to rendezvous with the Germans tomorrow, but they have already embarked across the Arm of Saint George."

"That wasn't the plan; we were supposed to join them first," Louis said.

"Komnenos would not allow the Germans to enter the city," de Breteuil explained. "They were confined to his summer palace outside the walls and food was brought out and sold to them. Komnenos refused to go to the German camp and Emperor Konrad would not enter Constantinople without his army. Each fears treachery by the other."

Odo of Deuil muttered something over his lectern about what could you expect from Germans and Greeks.

De Breteuil took a swallow of wine. "The Germans were ordered to cross the Arm and so were we. When we declined, our food supplies were cut off and we were harassed and set upon by infidel tribesmen — while the Greeks stood by and did nothing. At one point I thought we were all going to die." He touched his grazed temple. "When we sent a deputation to the Emperor, he claimed to have no knowledge of this and said he would set it right, but he was lying. He must have given the order to stop our food, and he did nothing to prevent the infidels from attacking us. He has made it clear we are as a plague of locusts to him, yet he wants us to do all the fighting and dying while his troops look on and pick their nails." De Breteuil's mouth twisted. "We are being used, sire, and by men who are no better than infidels themselves. The Emperor has made a twelve-year truce with these tribes who attacked us. What kind of Christian ruler does that?"

"But whether we like it or not, we need the Greeks to see us safe across to the other side with plentiful supplies and equipment," Alienor spoke up. "We must continue to speak the language of diplomacy."

Louis gave her a cold look. "You mean the language of deceit and treachery, madam?"

"I mean that which they regard as civilized. They treat us as they do because they see us as barbarians, with neither subtlety nor finesse. I do not say this is the truth of the matter, I say that this is how they perceive us, and if we are going to make any headway at their gates, it will not be by banging our shields upon them."

Louis drew himself up. "I am the sword of God," he said. "I shall not veer from my path."

Odo of Deuil nodded in the background and scribbled down Louis's words.

"No one is asking you to," Alienor said with weary impatience.

"Water wears away stone, no matter how solid. And it pours through the smallest crevices. We must be as water now."

"And you would know?" Louis said with contempt.

"Yes," she said. "I would." She rose and went to the tent entrance. It was fully dark now and the campfires glimmered at intervals like giant fireflies caught on a spider's web. She looked at Louis over her shoulder. "We need to rest, and we need to garner supplies. You might forgo those things because you distrust the Emperor of the Greeks, but if you were to conciliate with him, think of what you might gain that Konrad of Germany has not."

"And what would that be? Why should I wish to clasp the hand of a man who agrees to truces with infidels and sets them on my men?" Louis asked with a curl of his top lip.

"You travel this road not just as a warrior, but as a pilgrim," Alienor said. "Think of all the churches and shrines in Constantinople that Konrad has not seen. Think of the precious relics: the crown of thorns that pierced Our Lord's brow; a nail of the crucifixion stained with His precious blood. The stone that was rolled away from His tomb. If you are desirous of seeing and touching these things, it behooves you to deal with their guardian, whatever your opinion of him." She waved her arm, and her full sleeve wafted a scent of incense. "Of course, if you do not care for such things and to have such advantage, then go on your way with your sword in your hand."

A muscle flexed in Louis's cheek but he remained silent.

"The Queen makes a good point," said Robert de Dreux. "We shall have greater prestige than the Germans. You can have words with the Emperor about the treatment of our men and make a diplomatic triumph out of this that will add to the glory of France."

Alienor deemed it prudent to leave then.

Geoffrey would remain as her eyes and ears. She knew Louis would acquiesce, but not in her presence, because he would never agree openly with her point of view. He was a fool who could barely find his hindquarters with his hands.

28

Constantinople, September 1147

The great citadel of Constantinople occupied a triangle of land bordered on two sides by the sea and enclosed within great walls. On the eastern side of the city, and within another enclosure, its right flank was guarded by a stretch of water known as the Arm of Saint George. A massive chain protected the end of that stretch, preventing ships from sailing up the wide estuary and attacking the city.

On a hot morning in September, the French army arrived before its walls and set up camp. Alienor exchanged the gray cob that had borne her all the way from Paris and mounted instead the spirited golden chestnut palfrey sent to her by Empress Irene. His coat had a metallic gleam and his gait was like the smoothest silk, hence his name: Serikos, which was Greek for the cloth. Louis too had been presented with a horse: a stallion with a coat that glittered like sunlit snow. Both mounts were glossy and well nourished, unlike the crusader horses, which had lost condition during their hard journey and were unsuited to the parching heat of the Middle East.

Alienor rode beside Louis, her head up, her spine straight. She wore a gown of coral-red samite stitched with pearls. The coronet set over her silk veil was a delicate thing of gold flowers studded with sapphires. Louis was more somberly clad in a tunic of dark blue wool, but he wore a jeweled belt, rings on his fingers, and a coronet. After a single glance, Alienor did not look at him again, because she could not bear to see the gaunt, tight-lipped man riding in the place of the smiling youth who had once taken her hand and looked at her with his heart in his eyes.

They were greeted by nobles of the Greek court, their colorful silk tunics worn with the casual ease of everyday garb. In France only magnates could afford such fabric and even then it was a rarity. Despite their own efforts to appear magnificent, Alienor knew they must look like creased and shabby barbarians to the Greeks and reinforce their jaundiced view of Christians from the north.

They were escorted to the imperial Blachernae Palace, parts of which were still under construction. Cages of scaffolding enclosed sections of wall and laborers toiled, hoisting hewn blocks of stone and buckets of mortar onto the working platforms. The clink of chisel on stone, the creak of the winch wheel, and the shouts of the laborers caused a permanent clamor. However, the main palace was complete and faced with decorated arches worked in marble and patterned with different-colored bands of stone.

Servants came running to take their mounts and escort Louis and Alienor to the portico of the palace where Emperor Manuel Komnenos waited to greet them, together with his consort, the Empress Irene. Manuel was of Louis's age and stature, but there the similarities ended. Manuel resembled a fabulous mosaic, his robes of royal purple so heavily encrusted with gems that they were as stiff as a mail shirt, and when he moved, he glittered. He was dark-haired and dark-eyed and bore himself as if he were a deity condescending to supplicants. Beside him, Louis looked insipid: a lesser being caught blinking in the Godlight.

The sovereigns embraced each other and exchanged the kiss of peace. Alienor too was greeted by the Emperor with stiff formality. She curtsied deeply to him, and he raised her to her feet and brushed her cheek with his lips. She inhaled the scent of incense and sandalwood. His eyes were inscrutable and cold, the irises so dark that they blended with the pupils.

Alienor then curtsied to Empress Irene. She

was slender and tall, matching Alienor in height, but her eyes were dark hazel and her complexion olive. She was a little older than Alienor too, but still with young, smooth skin. She wore a dalmatic of royal purple silk, edged with gold braid and strings of pearls hung from her crown creating a curtain of milky raindrops over her coiled hair. Unlike many of the ladies of the court, she did not paint her face, save for subtle smudged lines to enhance her eyes.

"Be welcome," she said in Latin. "I have heard so much about the Queen of France."

"As I have heard much about the Empress of the Greeks," Alienor responded gracefully.

The women assessed each other with formal courtesy masking curiosity and caution.

"You have traveled far and still have a great distance to go," Irene said. "Come within and take refreshment. All we have to offer in the Blachernae Palace is yours for the time you are here."

Entering the palace, Alienor felt as if she had stepped into a gilded treasure chest. The walls were painted with life-size figures decorated with gold leaf and vibrant primary colors. Crushed lapis, kermes red, ochre. Surfaces of marble, crystal, and gold created a layered and watered effect so that reality shimmered. The polished, inlaid floor reflected Alienor's footsteps and she felt as if she were walking on illuminated water.

Eventually, they came to a great council chamber lined with arches. Two chairs were set upon a marble dais, one for Manuel, one for Louis. Everyone else was expected to remain standing, Alienor and Irene included.

An interpreter with a curled and oiled beard stood ready between the King and Emperor, for although Louis spoke Latin, Manuel did not. The conversation between the sovereigns was as elaborate as the surrounding architecture and decoration, for while Louis's responses were terse, the interpreter embellished his words with the flowery speech and mannerisms of the Greek court. Listening to Louis's replies, Alienor understood that opening pleasantries were being exchanged. In the Greek way, there would be no serious discussion today, tomorrow, or even the day after.

Preliminaries concluded, she and Louis were escorted to dine with the Emperor and his court in another chamber, once more reached through painted corridors with shining marble floors. The dining tables were marble too, pink and cream, ornately carved and draped with white napery. Fragrances of rose water, cinnamon, and nutmeg permeated the sumptuous dishes, served on plates of ceramic and silver gilt. There was tender lamb with apricot sauce, crisp golden game birds stuffed with wild rice, and platters of glittering silver fish from the rich waters of

371

the Golden Horn.

The Greeks ate their food with a two-pronged implement that speared the pieces of lamb or apricot and held them securely to be dipped in piquant sauces, or in olive oil, pale green as liquid glass. Seeing Alienor's interest, Irene presented Alienor with her own as a gift. "You will soon wonder how you ever managed without one of these," she said.

Alienor thanked her and admired the ivory handle inlaid with small squares of iridescent mosaic.

"You must see the great sights of our city while you are here," Irene added. "I will show you myself, and we can become better acquainted."

"I should like that; you are most gracious," Alienor replied, smiling.

Irene returned the smile, although the curve of her lips was not echoed by her eyes, which were deep and watchful. "Your husband: he has the reputation amongst us already for being a pious man. We hear from our merchants that he spends much of his time in prayer."

"That is so." Alienor lifted her cup, thinking that "merchants" was a euphemism for "spies." "My husband was trained for the priesthood as a child before he became the heir to the throne."

"He will find much to inspire him in our city. We have churches, shrines, and relics of value beyond price that the emperors have guarded and protected from enemies for a thousand years. Long may they continue to do so."

Alienor did not miss the warning and challenge in Irene's seemingly bland words. Louis was welcome to look, but not to touch, and the French were not so much allies as an expedient way of distracting Constantinople's enemies. "I believe we have a great deal to learn from each other," Alienor said.

"Indeed," Irene replied smoothly, lifting her own cup. "Just so."

Alienor settled into life in Constantinople. The opulence was seductive. She, Louis, and their retinues were housed in a hunting lodge that made Talmont look like a peasant's hovel by comparison. On the first night, Alienor bathed away the aches of the long journey in hot water scented with rose petals. Attendants rubbed her body with exotic oils and massaged out the knots and pains of traveling until she felt light-headed and languorous. The Emperor provided them with servants in addition to their own to wait upon their every need.

"Spies," Louis said, his nostrils flaring as he pushed aside a platter of small almond cakes decorated with colored sugar. "They set spies on us, and we cannot do the same to them."

Alienor shrugged. "What are they going to

find out?"

"Nothing, because we will tell them nothing." He caught her wrist as she walked past him and pulled her to face him. "I do not want you talking to the Empress and giving things away, do you hear? I know what gossips women are."

"I am not a fool," she retorted. "The Empress and I understand each other well." She wrenched herself free, rubbing the place where his fingers had dug in. "You should be encouraging me to talk to her and probe for information, but you do not want me to have that kind of power, do you?"

"This is men's business. You will not meddle."

She set her jaw.

"I am warning you." He wagged his forefinger in front of her face. "I will not brook plotting of any kind."

"It does not occur to you that I might be trying to help you?"

"No," he said. "It doesn't." He stamped from the room and across the corridor to his own chamber. Thierry de Galeran was standing on guard outside it, and he gave Alienor a knowing smirk. She rubbed her wrist where Louis had seized her, and her irritation at his stupidity churned into anger. The Greeks would swiftly know from their spies that the King and Queen of the Franks were not in accord. What point was there in ordering her to be careful when his own actions left the door wide open to all?

The opulence and luxury of Constantinople continued to take Alienor's breath away. At sunrise and sunset the city shone, every surface lustrous with gilt and bronze and gold. Irene took her to the roof of the Blachernae Palace and, on a glorious day of white sunshine and soft breezes, pointed out to Alienor the hippodrome, the forums of Emperor Constantine and Theodosius, the cathedral of Saint Sophia. Across the river the quarters of the Genoese traders at Galata shone like a separate golden casket. Irene spoke rapidly and she indicated everything with swift movements, as if determined to fulfill her duties as hostess by leaving nothing out.

Constantinople in the flesh was exhausting. Whisked all over the city by their hosts and shown one astonishing site after another, Alienor found them becoming an amorphous blur of crystal, marble, and gold. It was almost like being drugged, or smothered, and for all its beauty the city was intensely claustrophobic. Louis spent hours worshipping at jeweled shrines beside which the church of Saint-Denis paled into insignificance.

The French army was forced to remain outside the defensive walls under canvas and only permitted through the gates in strictly controlled small numbers. The Emperor was not about to let a mob loose in his city. The soldiers' experience of Constantinople was different to that of their liege lord and lady for they saw the parts that Louis and Alienor did not, yet it was just as edifying. The troops experienced the stinking, fetid underworld of the poor, riddled with disease and thievery. In the dark, narrow streets in the bowels of the greatest city in Christendom, where even full daylight was dim at ground level, the denizens lived a squalid, subterranean life. Pilgrims and soldiers reported back to their fellows that the city resembled an enormous golden stone turned over to reveal the mud and wriggling creatures underneath, and, by comparison, even the dankest, most unpleasant parts of Paris were places of high illumination.

A fortnight passed and Louis continued to wait for the arrival of the part of his army that had traveled by a different route. The feast of Saint Denis fell on the eve of that arrival and the Emperor sent Louis a select group of clergy to sing the service in celebration of the saint. Each monk was furnished with a tall taper elaborately decorated with gold leaf and vivid colors. There were eunuchs among the Greeks, castrated before their voices had broken. Their bodies were soft and plump and they sang in sweet high tones that blended with the deeper resonance of the other men, and the wonderful sounds brought Louis to tears.

Alienor wondered at the purpose of this musical gift, because she knew the Greeks were too wily to give anything purely for itself, even if they too celebrated the feast of Saint Denis in their calendar. Nevertheless, the service was beautiful and she thanked Irene graciously.

The Empress smiled and arranged the drape of her dalmatic on her sleeve so that the gold edge fell in a precisely straight line. They were seated in one of Irene's many chambers at the Blachernae Palace with glorious views of the Golden Horn through the open windows. Servants had come on quiet feet to pour sweet wine and serve delicate rosewater pastries. "The Emperor and I have done our best to make you welcome in our land, and we felt that it was a fitting culmination."

Alienor picked up on the last word. She reached to the delicate glass cup on the mosaic-inlaid table. "Culmination?"

Irene waved a smooth, manicured hand. "Naturally once your contingent from Italy has arrived, you will want to continue your journey."

"Indeed," Alienor said. "But our companions will need to rest before we set out."

Irene inclined her head. "We are happy to

welcome them while we make ready boats and supplies. However, your kin in Antioch must be anxiously awaiting your arrival." She affected a concerned expression.

So the Emperor wanted them gone, Alienor thought, and the celebratory service for Saint Denis was a punctuation mark on their stay. "My uncle will be glad to receive us," she replied, "but he understands the dangers of our journey and he would want us to set out well prepared and in strength."

"Indeed, but you should leave before the winter sets in." Irene leaned toward her as if speaking in confidence. "My husband hears reports that the German army has defeated all resistance it has met thus far. There has been a battle and thousands of Turks have been killed. Your way will be clear if you follow now."

Alienor was surprised. "That is news I have not heard."

Irene looked smug. "Indeed not. The messenger has not long returned with the tidings. The Emperor will send word to your husband this very day."

"Even so, we should wait for our contingent from Apulia and then travel together. That has always been the understanding."

Irene dipped her head. "Naturally you must do as you see fit, but the Emperor intends to set up a market for you on the other side of the Arm of Saint George so that you may prepare from there."

Alienor thanked her hostess, and the conversation turned to other matters, but the moment she could politely leave, Alienor made her excuses and hastened to find Louis.

He was in his quarters with his senior barons and churchmen. His preoccupation was telling in that he neither glared at her as she entered the room, nor sought to put her in her place. Geoffrey and Saldebreuil de Sanzay were there too, and the former exchanged a swift glance with her.

"The Empress has just told me about the German victory," she said.

Louis's cheeks were flushed and his eyes bright. "Fourteen thousand Turkish dead," he said.

"That is a large host. Do you think it is true?"

Robert de Dreux shrugged. "Who knows? Numbers are always difficult to interpret and the Greeks cannot be trusted. If true, it means the way is clear to advance and that the Germans have made great progress."

"The Emperor says the Germans have agreed to do him homage for every place they capture along the route," Louis said. "He demands it of us also in exchange for guaranteed supplies along the way. But I say it is his Christian duty to supply us as a given, not as a matter of coercion and barter."

There were mutters of approbation. Alienor

went to sit in an unoccupied chair and rested her hands along the gilded arms. "He wants us to leave before the Apulia contingent arrives. The Empress Irene said as much to me just now. Perhaps he is exaggerating German successes."

"He fears that once our reinforcements arrive, we will prove too mighty for him," said the Bishop of Langres. "If we unite with the Germans and the Sicilians, we could seize Constantinople and use its wealth to fund our objectives."

Louis cupped his chin and gazed narrow-eyed at the Bishop.

"Indeed." Langres warmed to his theme. "If we put our minds to the deed, it would be easy to take the city. There are places where the walls are crumbling and would not withstand an assault. The people are inert — like gaudy slugs — and would easily be overcome. They have no stomach for war. They employ others to do their fighting and prey on those they think they can dominate — whether by threat of arms, or by treachery and subterfuge. All we need do is cut off the water supply to their conduits."

Alienor felt a frisson of alarm. If Louis turned their army on Constantinople, it would divert them from their original purpose and they might never reach Antioch.

"The Emperor is no friend to us," the Bishop continued in a belligerent tone. "This city is Christian in name, not in fact. Her emperor prevents others from bringing aid to the oppressed, and he is himself the oppressor. Did he not intimidate Antioch recently and demand the homage of Count Raymond? Does he not make pacts with infidels? Does he not expel Catholic bishops from cities under his sway and replace them with his own priests? Far from uniting Christian forces, he divides them." He jabbed his crozier toward Louis. "Ought you to spare the man under whose rule the Cross and the Sepulchre of Christ are not safe?"

They were emotive words and had some validity. Alienor could see men nodding.

"But we did not come here with the intention of seizing Constantinople," Louis said. "What does it say of our own Christianity if we attack the wealthiest city in Christendom and then enrich ourselves? In so doing, we must kill and be killed. Will plundering this place expiate our sins?" He gazed around the gathering with disapproval. "Do you truly believe this? The Emperor should not have attacked Antioch, but that hardly makes him the Antichrist." Louis opened his hand toward the red-faced Bishop. "Is it as important to die for the sake of gaining money as it is to maintain our vows on this journey? Our priority is to protect Jerusalem, not destroy Constantinople. How would we control it without weakening ourselves for the remainder of our journey?"

"If the Germans have had such great success in Anatolia, we should follow swiftly," said Robert de Dreux. "Otherwise they will gain all the glory and carve up the territory between themselves and Manuel Komnenos. I say we cross now."

"You are making a mistake," the Bishop countered. "The Greeks will betray us at every turn. You may wrap a turd in gold, but it remains a turd nevertheless."

"Enough, my lord bishop," Louis said tersely. "I take your point and I shall consider it, but for now we do nothing to upset the balance."

The meeting broke up with the Bishop stalking from the room, shaking his head and muttering that Louis would regret his decision not to take Constantinople by force. The barons fractured into groups to discuss the matter among themselves. Alienor retired to her own quarters, but summoned Geoffrey and Saldebreuil.

"The King made a good speech," Geoffrey said. "No matter what the Greeks do to us, it would shame us as Christians to turn on Constantinople."

"But you are a man of honor and chivalry, my lord, not a covetous bishop with a bellyful of bile." She gave him a taut smile. "And you are a man of Aquitaine, and therefore see the situation more clearly than most. I agree that the King lived up to his role just now, but Antioch and my uncle matter nothing to him. It is his conscience before God that drives him. That it is doing so in our direction is to our advantage, but we cannot take it for granted. Louis is fully capable of digging in his heels, but he can also be swayed, especially by the Church."

"The Bishop was right about not trusting the Greeks though," Saldebreuil said with a shake of his dark ringlets. "They are plotting something. I fear to turn my back lest I feel the prick of a dagger between my shoulder blades."

"Who is not plotting?" Alienor asked with a sour laugh. "We are all seeking gain of one sort or another. They want rid of us before we grow too powerful and turn on them. Can you fault them for that?"

Saldebreuil shook his head. "No, madam, but I dislike the way they go about it by such underhand ways and means."

"Indeed, we should be vigilant," she said. "But that does not include making war on them. Our duty is to bring an army to my uncle so he can deal with his enemies. We must bolster the King in this effort and keep his resolve strong. That is my direction to you. The goal is Antioch."

"How long before it's our turn to cross the Arm of Saint George?" Gisela asked. The young woman was playing with a pretty gray and silver kitten, dangling a length of red ribbon for it to chase and pounce upon.

"Soon," Alienor said. They were waiting in the Blachernae for the call to go to their ships. Most of their baggage was packed and ready, and only the small fripperies remained, such as games and sewing to while away the time. Muttering to herself, Marchisa was busy checking her pouches of remedies and nostrums. She had stocked up on syrup of white poppy this morning, and Alienor was still feeling the hole in her purse, but better to have it than not in the months to come.

"How soon is soon?" Gisela danced the silk strip just out of reach of the kitten's paws. "A few hours, a few days — a few weeks?"

Alienor swallowed her irritation at Gisela's whining tone. They were all on edge and she had to make allowances. "Hours, I should think, certainly no more than a day." She went to look out of the window. The river bustled with ships traveling up and down the Golden Horn. The sky was overcast this October morning and the waters of the inlet choppy and gray. If it weren't for the lateen rigging on the ships, it could almost have been the Seine.

Louis had begun ferrying their army across to the markets on the other side of the Arm of Saint George. This was partly because the Emperor had cut supplies to the existing camp to a dribble, so he had no choice, and partly because the French soldiers were itching to be on their way before the Germans claimed all the land and the glory. Emperor Manuel had been most accommodating with ships for the crossing and the embarkation was going forward at speed.

Gisela sighed. "In Paris the trees will be shedding their leaves," she said, "and they will be harvesting the apples. I wish I could drink a cup of new cider this instant."

"You risk being accused of being a barbarian," Alienor teased. "Why is Greek wine not to your palate?"

"Because it goes down so smoothly and only kicks you later," Gisela said.

Alienor had to nod at her sagacity.

The kitten tired of its game and went to curl up on a cushion of plump red silk. The last group of soldiers embarked and set off down the Golden Horn toward the lower chain across the mouth of the inlet, leaving their campsite no more than an area of bare ground, pocked with black scorch marks where the cooking fires had been.

Alienor expected an imminent summons to the quay, but the sun moved another hour on the dial without any word. Growing impatient, she sent Saldebreuil to find out what was happening. He returned looking grim. "Madam, the Greeks are delaying again. They say they are waiting for ships to return from the other bank and that there have been difficulties with the money changers at the new market, but I can glean no more than that. They either do not know, or will not say."

Food arrived: vine leaves stuffed with a spicy meat mixture and flagons of dark, Greek wine. The eunuchs pretended not to speak French or Latin, and to every question the women asked, they merely shook their heads and gave them bovine looks from kohl-rimmed eyes.

Sunset turned the waters of the Golden Horn the color of blood and as darkness cloaked the room and the servants lit the scented lamps, Alienor gave up waiting and retired for the night.

By dawn there was still no summons. Looking out of the windows on a world lit by pale sunlight, Alienor noticed fewer vessels traveling on the waterway and none going in yesterday's direction. Her sense of unease increased.

Geoffrey de Rancon arrived and was ushered into her presence. He knelt at her feet. "Madam, there is news," he said. "The contingent from Apulia will be here by noon."

"Well, that is all to the good." She gestured Geoffrey to rise. "When do we embark? Have you heard from the main camp?"

"Yes, madam, a moment ago." His eyes were troubled. "The Emperor is withholding his ships — keeping them all on the city side and refusing to trade supplies with us. We had to cross over to you in a fishing vessel."

"What?" Alienor looked at him in angry alarm.

Geoffrey grimaced. "There was rioting yesterday at the money changers' camp. Some of Count Thierry's Flemings ransacked the Greek tables and caused mayhem. The King and the Count have punished those responsible and made reparation and the Emperor says he will restore the market once he is sure there is decent order, but he desires securities."

"Such as?" Alienor's unease deepened.

Geoffrey drew a deep breath. "He demands the homage of the King and his senior barons and the promise that any towns we take will be handed over to him."

Alienor waved her hand impatiently. "That was discussed earlier. We knew it was likely. It is not worth fighting over, because once we are clear, we can do as we please."

"If that were all, madam, it would be simple," Geoffrey said. His gaze flicked to Gisela. "He also wants to seal the bargain with a marriage alliance between one of his nephews and a lady of the French royal house."

Gisela's eyes widened with shock. "I came as an attendant to the Queen, not as a piece of merchandise to be bartered for goodwill."

"What does the King say?" Alienor asked.

"He is considering the Emperor's requests, madam," Geoffrey replied neutrally. "He thinks it might be a reasonable price to pay."

"No!" Gisela cried. "I won't do it! I would rather die!"

Alienor's irritation stirred. What choice had she had when Louis entered Bordeaux in the summer of her thirteenth year? What would she have given to be able to refuse him? What would she have given for a rescue? "Be quiet," she snapped. "Weeping and railing will not help matters. Use your head, you foolish girl."

Gisela swallowed and sent Alienor a beseeching, terrified look.

"There are fates far worse, believe me," Alienor said grimly. "You would live a life of luxury here. You would dress in perfume and silks and want for nothing."

"Madam, I would lose my soul." Gisela wept. "Please do not let this happen to me. I would die."

"You only think you would. I tell you this because it happened to me ten years ago, but I live still." Alienor turned to Geoffrey. "That was why the Emperor wanted everyone across yesterday. If he withholds his ships, he can ransom us for whatever price he wants — or so he thinks." Her lips hardened. "He may have withdrawn his ships, but the Genoan traders still have theirs, and there are always those who can be bribed to take us across. Louis may do as he wishes in the matter of

homage, but I will not stay here to be used."
She placed her hand on Geoffrey's sleeve.
"Find a way for us to leave, and swiftly."

He put his own hand over hers in reassurance — a steadying gesture to others
but conveying much more to Alienor. "Trust
me, madam." He squeezed her fingers,
bowed, and left the room.

"I should have known," she said. "I cannot
fault the Emperor's politics, but we should
have been more wary." She looked at the
trembling Gisela. "Do not worry. I have more
compassion than to leave you to the fate
Louis would seal for you."

Gisela swallowed. "When you said I would
live a life of luxury here, I thought —"

"I know what you thought," Alienor said.
"Indeed there are some advantages to being
a bride here, but I would not leave you behind."

Gisela knelt at Alienor's feet. "Thank you,
madam, thank you!"

"Oh, get up," Alienor snapped. "The
women who serve me are not milksops. Make
yourself useful. Our baggage is prepared, but
we may have to travel light. Take the things
you truly need and tie them in a bundle, and
have your cloak ready. Who knows how
quickly we may have to move."

Geoffrey returned at noon with six serjeants
dressed as servants, tunics covering their

mail. "I have hired a ship from the Geno-
ans," he said. "We should make haste. They
have not tried to stop us by force, but they
may change their minds. The sooner everyone is on the far bank, the better."

"We are ready." Alienor fastened her cloak
and, beckoning her women, followed Geoffrey
to the door.

At the foot of the stairs, one of the Emper-
or's eunuchs barred their way, but Geoffrey
showed him a foot of drawn sword and after
a moment the man lowered his gaze and
stood aside. The guards on duty at the gate
were reluctant to let them pass and pretended
not to understand at first even under the
threat of Geoffrey's blade. Alienor turned to
Marchisa. "Tell them that I am going to the
new camp to talk to the King about the marriage arrangements for his kinswoman and I
will make it worth their while if they let me
pass."

Marchisa spoke to the men in Greek with
much supplication and elaborate hand gestures, augmented by a bribe in the form of a
casket of gold rings that had originally been a
gift to Alienor from the Empress Irene.

The jewelry changed ownership in a metallic flash and the guards opened a postern
door to let them through. Beyond, waiting on
the riverbank, two shallow fishing boats rode
at their moorings, waiting to cast off.

Alienor's heart drummed against her rib

cage as Geoffrey took her hand and helped her into the first one. His firm grip steadied her, and she sent him a grateful look.

The soldiers took up the oars and rowed out from the bank to a waiting Genoese galley laden with men from the contingent of Louis's army that had traveled via Apulia. Aboard the ship was Louis's brother, Robert de Dreux, who had been talking with its commanders.

"Thank God, madam," he said, as Alienor stepped aboard. He turned to embrace Gisela. "You are safe now, cousin."

Gisela gave a small gasp and leaned into him, trembling. "I prayed you would not throw me to the wolves."

"I won't let them have you," Robert growled. "I would rather swear fealty to a dog than Manuel Komnenos. Let my brother do as he sees fit, but they shall not have my oath, and they shall not have you."

Alienor gave him a sharp look. "Louis still intends swearing fealty?"

Robert shrugged as the Genoese ship made its way down the Golden Horn. "He must if he wants to obtain the supplies and guides the Greeks have promised, but if it is like all their other promises, I doubt we'll see much in exchange. I have told him I refuse to take it, and as to a marriage between Gisela and the Emperor's nephew — let Louis agree if he wishes, but he cannot hand over what he does not possess."

Alienor raised her brows at him. "You would abduct Gisela?"

Robert shrugged. "I would rather call it taking her under my wing."

"Do what you must," Alienor said with a brisk nod. "I applaud you for it, although you risk your brother's anger."

"I do not fear him," Robert said with a steely gleam in his eyes.

Robert disembarked his charges at the French camp on the far side of the Arm and made swift preparations to ride on to the outpost scout camp at Nicomedia, two days' journey away. "Madam, I am in haste, or I would offer to bring you too," he said as he swung into the saddle.

Alienor smiled and shook her head. "I can fight my own battles. Godspeed you now, and bless you too." She watched him clap spurs to his mount and ride out with Gisela at his side. Not for the first time she wished that the birth order between Louis and Robert had been reversed. She could have better borne her burden and perhaps even found a modicum of happiness as queen to Robert's king.

Shortly after noon, Louis arrived at the dwelling where Alienor and her ladies were being accommodated. Exhaustion had set dark shadows under his eyes and deepened the lines between his nose and mouth. He glanced around the room at the women making up the beds and bringing water for washing. "Where is Gisela?" he demanded.

"With Robert," Alienor replied. "She has gone with him to Nicomedia. She does not wish to wed one of the Emperor's kin and Robert has taken her part."

"You stood by and let him do so?"

Alienor shrugged. "Whatever treaty you have planned with the Emperor will not be sabotaged for the loss of an unwilling bride."

His face darkened. "You have no notion how difficult it is keeping a balance between all factions. If I do not agree to the Emperor's requests, he will cut off our supplies and leave us stranded. If I do agree to them, my own men call me a weak fool. What am I supposed to do?"

The retort on the tip of her tongue was "Be a man," but she curbed herself. "I realize how difficult it is, but who has your best interests at heart? And who will guard your back?"

"Precisely," Louis snapped. "Do I trust the Emperor who makes stealthy plans while facing me like a dog doing his business, or my precious brother and my wife, who do exactly the same? Which should I choose?"

"Why don't you ask God or your precious eunuch and see if they will give you an answer?"

He struck her across the face so hard that

she staggered against the wall. "You are poison!" he shouted, his face contorted with fury. "You are a foul viper, clad in all the sins of Eve! You sicken me!" Turning on his heel, he slammed from the room.

Alienor put her hand up to her face. She had bitten her tongue and there was blood in her mouth. She hated him, how she hated him. Antioch could not come soon enough.

That evening she held court lavishly with musicians, entertainment, food, and copious amounts of wine. It was an act of defiance both to the Greeks and to Louis, who did not put in an appearance. Alienor had not expected him to do so, and even while she felt like crying inside, she raised her head in defiance and set out to dazzle all who came within her orbit.

Geoffrey and Saldebreuil arrived from arranging matters for the march to Nicomedia and found their lady at the center of the dance, a shield of laughter brightening her face. She wore a dress of dark green silk embroidered with stars, the long sleeves and skirt flowing around her as she swept and turned.

"Something has upset our lady," Saldebreuil said wryly. "Best beware on the morrow."

Geoffrey said nothing, because the sight of her had stunned the words out of him. He had always loved her, first when she was a bright, precocious child and the daughter of his seigneur, Duke William. He had been a very young man then, with a wife and a growing family, and Alienor had been a general part of that group. But then Burgondie had died bearing their fourth child and Alienor had begun to grow up and, as his grieving eased, he had started to dream of a future with her. Duke William was a widower himself and considering a new marriage in order to beget a son. Had such a thing come to pass, Geoffrey knew he would have stood a chance of wedding Alienor. Fate had decreed otherwise when William had died untimely. Geoffrey was sufficiently pragmatic to accept what had happened, but still romantic enough to remember the dream. Alienor had matured and changed, but she remained his Alienor, shining with all her different facets, and the wanting never went away.

Geoffrey followed Saldebreuil and joined a group of knights in conversation, but he was still intensely aware of Alienor. She turned this way and that and he saw the pale skin of her wrist and the gold silk of her sleeve lining, the suppleness of her body and the grace of her movements. And then he saw the bruise on her cheek and he felt sick. There was only one person who had the right to strike her, which was no right at all when he should have valued her above all things; yet he was Geoffrey's liege lord and entitled to all that Geoffrey was not.

He turned on his heel and left the chamber. To join in the merriment and dancing was impossible. That was Alienor's way of coping, not his. Leaning against a pillar, he closed his eyes and drew a deep breath, seeking calm to settle his anger, but it would not come. Had Louis been present, Geoffrey would have throttled him.

He heard Alienor's bright laughter and her voice telling whoever was with her that she would not be long. And then her footsteps, shadow soft; the rustle of her gown; and the subtle scent of her perfume.

"Alienor . . ." He stepped out from behind the pillar. She gave a gasp of surprise and after a hasty glance over her shoulder, hurried toward him.

"Why did you leave?" she demanded in a low voice. "I wanted to talk to you."

"I left because I could not trust myself to pretend anymore." He drew her further into the shadows where no one could see them. "What has he done to you?" He brushed her cheek with the back of his hand.

"It does not matter," she said impatiently. "He is furious that Robert has gone and taken Gisela. He needed a scapegoat, and as usual it was me. This will all end once we reach Antioch."

"So you keep saying." His voice was grim.

"Because it is true." She stroked the side of his face, reciprocating his action. "Geoffrey . . ."

He pulled her against him. "It does matter." His face contorted. "You do not realize how much. I cannot bear it."

"But you will bear it, even as I do — because we must. There is no choice for now."

He made a sound of despair and kissed her, his grip tightening on her waist. She put her hands in his hair and parted her lips and he came undone because the kiss was such a blend of sweetness and pain. They had been so careful for so long, keeping their distance, behaving as vassal and lady, but it was as if the underground river had risen in full spate and, bursting its banks, had overwhelmed them and swept them to a place where all that existed was this moment and themselves. He leaned against the pillar, lifted her, and entered her with all his pent-up love and frustration. She wrapped her legs around him and buried her face against his throat with a sob. And in those moments they lived a lifetime, knowing it was all they might ever have of each other.

29

Anatolia, January 1148

Alienor turned over and, pulling the furs up around her ears, snuggled against Gisela for warmth.

"Rain," said Marchisa who had stuck her nose outside the tent flaps to sniff the dawn air. "It might even turn to snow."

Alienor groaned and burrowed further under the covers. Everyone spoke of the burning heat of Outremer, but the cold on the high ground was bone-biting.

Today they were due to make the grueling climb and crossing of Mount Cadmos on their journey to the coast at Antalya. The notion of riding up a mountain in the face of a sleety wind made Alienor reluctant to stir. If only she could wake up at home in Poitiers or Antioch without having to travel in either direction.

Outside Alienor could hear the camp stirring to life: men hacking and coughing, snatches of conversation around the campfire, the stamp and nicker of horses as they received their rations of fodder. The ominous rasp of a sword on a whetstone.

Marchisa was building up the brazier in their tent and setting out portions of cold lamb and flat bread with which to break their fast. With great reluctance, Alienor sat up and rubbed the sleep from her eyes. She could smell smoke and grease on her hands from the previous night. The urge to observe the niceties of staying clean and fresh had dwindled to nothing when set against the need to keep dry and warm. She had not bothered to unpack her mirror for the last five nights, and the silk gowns she had worn in Constantinople had been relegated to the bottom of her baggage pack.

Alienor braced herself and left the bed. She had slept in thick socks, her chemise, and a woolen gown. Now she donned a pair of soft linen braies and attached men's leather riding hose to them. She and her women had adopted such clothing since leaving Constantinople because of its comfort and practicality in the advancing winter season and hostile terrain. A highly amused Geoffrey de Rancon had called them "the Amazons" on first discovering the apparel while helping Alienor into the saddle. The nickname had quickly become common parlance among the men. Louis had not been best pleased. He said it was beneath the dignity of the Queen of

France and therefore reflected poorly on himself, but since Alienor and her ladies wore perfectly respectable gowns over their hose, and since it helped them to keep up the pace, he let it pass with no more than scowls.

Alienor covered her hair and went to look outside. Pungent wood smoke drifted from the cooking fires set up under tent awnings. She noticed dashes of white in the rain and knew it would be snowing higher up the mountain. As she stood considering the dismal prospect of riding into the bad weather, a guard detail returned from overnight picket duty.

"The Turks are out there," she heard one soldier telling the men around the fire. "They'll be circling like vultures, just awaiting their moment, the devils. We found two more German corpses butchered and stripped, poor bastards. Skulls stove in like smashed apples."

Alienor's stomach contracted. Glancing around, she saw that Marchisa had heard. Gisela and the others were fortunately too busy dressing. Marchisa was by far the most pragmatic and practical of her ladies. Nothing discommoded her as they toiled through the inhospitable wastes of Anatolia: neither weather, nor sickness, nor scant supplies. Becoming lost for half a day when their Greek guides deserted them had scarcely disturbed her equilibrium, and she had been a steadying influence on Alienor's entire household, including Alienor herself, when they discovered that Emperor Manuel had fed them a pack of lies. Contrary to what they had been told in Constantinople, the Turks had in fact decimated the German army. The latter had turned back, leaving the road littered with their dead. With no one to bury the corpses, they were slowly rotting where they had fallen. Day upon day the French army passed the grim way markers: testimony to what had really happened to their allies and to the web of deceit in which Manuel Komnenos had snared them. The promised guides had slipped away within days and the supplies had also dried up. The French had no choice but to forage, antagonizing the local populace and making themselves vulnerable to Turkish attack. Every day brought fresh casualties and growing anxiety. They should have been in Antioch to celebrate Christmas, yet here they were, still weeks from their destination with the long and treacherous track over Mount Cadmos to negotiate.

Geoffrey was leading the vanguard with Louis's uncle Amadée de Maurienne. Alienor worried for Geoffrey's safety but showed nothing outwardly. They had become even more careful around each other since that brief loss of control in the camp at Constantinople, for they both knew the danger and how vulnerable they were.

, She turned back into the tent. Gisela was shivering as she donned a fur-lined pelisse. The hem was dusty and the pelts, once a warm squirrel red, were matted and draggled. "I don't want to ride across that mountain," she said querulously.

"It could be worse," Alienor said with small patience. "You could have remained in Constantinople as a bride."

Gisela compressed her lips and finished dressing in silence.

Louis arrived while the women were waiting for their mounts to be brought. "Stay in formation and don't straggle," he warned. "I want everyone across by nightfall. No foolishness."

Alienor eyed him with irritation. What did he think they would get up to on a freezing rough mountainside? And why would they wander off when it might mean death from Turkish arrows or tumbling down a stony slope?

"I have told the vanguard to be vigilant and to wait at the summit for the baggage to catch up." Louis nodded briskly, wheeled his stallion, and rode back through the camp, leaning down to have a word here and there, bolstering men's resolve. Alienor watched his progress and grudgingly acknowledged that for all his flaws and the things he had done that made her despise him, he sat a horse well and was an inspiration to his men when he made the effort. He was a strong and skilled swordsman, possessing grace and coordination. If there was anything left that sparked feeling in her, it was the manhood he showed astride a horse.

Saldebreuil brought Serikos around to the tent which the servants had begun dismantling. A thick rug covered his rump this morning and under it, her groom had packed Alienor's bow and a quiverful of arrows. Everyone carried weapons of some kind; even the poorest noncombatants had a knife and a cudgel.

"The seigneurs de Rancon and de Maurienne have already set out with the van," Saldebreuil said as he boosted Alienor into the saddle. "The middle will have to move sharpish to keep up. The van will have a long wait at the top if they get too far ahead."

"They know their part," Alienor replied as she gathered the reins. "The sooner we are over the summit the better for all."

Together with her women, Alienor set out on the stony track that led up the steep, partially forested slopes of Mount Cadmos. Saldebreuil, ever watchful, rode as close to her as possible, although sometimes before or behind because the path was often too narrow for two horses to go abreast. "Make way!" he shouted. "Make way for the Queen!"

The heavily burdened sumpter horses

struggled as the steepness of the climb increased. Pilgrims meandered, trying to find the easiest way, planting their staffs in the ground, hauling themselves up step by step and cursing the weather. Alienor heeled Serikos's flanks, urging him on. Pellets of sleet stung her face. She pulled a scarf across her nose and mouth and felt her breath moisten the wool, each exhalation a momentary burst of warmth that swiftly became an icy chill over her lips and chin. She fixed her mind on the thought of reaching the other side and the welcome of fire, shelter, and wine laced with pepper and ginger. Each stony step brought her closer to Antioch, to her uncle Raymond, and release.

Only lightly encumbered and riding good horses, the vanguard progressed swiftly toward the summit of the mountain. Geoffrey de Rancon and Amadée de Maurienne kept their men moving in tight formation. Sometimes they heard the ululation of the Turks who had been shadowing and harassing them all along the route since crossing the Arm of Saint George, but they did not see them. A few desultory arrows curved out of the trees, but they fell short and posed little threat. Nevertheless, the space between Geoffrey's shoulder blades felt extremely vulnerable. The threat came not only from the Turks. There were men in the train behind who would rather he was dead. He knew of the whispers behind his back: that he was the Queen's lapdog and not to be relied upon. There was all the prejudice of the northern French nobles for a southern lord, and one beholden to a woman as his liege lady rather than to the King of France. That was why they had paired him with Amadée de Maurienne to take the vanguard over the Cadmos Pass, because the latter was the King's uncle and considered experienced and trustworthy.

Geoffrey knew that if his deeper intimacy with Alienor were discovered, he would be found guilty of treason against his king and he would die. Perhaps Alienor would too or else face incarceration for the rest of her days. He did not care about his own fate, but for her sake, he had to keep his distance, no matter how difficult it was. That moment at Constantinople had filled him with a maelstrom of conflict. He was ashamed for his loss of control and the danger in which he had put her, but the moment itself had felt sanctified. He had no sense of betraying Louis, because Alienor had been a part of his soul for far longer than Louis had been her husband. She said once they reached Antioch things would change. He did not know how that was going to happen, but since the day was not far off, one way or another, the waiting would be over.

The wind drove a fresh flurry of sleet into

his face. The higher they climbed, the colder and more exposed they became. Drifting curtains of snow-laden cloud obstructed their vision. The desultory assaults ceased, but the weather continued to batter them all the way to the long summit. Geoffrey drew rein and stopped to listen for the jingle of pack pony bells and the horns blaring from the unwieldy midsection of the army. The sound was faint and variable depending on the direction of the wind, which had its own banshee voice and demonic force. There was no judging how long it would be before the center arrived. Their standard-bearer planted the French lance in the sparse soil of the summit and the silks snapped in the wind, their edges faded and frayed by the months of hard traveling. Geoffrey peeled off one of his sheepskin mittens and, having fumbled his wineskin from his saddlebag, set it to his lips. The sour, tannic taste made him screw up his face and he spat out what was essentially vinegar over his mount's withers. De Maurienne huddled in his thick squirrel-lined cloak. His bony beak of a nose made him look like a disgruntled vulture.

Geoffrey pulled up his hood as yet again it blew back off his head. His teeth ached and he had to half close his eyes to see through the whirling flakes. He sought the lee of a large boulder. His stallion put down its head and hunched its body, tail streaming between its hind legs.

"Good Christ," de Maurienne muttered, his eyes streaming. "By the time the others arrive, we'll be frozen rigid."

Geoffrey glanced at him. De Maurienne was not a young man and although he had been robust when they set out, the long journey had taken its toll on his health. "We could seek shelter farther down off the mountain," he suggested. "We can put up the tents we have with us and light fires for when the others arrive."

De Maurienne looked doubtful. "The King said to wait here and move off together."

"I do not think he realized how much the weather would close in. It's madness to stay here and freeze. I doubt I could hold my sword if I had to use it."

The wind veered again, bringing to them the scrape of hoof on stone and the sound of the outriders blowing their horns.

"I suppose they are not far away," de Maurienne said. "If it weren't for this weather, we'd be seeing them by now."

"Indeed. There won't be room for all of us on the summit; we should move on and make camp."

De Maurienne stroked his white mustaches. "Yes . . ." he said doubtfully, but another blast of wind-blown sleet decided him. He summoned a squire and sent him down the mountain to liaise with those following on.

Heaving a sigh of relief, Geoffrey ordered the standard-bearer to uproot his lance and take the track to the shelter of the valley.

"Make way! Make way for the Queen!" Saldebreuil's voice rang out again and again, a little hoarse at the edges now. The path had grown steeper and stonier as they climbed, and Alienor and her women had dismounted to go on foot because the horses had become skittish. Alienor had already seen several animals and their riders come to grief, which only added to the ranks of the wounded and to the weight of the packs that everyone else had to carry up the pass.

Gisela's little gray kept trying to turn back the way he had come and had to be forced forward with flicks of the whip. He obeyed, but all the time showed the whites of his eyes. Alienor clucked her tongue to Serikos, urging him on, offering him small pieces of bread and dried dates as encouragement. His whiskery muzzle gusted at her shoulder. She could feel the hard stones of the track through her shoes. Despite the weather, the cold, and the hardship, the connection gave her a certain sense of satisfaction in the reality of the moment. There was a challenge in going forward, in working her way through the ranks. As a child she had run races against the other palace children, seeing who could be the first to the top of the hill, and there was an element of that feeling now, a testing of her own stamina and strength.

Suddenly an arrow whined through the air and drove into the chest of a man in front of Alienor, hurling him off his feet. He sprawled, drumming his heels and twitching in his death throes. His horse jerked the rein free from the bend of his elbow and plunged back down the track, barging Serikos's shoulder and narrowly missing Alienor. More arrows showered down, bringing death, injury, and panic.

Alienor grabbed Serikos's bridle close to the bit and ducked under his chin and around to his other flank, intent on reaching the protective quilted tunic in her saddle baggage. The yells of the Turks were clearer now. She saw the flash of a turban from behind a boulder as a Saracen rose to deliver his shot at a burdened pack pony. The initial hit did not down the sumpter immediately; it lumbered and staggered, crashing into pilgrims, creating mayhem. Already the Turk had another arrow at the nock.

"Good Christ," cursed Saldebreuil. "Where in God's name are de Rancon and de Maurienne?"

Alienor shuddered. She had a terrible vision of Geoffrey's arrow-quilled body sprawled across the rocky path. What if the vanguard had been hit and destroyed? Surely she would have heard the noise of battle and their horns summoning help. Where were they?

Pilgrims screamed and ran, were caught and cut down. Serikos lunged and tried to rear. She staggered against his surging shoulder. Turkish fighters hurled out from the rocks, brandishing scimitars and small round shields. Saldebreuil and another knight engaged them, their larger kite shields protecting their bodies. Alienor heard the grunts of effort, saw the chop of swords and the crimson spurt of blood as Saldebreuil dealt with the first Turk and then took down another. She grabbed Serikos's reins and struggled into the saddle. "Ride for higher ground!" she cried to her ladies. "Ride for the clouds!"

Gisela screamed. Alienor whipped around to see the gray staggering, an arrow deep in its shoulder. "Climb up behind me," Alienor commanded. "Ride pillion!"

Weeping in terror, Gisela set her foot on Alienor's and hauled herself onto Serikos's rump. Alienor struck her heels into the gelding's flanks and urged him upward. The higher they climbed the better their chances: safer than trying to turn back through a net of Turkish swords.

Below, Alienor heard the vicious clash of weapons and the screams of people and horses as the slaughter continued. She felt the first stirrings of panic. Behind her,

410

Marchisa and Mamile were praying to God to spare them, and she added her own entreaties to theirs, her voice tight in her throat.

They came upon a loose palfrey, its reins dangling dangerously near its forelegs, its dead young rider sprawled across a boulder. Alienor's blood froze as she recognized Amadée de Maurienne's squire. Dear God, dear God. She stared around wide-eyed but there was no sign of the rest of the vanguard, just this sole corpse. Swallowing, she turned back to the matter in hand. "Take the horse," she urged.

Gisela shook her head, staring at the blood-drenched hide. "I can't, I can't!"

"You must! Serikos cannot bear us both! Quickly now!" Alienor caught the palfrey's reins.

Making small sounds of distress, Gisela slid from Serikos's back. A Turk leaped out at her from behind a rock, his scimitar drawn, and Gisela's whimpers turned to screams. The Saracen prepared to strike, but never completed the move because Saldebreuil arrived at a gallop and cut him down with a swipe of his sword. He had two more knights of Alienor's escort with him, and a serjeant. Swiftly he dismounted, bundled Gisela onto the dead man's horse, and swung back into the saddle. "God knows where the vanguard is," he snarled. "We're being slaughtered!" He spurred his blowing, bleeding horse and smacked Serikos with the flat of his gory blade.

The journey down the other side of the mountain was terrifying. The horses scrambled and slipped on the precipitous, uneven ground and Alienor feared they were going to take a tumble and shatter their bodies on the bones of the mountain. The cloud was thick here and boulders and scree loomed out at them without warning. She was certain that at any moment they were going to ride off the edge of the world and vanish into oblivion. She kept expecting to come upon more arrow shot and butchered corpses from the vanguard, but there was nothing. Perhaps they had indeed taken that leap into the void.

The ground became softer and flatter, the boulders and humps diminishing to scree. At their backs, stones pelted and bounced down the mountainside, disturbed by their passage, and the horses skidded. Saldebreuil led them at a rapid trot along a track where piles of fresh horse droppings showed that the path had recently been used. Eventually they came to an open area in the valley with a swift-running stream. Soldiers had pitched tents and the horses had been put to graze. Twirls of smoke rose from fresh campfires, and the scene was so pastoral and calm that Alienor had to fight disbelief. Only when the guards on picket duty saw the riders approaching at a fast gait did they stand to attention.

"The middle is under attack!" Saldebreuil bellowed at them. "Get back there, you craven fools! We're being massacred and robbed. The Queen is safe by the grace of God, but who knows what will happen to the King!"

A soldier ran to fetch Amadée de Maurienne and Geoffrey de Rancon, while the knights scrambled to resaddle their horses.

"Why didn't you wait?" Saldebreuil snarled at Geoffrey as the latter arrived at a run, buckling on his sword. "The Turks are slaughtering us on the mountain and we're caught like lambs in a pen! It's your fault, but all of us from Aquitaine will carry the blame!"

Geoffrey's olive complexion was yellow. Without a word he turned and began shouting orders. De Maurienne was already astride his stallion and rallying the men.

"Guard the camp," de Maurienne bellowed to Geoffrey. "Prepare for attack. I will deal with this." He spurred back the way he had come at a hard gallop.

Geoffrey clenched his fists, his chest heaving. Alienor was furious with him, but was not about to upbraid him in the midst of a desperate situation, and above all else she was limp with relief that he was alive. "Do as de Maurienne says, and be swift about it," she said curtly. Without waiting for aid she dismounted from Serikos.

"I swear I did not know. I thought to make a camp out of the weather as a refuge." His voice almost cracked. "If I had thought for one minute that the Turks would attack, I would never have ridden ahead. I would never risk your life."

"But you did." Her body shook with reaction. "Your decision carries a high price. If you have a tent prepared, as you say, have your squire escort us there."

"Madam . . ."

She set her jaw and turned away before she either struck him or fell upon him in weeping dissolution.

Geoffrey's squire escorted Alienor and her ladies to a tent in the middle of the camp. A pot of hot stew bubbled softly over a brazier. Sheepskins had been placed on the floor and covered several benches arranged around the coals. Marchisa, practical as ever, prepared a hot herbal tisane and pressed one of the fleeces around Gisela's shoulders, for the young woman's teeth were chattering.

Alienor could hear Geoffrey bellowing orders and men running to obey. She tried to compose herself, but inside still felt as if she were tearing down that slope of rocks and scree toward a shattering impact. Thank God Geoffrey was alive. Thank God they had not betrayed each other. But his error would have terrible repercussions, both in the wider field and the personal. She felt sick. She drank the tisane and left the tent to do what she could for the survivors who were straggling into camp, dazed, bleeding, and disoriented.

Night fell and the trickle into the camp continued from the decimated pilgrim middle sector, and then men from the rearguard in a disorganized scatter. No one had seen the King. Some said they had seen him riding to the aid of the embattled middle with his bodyguard, but not since then.

Robert de Dreux arrived, his shield almost in pieces and his horse cut about the haunches and lame. Amadée de Maurienne was with him, looking shaken and old. "We could not find the King," he said in a trembling voice, "and the Turks and the natives were all over the mountain, looting and butchering."

Alienor absorbed the news with an initial surge of shock, but as the jolt left her, she shook her head. Louis was not the world's best commander, but when it came to fighting ability in a crisis, and sheer luck, he had few equals.

"God preserve him. God preserve us all." Robert crossed himself. He was quivering and his eyes were wide and dark. If Louis did not return, then Robert, here and now, would become King of France. The air was huge with tension. She knew how ambitious Robert was, and already she could see the glances being cast his way, each man wondering if he should dare to be the first to kneel and give his allegiance.

If Louis was dead, then she was no longer Queen of France. Robert's wife Hawise would bear that burden instead. She could return to Aquitaine, with her daughter, and this time marry as she chose. The notion was like a prison door opening, but she dared not allow herself to think it might be true and pulled back from the thought as if she had touched a hot iron bar.

Throughout the evening, stragglers continued to arrive. The guards were tense, challenging each one, afraid that the Turks would creep up under cover of darkness and encircle the camp. The cloud on this side of the mountain was sparse, and the stars shone like chips of rock crystal in the bitter night.

Alienor was crouching beside a wounded knight, offering him words of comfort, when she heard the shout go up. "The King, the King is found! Praise God, praise God!" She rose to her feet, clutching her cloak around her, eyes wide. She had been hoping and fearing. She had expected him to succeed and survive, but her thoughts, although controlled, were on a knife-edge. She hurried toward the shouting and then stopped abruptly because Louis, filthy, bedraggled, and blood-spattered, was swaying where he stood, legs wide-planted for balance, and on their knees before him, heads bowed, were

Geoffrey de Rancon and Amadée de Maurienne.

"Where were you?" Louis was demanding. "You are to blame. You rode off to see to your own comfort. You hid like cowards and left me and my men to die. De Warenne, de Breteuil, de Bullas: hacked to death before my eyes. This is betrayal that amounts to treason!"

"Sire, we did not know," pleaded de Maurienne. "We thought it was safe. If we had known, we would not have come down to make camp."

"You disobeyed my orders and men whose names you are not fit to utter have died today because of your incompetence and cowardice."

"I will give my life if you ask it, nephew," de Maurienne volunteered.

Louis's gaze stabbed the kneeling men. "I am inclined to accept your offer," he snarled. "Neither of you is worth a pot of piss! You are both under arrest, and I will deal with you as you deserve in the morning. Prepare your souls. My household guard sacrificed themselves for me and their bodies are lying out on that mountainside, stripped and butchered by infidels." His voice cracked with rage and grief. "Their blood is on your hands for eternity, do you hear me? For eternity!" He raised his dirty, bloodstained fists to emphasize the point, and then slowly lowered them. "Bring me maps," he commanded. "Find me de Galeran — if he survived." He pointed to de Maurienne's tent. "I will take this for my own. See to it."

Geoffrey and de Maurienne were dragged away through a crowd clamoring to see them hanged here and now, especially Geoffrey. Men spat at them and struck out as they passed amid cries of "Shame!" and "Treason!" Alienor's heart began to pound. Sweeping her cloak around her, she hastened to the tent that Louis had just commandeered and forced her way past the soldiers guarding the entrance. "Husband," she said to Louis, invoking the familiar form as she dropped the flaps.

He was standing in the middle of the tent, his face in his hands and his body shuddering with sobs. He made an abrupt turn to her and raised his head, tears streaming down his grimed cheeks. "What do you want?" he said raggedly.

She lifted her chin. There was no falling into each other's arms. No "Glad you are alive." They were far beyond that. "I am sorry for the good men we have lost, but you cannot hang your uncle and my seneschal on the morrow, and you must make sure your men do not do so tonight."

"Are you trying to rule me again?" He bared his teeth. "Do not dictate to me what I can and cannot do."

"I am telling you that if you do this thing, you will have a war between our troops that will finish what the Turks began." She drew herself up. "Geoffrey de Rancon is my vassal and it is my prerogative to chastise him for what he has or has not done. You shall not hang him."

"They disobeyed my orders," Louis snarled, "and because they did not do as they were told, my men — my friends — were slaughtered. I shall do as I see fit."

"They did what they thought best. They made a mistake, but it was folly, not treason. You have no right to hang Geoffrey, because he is my vassal. If you do, then the Aquitaine contingent will rise in revolt against you. Do you really want to contend with that? And if you hang Geoffrey, you will also have to hang your uncle — your own mother's brother — because they share the blame. Are you willing to do that, Louis? Will you watch them both swing? How will that sit with your men?"

"You know nothing!" he sobbed at her. "If you had been there, seeing your friends cut to pieces in front of your eyes, you would not be so swift to leap to their defense! My bodyguards gave their lives to protect mine, while de Maurienne and de Rancon were warming their backsides at the fire and taking their ease. This is all their fault, all of it. If you were any kind of wife to me, you would be supporting me in this, not casting obstacles in my way."

"You have a penchant for always seeing reason as an obstacle. If you hang these men, you will lose two battle commanders and all of their vassals who will no longer cleave to your banner, and that means you will only have yourself to blame when what remains disintegrates in your hands."

"Be silent!" He raised his clenched, bloody fist.

Alienor did not flinch. "If you do this, you doom yourself," she said, her voice quiet but hard. She turned her back on him and left the tent.

Behind her she heard a crash as if something had been kicked over. A real man would not succumb to a boy's tantrum, she thought, and the sound only served to increase her contempt for him and her fear of what he might do.

Alienor went with Saldebreuil to the tent where Geoffrey and Amadée de Maurienne were being held under house arrest. A crowd of knights and serjeants, survivors of the rearguard, had gathered outside and were shouting insults, most of them directed at Geoffrey. "Poitevan coward!" and "Southern softsword!" were the least of them. Chanted threats to hang the men surged and receded, and more soldiers were drifting toward the tent and joining the crowd with each moment. "Find Everard des Barres. Quickly!" Alienor commanded Saldebreuil.

He snapped swift orders to one of his men, and then, with a handful of household knights, made a corridor for Alienor to approach the tent entrance. "Make way for the Queen!" he bellowed.

Soldiers fell back, but Alienor was aware of their muttering and resentment. A real sense of danger tingled down her spine. At the tent entrance she paused, drew a deep breath, and then parted the flaps.

Geoffrey and de Maurienne sat at a trestle table with a flagon between them and a platter on which stood a loaf of hard bread and a rind of cheese. They looked up with taut faces as she entered; both then rose and knelt to her.

Alienor knew she dared not betray her emotions by a single look or gesture. "I have spoken to the King," she said. "He is furious, but I believe when it comes to the crux, he will spare you both."

"Then we must believe in your belief, madam," said de Maurienne, "and my nephew's good sense. But what of them?" He nodded toward the tent flaps. Something struck the side of the canvas with a heavy thud. A stone, she thought, and the volume of the shouting increased.

"Help is at hand," she replied, praying that it was, and hoping Louis would indeed see sense by the morning.

"Well, if it is French help, they are likely to string us up," Geoffrey said grimly, "and if you have summoned our men, there will be bloody fighting in the camp between the factions."

"Credit me with more sense than that," she snapped. "I have sent for the Templars."

A look of relief passed between the men, but then Geoffrey shook his head. "Perhaps we do deserve to die," he said.

"You have already committed enough folly to last you into your dotage, without adding more," she said, covering her fear with anger. "When we reach Antioch, my lord, I am sending you back to Aquitaine." He inhaled to protest and she raised her hand to silence him. "My mind is made up. It will benefit me and Aquitaine far more than if you remain here."

Geoffrey stared at her, his eyes glittering with tears. "You will shame me before all."

"No, you fool, I will save your life, even if you seem keen to throw it away. Listen to them." She gestured to the tent flaps. "They will make a scapegoat of you. Someone will put a knife in you before this journey is done. It is different for my lord de Maurienne. He is the King's uncle, and they will say he followed your lead. They may not hang you today, but nevertheless they will find some way of murdering you. I will not let that happen to . . . to one of my senior vassals. Besides, I need your strong arm to prepare Aquitaine for when I return. So much will have changed." She raised her brows in emphasis.

"Madam, I beg you . . ." Geoffrey looked at her with his heart in his eyes, then he swiftly dropped his gaze and bowed his head. "Do not send me away."

Alienor swallowed. "I must. I have no choice."

There was a taut silence, then Geoffrey said, "If that is your wish, I must yield you my obedience, but I do it at your will, not my own."

De Maurienne had been silently watchful throughout the exchange, and Alienor wondered how much they had given away. "The Queen speaks wisely," the older man said. "I can weather the storm, but you are vulnerable; you have enemies. It is best for all that you leave."

Outside the tent, the shouting and insults had fallen silent, replaced by the sound of a heavy tread in unison and the clink of weapons. Alienor turned to the entrance. A row of Templar knights and serjeants was lining up facing the crowd, shields presented, hands on sword hilts.

"Madam." Their commander, Everard des Barres, gave her a stiff bow.

Alienor returned the courtesy. "Sire, I ask

you to guard these men. I fear for their lives. There will be more bloodshed among us should anything happen to them tonight before the King has made his decision. We have problems enough in the camp without adding to them."

Des Barres gave her a shrewd look from narrow dark eyes. He and Alienor had never been particularly cordial with each other but were both pragmatic enough to deal on political and diplomatic terms. "Madam, you have my personal oath that these men will not be harmed."

There would be a price to pay at some point, she knew, but des Barres was a man of his word. The Templars had no affinity apart from God and were the best soldiers in Christendom. "Thank you. I leave this in your capable hands, my lord."

Alienor left the tent without looking back because she did not want to meet Geoffrey's gaze. The Queen's traditional role was that of peacemaker; let it rest at that and pretend that her heart was not breaking.

Having passed a worried, sleepless night, Alienor had just finished her morning ablutions when Louis arrived. In the morning light, his face was pale and ravaged, with eyes red-rimmed from exhaustion and weeping. "I have decided to spare my uncle and de Rancon," he said. "It will be a far greater punishment for them to live with their shame."

"Thank you," Alienor said, her tone concil-iatory and subdued. She felt weak with relief, for he could so easily have chosen execution and in the end she could not have stopped him. "Geoffrey must return to Aquitaine."

Louis gave a curt nod. "Indeed. I am not inclined to protect him from the men, and I can no longer trust him with any kind of military responsibility. The Templars will command the vanguard for the rest of the way."

He left the tent in a brusque flurry and Alienor released the breath she had been holding. She could not even bear the scent of him now. Overcome by nausea, she had to run to the slop bowl.

Marchisa left what she was doing and hastened to tend to her.

"It is nothing," Alienor said, gesturing her away. "I am all right."

"I am here if you need me, madam," Marchisa said, giving her a long, thoughtful look.

The Templars led off the army later in the morning. Louis kept de Maurienne close to his side, and Alienor had Geoffrey ride as part of her escort, near enough that he was under her protection as much as he was protecting her. It was unsettling and bitter-sweet. Each time she breathed him in, the sensation was almost unbearable, as it was with Louis, but for the opposite reasons. She dared not touch him or favor him because people were watching closely. It all had to be worn on the inside. No one must ever know.

30

Antioch, March 1148

Alienor and Louis sailed into the port of Saint Symeon on a glittering morning in mid-March. The breeze was soft, the sky clear blue, and the sea rocked with a gentle swell. Alienor walked on to the harbor side, thanking God for their safe deliverance. It was impossible to believe that the voyage from the port of Antalya to Antioch, usually of three days' duration, had taken almost three weeks, during which their vessels had been buffeted on rough seas and blown far off course. The Greek sailors had demanded an extortionate fee of four silver marks for each passenger they shipped. The alternative was a forty-day journey through rough and hostile terrain, which was what the bulk of the army had had to do despite being weakened by sickness and hunger.

Alienor had been nauseous throughout the sea journey, even during the times when the weather was calm. Marchisa had tended to her and said nothing, but her gaze was astute. Alienor knew that sooner or later she would have to confide in her. She could not keep her condition secret for much longer without help.

Antioch stood on the River Orontes, the city wall rising in massive crenellations up the sides of Mount Silipus. It was home to the Holy Saint Peter, first disciple of Jesus, and housed the church where the word "Christian" had first been coined. That church still existed, built into a cavern in the mountainside, and was a place of reverence and pilgrimage. Louis was eager to worship there and tread in the footsteps of heaven's gatekeeper.

Alienor's own thoughts were more directed toward meeting her uncle and claiming his protection. Preparing to meet him, she dressed in a red silk dalmatic given to her by the Empress Irene. The loose-fitting gown was ornamented with precious gems, pearls, and gold beads. Sapphires and rubies adorned her fingers and she covered her hair with a veil of Egyptian linen, so fine that it was like mist. Despite the rigors of the journey and her recent uncertain health, she was determined to greet her uncle with regal dignity.

She had last seen him when she was nine years old and had a vague memory of a tall young knight with deep blue eyes and hair the same dark golden hue as her own. Her stomach was queasy with anticipation and the knowledge that she was about to begin a new phase of her life, a phase that did not include Louis, although for the moment she would play her role as Queen of France.

They were greeted by a crowd of people singing hymns and scattering blossom petals before them in a pink and white cloud. Louis's jaw tightened. "Let us hope that this place is not another Constantinople," he muttered with a curl of his lip.

"Why should it be?" She gave him a sharp look. "It is ruled by my father's brother and his wife is your cousin."

"Because the ways of the East are tainted, and the fine flourishes only serve to conceal and gild their treachery," he said.

She stared at him. "You believe our own kin to be treacherous?"

"Until I have been given good reason to think otherwise," he said grimly. "After all, I have encountered treachery and deceit close to home on more than one occasion."

Alienor swallowed nausea. Just a little longer, she told herself, just a few days more and she would be free. "Antioch is not Constantinople. My uncle and his wife are of our lands even if they have made lives here, and we have come to help them — that was our original purpose."

"Not our only one," he said. "Our duty to

God is the more important."

Outside the palace, her uncle Raymond waited to greet them with his wife, Constance, who was kin to Louis. Many years in the Middle Eastern sun had bleached Raymond's hair to the white gold of ripe wheat, and his blue eyes were surrounded by deep creases from staring into harsh light. He was taller and broader than Louis and had such a look of her father that she wanted to fling her arms around him and sob on his neck, but she restrained herself. Constance was slightly younger than Alienor, slender and dark-haired with light green eyes and fine features. She had a look of Louis around her nose and cheekbones, but there was something a little exotic about her too, as if the East had added its quality to her blood.

Their marriage had begun in scandal and subterfuge. At the age of twenty-two, Raymond had been invited to Antioch to become its ruler by marrying Alice, widow of the recently deceased Count Bohemond. But Alice was headstrong and not of the bloodline, whereas her nine-year-old daughter Constance was. Traveling in secret to avoid enemies, Raymond had arrived in Antioch, ostensibly to marry the mother, but had taken the daughter to wife instead, thereby thwarting Alice's ambitions and setting himself up in dominance. Although under heavy threat from the Seljuks, he remained a powerful player in the game and was still only in his thirties.

"Welcome," Raymond said, his voice deep and mellifluous. He spoke the French of the north as he greeted Louis with the kiss of peace and embraced him, but he did not kneel. Then he turned to Alienor and his gaze filled with warmth and compassion. "Niece," he said in the *lenga romana.* "My brother's child."

When he kissed her cheek, she clung to him, feeling like a shipwrecked sailor being thrown a rope by the master of a seaworthy boat. "You look so much like my father," she said, a quiver in her voice.

Raymond smiled, revealing large white teeth. "I hope that is a flattering comparison. We are so glad to see you and welcome your aid. I hope you will find Antioch pleasing."

"I feel as if I have come home," Alienor said, her throat tight with emotion. She turned to Raymond's young consort and embraced her too. A perfume of incense hung around Constance, smoky and spicy at the same time. Louis's jaw was tight with tension, but he was not hostile, just wary.

"The bulk of my army is taking the overland route and will be here in a little less than two weeks," he said. "We will be glad of your succor until then."

Raymond raised his brows. "You are welcome to stay for as long as the campaign requires," he replied. "I had heard that your troops were on their way overland. You have found to your cost that the Greeks charge extortionately for their services."

"Indeed, I have found to my cost that trust and loyalty are rarer than Tyrian purple and the horn of the unicorn," Louis replied grimly. "And that everything has its price, and it is always more than it is worth."

"That is so," Raymond replied. "Welcome to Outremer."

For the first time in months, Alienor was able to truly relax and feel safe. Raymond reminded her so much of her father, but a version that was larger than life and filled with vitality and exuberance. He was secure in his manhood and he occupied his space effortlessly. He casually tousled the heads of his children as he introduced them. Baldwin his heir, four years old and shining gold like his father, and two dark-haired enchanting daughters, Maria, who was two, and Philippa, a babe in arms. Alienor felt a pang as she looked at Maria and thought of her own daughter of that name. She would be running about now and learning to say "Mama" to other people — to Petronella and the women of the court. It was a world away — another life, and one to which she did not intend returning. There was another child to consider also, its life a tiny flickering secret within her womb.

The palace at Antioch was not as large or as opulent as that of Constantinople, but still gracious and filled with riches beyond anything that the courts of France possessed. The floors were dressed with iridescent tiles and mosaics. Marble fountains splashed in flower-scented courtyards and the courtiers wore silk just as they did in Constantinople. Alienor and her ladies were afforded a set of chambers with cool marble floors and high latticed windows to sift the breeze. Although the outward trappings were similar to Constantinople, the ambience was very different. She could feel her power here, and it was the power of Aquitaine, not France. She had presence and influence. As Duchess of Aquitaine and the niece of the Prince of Antioch, she was treated with respect and reverence. Her ideas and her abilities were valued, and the way she chose to dress and comport herself was regarded as normal and the right thing to do. It was in such contrast to her treatment at home and on the journey that it made her throat ache.

Indeed, Antioch felt close to Aquitaine in many more ways because her uncle had imbued his palace with that land's energy and traditions. The court's official language was the *lenga romana,* and the culture and music were all of the southern lands. Alienor and Raymond had memories to exchange — he of the times before she had been born, when he had been a child growing up with her father, and she of the years after he had gone.

"I would love to see Poitiers again before I die," Raymond said, "but my life is here now and I know I shall never go back." He squeezed her hand in his and kissed her cheek. "You must do it for me, niece. Govern wisely and well."

Alienor looked down at his broad, capable hand over hers and drew a deep breath. "I want to annul my marriage with Louis," she said. "I loved my father dearly, but he did me no favors when he made the match."

Raymond's expression grew very still. "That is a serious undertaking. Does Louis know your intent?"

She shook her head, feeling tense. What if Raymond took Louis's part and refused to help her? "Not yet. I wanted to be in a safe place before I broached the subject with him."

"Why do you desire an annulment?" He fixed her with an intent stare. "What makes the match untenable?"

She could not tell from his words and his expression whether or not he was sympathetic. "Because it is not right for Aquitaine," she said. "Louis hems me in and belittles my abilities. He is no husband to me in any sense of the word." Her mouth twisted bitterly. "He might as well be married to Thierry de Galeran. The Templar has shared his tent throughout this campaign and sleeps in his chamber. Louis is swayed by the advice of men who have no love for me or for Aquitaine. And because you are of Aquitaine and keep a southern court, he will not love you either."

Raymond leaned back in his chair. "An annulment would leave you vulnerable and open to predators."

"I know I would have to remarry, but I would be able to choose my own consort and not be forced by the dictates of others."

He stroked his chin. "But your choice would be dictated by the needs of Aquitaine."

"And I shall make it carefully indeed."

"Do you have a choice in mind?"

Alienor closed her face. "Let that come later."

"You can trust me, you know that." His voice was as warm as sunlight.

She gave him a straight stare. "I have gotten out of the habit of trusting anyone."

"Well then, you are wise, because I am of the same mind myself." He patted her hand. "I need your husband's support for the campaign against Aleppo, but when that matter is concluded, I will offer you what aid I can."

Alienor's caution did not completely dissipate, but she was relieved at his favorable, if qualified, reply. "And you will succor me here in Antioch?"

Raymond embraced her. "Your home is mine for as long as you have need, niece."

It was late in the evening and most folk had retired to sleep, although the oil lamps in the palace corridors were still burning. Alienor had stayed a long time in her uncle's chamber, catching up with the past and discussing future policy. Louis had his own apartments and had gone early to bed, pleading tiredness and a need to pray. Thus far she had managed to avoid him, only joining him for formal occasions and mealtimes, and had steeled herself to smile and put on a courtly facade for the duration.

As midnight approached, Alienor finally retired to her own chambers, escorted by her ladies and the protective presence of Geoffrey de Rancon and Saldebreuil de Sanzay. The latter bowed at her door and went off to check that all was well with the men. Alienor dismissed her women to their beds in the anteroom, all save Marchisa, and with her as chaperone bade Geoffrey enter her own chamber.

"Wine, Marchisa," she said, "then you may go, but stay within call, and leave the door open a little."

"Madam." Marchisa performed the duty with quiet efficiency and left the room, skirts softly whispering on the tiles.

"That will go some way to satisfying propriety," Alienor said, "but it still affords some privacy."

Geoffrey raised his brows. "You are optimistic," he said, but sat down on the long couch beside her.

"I fear nothing at my uncle's court. He only has my well-being at heart." She watched him sip the wine — the flexion of his throat, the curl of his hair near his earlobe. He would be leaving with the dawn, returning to Aquitaine by the swiftest routes. He would be free and clear and she was glad, but her heart was aching. She set her hand over his. "I am with child," she said. "That moment in Constantinople . . ."

His gaze sharpened and filled with shock and anguish. "Dear God . . . Why didn't you say before?"

She could see him calculating the months and put her forefinger to his lips. "Hush. There would have been no point in telling you sooner. What you did not know was protection for you."

"I was a purblind fool," he said grimly. "I should have had more control."

"Then so was I. We were both a part of it, as we are part of it now — and I am glad." Taking his hand, she placed it on the gentle curve of her belly. "I cannot regret this."

"But I am leaving." He swallowed. "I cannot let you face this alone."

"You can and you must."

"I don't —"

"No." She cut him off. "I need to accomplish this in my own way and it will not help to have you here. We might give something away and no one must ever know, for the sake of all of our lives." She drew a deep breath. "I intend to have my marriage with Louis annulled. I have already written to the Archbishop of Bordeaux to set matters in motion. My uncle will make me welcome here for as long as I choose to stay, and I shall do so until the child is born."

"Does your uncle know of your condition?"

She shook her head. "No, and he does not have to know either. There are places I can go when the time comes, and the child can be raised honorably in my household without anyone knowing but us. He or she will receive a fine education and career and never have to be bound by the constraints that have bound us."

Geoffrey dug his hands through his hair. "What if Louis refuses to consent to an annulment?"

"He will see that it is in his best interests."

"And if he does not?"

Her voice filled with steely determination. "I shall persuade him."

"Might he think the child is his?"

Alienor exhaled a bitter laugh. "It would be a miracle. He hasn't been near my bed since we left France." She met his gaze without looking away. "I am not sorry that this has happened," she said forcefully. "I may not have chosen such a route, but I am glad."

He was not reassured. "There is more at stake now than there has ever been, yet you want to send me away where I am powerless to do anything."

She pushed his hair back from his brow in a tender, intimate gesture. "I know it is difficult, but it is the safest path for us and our child — trust me."

He groaned and wrapped his arms around her. "I do trust you. It is myself I find wanting."

"Do not," she said. "I will not hear you say that." She sealed his mouth with a kiss when he inhaled to protest and instead took his breath into her own body and imagined it traveling down to her womb, giving their child life and sustenance.

It was deep in the night when Geoffrey finally left Alienor's chamber, his footfall stealthy as he crossed the anteroom. Alienor accompanied him, and Marchisa walked before them, shading a small oil lamp in her hand. The other women slept behind their gauze curtains. At the door, Alienor bade Marchisa go to bed. The maid curtsied and silently withdrew.

Beyond the doorway, lit by stars and a large crescent moon, the fountain glistened with dark rills of water. "God speed your journey and make your way fair and good," Alienor whispered. "I will pray for you every moment."

He brushed her face with his hand. "As I will pray for you and our child." His throat worked. "I would have stayed . . ."

"I know you would, but someone would put a knife in your back even here in Antioch. You are better gone from this, and there is much work to do in Aquitaine when you return. While both of us are in this world we shall always be together."

They had kissed their farewell within her chamber, but now he took her hand and lifted it. She felt the soft brush of his lips on her skin. And then he drew back, bowed, and walked away. Alienor watched until he was out of sight and then closed her eyes, letting him go.

She was turning to retire when Raymond stepped out of the shadows soft-footed as the cheetah he kept for the hunt and which slept in his chamber. "Ah, niece," he said. "You are fortunate there was only me to witness that tender farewell. What would others construe from so fond a parting?"

Alienor drew herself up and concealed her fear by meeting his gaze full on. "I do not think 'fortunate' is the right word, Uncle, but since you used it, I take it you are not going to expose us?"

Raymond sat down on a bench facing the fountain and gestured Alienor to join him. "He is leaving tomorrow, is he not?" he said.

"You do not know how difficult my life is with Louis," she said with quiet intensity.

"A veritable monk," Raymond said. "With all a monk's proclivities and vices, no?" He spread his arms across the back of the bench and crossed his legs.

"You might say that. My only value to him is because of Aquitaine. For the rest he treats me as a necessary but worthless appendage. And I have long since ceased to have any respect for him."

"And this other man, de Rancon?"

Her uncle's tone was mild but she was not deceived. "I would have married him, not Louis, if I had been given the choice."

"Would you indeed?" Raymond looked thoughtful, his posture that of a great indolent lion. "But not such a good choice for Aquitaine. Would the people follow him? Would they account him Duke? Louis may have proved to be a fool, but your father's policy was sound at the time. De Rancon would not be a wise choice to make even if you were free; I strongly counsel you against it."

Alienor swallowed her anger and a frisson of alarm. She could only be thankful again that she was sending Geoffrey back to Aquitaine. She liked her uncle, but she had no illusions. He was ruthless, because only a ruthless man could survive in this environment. "I am not foolish," she said. "I see further than I did at thirteen years old. My decision will be the best one for Aquitaine."

"Some might consider Louis expendable," Raymond said after a moment.

Alienor looked down at her hands. "That is up to them, but he is an anointed king, and I believe they would only create more difficulties by solving the one."

"Indeed," Raymond replied and smoothly continued as if he had not just broached the matter of having Louis removed: "I have still to gain your husband's measure in terms of how far he can be persuaded on matters of policy and whether he will agree to a campaign against Aleppo."

"His desire is all for Jerusalem," she said. "I doubt he will heed you, because you are my uncle and of Aquitaine. You have seen how it is between us. He will not listen to me, and neither will those around him, although his brother may be more open to reason."

"Ah, Robert. And he too has ambitions, I think."

"He would be King of France, but he is cautious. He may agree with your policies, but do not expect him to support you unless it suits his purpose."

Raymond drummed his fingers on the back of the bench. "The men of Aquitaine? They would stay?"

"You are my father's brother; they would follow you — I think you know that. Certainly they would stay with me rather than follow Louis."

He nodded purposefully and stood up. "Time I retired," he said. "There is much to consider. I shall speak with Louis on the matter of Aleppo . . . and if I cannot bring him to agree, then we shall have to think of a different way around the dilemma."

She rose too and he tenderly kissed her brow. "All will be well, I promise you."

Alienor's throat tightened. "My father always kissed me and told me the same thing — but it wasn't true."

Raymond gave a mordant smile. "We were both speaking of the future, my dear, not the present."

A noise in the darkness to their left made them turn swiftly, but there was nothing to see, and when they listened they could only hear the splash of the fountain and the soft chirring of crickets. "There are many cats abroad at night," Raymond said with a curled lip, "all with their ears pricked and their eyes shining like mirrors. Go now, quickly."

Her heart hammering, Alienor stepped inside her chamber. Marchisa was waiting to light her back to her room, and Gisela was sitting up on her pallet with the gauze curtain drawn back and her eyes wide. "Madam?"

"Go back to sleep," Alienor said, her voice

quiet but terse.

"Madam." Gisela's curtain swished back down.

Alienor stretched out on her own bed. Marchisa left quietly, having placed the lamp in a chain holder. The flame softly flickered, creating reflections and patterns on the marble floor, the fire drawing in the direction of the faint breeze from the lancet windows high above the bed. She lay awake for a long time, her hand on her womb, and watched the flow of the light over the floor and walls until the lamp guttered and went out.

Louis found Raymond of Antioch disturbing and irritating in equal measure. His height, strength, and golden presence made Louis feel that he had to puff out his own chest and try to match him, yet his best always seemed inadequate.

"We should strike at Aleppo," Raymond said firmly. "That is the greatest threat to Antioch now that Edessa has fallen to the Turk. If we can take it, then we will have stability for years to come."

"I am not convinced it is a good idea," Louis said. "Edessa is already lost. Aleppo may be important to you, but we must listen to what the King of Jerusalem and his barons have to say. I say it would be better to concentrate on Damascus." He shot Raymond a challenging look and was gratified and also a little afraid to see the flash of temper in the Prince's blue eyes.

"That would be folly," Raymond snapped. "It would be much simpler and more sensible to take Aleppo first and then deal with Damascus."

"From your point of view, yes, but that may not be the opinion of Jerusalem." Louis looked over his shoulder at Thierry de Galeran and his uncle William de Montferrat, who both nodded agreement.

"We are like a row of pins. Knock one down and it will crash into another and then another. Edessa has already fallen and Antioch is the next pin in that sequence. If I fall, then Tripoli follows, and then the precious Kingdom of Jerusalem. And all for the want of a decisive strike now."

Louis eyed Raymond's clenched fist and took a perverse pleasure in saying, "So you say, but I well know the situation and wish to take other counsel."

Raymond raised his eyebrows. "Indeed, sire? Then in knowing, you must have great insight, since you do not dwell here."

"Sometimes it takes someone with a longer view." Louis leaned back, aping the indolent pose Raymond often assumed. "My intent is to ride down to Jerusalem and fulfill my pilgrimage. Once that is accomplished, I shall consider the battlefield again."

"Some of us do not have that choice," Raymond said with asperity. "You came to help, but I see now you have no intention of doing so."

Louis gave him a steely look. "I shall do what I consider best, not what you would have me do to suit yourself."

Raymond swallowed and Louis could almost see him grinding his teeth. It made him want to smile. He could play the game and beat this man whom he had disliked and distrusted on sight.

"Sire, I hope you will reconsider," Raymond said stiffly. "Perhaps we should talk again on another occasion when you have had opportunity to reflect."

Louis dipped his head. "I shall think on the matter, but I doubt I shall change my mind."

Raymond left quietly, but the atmosphere around him was tense with suppressed rage. Louis was wary, but content. It gave him a sense of power and achievement to know he could defeat Raymond just by refusing. And after all, the opinion of Jerusalem was what really mattered.

His brother Robert cleared his throat and folded his arms. "I think we should help him to take Aleppo," he said. "We need to look at the future when we are gone from here. He does have a point."

Louis scowled. "I will not have my hand forced. I do not trust him. He is little better than a Greek and a bad influence. He courts people with fine words and gilded trappings, but it is all false. A snail may produce the color purple from its shell, but it still leaves a trail of slime." Louis affected an imperious air. "I shall go to Jerusalem. The honor of Christ stands far above the needs and conceits of this man."

Alienor waited until she was certain Louis was alone in his chamber. Having spent an hour at his prayers, he was composing messages to Abbé Suger using a stylus and a waxed tablet before retiring to bed.

"I must speak with you," she said.

Louis gave her a supercilious look. "Can you spare the time away from your precious uncle to do so?"

She gave a sigh of annoyance. "He is my closest living kin on my father's side. We have much to talk about."

"I am sure you do," he sneered.

Alienor wanted to slap him. "He is right about Aleppo. You said you would help him, so why are you refusing now? Do you not see how important it is?"

"Warfare is men's business and you should not meddle." Louis gave a dismissive wave of his right hand. "If he has sent you to plead on his behalf, then his cause is worthless. I only take advice from men I trust and certainly not from you."

"You insult him, and you insult me."

"I insult no one; I speak as I find." He flashed her an angry look. "You both have your agendas and I will not be a pawn."

"You are already a pawn," she said scornfully. "The men of your own faction play their power games with you, but you are so much in their thrall that you do not see it, or perhaps you do not want to see it."

"I am my own man," he snapped.

"And on your own. How much of a man are you, Louis? How much of a king? I have seen precious little of either in you."

"Enough!" He cast down the stylus with a metallic clatter.

Alienor made a throwing gesture that rippled her long silk sleeve. "If you go to Jerusalem, you go alone. I am staying in Antioch."

"You are the Queen of France and by God you will go where I go."

"I will not." She stood tall. "It is finished between us, Louis. I want our marriage annulled."

A look of astonishment crossed his face, swiftly followed by fury. "Your uncle has put you up to this, hasn't he?"

"He has no need to. I am the one broaching the subject. Our marriage is consanguineous — something we both know and have ignored, but clearly God has not looked on our match with favor. Better we part now than drag it like a corpse behind us for the rest of our lives."

"Is this what you and your uncle have been talking about at all hours of the night?" Louis demanded. "By Christ, you are unfaithful and unchaste."

"Then why keep me when I am so unsuitable?" she spat. "Why stay wed to a wife you neither trust nor desire? You would be free to beget a son on someone else if you set me aside. Your barons and clerics would no longer have cause to make their petty complaints about me. This is a practical time to agree an annulment. You can hand me into the keeping of my uncle and it will be an honorable exchange — the more so since his wife is your own second cousin." She saw the glint of uncertainty in his eyes and pressed home her point. "Do you really wish to continue with this travesty of a marriage? If so, you have given no sign of it since we set out from Saint-Denis."

He looked away. "I took a vow not to sully myself, you know that."

"*Sully?* Does that not say it all?" Her anger burned very close to white heat but somehow she held it down.

"I will have to consult with my advisers," he said.

"You mean seek their permission?" Alienor scoffed. "Do you have to do everything by order of Abbé Suger and that codless Templar? Does Thierry de Galeran rule your mind as well as your bedchamber? You say you are your own man? Well, prove it."

Louis gave her a look filled with distaste. "I am God's man first, and it is His will I do."

"Then ask Him."

"Let me be," Louis said through clenched teeth. "I will give you an answer when I am ready."

"Do as you will, but know this: I am not going with you. My choice is made and I am staying here in Antioch."

As she left the chamber, Thierry de Galeran was waiting to go in and from the look on his face had plainly been eavesdropping. He wore a soft silk robe embroidered with small silver crosses and over the top, incongruously, his scarred leather sword belt. Alienor gave him a glare filled with loathing. "It is for the best," she said. "Tell him that while you are both at your prayers."

Thierry returned her look before sweeping a supercilious bow and entering the chamber.

Slumped in his chair, Louis glanced up as Thierry closed the door. "You heard?" He pinched the bridge of his nose.

"Some of it, sire," Thierry said cautiously.

"She wants to dissolve the marriage on the grounds of consanguinity and stay here when we leave." Louis lowered his hand and looked up. "I am half inclined to grant her wish."

Thierry frowned and hitched his belt. "I advise you not to be hasty, sire. If you agree,

450

it will damage your prestige. People will say you cannot keep your wife and that another man has taken her away, albeit that the man is her uncle. It would mean that the men of Aquitaine would look to Antioch for leadership, not France. You are Aquitaine's overlord in law, but if the Queen repudiates you, your position will be difficult."

"She is a thorn in my side." Louis's expression contorted. "And all the more painful because I still remember the beauty of the rose."

"Many beautiful things are sent by the Devil to do us harm," Thierry said. "Look at the beauty of a viper's gleaming skin, but know that it has a deadly bite. And did not the serpent entice Eve into tasting the fruit of the tree of knowledge, and did she not then persuade Adam to eat of it?"

"I will write to Suger," Louis said with a sigh. "He will advise me, but you are right. In the meantime she should not remain in Antioch."

"I do not think you should bring your army into Antioch. Rather let them join us farther on."

Louis's gaze sharpened. "What are you saying?"

"Sire, I have heard disquieting rumors."

"What kind of rumors?"

Thierry screwed up his face as if he had been drinking vinegar. "I believe that the lord

451

of Antioch plots against you."

"Think or know?" Louis's breathing quickened and panic tightened his chest.

"I have seen the Prince trying to drive a wedge between our people. He speaks fair words in your brother's ear, and I believe he is plotting with the Queen too." Thierry's tone dripped with revulsion. "I suspect Raymond and the Queen have been inappropriate together. I have seen them sitting as close as lovers, alone without attendants when everyone else is asleep." His voice slurred a little on excess saliva. "I have seen them embracing. She has behaved inappropriately with other men too. Geoffrey de Rancon was in her chambers until long after midnight on the night before he left Antioch, and my spies report that they parted tenderly. It makes me wonder if what happened to the vanguard on Mount Cadmos was purely an accident."

Louis stared at him in horror. "By Christ and Saint Denis, are you sure of this?"

"Sire, I would not have spoken if I did not have grave doubts. I say we should leave Antioch the moment our army comes within reach and ride immediately for Jerusalem, bringing the Queen with us. With her at your side, her uncle will not dare to move against us, and where she goes, the men of Aquitaine will follow like drones."

Louis swallowed. "What do you advise?"

"That we make plans to leave by stealth the

moment we know our troops are close. We shall need to move swiftly and only tell the people we trust. Raymond cannot stop you riding away, nor can he prevent you from taking your own wife. You must remove her from his influence and keep her at your side where she will have no opportunity to plot and scheme."

Louis felt sick. He could not encompass the enormity of what he was being told. He did not want to believe it, and yet Thierry was his eyes and his ears and could nose out plots like a rat discovering a piece of rancid cheese. He had had a sense of danger for a long time now, and it did not surprise him, but he did feel very afraid.

"Let me deal with it, sire," Thierry said smoothly. "I shall make sure that the Queen is ready to leave when the moment comes."

Louis nodded, relief flowing through him. "You always know what to do for the best," he said.

31

Antioch, March 1148

The night was close and Alienor had told her women to leave the shutters open to encourage what little air there was to circulate. Somewhere in that vast, spangled darkness, Geoffrey was on the road. She remembered their conversation about the stars on the plains of Hungary and hoped he was making swift progress.

This morning she had visited the church of Saint Peter to offer up prayers and silver for his safety and that of their child. She was eager now for Louis to leave for Jerusalem so she could relax her guard and have peace. Under cover of the square of embroidery on which she was working, she gently cupped her womb and whispered words of love and comfort to the child.

"Did you speak, madam?" Gisela asked.

"Only to myself," Alienor said. Gisela had been acting strangely: jumping at the slightest thing, yet withdrawn and preoccupied at the same time. "You do not have to stay in Antioch with me," Alienor said. "I am not stopping you from leaving with the King."

"I know that, madam."

Alienor's voice sharpened with impatience. "Then what is wrong with you?"

"Nothing, madam, I am just tired." Gisela looked down at her own needlework and bit her lip. "I have had a headache all day. May I have your permission to go outside and take some air?"

"Yes, but do not be gone long. I am close to retiring."

Gisela rose to her feet, slipped on her cloak, and left the chamber.

Alienor turned to Marchisa. "Do you think she has a lover?"

The maid raised her eyebrows. "If she does, I do not know who it could be. The only young man I have seen her talking to is Thierry de Galeran's squire, and he is not the type to conduct a flirtation."

Alienor thought of the dour youth with his large Adam's apple and pockmarked face. "Spying then," she said, and her stomach sank. Could no one be trusted?

Marchisa shrugged. "It may well be, madam."

"Do you think she knows about the child?"

"She may suspect, but she has no proof."

Alienor bit her lip. She had been careful ever since she realized she was pregnant to show the evidence of her monthly fluxes, even if the rags had been stained with chicken blood smuggled into her chamber in vials by Marchisa.

Gisela returned looking flushed and sparkle-eyed. Alienor vacillated. Perhaps she did indeed have a lover. If she could conceal a pregnancy, then Gisela might be just as adept. Perhaps he was a non-Christian or a man of a lower rank and therefore the affair had to be clandestine. She resolved to get to the bottom of it tomorrow.

Alienor retired to her chamber with Marchisa and Mamile helping her to bed, while Gisela prepared the maids' room, dousing the lamps and tidying away the needlework. Marchisa took a comb to Alienor's hair, smoothing after each stroke with the palm of her hand, creating a wave of heavy, shining gold.

There was a sudden soft gasp from Gisela. Alienor looked up and froze as dark-clad figures entered her sleeping sanctum and then closed the doors between the rooms.

Soldiers! They wore swords, and she could see mail gleaming under their cloaks and surcoats. The acrid smell of their sweat pervaded the room. She could feel their eyes raking her figure and her unbound hair. From their midst, Thierry de Galeran stepped forward, his dark eyes filled with satisfied malice, and Alienor knew terror.

"What is this?" she demanded. "How dare you?"

"Madam, the King is leaving Antioch now and he desires you to join him. Come, we must go. It is of the utmost urgency."

"Let the King do as he wishes," she retorted. "I am staying in Antioch."

"Madam, that is not possible. The King has asked me to make provision for you now." He had a bundle over his left arm, which proved to be a man's cloak of heavy dark green wool, edged with sable.

"The King knows very well I am remaining here." She held herself rigid. The other men stared at her with hostile eyes, not one lowering his gaze in deference to her as a queen. There was no sympathy here, no way out. "Or have you come to kill me?" She realized as she spoke that her murder was a very real possibility. "Where is Saldebreuil?"

"Let us say he is indisposed," Thierry said and reached for her.

She batted him away. "Do not touch me!" she hissed, revolted at the very thought of his hands on her.

He seized her wrist and she bit him. Marchisa rushed to the attack, using the comb to rake Thierry's face. He hit her across the cheek and sent her staggering against a painted chest. Mamile began screaming and one of the other men seized her and set a hand across her mouth. "Silence, mistress," he growled, "or I shall squeeze the voice from your throat."

Alienor kicked Thierry in the shins and ran from him, but the doors were shut and she was cornered. Even so she turned to fight, grabbing a poker from beside the brazier and jabbing it at Thierry. He laughed, feinted, and seized her wrist, twisting it until she was forced to let go. She tried to drag his knife out of his belt, but he spun her around and bundled her in the cloak with aid from his henchmen, parceling her up and tying ropes around her until she was immobilized. Still she tried to fight. Her mind filled with visions of being thrown into the Orontes to drown, or being taken from here, stabbed, and left for the wolves and wild dogs to devour.

Thierry stood back panting, blood running down his face where the comb tines had raked him. "Hellcat." He wiped his cheek with the back of his hand. "Bitch." He gave her a nudge with his foot.

She glared venom. "I will have vengeance for this. I call upon my father's soul to witness what you do now and curse you forever! Let me go!" She struggled against her bonds.

"It is for the King to say what happens to you. I leave it to him to deal with the traitors and whores in his own household." Stooping, he tightened the binding again until Alienor struggled to breathe.

"There is only one whore in this room," she panted. "And he is standing before me."

De Galeran kicked her in the region of her belly. "The truth of that will out soon enough," he snarled.

She couldn't scream; she didn't have the breath. Her vision darkened and blurred, but she was dimly aware of the men seizing Mamile and Marchisa at sword point. De Galeran and another knight picked her up and carried her sideways as if she were a rolled-up carpet in a souk and bore her into the main room. Gisela stood ready, a cloak around her shoulders and a tied bundle of belongings in her hand. Her eyes were wide with fear, but there was a defensive jut to her chin, and Alienor knew that here was the traitor to match the whore.

After a brief, jolting journey and a clink of a money pouch, Alienor was dumped with unceremonious force onto stony ground. The heavy cloak cushioned some of her fall, but not the entirety. If before it had been an effort to breathe, now it was a supreme struggle. She was going to die, she was certain of it now, and the child with her. She was suffocating inside the cloak. There was liquid in her throat and she was gagging.

Thierry stooped and cut the bindings. Alienor sucked in lungfuls of air, gasping and retching. "You will die for this!" she choked.

"I doubt it," Thierry said. "But you might."

He seized her and with the help of another knight brought her over to a stamping, unsettled horse. One of the soldiers was already mounted and she was bundled up in front of him. When she began to scream, he clapped a hard, calloused hand across her mouth and under her nose, almost cutting off her breath.

"Any more, and it will be death for you."

She tried to bite him and he swore.

"Gag her," Thierry said and handed up a strip of bandage, which the soldier wadded and stuffed in Alienor's mouth. "Blindfold her too. The fewer senses the bitch has, the better."

She struggled and fought, but the men were stronger and in a vicious mood. "Hah!" said the soldier and dug in his heels, and the horse sprang forward. She was astride the saddle and there was a terrible feeling in her stomach, as if her muscles were being stretched until they tore. She was jolted and bumped. The wind stung her eyes. She was helpless and terrified, certain they were taking her somewhere isolated in order to kill her and dispose of her body.

It seemed to her that they rode for several hours. The horse's rapid jog trot slowed to a walk, then a plod. Eventually, she smelled smoke and heard the sound of voices and her captor drew rein. She felt him dismount, and then he pulled her down off the horse and threw her to the ground. Alienor could not prevent the whimper that rose from her throat. "Don't go anywhere," he said. She sensed him walking away from her and she heard him greeting the men at the fire, followed by the slosh of liquid into a cup.

"Perhaps it would be better if she did not live," she heard someone say. "Better dead than the scandal this will bring on us all."

"It is the King's decision," another voice said sharply. "We should wait until he arrives."

"I do not see why. We can say it was an accident. He is better rid of her, and Christ alone knows what she was plotting with that uncle of hers — if plotting was all she was doing."

Alienor's teeth would have chattered with terror if she had been able to close her mouth around the gag. Would they dare murder her here and now without giving her the grace of confession and shriving? She forced herself to lie quiescent while she strained her ears. She would play dead, and if given the slightest opportunity, she would escape.

Eventually the discussion between the men ended as the decision was taken to leave her fate in the hands of the King. She felt footsteps approaching and her nostrils drew in the scent of some kind of hot stew with onions and garlic.

"Here," said a gruff voice. "If I untie you,

do you want something to eat?"

Alienor heaved up and lunged toward him and heard him curse as the hot stew splattered over his hands. He swore at her, and she heard the laughter of the other men from around their fire.

"Leave her!" one of them shouted. "What do you expect if you try kindness on a she devil?"

Alienor slumped, tears wetting the blindfold.

Moments later she heard more hoofbeats and the sound of troops dismounting. Then Louis's voice demanding to know what was happening.

"The Queen is here, sire," Thierry said. "We had to bind her because she refused to come of her own accord. We also thought it best to disguise and conceal her."

"Let me see her," Louis demanded.

Aware of an approaching footfall, Alienor writhed and thrashed.

"We would have fed her, sire, but she spilled the food all over Simon when he offered it to her."

Alienor felt fingers on her face and struggled frantically.

"See," said Thierry. "She is possessed, sire."

"Be silent," Louis commanded. "Did I order you to do this? I think not."

The fingers worked at the knot on the blindfold and pulled it away. The gag came out next and Alienor coughed and drew in enormous breaths of unrestricted air.

"Dear God," said Louis. "Dear God!" He turned to Thierry. "I did not order this. Give me your knife."

Stony-faced, Thierry drew his long dagger from its sheath and handed it to Louis.

With jerky movements, Louis cut the bindings around the cloak and set Alienor free. She fell forward into his arms and immediately recoiled.

"I never meant them to do this to you." Louis's expression filled with shock. "I wanted you to come with me, and we had to leave by stealth at night. I would never condone this — never!" He looked over his shoulder at the now tense and worried knights who had kidnapped her. "You have overstepped your bounds." He glared at Thierry. "Is there no maid to assist the Queen? Where are her women?"

Thierry made a terse gesture and Gisela was brought forward from the other side of the campfire. Tears streaked the young woman's face and she hung back. "I am so sorry!" she sobbed.

"Attend your mistress," Louis said.

Alienor raised her head. "I want Marchisa," she said with a last vestige of strength. "I will not have this one attend me ever again!"

Louis flicked his fingers and Gisela was led away, weeping bitterly. Marchisa stepped forward, her own face bruised, one eye swelling shut.

"You beat her maids too?" Louis was shocked.

Thierry touched the comb rakes on his cheek. "That one is as wild as her mistress," he said.

Marchisa shot him a glare. "I would have cut out your black heart if I could," she spat and knelt over Alienor. "Madam, it is all right, I am here now. I am here."

Alienor clung to Marchisa. Now that the immediate danger had passed, she was numb. Marchisa propped her against a pile of saddle blankets and clothing packs and brought her a cup of wine.

Alienor bowed her head. "He will pay for this, I swear," she said. "I shall still have my annulment." She closed her eyes. She was too tired and damaged to think. To feel only filled her with bleak despair. But come the morning she would set about planning her return to Antioch.

She was shaken out of the blackness of deep sleep to a sky that had the milky appearance of predawn but was still scattered with stars. The men were mounting their horses. Her bruises had stiffened and the pain made her gasp as she tried to move. "I cannot ride," she whispered as the previous day's horse was brought to her. "It is impossible."

Louis came over to her and studied her with hard eyes. "You should not have resisted Thierry when he came to fetch you," he said. "It is your own fault that this has happened. Some might say you deserve it; nevertheless, I have chastised him for his conduct."

"I will not speak with you." She turned her head away. "It was my right to remain in Antioch."

A look of revulsion crossed Louis's face. "Antioch is a den of iniquity. Do you know what people are saying about you? Do you know how much you have sullied your name — and mine into the bargain? Do you care that you have made France a laughingstock?"

She closed her eyes, refusing to engage. It was all as nothing.

Louis exhaled hard. "I need us united. How can I lead an army if you are in Antioch encouraging rebellion against me and fomenting discord? You shall come to the Holy Sepulchre and you shall be washed clean. Make no mistake, you will never return to Antioch. Do you hear me? Never!"

The French army, reunited, made its way toward Jerusalem. They were traveling in the Christian states now and the way was easier, but the days were hot with encroaching summer and the spring campaigning season had been lost. Louis paused to worship at shrines along the way as they covered the two hundred miles between Antioch and Jerusalem. There was no word from Antioch, but the silence itself burned like the tips of the soldiers' spears in the baking summer heat and Louis was constantly looking over his shoulder.

Alienor traveled in a litter, enclosed and unseen. It suited Louis because she was with him but out of sight and Alienor did not complain because it fell in with her own needs. She did not have to interact with anyone except when they made camp or she required the necessary screens for her ablutions. She could be alone with her thoughts while her body recuperated. Louis had not been near her since that night. She knew she was being closely watched lest she try to turn back for Antioch, but with each mile that passed, it became less and less possible.

Seven days into their journey, Alienor woke in the night certain that something was wrong. She had been dreaming of a baby, its downy golden head nuzzling at her breast, but when she looked down into its tiny face, it began to change, its rosy color becoming ashen and its eyes turning as dull and dusty as wayside stones. It flopped in her arms, lifeless, and as she clutched it to her, it crumbled to dust. She sat up gasping and pressed her hands to her belly. It felt heavy and solid under her touch, like a stone. There was no feeling, no flutter of soft limbs against the wall of her womb. She tried to go back to sleep but eventually gave up and went to sit by the embers of the fire until it was time to move on.

Louis wanted to visit the holy sites of the Lebanon, including the place where Saint Peter had been given the keys to the Kingdom of Heaven. The land was fresh and green, known as the "valley of springs," and there was some respite from the burning heat. Alienor tried to drink of the tranquility and absorb some peace into her soul for the sake of herself and the child. Louis's mood was bright, but then he enjoyed being royalty on the road when all he had to do was parade and be gracious. She had watched him from a distance, effusing to the men and smiling broadly, even at Thierry de Galeran, whom he seemed to have forgiven in short order. All was well in his world. Raymond of Antioch had been outwitted and Alienor was contained in her curtained litter where she belonged and could do no harm.

As the day's journey progressed, Alienor began to feel unwell. The jolting of the litter was like being on a boat on a rough sea and there was a band of pain across her belly. At first it resembled the niggling ache that came with her monthly fluxes, but gradually it intensified to the surging pains of true labor. "No," she gasped. "No, it is too soon!" Her waters broke on a sudden gush, and they were streaked with blood and a greenish-black substance. She pulled back the curtain and leaned out to scream for Marchisa who was riding on a mule at the side of the litter.

"Madam?" Marchisa bade the men halt the litter and peered in at Alienor. "Holy Mary," she breathed and for a moment even her aplomb was shaken.

"No one must know," Alienor gasped. "At whatever cost."

Marchisa shook her head. "You cannot continue, madam," she said. "We have to find you shelter." She looked around. There was a shepherd's hut a little off the track. It was no more than a crude stone shelter, but there was nothing else; Louis's pilgrim site was much farther on.

"The Queen is unwell," Marchisa said to the litter-bearers. "Take her to that hut and I will tend her there."

"But we cannot leave the line, mistress," one of them said.

"If you do not, she will die," Marchisa said fiercely. "And you will be to blame. Do as I say."

"But the King —"

"I will deal with the King." Marchisa drew herself up. "My lady's ailment is a recurrence of the sickness and flux she suffered in Hungary and worsened by the treatment she received when she was forced to leave Antioch."

Having prevailed on the men to bear the litter to the hut, Marchisa sent a squire to Louis with the same story she had given the litter-bearers and had Mamile brought to the hut too. "As you are loyal to my lady, say nothing of this," she whispered fiercely to her. "If anyone asks, the Queen has the bloody flux."

Mamile looked at her in fear mingled with angry indignation. "I know full well what ails her," she said. "But I am not Gisela and my loyalty is staunch."

Together they helped Alienor into the hut. The litter-bearers, having heard the word "flux," were keen to keep their distance and Marchisa encouraged them to do so. A messenger arrived from Louis saying he would continue to the pilgrim site and that Alienor should rest where she was until she was strong enough to rejoin the main troop. However, he would leave guards to protect her, who would camp beside the hut. The messenger insisted on seeing Alienor to make sure she truly was ill and not just pretending in a ploy to make an escape back to Antioch.

He took a single glance at Alienor writhing in the straw on the floor of the hut and made a swift exit.

A fresh spring bubbled beside the hut and Marchisa filled a bucket with fresh, cold water. She lit a fire in the small stone hearth. There was dung for fuel and she had a sack of charcoal among her supplies. She stuffed a linen palliasse with some of the straw to make Alienor a bed and, once the fire was established, brewed her a tisane that would take away the edge of the pain, although she knew she could not dull what was to come. The blood in the waters and the green smears of the unborn infant's feces told their own story of impending tragedy. She suspected that the blows Thierry de Galeran had inflicted on Alienor as they left Antioch had been deliberate in more ways than one.

Alienor opened her eyes and stared at smoke-darkened rafters. There was a burning pain in her belly and between her thighs, constant and duller now, rather than cresting surges. Her throat was raw, as if she had inhaled too much smoke, or screamed until her voice was ragged. She put her hand down to her belly and it was flaccid. Her breasts were tight and someone had bound them with linen cloths. There were pads between her thighs too. She felt weak and wrung out.

"Madam?" Marchisa leaned over her and pressed a hand to her forehead. "Ah, the fever has dropped at last," she said. "You have been very ill. Here, you must drink more of this."

Alienor sipped the cool, bitter brew from the cup that Marchisa pressed to her lips. "My child," she said. "Where is my child? He will need feeding." She looked around the hut. A linen curtain hung across the doorway, screening the outside but letting in weak light. A thread of blue smoke twirled from the hearth. Mamile was stirring some sort of stew in a pot, but she looked across at Alienor and then swiftly away. "What have you done with him? Show him to me!"

Marchisa bit her lip. "Madam . . . he . . . was born dead. That was why you went into travail early — because he had died. I am so sorry."

"I do not believe you!" Alienor could feel panic and grief gathering like a surge behind a crumbling wall. "Show me."

"Madam . . ."

"Show me! If there is a body, I will see it and know all there is!"

Marchisa turned to a basket covered with a linen cloth on top of which she had laid the cross on its chain from around her own neck. "I was going to bury him at sunrise," she said. "Truly, madam, I am not sure you should look."

"I must."

Marchisa drew back the cloth and Alienor gazed on what lay within the basket. She let out a single wail and then absorbed the grief, curling over, clutching it to her in lieu of a living, breathing infant. Even as the child had died, so now too did a fragile part of her hopes and dreams. She rocked back and forth, nursing her pain. "I do not care what happens to me," she said. "Let me die. This is no holy land; this is my hell."

32

Jerusalem, September 1148
A ceramic platter of the dainty almond and rosewater confections the Arabs called *faludhaj* stood on the inlaid table between Alienor and Melisande, Queen Mother and coruler of the Kingdom of Jerusalem. Melisande bit into one with pleasure. "Too many give you the toothache and gripes," she said ruefully, "but they are delicious." She had a golden complexion and sparkling dark brown eyes that, while full of humor, were shrewd and knowing. "These are women's dainties. Men devour them in one bite, and never discover the joy of true appreciation, but even so, they are a useful lure, I find."

"Is that not typical of all male behavior?" Alienor smiled and took one herself, playing the role of the gracious French queen. It had been her anchor in the terrible months since the birth of her stillborn son in the Lebanon and the only way out of the darkness that had threatened to engulf her. She dared not lower her guard for the pain was too great when she did, and her nights were disturbed by vivid, terrifying dreams. Nevertheless, she was living through each day, surviving the nights, and time by infinitesimal increments was thickening the scab over the wound. Saldebreuil had rejoined her in Jerusalem a fortnight ago, still weak from his beating at the hands of Thierry de Galeran and his henchmen, but able to resume his duties, and that at least had comforted her a little, because she had thought him dead.

She and Melisande were sitting on a flat rooftop of the palace of Jerusalem, protected from the sun by an open tent with gauze linen curtains blowing in the breeze. The women wore comfortable loose silk robes and turbans in the way of the Jerusalem Franks and were enjoying each other's company while they rested during the hottest part of the day.

Melisande laughed. "I fear you are right on the whole, although sometimes there are men who are different, and we should treasure them."

Alienor looked out across the blue sky and the heat haze rippling from the ancient golden stones. "Yes," she said softly. "But so often we do not get to keep them, do we?"

She was aware of Melisande's thoughtful scrutiny, but it did not disturb her. Melisande's blood carried the right to the throne of Jerusalem, but her husband Fulke in his lifetime had tried to seize power from her and she had had to fight for every shred of authority she possessed. She had also been accused of conducting an affair with Hugh le Puiset, lord of Jaffa, one of her closest courtiers, but she had brazened out the storm and emerged from the scandal with her strength intact.

"No, we do not," Melisande said. "It is a sad fact of life." She gave Alienor a look that was both piercing and gentle. "You can tell me what you will and it will go no further. I know enough of you and your situation to listen and understand. See me as a point of respite on your journey from which you will move on in good time."

Alienor was silent for a moment, then she drew a deep breath and said, "I asked Louis for an annulment. Our marriage is consanguineous . . ."

"As are many," Melisande replied to the point. "Most people are related to their spouse in some degree or other, but it does not lead them to annulment unless they choose." She tilted her head to one side. "You say you asked Louis — not the other way around? Why is that?"

"Because . . ." Alienor looked away, her throat tightening and tears pricking her eyes. "Because it was a mistake from the beginning. I love my father and honor his memory. I know he did what he thought was the best for me, but it wasn't. Louis is . . ." Her mind filled with words she could not bring herself to utter. "Neither of us has fulfilled the other's expectations. I am Duchess of Aquitaine and Queen of France, but it means nothing. I desire only to be rid of him and have this marriage dissolved. I want my own power and the wherewithal to make my own decisions. I have been forced to take roads I would never have set foot upon without being coerced." She looked at Melisande, who was watching her intently. "Louis is weak and foolish. He takes bad counsel from those around him and will not listen to sense. I do not wish to be at the beck and call of a dolt and his minions for the rest of my life."

"Ah," said Melisande. She clapped her hands and a servant appeared to refresh their cups with wine that had been cooling in a cistern. "I well understand that. It is difficult when men prefer to take the advice of other men and make unwise choices. That decision to attack Damascus was a case in point."

Alienor grimaced. "Indeed," she said. "How different things might have been if they had made Aleppo their objective." She had still been recovering from the stillbirth of her son when she had arrived in Jerusalem. No one knew of it even now save for Marchisa and Mamile. There were scurrilous rumors doing the rounds of the barons and clerics, but those rumors concerned impropriety between herself and her uncle and were being spread by the likes of Thierry de Galeran in an attempt to blacken Raymond's name and turn against him men who might otherwise have listened to his pleas to strike at Aleppo. A council had been held at Acre and Melisande had been present in her capacity as coruler of the Kingdom of Jerusalem. Alienor had been excluded by Louis and had been too unwell and powerless to protest the exclusion anyway. Melisande had tried to persuade the other attendees that it would be more to their advantage to ride on Aleppo, but she had been overridden. Damascus was a far more tempting prospect to all in the short term, rather than looking to any longer gain. Raymond had refused to come to Acre to argue his point, declaring that there was too much treachery abounding for him to consider risking his life for what was obviously a foregone conclusion.

The army of Jerusalem, bolstered by the French, had assaulted Damascus and been routed, the campaign a disaster. Louis's reputation had suffered another setback as all the impetus and opportunity to improve the security of the Christian kingdom had been squandered. Louis had now firmly exchanged the mail shirt of a soldier for the robes of a pilgrim. He said it was a precious thing to breathe the same air that the Savior had done, walk in the same dust, touch the same temple walls. So it was, and Alienor had visited many of the places herself and been humbled and moved, but pilgrimage had become Louis's obsession and bolt-hole from reality. He was currently absent on an expedition to Lake Galilee where he intended collecting vials of the precious water on which Jesus had walked and where he had declared he would make his disciples "fishers of men."

Melisande gave a flick of her wrist. "Indeed," she said. "Beware all men. I grew to be fond of the husband I was forced to wed, but in our early years, he did his utmost to lock me out of power even though I was his key. It took him a while to learn the ways of this land, and just as we came to an understanding, the fool fell from his horse and broke his skull." Her eyes filled with pain, and then she shook herself and reached for her wine. "What did Louis say? Has he agreed to give you an annulment?"

"He would if left to decide on his own, but others have advised him against it," Alienor said. "He does not want me because he says I am sullied and I do not obey God as I should, and therefore God declines to bless us with an heir — although if Louis will not lie with me how can he beget that heir? But he knows if he does agree to an annulment, he loses Aquitaine and he loses face. Men will call him a failure on all fronts." She gave a sour smile. "He cannot live with me, he cannot live without me, and so he hides on his little peregrinations, where he can be the King of France with all the dignity and none of the problems. He can fulfill his spiritual needs and forget he has a wife at all. It is an annulment of sorts, just not official." Her expression hardened. "We shall be visiting Rome on our way back to Paris, and when we do, I hope for a positive outcome."

Melisande looked troubled. "You are set on this?"

"I already have deputations at Rome working on my behalf."

"What will you do if your annulment is granted?" The Queen of Jerusalem shook her head. "You will be an irresistible marriage prize to someone. You will be immensely wealthy and still with many years of child-bearing ahead of you. What ambitious noble would not snap you up and devour you?"

"I have loyal protectors," Alienor replied with bravado. "I shall do what I must."

"Then I wish you well. The world is a murky place, as well you know, and it is wise to look ahead and to plan for more than one situation."

"I have always tried to do so," Alienor replied. "I was taken by surprise in Antioch. I underestimated my enemy and it was my downfall."

Melisande gave her a sidelong glance. "You must be aware of the rumors about you and your uncle in Antioch. I do not for one moment believe them, because I know what it is to have defamatory tales spread about your moral reputation by those intent on bringing you down, but the smear remains."

"Yes, I have heard the gossip," Alienor said with stiff composure and drew back a little, because Melisande was touching on ground that was still too raw to bear a footfall.

"You should bear a son and become a widow," Melisande said. "That is the best power you will ever have as a woman, believe me — unless you become a nun of your own volition. And even then, sons grow up and demand power in their own right. They will fight you for it, even as a husband will take it from you. That is the way of the world."

"What comfort am I supposed to take from that?" Alienor asked, her throat tight with suppressed emotion.

"I was not offering you comfort," Melisande replied coolly, "but if you are going to plan ahead, you should take these things into account so that you may deal with them should they arise."

"My heir is a daughter," Alienor said. *My sons have died.*

"As I was to my father, and as you were to yours." Melisande leaned forward in emphasis. "You are still young enough to have a different life."

Alienor took a drink of wine and steadied

herself. "I intend to," she said.

Louis celebrated the Nativity in Bethlehem under a cold star-glittered sky, kneeling at the shrine covering the site of the stable where the Christ child had been born. Tears of exalted rapture streamed down his face. Alienor celebrated at his side, although it was almost more than she could bear, this joy for the birth of a holy infant, when her own son lay in an unmarked grave, never to be acknowledged except by her. She was tired of being a guest of the Kingdom of Jerusalem. Much as she enjoyed Melisande's company, she was ready to leave. All the commands, all the arrangement, all the government was by another's will and it was not her home. Louis remained obsessed with his pilgrimages. Like a little child craving sweets, he was greedy for more even though he had had a surfeit.

The French army had broken up in September and the troops had begun wending their way home. Louis's brother Robert had set out with most of the French contingent, leaving a nucleus of soldiers and servants — enough for an entourage, but not an army. Louis said he would follow shortly, but the intent went no further than words and was soon forgotten.

Alienor paced her chambers in Jerusalem like a prisoner, albeit she had every comfort. She went to the souks and the bathhouses.

She attended the local shrines; she prayed at the sepulcher. She read, embroidered, played chess, wrote numerous letters and marked time. Still Louis made no effort to return home. There were more shrines and holy places to see and others to revisit to fix them in his mind. While he was thus occupied he did not have to think about what was waiting for him: the hardships of governance and the decisions about the future. He hid himself amid the glories of God and made them his only reality.

Suger sent letters urgently requesting Louis's return, and Louis cast them to one side after barely scanning the contents. Alienor had received letters too, from her nobles and clerics, and although Suger had not written to her, she knew full well what was happening.

"Suger is losing control," she said, pinning Louis down to a conversation before he could disappear on yet another excursion. "There is no reason for us to stay here. You have seen every site of importance and numerous others more obscure. France will descend into chaos if you do not return, and Aquitaine too."

"You exaggerate," he growled with a dark look. "Suger is an old woman; he fusses too much, but he is still capable of holding it all together."

"No," Alienor said. "Suger is an old man

beginning to fail. It is your duty to rule France, not his. And I have a duty to my people in Aquitaine — how can I fulfill that duty while I am here? How much longer can we govern from a distance, Louis? Your brother is threatening to seize the regency from Suger and your mother is egging him on. Raoul de Vermandois sits on the fence. Even if we set out today, by the time we arrive in Paris, we will have been gone for three years. And we won't set out today, or tomorrow, or the next day, or even next week, and all the time your rule at home falls into chaos. How long since Suger wrote to you?"

"Do not badger me," Louis snapped. "There is time enough, and Christ must come first."

"Then in all that time enough, tell me when shall we leave? At least I can begin to make preparations."

"Easter," he said. "I shall celebrate Easter in Jerusalem, and then I shall see about departing."

"That is more than two months away."

"Then it gives you time to prepare," he said coldly. "I refuse to go until then. I worshipped in Bethlehem at His Nativity. Now I shall celebrate His death and resurrection in the time and place where it happened."

He had the stubborn glint in his eye that told her she would get nowhere by arguing. "When we reach Rome, I shall still have my annulment," she said.

Louis shrugged. "If the Pope agrees, then let it be done." His tone was indifferent, but there was tension in his jaw. She knew Suger kept advising him not to agree to an annulment. People would say that a man who could not keep his wife or beget heirs was a poor warrior and a weak excuse for a king, and when a king was not virile and in command, then the country suffered. To her advantage was the fact that Louis was ambivalent about Suger's advice. An annulment would mean a fresh start, and to offset the loss of Aquitaine, Louis could find a new queen with a good dowry and whatever affinity she brought to the match.

When he had gone, Alienor called for parchment and quills and wrote to Geoffrey de Rancon. It took several months for correspondence to reach Aquitaine and the same the other way, and she had to be certain there was nothing within her letters to give her away. It was the same with him. He wrote her reports that on the surface were no more than the words of a loyal vassal discussing business with his liege lady, but they were both adept at reading between the lines.

She had told him of the loss of the child and he had grieved. He was doing his best to hold Aquitaine steady during her absence but was finding Suger and the meddling French a trial. He thought of her often and prayed for her return and a positive outcome in Rome. He had accompanied his most recent letter with a brooch bearing the symbol of an eagle enameled in jewel colors with its wings outspread. She wore it every day and she touched it now before dipping her quill in the ram's horn of dark ink and writing that she would be home by the time the next harvest filled the barns, and that, God willing, she would be free.

33

The Mediterranean Sea, May 1149

Alienor gazed at the sun sparkle on the sea as the Sicilian galley plowed white furrows through the deep sapphire water. A stiff breeze filled the sails and they were making swift headway toward their intended destination of Calabria. The cook was frying freshly caught sardines on deck and preparing to serve them with hot flat bread flavored with garlic and thyme.

By narrowing her eyes, Alienor could make out the other vessels in the French fleet. Louis's ship was naturally the largest and flew a blue-and-gold fleur-de-lis pennant from the top of the mast. Her own vessel, bearing both the fleur-de-lis and the eagle of Aquitaine, was smaller but she was glad not to be sailing with Louis. Being in his company was like having a stone in her shoe.

They had been at sea for four days and it would be another fortnight before they reached Calabria, ruled by their ally King

Roger of Sicily. And then from Calabria to Rome and the blessed relief of annulment.

The cook slid the sardines onto a platter and added a sprinkle of herbs. A squire presented the dish to Alienor and she had just taken the first, delicious bite when they heard a shout from one of the other vessels and horns sounding across the water.

She hastily chewed and swallowed. "What is it?"

The crew began shouting to each other and hastened to trim the sails, seeking to gain more speed. The cook took a jug of water and doused his fire. "Greeks, madam," he said tersely.

Filled with alarm, Alienor set her food aside. The Greeks were at war with the Sicilians, and since Louis had declared himself Sicily's ally and their ships belonged to King Roger, they were open targets. Emperor Manuel Komnenos had promised a reward should any captain take the King and Queen of France hostage and bring them to him in Constantinople.

Alienor stepped aside as the crew hauled on the sail. They were on the outer edge of the convoy and, despite the efforts of the sailors, they were being left behind except for one other vessel. The others, rather than turning to fight, were breaking out the oars and running for all they were worth.

Tight-lipped she watched the enemy bearing down on them. The newcomers had more oars and were closing the gap so swiftly that there was nothing to be done. The Greek ships shone with bronze cladding at their prows, formed into the shape of elongated animal snouts. When primed, the tube at the end of the snout would blaze out deadly Greek fire.

"I would rather throw myself overboard than go back to Constantinople," Alienor said to Saldebreuil, who was standing beside her, his hand on his sword hilt.

"Madam, it will not come to that. Help will come."

"It had better." Briefly she put her face in her hands. Once again she was powerless because she could do nothing to avert what was happening.

The Greeks soon overhauled their smaller galley, forcing them to surrender. The Greek shipmaster was delighted at his prize and although he treated Alienor with deference, she could sense his smug satisfaction as he "welcomed" them aboard his own vessel.

"The King of France will make you pay for this," she said. She felt like a hissing cat cornered by a large dog.

He was highly amused when her words were translated to him. "Oh no," he said with a grin. "He will pay me!" And patted the coin pouch at his hip to make his meaning clear.

Alienor retired to the deck shelter provided

for their use. Some of the crew from her galley were taken prisoner and locked in irons. Others were left on board their own ship with the mast removed and all oars but six thrown overboard. Saldebreuil's sword was confiscated; however, he had managed to conceal a short dagger down the side of his boot.

Alienor's possessions were treated as booty by the Greek captain. A beautiful ivory-cased mirror and comb that Melisande had given her disappeared into his baggage, as did a crimson silk dalmatic embroidered with golden eagles.

"Sons of whores," Saldebreuil muttered. "I will slit their throats while they are sleeping."

"You will do no such thing!" Alienor hissed. "You would be caught and we would all suffer. I cannot afford to lose you on top of everything else. Mark who takes what so we can retrieve it later."

"I will geld the one who has my sword," Saldebreuil said, his dark eyes gleaming.

They were sitting in a morose huddle when another shout went up and suddenly the Greeks were hoisting sails and running to their oar benches. The ship shuddered as the rowers began to pull, propelling her forward in long sweeps, gaining momentum with each surge. Alienor stood up and shaded her eyes. They were being pursued and even as the Greeks had caught her galley with ease, so they in their turn were being overhauled.

Saldebreuil stood up beside her. "Well, here's an interesting pass," he said. "The big fish swallows the little fish, and then the whales swallow all."

She looked up at him. "Do we want to be swallowed by a whale?"

"Yes if it's a Sicilian one." He narrowed his gaze and said softly, "Twenty biremes of a hundred oars apiece, and they'll be carrying Greek fire. This ship only has sixty oars and the men have already fought once today. They'll be on us before sunset."

The Greek captain had Alienor's knights put in fetters and chained to the sides of the ship and set a soldier to guard their group. "What a unique experience to tell my grand-children, should I live long enough to beget their father," Saldebreuil said, rattling his iron bracelet. "Does it become me, madam?"

"Be quiet, you fool," she snapped.

"It doesn't then." His smile flashed. "I must needs be rid of this jewelry swiftly in that case."

Alienor met his gaze and then glanced the slight bulge at the top of his boot.

The Sicilian biremes caught the Greek ships as the sun began to sink toward the horizon. An evening wind had gotten up, making the waters choppy, and clouds were chasing in from behind their pursuers, threatening a summer storm. Their ship, unable to outrun her pursuers, turned to fight. Alienor pressed her lips together as the Greek galley wallowed on the water. The crew at the bow was preparing the Greek fire to spew out of the bronze snout at their enemy and Alienor inhaled an alien smell: oily, greasy, chest-squeezing.

The two groups of ships closed on each other and spouts of flame roared from the brass tubes. Amid a chaos of bellowed orders, ships tacked frantically to avoid being hosed by deadly fountains of fire. Sails turned to blazing rags of red and gold, matching the sky. Men became living torches and leaped into the sea, where still they burned as the unquenchable Greek fire spread over the water like a fallen sunset.

Grapnel ropes clawed the wale of their ship and the crew sped to repel boarders with swords, clubs, and axes. Saldebreuil delved into his boot, seized the knife, and, in a swift motion, plunged it into the thigh of the soldier watching over them. As the man screamed and fell, Saldebreuil dragged him down, withdrew the knife, and finished him. Then he used the man's ax to strike through the fetter chain and stood in front of Alienor to defend her, although in the event it proved unnecessary. The battle between the Greeks and the Sicilians was bloody and brutal, but over swiftly.

Once more Alienor changed ships as the remnants of the Greek flotilla were either scuppered or taken into Sicilian hands. All that remained of the light was a dull red streak on the horizon, and numerous small fires on the water like fallen stars, illuminating bodies and flotsam.

The Sicilian captain, a solidly built olive-skinned man of middle years, escorted Alienor and her entourage to the deck shelter at the stern of the boat with deference. "We have been chasing these wolves for several days, madam," he said, "and looking out for your fleet."

"A pity you did not find us a few hours earlier," Alienor replied, "but I thank you nonetheless." She saw him looking expectantly at the items of baggage his men had transferred from the Greek ship. "Of course you must be rewarded." It was better to give them something than have her possessions rifled through yet again, and better too to keep the crew on good terms. But they were all pirates of one kind or another, and she still felt as if she had been captured all over again.

The captain bowed to her with a flourish. "Madam, to serve the Queen of France is enough, but I accept your generous offer."

Alienor raised her brows. She had not said she was going to be generous.

It was full dark by now and the increasing wind caused the ship to buck like a frisky horse. She heard the sailors shouting to each other as they secured the vessel against the worsening weather and she swallowed a laugh. To have gone through all this only to succumb to a storm at sea would be the greatest irony.

Louis stood on the headland looking out to sea on a calm glittering day in late spring. The Sicilian sun was hot on the back of his neck, and the breeze was pungent with the smell of thyme and salt. "I do not know if she is alive or dead," he said to Thierry de Galeran. "No word comes, and it has been many weeks. If she had been captured by the Greeks, then I would have heard by now. They would have sent me gloating letters." He bit his thumbnail, which was already down to the quick.

"Then that is obviously not her fate, sire," said de Galeran.

Louis grimaced. "I dreamed last night that she came to me in drowned robes, all glistening with weed, and she accused me of her murder."

Thierry curled his lips. "It was but a nightmare, sire. You should pray to God for succor and peace."

"I should have turned back for her when the Greeks attacked."

"Would she have turned back for you?" Thierry asked.

"That is not the point," Louis said impatiently. "As we stand now, we do not know her fate. If I truly knew that dream was a portent and she is dead and drowned, I could mourn her and remarry the moment I return to France and govern Aquitaine on behalf of our daughter. Instead there is silence, and what do I do about that? How much longer do I wait?"

The Templar laid his hand on Louis's shoulder, his gesture sympathetic, intimate, and controlling. "You should make arrangements to leave and if the Queen has not returned by the time you are prepared, then you must consider her lost."

Louis pressed his lips together. Although at times he hated her, there were moments when his feelings from the early days broke through to trouble him. He needed to sever the ties, but when it came to the cut, he could not do it. And if that cut was to be her death at sea, he would bear the guilt to his own grave, no matter what Thierry said.

Alienor opened her eyes to a room glowing with rich and subtle color. The bed was solid and firm. It didn't sway with the waves; there was no roar of water against the hull, no flap of sail or rub of oars in their ports. Instead there was birdsong, the hushed murmur of servants and peace. Facing her bed was a mural of spotted leopards wearing superior expressions, their perambulations interspersed by date palms and bushy orange trees.

Slowly she remembered that she was safe in the Sicilian port of Palermo having finally made landfall last night. Severe weather had blown the bireme off course. Having survived two storms that had hurled them far to the south, they had repaired their damage at Malta and sailed for Sicily, only to be battered by another storm and involved in more skirmishing with the Greeks. By the time the ship dropped anchor in Palermo, Alienor had been at sea for more than a month.

The whisper of servants grew louder. The door opened and Marchisa tiptoed in, bearing a tray laden with bread, honey, and wine. Alienor was not hungry. Indeed, she felt wretched. The period at sea had been a holding point, a time in limbo when she had not had to respond to anything but the simplest of needs. Now she had to take up the reins again, and it was an effort to do so.

She forced herself to eat and drink, and then donned the loose silk robe that was brought for her to wear. Palermo was the dominion of Roger of Sicily, one of the most powerful monarchs in the Christian world. Roger himself was elsewhere in his kingdom, but his son William welcomed her: a handsome, dark-eyed youth of eighteen, who showed her around the palaces and gardens with pride and courtesy.

The latter were drenched with the intense perfume of the roses that blossomed everywhere, deep crimson, their stamens tipped with powdered gold. Peacocks trailed the paths, their tails like iridescent brooms, their breasts sequined with sea colors. Butterflies, dark and soft as purple shadows, lit among the blooms.

"I will have our gardeners give you some roses to take back to France," William offered gallantly. "Have you seen these with cream stripes?"

Alienor found a smile for him, although it was difficult. While she appreciated the wonders, her feelings had become disconnected and she had seen so much that was similar, that it all seemed the same. "That is kind of you," she said. "They will look well in the garden at Poitiers."

A servant was waiting for them as they reached the garden entrance and immediately knelt to her and the young Prince. "Sire, there is news from your father, difficult news." The servant's gaze flickered to Alienor as he presented a scroll to his lord.

William broke the seal, read what was written, and turned to Alienor. "Madam, perhaps you should sit down," he said, gesturing to a carved bench near the wall.

She stared at him. Dear God, Louis was dead, she thought. She did as he suggested. Roses overhung the seat, heavy and red, their perfume filling each breath she took.

A frown clouded William's smooth brow. "Madam," he said gently, "I grieve to tell you that Raymond, Prince of Antioch, has been killed in battle against the Saracens."

Alienor continued to stare at him. The smell of the roses intensified and the air grew so thick that she could barely breathe, and what air she did inhale was drenched with the syrupy sweet scent of flowers on the edge of corruption.

"Madam?"

She felt his hand on her shoulder, but it was a flimsy anchor. "How did he die?" she asked in a constricted voice.

"It was honorably, madam. His men were camping in the open; they were surrounded by Saracens and attacked. Your uncle could have fled and saved his life, but he chose to remain with his men."

Alienor swallowed. There was bile in her throat. Her uncle was not a fool in matters of warfare; there was more to it than that: either he had been betrayed by his supposed allies — which was commonplace enough — or perhaps he no longer wanted to live as a wounded lion beset on all sides. Better a swift death than lingering in a net being drawn ever tighter. The latter thought was so painful that she doubled over, clutching her midriff.

Alarmed, the young man called for her women, but when they arrived Alienor fended them off. "I will never forgive him," she said vehemently to Marchisa, "never as long as I live."

"Forgive who, madam?"

"Louis," Alienor said. "If he had agreed to march on Aleppo and aided my uncle as he should, this would not have happened. I hold him and his advisers accountable for my uncle's . . . murder. There is no other word for it."

Alienor rested in Palermo for three weeks before traveling by gradual stages to Potenza where Louis waited for her. She would rather not have seen or spoken to him ever again, but since they had to make a joint petition for annulment in Rome, she had no choice but to go to him. Doing so made her feel physically ill and when Louis embraced her, declaring how relieved he was to see her, it was all she could do not to push him away in public.

"My only relief in all this is that we can go on together to Rome and have this marriage annulled," she said, her jaw clenched. "You shall force me no further."

Louis looked hurt. "I barely slept for my worry over what had happened to you."

Alienor raised a cynical eyebrow. She did not doubt his words, but she doubted his sleeplessness had been caused by concern for her. For himself perhaps . . . To one side of

Louis, Thierry de Galeran was doing his best not to curl his top lip and not quite succeeding.

"By all means let us hear what the Pope has to say," Louis said. "We must be ruled by God's holy law." He took her arm to lead her to a couch and commanded a servant to pour wine into a rock-crystal cup.

Thierry remained standing behind Louis. "We were all deeply sorry and shocked to learn of the death of the Prince of Antioch," he said in his smooth, cold voice. "We heard he fought bravely, even if he brought death upon himself by his folly."

Alienor felt as if Thierry was twisting the knife. She could sense the hatred emanating from beneath his cool, urbane exterior, but hers was a match for it. "Had we kept our promise to help him, he would not have been put in that position," she said. "I hold you responsible."

"Me? Ah, come now, madam." Thierry bowed and gave a supercilious half smile. "I did not send him out into the desert to make camp in the open; that was entirely his own choice and a poor commander's decision."

"As were your own at Damascus. Had you marched on Aleppo, my uncle would be alive now."

"Alienor, you know nothing of the business of war," Louis warned.

"And you do? All I have ever seen of you

and warfare is one disaster after another as you are led by the nose by your so-called advisers. I do not have to be a man to know strategy. You left my uncle no choice. His blood is on your hands."

Louis flushed under her scathing assault. Thierry recoiled as if he had been struck by a snake. "Forgive me," he said. "Your uncle did have a choice and he made the wrong one and it cost him his head. I understand the emir Shukira struck it from his shoulders and had it embalmed and borne in a silver casket to the Caliph of Baghdad as a trophy."

Alienor sprang to her feet and dashed her wine in Thierry's face. "You misbegotten whoreson! Get out, get out now! How dare you!"

Thierry gave her a look that flashed daggers. "I am sorry, madam, I thought you knew all of the circumstances."

"Then there was no need to tell me now except to gloat."

"Leave us, Thierry," Louis said. "Go and wipe your face." De Galeran compressed his lips, bowed to Louis, narrowed his eyes at Alienor, and left the room, his great cloak sweeping behind him.

"Why do you keep him by you?" Alienor was shaking. "He poisons everything he touches. You let him whisper in your ear; he slept in your tent and in your bed all the time we were traveling on crusade while you barred me from ever entering."

"He cares for my welfare in ways you could not begin to understand," Louis said, and there was an almost bleak note in his voice.

"Indeed that is true," Alienor said bitterly. "And he makes you less of a king because of it, and even less of a husband. With his advice you made the decision to go to war against Damascus and you let others pay the cost. All that you lost was the final shreds of your reputation as a leader of men. They will remember my uncle as a hero; they will remember you as a weakling under the sway of others who pulled you in all directions and warped your spirit out of true. And I shall never forgive you for the decisions you made that led to his death. Never, for as long as I live."

"Madam, enough." Louis set his shoulders. "You wonder why I barred you from my tent — then look no further than your behavior. I thought I might find you in a mood for conciliation after all we have endured on our journeys, but that is plainly not the case."

"Why should you think that?" Suddenly she was weary — exhausted with the futility of it all. "Neither of us has changed. I have no wish to continue this conversation. I am going to pray for my uncle's soul, that it may find peace. There will be none for me."

She left him standing in the chamber, clenching and unclenching his fists. Thierry was standing by the door waiting to go back in to Louis. He had wiped his face, but his hair was still wet at the front and she could smell the wine on him. She was afraid of him and hated him at the same time.

"You deserve no mercy for what you have done," she said in a shaking voice. "God sees all and you will be judged."

He bowed to her with a cynical flourish. "As shall we all. I do not fear His judgment when all I have done is to protect my king and serve my God."

"Truly you are sick in mind and deed," she said.

He gave her a look filled with venom. "Believe what you will, madam. I know what God tells me about the Serpent and the Whore of Babylon. I am the one with the King's ear. What power do you have?" He entered Louis's chamber and closed the door behind him.

Alienor clenched her fists. She was trembling with anger, shame, and grief. She should not have had to hear about her uncle from Thierry's lips and forever have it associated with the Templar's gloating. She should not be standing out here while Louis and Thierry were closeted together. But then perhaps if Thierry did not deserve mercy, he and Louis certainly deserved each other — and she deserved better.

34

Papal Palace at Tusculum, August 1149

Pope Eugenius leaned forward on his chair, pale hands tightly clasped, and peered intently at Alienor. He was a small man, made smaller by his posture, and resembled a shrew clad in magnificent episcopal robes.

"Your Eminence, I am ready to hear your judgment," Alienor said. This was it, the fulfillment of the journey. Louis had agreed to the annulment and had spoken to the Pope earlier that morning. She had not seen him since, but he had resolved to go forward with the matter. All that stood between her and the dissolution of her impossible marriage were a few words from this elderly little man and the necessary documentation.

Eugenius rubbed the shining sapphire in his pontifical ring with the pad of his thumb. "As I told your husband earlier, this is a matter for God, not for man, and God forbids the separation of those he has joined together, except in very serious and complex situations, neither of which pertain in your case."

He had a habit of slurring his words at the end of sentences so that it was difficult for Alienor to tell what he was saying, but she understood enough to know he was not taking the tack she wanted.

"But our bloodlines say our marriage is consanguineous in the fourth degree. Louis and I share the same ancestors."

"By all means laws should be kept, but sometimes they are used as conveniences without due sincerity." His voice was an old man's, thin and gravelly, but nevertheless imbued with power, not least because he was passionate and sincere about what he was saying. "I trust you will put your faith in God. You do not wish to raise His anger. Be meek and bend your will to His. That is what I told your husband." He raised a warning forefinger. "I was much disturbed when I heard that he too desired an annulment. It is not the behavior I would expect from a true son of the Church. Too many people sue for annulment when they should be doing their best to cherish their marriages. I told him he must reconsider, and he agreed to do so."

Alienor gazed at him in growing, sick dismay.

Eugenius now pointed his forefinger at her. "It is not your place to deny God's purpose. I do not sit in judgment beyond that which God allows me. I urge you with all my heart to come together with your husband as you were once before and go on your way united. From your union you shall bear an heir for France." His brow furrowed in bafflement. "You are a young woman still and have no need of resorting to such stratagems in this matter. You must beg God's mercy for the waywardness of your thoughts." A sad but almost kindly smile curved his lips. "You have come to the proper place to make it right. All it needs is the determination and everything can be made whole again."

Alienor was in shock and turmoil, but she set her face and held onto her dignity. Eugenius's gaze was filled with compassion and concern and also a little troubled censure, as if he were rebuking an erring child. It was plain that the pontiff was not going to agree to annul the marriage and that his mind was set on a very different path.

"Daughter, you should go to confession and pray upon what I have said, even as I have entreated your husband to do. Let today be a renewal of your marriage vows with your husband, not an ending." He held out his hand for her to kiss his ring. "I shall hear no more on this foolish matter of annulment. Go and prepare yourself to be your husband's bride and you will be vouchsafed a son."

There was nothing Alienor could do but make her obeisance and leave. She was numb, unable to believe the meeting with Eugenius had ended like this. There was no room to appeal his decision. She and Louis were more irrevocably bound than ever.

That night Alienor walked barefoot in her shift and cloak through the corridors of the papal palace at Tusculum, her right hand set lightly on Louis's left wrist. He too was barefoot and similarly clad. They both wore the gold crowns that had traveled in their baggage from the outset of the crusade. Alienor's hair fell in burnished ripples to her hips. The scent of roses and incense wafted from her garments and her body as she walked. Louis too was bathed and groomed. Before and behind them a choir of secular canons sang God's praises, and attendants strewed rose petals from the palace gardens across the floor tiles.

Eventually they came to a polished oak door decorated with wrought iron curves and scrollwork. With great ceremony an usher knocked upon it with his ebony staff and, at a command from within, turned the latch and admitted them to a bedchamber ablaze with light and color. It reminded Alienor a little of the stained glass glory of Saint-Denis because here too the effect was of walking into a reliquary. It felt sacred, and she was filled with trepidation and uncertainty.

Pope Eugenius was waiting for them, standing before the bed as if officiating at an altar.

His small, ferrety frame was drowned in a white cope gleaming with embroidery of silver and gold. In his right hand he bore a staff on which was set a reliquary cross, the gold almost obliterated by gemstones. A bishop stood at his side, holding a silver pot containing holy water, and another stood ready with a vial of oil. The scent of incense permeated everything, but especially the bed, which was a confection of white and gold matching the papal robes. Candles and lamps blazed in every niche and crevice, giving off the sweet aromas of beeswax and perfumed oil, filling the room with heat. Eugenius's lined forehead glistened with drops of sweat like beads of rock crystal.

"My children," he said, opening his hands in welcome. His eyes were as bright as berries and filled with benevolence. "This is a moment of renewal, of hope and fruitfulness, endorsed by God. I have sanctified the bed in which you shall lie tonight as husband and wife, and now I shall sanctify you that you shall be blessed with a male heir for France."

He bade them kneel and Alienor felt his trembling thumb anointing a cross on her brow with holy oil as he spoke words of blessing and sanction. "In the name of the Father, the Son, and the Holy Spirit, let it be done," he said.

The gathered clergy left the chamber in an orderly procession, singing as they went, swinging censers, leaving behind drifts of the heavenly scent of frankincense resin.

Alienor and Louis faced each other, two strangers as they had been on their first wedding night, and yet with all the knowledge of years between them like a poisoned chalice containing a brew of hurt, betrayal, treachery, and abuse. Eugenius wanted them to start again, but Alienor knew it was a vain hope. All of this was taking her further onto the wrong path. Her first wedding night had led her into a marriage that had soon turned sour. How was this going to be any better? Knowing what to expect only made it worse.

Louis put his arms around her and, drawing her against him, kissed the cross of oil on her forehead. "If it is the will of God, then it is our duty to follow what must be done," he said somberly. "The Pope is right. We should put our personal desires aside and be a king and queen."

As Alienor lay back on the great, blessed bed with its priceless hangings and perfumed sheets still damp with sprinkles of holy water, she felt as if not just her heart but her whole body was breaking. How could this be happening when this morning she had expected to be in receipt of an annulment? She barely responded to Louis, but that only served to arouse him, because a passive wife was an obedient wife, and as far as he was concerned, she was obeying the advice the Pope had given to them, and submitting to God's will.

In the end, Alienor found the physical act itself not too unpleasant. Louis was thoroughly immersed in his role and since there could be no greater sanction to the marriage bed than having it personally overseen by the Pope, he had no difficulty in performing his duty in a way that honored their surroundings and the sacrament of the moment. Afterward, he lay back, his hands pillowed behind his head, and gazed up at the bed hangings with a slight smile on his lips. "We shall yet have our heir," he said, "and then everything will be different, you will see."

She doubted that. Even if she bore a son from this mating, the same courtiers would cause the same problems and marginalize her power. She could not see Louis returning to her bed on a regular basis. It might happen for a short while with the Pope's exhortations fresh in his mind, but she knew him well. As soon as the glamour began to fade, he would return to his other proclivities.

She needed freedom above all else, but she had just been burdened with yet more chains.

35

Paris, December 1150

Alienor had never known a winter so bitterly cold. The hard frosts had begun in late November and a fortnight later the snow had followed. Although the shortest day had passed, there was no sign of a thaw, and dawn still came late and the dusk early. There was privation. The queue for alms at abbey gates grew ever longer as food supplies dwindled and increased in price. The poor starved — and froze. The Seine was solid and river commerce had ceased. Supplies were hauled on sleds, and people had to melt ice to obtain water for their cooking pots. The price of kindling rose until folk could scarcely afford to build fires.

Alienor had been out giving alms to the needy and visiting the sick, as had Louis. Their plight concerned her, but they had been born to their lot in life even as she had been born to hers. She did what she could for them within her remit.

Under a hard, bright moon in the winter dusk, she walked with Petronella in the frozen palace gardens. Her heavy cloak was lined with ermine and her shoes insulated with thick, soft fleece. Petronella carried a hot stone wrapped in a layer of sheepskin. An ostentatious ruby ring glowed on her wedding finger to remind the world she was now officially the wife of Raoul de Vermandois. His first wife had died, thus removing the impediment to their match, and they had been received back into the bosom of the Church.

Children dashed and played around the sisters, throwing snowballs, taunting each other, their voices sharp as crystal on the still air of dusk. Alienor's four-year-old daughter belonged in this landscape with her long flaxen hair and twilight blue eyes. She was a slender faerie child, but her build masked her vigor and she possessed a robust will that made her ready to tackle her Vermandois cousins fearlessly. Alienor had left her barely walking, still a babe in arms, and had returned to a demanding spindle-legged little girl. There was a gap where maternal emotion should have existed. Alienor felt little connection with her daughter; there had been too long a separation. All she could summon was a feeling of wistful regret. She was with child again, the fruit of their stay in Tusculum on their way home, and she was cutting off from that too, because it was too painful to think about.

"You will have to tell Louis soon," Petronella said as they paused beside a snowy bench to look out over the dormant beds. Alienor had brought home roses from the garden at Palermo, but they would not bloom until the summer. "I saw him looking at you earlier today when you refused the trout with almonds."

"And then he will turn me into a prisoner," Alienor said bitterly. "The moment he knows I am with child, he will confine me to my chamber and send in his physicians and priests. He will have me watched day and night. He is almost unbearable now. What will it be like when he does know? Do you think he would allow me to walk in the garden now with you? He would say the night air was bad for the child and I should take more care. He would accuse me of negligence."

"But you will still need to do it soon," Petronella persisted. "He may be a man, but he can count. You are always telling me I should think about the practicalities."

Alienor grimaced. "Yes, but not quite yet. I intend to have a few more days of freedom."

Petronella's gaze narrowed. "There is much you are not telling me. Raoul saw Abbé Suger's correspondence in your absence. You sought an annulment when you were in Antioch, and you were still seeking it when you went to Rome. Raoul said Louis would have to be the greatest fool in Christendom to agree to it and lose you and Aquitaine."

"Yet he would have agreed," Alienor said. "It was the Pope who bound us together and refused to dissolve the marriage, the sentimental old fool. He made us share a bed and promised Louis a son." She pressed her hand to her belly and breathed out a puff of white vapor.

"But if he had agreed to the annulment, what then?" Petronella demanded. "What would you have done? You wouldn't have been free — not as a woman alone and without a male heir but with many years of childbearing left. Someone would seize you. Raoul said you were being just as foolish as Louis."

"Raoul seems to have a lot to say on many things, and you seem very keen to take his word as the truth," Alienor snapped. "Raoul knows nothing of my situation. I do not choose to share my plans with him and with good reason."

Petronella's eyes flashed with anger. "He has been loyal to Louis throughout."

"But I have no doubt that he was busy covering all exits and entrances. And who is Raoul to speak of foolishness with his reputation? Ah, enough. I shall not quarrel with you."

Ahead of her the children were flurrying through the snow. Little Marie slipped on a patch of ice and fell hard. Her bottom lip quivered and she began to wail. Her cousin Isabelle pulled her to her feet, but it was to Petronella that Marie ran for comfort.

"Hush now, my love, hush," Petronella said and crouched to stroke Marie's cheek with a hand that was warm from the stone. "It's nothing, a little scrape, hmmm? Such a fuss." She gave her a cuddle and a kiss.

Alienor watched, feeling empty and heartsick. "Come," she said curtly, turning toward the garden gate. "We should go inside; it is growing colder."

A week later, with the bitter chill still straining people's endurance at the seams, Louis sat in his chamber of the Great Tower in the late-winter afternoon. Dinner was over, the candles had been lit, and everyone was taking their ease. For once Louis was not at his prayers, but sitting in conversation with members of his household. For once, too, Thierry de Galeran was not at his side, having business at his estates of Montlhéry, and as a result the atmosphere was more relaxed.

The court children were playing a simple game of dice near the hearth and their quick cries rang out. It would soon be their bedtime and the nurses were keeping close watch. Raoul's son and namesake was overexuberant and the dice bounced from the table and rolled under the trestle where the adults were talking. Little Marie crawled under to fetch them and then squealed as a dog took this as an invitation to lick her face.

Raoul called the hound to heel and peered under the table. "What are you doing, child?"

"Finding the dice, sire," she lisped and held them out on the palm of her hand.

"Ah, you weren't spying on us then?" Raoul said with a twitch of his lips. His words elicited an uncomfortable silence from the adults.

"What's spying, sire?"

"Listening to what other people say without them knowing you are listening, and then reporting what you have heard to others. If you're lucky, they'll pay you for the information."

She continued to stare at him. "That's telling tales."

Raoul's shoulders shook with suppressed laughter. "I suppose it is. Just remember that all knowledge is profit." He smiled briefly at Alienor and, rising from his stoop, went to join the dice game and show the children one of his tricks.

Louis shook his head and snorted with amusement. "Fool," he said.

"A knowing fool though." She watched him bend over the table and perform a vanishing trick with the newly retrieved dice. Marie leaned against his leg like a kitten after milk and he patted her head.

Alienor looked down at her lap. She knew she had to tell him. That smile from Raoul had been a warning. "Louis," she said. "I am with child. You are to be a father once more."

His expression went very still and then, like raindrops hitting a pool, the emotion twitched across his face. "Truly?" he said. "You speak truly?"

Alienor nodded and set her jaw. She wanted to cry, but not with joy. "Yes, I speak truly," she said.

Louis took her hands in his and leaned forward to kiss her brow. "That is the greatest news you could give me! The Pope was right and wise. This is indeed a new start. I am going to protect you and look after you and make sure you have the best possible care." His chest expanded. "Tomorrow I shall send for the most learned physicians in the land. You and our child will want for nothing. I shall do everything in my power to keep you and the child safe."

Alienor tried to smile but could not for she knew that now her incarceration would begin. Already she felt as if she could not breathe.

If the winter had been long and hard, then the early summer of 1150 was hot enough to blister the paint from the shutters and warp doors, creating fissures and cracks in the gasping wood. Even in the top chamber of the Great Tower, with the shutters open and the insulation of the thick, cool stone, the air was warm and stale. Laboring to bear her child, Alienor's only relief from the heat came as successive layers of sweat dried on her body.

The midwives had told her all was well and progressing as it should be, but the hours still slipped by in the pain and endurance of Eve's lot. She could not help but remember the stillbirth on the road from Antioch and it churned up all her terror, rage, and grief from that time. Those emotions had never gone away and rode her hard as she sought to push this new child from the womb and be free of the burden.

There came the last moments of struggle, the final effort, and the baby was born, pink and wet and living, with a set of lungs that filled the still air in the room like a fanfare. But all the attendants and adults in the room were silent and the anticipation on their faces turned to blank expressions and sidelong glances.

Petronella leaned over the bed and held Alienor's hand. "It's another girl," she said. "You have another beautiful daughter."

The words meant nothing to Alienor. It was as if her mind was cut off from her feelings just as the cord severed her from the new baby. She had had no choice in Tusculum but to share Louis's bed and this child was a matter between the Pope and her husband. She had only been the vessel. That it was a girl did nothing to pierce her numbness. There was naught she could do about it and so it had to be accepted. She turned her head toward the window, to the faint breath of breeze.

"Perhaps the next one will be a boy," Petronella said. "Our mother had two daughters and a son, and so do I."

Alienor looked at her sister. "It doesn't matter," she said. "What God decides, He decides."

Petronella gently stroked Alienor's loose hair. Then she rose and stood aside for the midwives to deal with the afterbirth as the contractions gathered again. "Perhaps it is for the best," she whispered. "You can be free now."

Louis had been pacing and waiting for news ever since hearing that Alienor's labor had begun. As always such things seemed to take forever. This time he knew it would be a son. The Pope had given his word, and the child had been conceived in the papal palace. Everyone he consulted assured him that the child was a boy. He had made sure Alienor had had the best of care and protection throughout the pregnancy. He was to be named Philippe, and Louis was ready to take him to his christening before the altar of Saint Peter in the royal chapel the moment he was brought from the birthing chamber. He had even written some documents in his son's name, promising gifts to abbeys, penning the words himself without the use of a scribe so that he could form the inky nib around the name "Philippe" and feel that wonderful sense of destiny.

Abbé Suger sat with him. They had been at prayer together earlier and were now busy with matters of government. Suger had aged in the bitter winter last year, becoming gaunt and wizened, his words punctuated by a persistent dry cough. However, despite his physical frailty, he was still politically active and astute as they discussed their troublesome neighbors.

"It would be better to negotiate an agreement with Geoffrey of Anjou and his son, rather than going to war against them, sire," Suger said. "The Angevin support was vital to me during the time that I was regent during your long absence."

"You are saying I should ignore their impertinence?" Louis drew himself up. "They must be taught their place."

"Your brother attacked the Angevins when you were still on your pilgrimage. Geoffrey of Anjou is a powerful vassal. You have recognized him as Duke of Normandy and now he has conferred that title on his son. Better for now to have them in our camp."

"Geoffrey of Anjou conferred that title without my sanction, and the young man is a whelp who needs bringing to heel," Louis snapped. "I shall not let upstarts dictate to me."

"Indeed, sire. But you should think of the future. Many favor the Angevin's heir to sit on England's throne rather than Stephen's son."

Louis's nostrils flared. "I will not see an Angevin wear a crown. They have already seized more than their due."

Suger persisted with firm but weary patience. "But you should leave your pathways open," he said. "And you should not keep risking yourself in war until you have your own heirs firmly established. The country is still recovering from the harsh winter and spring. The crops are barely in the fields. Make this a time of husbandry and rest."

Louis looked at his tutor, really looked, and noticed the shadows under his eyes and the hollows in his cheekbones. Suger had been elderly for a long time, but Louis had never thought of him as being frail or mortal. Certainly he had wished him gone or less interfering on many an occasion, but now, suddenly, he saw that what had been a constant in his life, taken for granted, was on the wane. This time of husbandry and rest might also be one of letting go for Suger. "I shall think about it," he said, and managed to keep his voice steady, even though the moment of realization had jolted him.

"That is all I ask of you for now, and I hope your wisdom sees you through." Suger gave Louis a shrewd look. "And you do have wisdom, my son, even if it is hard-earned and sometimes overridden by your own stubborn will and the foolish advice of others."

Not so frail that he was unable to lecture. Louis's moment of concern passed into the background.

A steward rapped on the door with his rod and announced that attendants from the Queen's apartments had arrived with news of the birth.

Louis's chest swelled as he commanded their admittance. Now he would see his son.

The midwife came to him, a bundle carried in her arms. Her eyes were downcast and her expression was neutral. "Sire," she said and, kneeling to him, spread the blanket open in her lap to show him the naked baby.

Louis gazed down at the tiny creature as it wriggled in the sudden exposure to cold air and gave a mewling cry. He was being shown a girl baby, but that was impossible and the sight rendered him speechless. He looked from the baby to the gathering of courtiers accompanying the midwife and back to the baby in utter disbelief. It was true, but it couldn't be. He set his jaw. "I have seen enough," he said with a flick of his hand. "Take the child away."

The midwife carefully folded the infant back in the blanket and, with her escort in tow, bore it from the room. Louis looked down at his hands, which were shaking. His mind was blank with shock; he couldn't think. It was as if the missing genitalia on the child had caused that part of himself to vanish too, and he felt as if all of his body was crumbling inward.

"Be steady," Suger said. "At least the Queen has proved she is fertile."

Louis paced the room numbly, touching this and that. He paused by his earlier working and the word "Philippe" stood out to him like a brand. "I had a son a moment ago," he said. "Now he is gone, usurped by a girl, and I have nothing." He seized the vellum and crumpled it in his fist.

"Sire . . ."

He cast Suger a look filled with anguish and fury. "What will people think of me that I cannot sire a son on this woman even with the blessing of the Pope upon us? What will people say?" He could feel a terrible pressure of tears growing behind his eyes and there was pain in his stomach. "It is all her fault. She has let me down again. If God cannot persuade her to produce a boy, then surely I cannot." He felt a moment of almost overwhelming bitter hatred against his wife for doing this to him, and then the shock surged again. He had been so certain it would be a boy. He had been convinced by the Church that he was doing the right thing. The Pope had promised. They had forced him into this and made him a victim. "No," he said to Suger, holding up his hand. "Do not try to console me and tell me all will be well. I should have had this marriage annulled long since."

"I know you are suffering, my son," Suger said, "but it is not your right to question God's will, and you have a healthy daughter. That is something to celebrate, because you may make a good marriage for her. You are both still young enough to try again."

Louis shuddered. "Not with her," he said. "She has let me down for the last time."

"But if you annul your marriage, you will lose Aquitaine, and in truth, that is a greater consideration than losing your wife. I counsel you not to act in haste, but to think the matter through. Think of what it will mean to France, not just yourself."

Louis bit the inside of his cheek. His mind was made up but he knew Suger would fight him to the last because of the great wealth of Aquitaine. The fact was that Louis did not care anymore. He wanted to be rid of Alienor. When he had first seen her she had seemed like an angel to him and he had trembled with his love for her, but in the end all she had brought into his life was scandal and disgrace. She made him feel guilty and unclean, and she herself was unclean because all she could bear him were girls. Physicians said that a woman who bore only girls was too dominant in her humors and her unnatural imbalance caused her seed to override her husband's and thus produce females. The other way of looking at the matter was that the husband's seed was not strong enough to dominate, but Louis would admit no such weakness in himself. It was her fault, all hers, and he could no longer be saddled with a wife so flawed. He would begin the search for a mate more suitable; one who would bear him a living son. "Yes," he said to Suger. "I shall think matters through."

The elderly churchman coughed and took a drink of his wine. "You must see to the christening of your new daughter," he said. "You have decided on a name?"

Louis hadn't. All his focus had been on a son. He certainly wasn't going to change the name to Philippa even though it was in both families. "I leave that to my wife," he said. "She bore her. Let her have the naming."

36

Abbey Church of Saint-Denis, February 1151
Alienor signed her breast and rose from her prayers, her breath clouding the air. Saint-Denis was bone cold on this bleak February morning. The swords of light piercing the high windows to strike the tiled floor imparted no warmth. The only heat in the church came from the rows of votive candles flickering on their stands. Alienor paused to light one and place it beside the others.

Suger had been in his grave for several weeks. Saint-Denis had tolled a knell for its beloved abbot as he was laid to rest in the church he had glorified for so much of his life. He had died in fear for his mortal soul — afraid that he had spent too much time on politics and dealings with the world instead of attending to spiritual matters. He had begged Bernard of Clairvaux to attend his deathbed and pray for him, but Bernard, old and frail himself, had been unable to come, and instead had sent him a linen kerchief, which Suger had been clutching when he died, begging for constant masses and prayers to be said for his soul.

It was strange, Alienor thought. She had known Suger all the years she had been Queen of France. She had often found him obstructive and irritating. He could be devious in obtaining his own ends, but she had never felt any personal malice coming from him, and that raised him in her estimation. He had not allowed his private opinions to color his politics. Louis had wept like a child for his tutor and mentor. Nevertheless, when his tears dried, his eyes were hard.

She returned to the guesthouse where she was staying before her return to Paris. She had letters to write to various vassals and members of the clergy. Suger's death had been an ending and a beginning, but the latter was suspended in that moment following the resonance of the final note. Last night she had dreamed of Poitiers; a warm, thyme-scented breeze had brushed her eyelids, lifted her hair, and filled her with yearning.

Louis had not joined her at her prayers, preferring to hold his own separately, but waited for her now, his plain dark robes embellished by a gold reliquary cross on his breast. He was pale and hollow-cheeked, and he made her shiver. She acknowledged his presence and put distance between them as swiftly as she could. They had barely spoken to each other or shared company since the birth of their second daughter, whom Alienor had named Alix. She had borne her in early June and emerged from confinement at the end of July. She had handed Alix to a wet nurse on the day of the churching and her fluxes had begun again in early September. Louis had not visited her chamber to sleep with her and she had not encouraged him. Their marriage was as bleak and joyless as this raw February morning.

"I wish to talk to you about annulling our marriage," Louis said. His mouth had a sour downturn.

Alienor raised her brows. "As I have suggested to you many times before, but it has never come to fruition."

"It will do so this time, I shall make very sure of it."

"So you can make another match and beget a son?" She gave him an acerbic smile. "Perhaps you are only destined to have daughters, Louis. Have you thought about that?"

A muscle ticked in his cheek. "That is not so. Our match, whatever the Pope decreed, is consanguineous and a sin in the eyes of God. It is not meet that we should stay together."

"You knew it was consanguineous on the day you married me."

He flushed. "I did not; I had no inkling."

"But Suger did; he knew very well, but

nothing mattered save that Aquitaine be delivered to France. Many couples related in the fourth degree as we are live their entire lives married, and they are blessed with sons. Consanguinity is but a useful excuse on which to hang a parting." She opened her hands. "I am delighted to agree to an annulment, Louis, but if you had consented to my request in Antioch, you would have saved us three years of wasted time."

He scowled. "Antioch was a challenge and an insult to my kingship. I was prepared to grant your annulment when we came to Tusculum, but the Pope judged otherwise. I did my best, but clearly he was in error, and we must part."

Alienor felt a rush of relief, but there was also a bitter taste in her mouth and a stultifying sense of futility. She had not wanted to marry Louis, but once it was done, she had believed they could make a working partnership, and that the glint of attraction might become something deeper. Instead, the machinations of others had warped and twisted the relationship until it became untenable. To come to this point felt like failure. Yet it was a release too. There would be many months of negotiation ahead, but let the decision be made and let consanguinity be the coverall excuse, even if they both knew it was not the true reason. "Well then, if you can convince the Pope to reverse his decision, let us go forward." She gave him a hard look. "Of course you will no longer have a governing say in Aquitaine. You must remove all of your officials and garrisons from my territories."

"That will be attended to," Louis said curtly. "But our daughters are still your heirs, so I have an interest on their behalf. They shall remain with me and be raised in my household."

Alienor hesitated for a moment, and then acceded. What did she have or know of her daughters anyway? Marie had been barely walking when Alienor had gone to Outremer, not returning to France for three years. Alix was a babe in arms. Neither daughter knew her, nor she them. All she could feel was a sense of loss and regret for what might have been.

"Then we are agreed," Louis said. "I shall set matters in motion." With a stiff nod, he left the guest chamber. Alienor gazed at the door as he closed it behind him. She felt numb when she should have felt like an eagle set free from the mews. Having been constrained for so long and having striven to escape until her wings were battered and her spirit close to breaking, she needed time to prepare herself for flight and gain the courage to soar.

She could have Geoffrey now, but everything had changed. She could return to

Poitiers and feel the warm wind in her hair, but she would be a different person. When innocence was gone, one's life pattern changed forever. With Aquitaine no longer united with France, she had to find new strategies and policies to survive.

There was much to do, but today was a time for evaluation. Tomorrow she would begin.

37

Castle of Taillebourg, March 1151

Geoffrey de Rancon looked at the letter in his hand and then at the Archbishop of Bordeaux. Outside a strong March wind blew fluffy white clouds past the turret window of Taillebourg's great tower overlooking the Charente River. The day was chilly enough to warrant a good log fire in the hearth, but held that promise of spring.

"Our duchess is coming home," Geoffrey said and felt a lightning spark somewhere deep inside him. The pity was that she had ever had to leave.

"Yes," said Gofrid, "but not until the autumn, and even then the annulment will not be secure until well into the next year."

"She says Louis has found three bishops to pronounce the annulment," Geoffrey said. "But will the Pope agree?"

"I think he realizes there is nothing more he can do," the Archbishop replied, "and that beyond this point, concessions must be made.

It is not as if either party is contesting the matter or has a previous spouse in the background."

Geoffrey dropped his gaze to the piece of parchment and the elegant words of a scribe informing him that Louis and Alienor would be here in the autumn to tour their lands and take stock. French soldiers and officials were to be withdrawn during the visit and part of Geoffrey's brief was to find men of Aquitaine to fill the positions. There was a separate note to him from Alienor, written in code, telling him that the autumn could not come soon enough and that the only thing that filled her with hope each morning was her return to him. She had written "Aquitaine" but he knew it was a substitute for his name. He did not want to let her down, yet he feared it was already too late.

The Archbishop was watching him with shrewd eyes. "It will be a difficult time," he said. "Our duchess is a strong-willed woman, but nevertheless she will be a woman alone. She will need guidance and many will try to take advantage."

Geoffrey returned the Archbishop's look steadily. "Not if we are here to protect her. I will defend her rights as duchess with my life."

"Indeed. You are an honorable man and you will do the right thing."

Geoffrey said nothing because he could not

tell how much the Archbishop knew, or how much of an ally he was. He suspected they were both fencing in the dark. When Alienor returned to Aquitaine as duchess in full, she would need courtiers and clerics to advise her, and it was only wise to secure those affinities before she arrived.

The Archbishop sighed. "I had hoped for great things of the marriage between the King of France and our duchess, as did her father. It was his ambition that his daughter should be the matriarch of a great dynasty. How could we have known that it would come to this?"

"Indeed," Geoffrey said, and then fell silent, because there was nothing else to say. He pinched the bridge of his nose, feeling tired and dull. It was as if he were a fading footprint in the dust, rather than the man striding forward to make his destiny.

There was sickness in the palace. People were succumbing to high fevers accompanied by sore eyes, congestion, and an itchy spotted rash. Both of Alienor's daughters had caught it, as had their Vermandois cousins, and the nursery in the royal palace was full of sick, fractious children. Louis contracted the fever as he was preparing to go to war in Normandy against the young Duke Henry and his father Geoffrey of Anjou. On the day he should have set out to join his army and liaise with Eustace of Boulogne, who was already in the field, Louis was in bed, sweating and shivering in delirium. Beset by terrible dreams in which Abbé Suger threatened him with the fires of hell, terrified of dying, he sent for his confessor and had his attendants dress him in sackcloth. It became clear he was not going to recover in a day or even a week, and that the battle campaign — a major strike against the city of Rouen — would have to be postponed.

"Louis has decided to call a truce," Raoul told Alienor and Petronella when he came to see how the children were faring. "He cannot lead an army into Normandy in his condition, and there is no telling how long the contagion will last."

Petronella turned her head away from her husband and refused to look at him, her attitude one of angry rejection. She wrung out a cloth and laid it across her son's flushed forehead. The little boy whimpered and began to cry.

Alienor looked at Raoul. "How is the truce to be arranged?"

He cast an exasperated glance at his wife. "The Count of Anjou and his son are to come to Paris to discuss the situation and agree a cessation of hostilities in return for certain concessions."

"Such as?"

"Louis will recognize Geoffrey's son as

Duke of Normandy in return for their giving up the territories in the Vexin that they hold."

"And he thinks they will agree?"

Raoul shrugged. "It will be to their advantage. The King is too sick to campaign against Rouen and has too many other issues to deal with to start another campaign when he has recovered. If he can arrange a truce until next year and gain some land into the bargain, all to the good. The Count of Anjou and his son, for the exchange of a strip of territory, will buy valuable time to deal with their own concerns." He gave a half smile. "I am too old a warhorse to be disappointed that we are not riding out on campaign. It will suit me to sign a truce."

Alienor absorbed the detail that she had better prepare to receive guests and calculated how long she would have before their arrival. Even if Geoffrey of Anjou was a rogue and far too full of his own masculine dazzle, he would be a distraction from her cares. His son she had never met, although she had heard tales about his precociousness and fierce energy.

Raoul looked at the children. "I will go and say my prayers for them," he said. "There is little else I can do here. Petra . . ." He went to touch his wife's shoulder and she shrugged him off.

"Go," she said. "I know what kind your prayers will be, and at what kind of altar you will offer them."

"Oh, in the name of Christ, woman, the only thing that will drive me away are your groundless accusations. I can no longer hold any kind of sensible conversation with you." Turning on his heel, he flung from the room.

Alienor gazed at her sister. "What's wrong?"

"Other women," Petronella said, her lip curling. "It is always other women with him. He thinks I do not notice, but I do, and when I confront him, he denies it. Dear God, he is old enough to be my grandsire, but still he cannot stop the chase."

Alienor took a proper look at her sister. Petronella's dark hair was flat and draggled. Her eyes were pouched with dark circles and her dress was stained. She smelt sour and unwashed. She was like their grandmother Dangereuse. Her passions were so intense that they burned her out. She had a desperate craving to be wanted and loved, and Raoul could not sustain the fire at that kind of level. And perhaps Petronella was right to an extent. Raoul's nature was such that he would indeed be chasing women until the day he died.

"Come. You must eat and rest. How can you think when you are so tired and overwrought? Remember how you counseled me when I was heartsick?" She took Petronella's arm and gestured the nurses to attend the children.

"You know it's true, don't you?" Petronella said. "That is why you don't say anything."

"Because there is no point while you are like this."

Petronella shook herself free of Alienor's grip. "It is all your fault!" she burst out. "Without your annulment Raoul would still cleave to me. Once you return to Poitiers, he will cast me off because I shall no longer be of any use to him — indeed I shall be a hindrance. If my mind is in turmoil, you are to blame!"

There was no reasoning with Petronella when she was like this, and she spoke enough truth for Alienor to feel a stab of guilt. Once her marriage with Louis was annulled, Raoul would indeed have no reason but love to remain wed to Petronella, because all the affinity would be gone and there would be no gain in being shackled to the former Queen of France's unstable sister.

"Railing at me will change nothing. If you are to keep Raoul, then you need all your faculties."

Petronella tossed her head, but allowed Floreta and Marchisa to wash her and dress her in a clean chemise. She refused to eat, but she did drink the wine containing a soporific that Marchisa gave to her. Her lids grew heavy and she lay down on Alienor's bed. "If he doesn't want me," she whispered, "then I do not wish to live."

"Do not talk like a fool," Alienor snapped. "Raoul de Vermandois is not the beginning and end of the world. You have three children to call you Mother. You have kin and friends in Poitiers. How dare you say that?"

Petronella just rolled on her side away from Alienor, shutting everyone out.

Alienor went to find Raoul and discovered him, as he had said, praying in the chapel of Saint Michael. She knelt at his good side, where he had vision, and sent up her own prayer while she waited for him. He lingered as if reluctant to engage with her. His thick white hair was thinning at the crown, she noticed, and the flesh that had once been taut on his bones was sagging at the jawline. His clothes were immaculate and he still projected an air of power, but his years sat on him with more weight these days.

Eventually he stood up and she rose at his side. "Are you intending to annul your marriage to my sister?" she asked him bluntly.

Raoul's expression grew very still. "Why should you think that?"

"You know as well as I do. Do not play a courtier's game with me, Raoul."

He heaved a sigh. "You have seen how she is, and that is most of the time these days. If I so much as glance at another woman she throws a jealous tantrum. She demands my attention and does not understand that I have duties to perform. She falls into dark moods where she takes to her bed and will not bestir herself for days. The priests say it is judgment upon us for what we did, but I do not believe it. I believe she has always been like this, but now it has become much worse."

"That does not answer my question."

He shook his head. "Yes, I am considering the matter, and I must consult with the King. It seems to me that if you are returning to Poitiers, it would be better if Petronella went with you. She will fare better in the land of her childhood — in so many ways she has remained a child herself."

"So you would put the responsibility for her onto me?"

"She needs to be cared for and I believe it will be for the best."

"For your best or hers?" Alienor asked with scorn.

"For both our sakes, and that of our children."

"And when my marriage is annulled and I part company with the King, what then?"

"Then I shall have to decide."

Alienor inhaled to remonstrate but stopped as she saw the genuine pain in his expression.

"Then I hope your conscience steers you in the right direction," she said. "You swore to protect her. Do so now."

38

Angers, August 1151

Henry, Duke of Normandy, was enjoying himself. The young woman straddling his thighs was a beauty with thick ash-brown hair, wide gray eyes, and a full, cushion-soft mouth capable of rendering the most exquisite pleasure. Being eighteen years old, Henry's enthusiasm and capability had remained firm over several sessions of love sport, begun the previous evening when he had retired to bed with Aelburgh, a flagon of wine, and a platter of honey-drizzled pastries.

"I am going to miss you," he panted as she rode him. He admired the jiggle of her breasts and felt the twinges of crisis as she rose and dipped.

"Then take me with you, sire." She leaned over him to nip his shoulder. "I would keep you warm on your journey."

Henry briefly entertained the notion. He had been going to bring her with him on battle campaign. He appreciated the comforts she could provide and Aelburgh was not one to complain about life on the road; she would be no trouble. Regretfully he set the notion aside. His father would not be best pleased. "No, sweetheart," he gasped. "Much as I would enjoy having you in Paris, it would not be seemly."

"Hah, I did not realize you cared for what is seemly and what is not."

"I care when necessary. My father and I have some delicate negotiations with the King of France. There are things we want from him, and it behooves us to be perfect courtiers. What I need from you is a . . . fond farewell."

She tossed her head and laughed. "Then I will drain you dry, my lord. When I am finished, you will not desire a woman for a full month!"

Henry doubted it, but let her continue anyway.

As the morning sun climbed out of the dawn, Henry dismissed Aelburgh with a slap on the buttocks and a pouch of silver sufficient to keep her during his absence. He felt full of well-being but by no means exhausted. It took more than a few sessions of enthusiastic bed-romping to wear out his vivid, vigorous energy. He needed very little sleep; when awake his mind was always busy on several tasks at once and his overflowing energy would cause him to stride about the room and fidget. Remaining still in church was the most difficult routine duty of his life. He considered that God intended him to be a king and a duke and would excuse him time spent in prayer. That was what monks and priests were for.

Henry went to look out of the window as he donned a tunic of red wool, somewhat frizzy around the cuffs where he had been playing tug of war with one of the dogs. Henry knew the value of dressing for formal occasions, but for every day he liked the old and the comfortable. It was the man inside the clothes that mattered and how he used his power. His father disagreed with that stance, but then his father used clothing as part of his magnificence.

The courtyard was busy with activity as servants made ready for the journey to Paris on the morrow. There were horses to be shod, harnesses to be polished and equipment to be checked so that when they did set out, all would be smooth and brisk without delays. King Louis had pulled back from his intention to strike at Rouen and called for talks instead. He had claimed ill health, but in politics, unless you were face-to-face with someone, it was never possible to tell whether the claim was the reality or an excuse.

Whistling, Henry fastened his belt at his hips, combed his thick red-gold hair into a semblance of order, and went to find his father.

Geoffrey was in his own chamber with his bed curtains hooked out of the way and the bed itself made up with its day covers. His attendants and courtiers were already hard at work, his scribes toiling over sheaves of documents. Geoffrey sat at a trestle, his foot elevated on a padded stool. He was looking thoughtfully at a document in his hands.

"Ah," he said as Henry breezed into the room. "The sluggard arrives."

Henry poured a cup of wine and took a small loaf from the basket on the table. "I've been awake awhile," he said with a knowing grin.

His father raised his eyebrows. "Indeed? Let us hope you put your early rising to good use."

A moment of humor glimmered between father and son, although Geoffrey's expression had an irritable edge.

"Indeed I did. Experience is all to the good, as you are forever telling me." Henry gestured at the stool. "Is your foot troubling you again?"

Geoffrey continued to look irritated. He wanted to garner sufficient respect and attention for his ailment, the result of a wound sustained in a battle campaign more than ten years ago, but without attracting any hint that he was becoming incapable. His son was eighteen and a handsome young stallion arching his neck over the stable door, but Geoffrey was still in command and never let his heir forget it. "No worse than usual, but better to rest it on the day before a long journey." He gestured Henry to sit down. "There are still matters we need to discuss."

They had already talked about dealing with the French. Louis was demanding that the lands of the Vexin on the border between Normandy and France be handed over to him in return for his recognition of Henry as Duke of Normandy. There was also the matter of the rebellious castellan of Montreuil to be settled, but since Giraud de Berlai was in chains in their dungeon and Montreuil razed to the ground, it was a moot point. However, since de Berlai had appealed to Louis for aid against his Angevin overlords, he might prove a useful lever in negotiations. Henry was keen to have a truce arranged and Louis bought off or pacified. Keeping the French out of Normandy meant he could concentrate on England. If that meant greasing the wheels with conciliatory words and a strip of land, then so be it. All might change on another occasion. "What kind of matters?" He sat down on a chair facing his father.

Geoffrey said, "King Louis is in the middle of annulling his marriage. He needs a male heir and sadly his wife's seed is too strong and his own too weak to make this happen.

All he can get on her is girls."

Henry frowned, uncertain where his father's speech was leading. Surely this was not about the union between himself and Louis's eldest daughter. That had been mooted and rejected many years ago.

"That is his fault, of course. Your mother is far more of a termagant than Alienor of France and my seed still dominated hers to plant three sons in her womb. You will have no such difficulty."

Henry stared at him. The piece of bread he had been chewing almost stuck in his throat and he had to gulp.

"Think of how much prestige and power we would gain from such an alliance and how much France would be weakened."

Henry coughed and took a swallow of wine. He had not envisioned taking an older woman to wife — another man's leavings at that.

"Aren't you going to say anything?"

"I was not expecting this, sire," Henry managed to reply. His mind filled with the image of himself lying in bed with a world-weary hag. He could remember his father having dealings with Alienor and Louis when he was still trailing after his wet nurse with a comfort cloth in his hand. His epitome of a perfect bride was someone virginal, innocent, and younger than he was, but political reality was a different matter entirely. Caught between his ideal and brutal fact, he was briefly nonplussed, and that for Henry was disconcerting.

"Well, overcome your astonishment and accustom yourself to the notion," Geoffrey said curtly. "I expect your compliance in this."

Henry stiffened.

Geoffrey raised his right forefinger in admonishment. "You must see the advantage. You will gain Aquitaine for the taking of a marriage vow. Your rule as duke will stretch from the Limousin to the Pyrenees and give you the resources to go forward in England and Normandy. If you do not seize this opportunity, others will, and you will be the loser."

Henry grimaced.

Geoffrey's complexion flushed. "Do not look at me as if I have offered you a platter of dead fish! An opportunity like this will not come again. I will have Aquitaine for my bloodline; I have been chasing it for long enough. If you refuse, I am certain one of your brothers will be pleased to accept."

Henry glared at his sire. "I did not say I refused. Indeed, you are right. It is a great opportunity but you have sprung it on me. I was not thinking to wed just yet."

"I had been married to your mother for more than three years by the time I was your age."

"Hardly made in heaven though, was it? What did you say to your own father?"

"That is not the point, as well you know," Geoffrey said, his eyes brightening with anger. "Alienor of France is an entirely fitting match for you and I will hear no more on the matter. Is that understood?"

"Perfectly, sire," Henry replied. "Do I have your leave to go?"

Geoffrey flicked his hand. "For now, but we must talk more on the matter because we need to be prepared before we arrive in Paris."

Henry bowed to his father and managed to reach the latrine before he was sick, vomiting up the bread that had almost choked him. He hated being treated like a child and ordered around. He was Duke of Normandy and a grown man. He wanted to be free to do as he chose, not be directed by his father's hand as if he were still an infant. And yet his father was right, and it was an opportunity they had to seize. He wiped his mouth on the back of his hand and then he clenched his fist and struck the wall in temper.

"What's wrong?" His half brother Hamelin stood in the doorway. He was older than Henry by three years, a handsome, robust young man with tawny hair and changeable hazel eyes. For a short while until her death in childbirth, his mother had been Henry's father's mistress. Hamelin's full sister, Emma, was currently dwelling in the secular house for women at the nunnery of Fontevraud.

"Nothing," Henry said. He and Hamelin had a relationship built on grudges and rivalry, yet at the same time, they would fight side by side against the world. Henry's battles were Hamelin's battles, and if it came to a brawl between Henry and his two legitimate brothers, Hamelin always took Henry's side — from self-interest if nothing else.

"It doesn't look like nothing to me."

"It's a private matter between me and our father," Henry said, knowing he couldn't say anything, even to Hamelin. "You will know soon enough."

Hamelin pursed his lips while he decided whether or not to take offense.

"God, I need to get out of here." Henry strode out of the latrine cubbyhole. "Come, ride out with me."

Hamelin's gaze flickered. "Haven't you got more business with our father?"

"No," Henry said, his jaw taut. "We have discussed more than enough for now."

Hamelin shrugged, content to go with Henry because there was nothing he enjoyed more than a hard gallop with the wind in his face and a good horse at full stretch. There was the competition too. Usually Henry won, but there were golden occasions when Hamelin beat him, and they were worth striving for.

Today, however, Henry rode as if the hounds of hell were snapping at his heels, and Hamelin had to taste his dust, knowing that something had seriously riled Henry, but at a loss to know what.

39

Paris, August 1151

Henry wandered restlessly around the chamber in the Great Tower that had been allotted to him and his father. The wall hangings were of good quality cloth, thick and heavy, and the walls themselves were painted with a frieze of acanthus flowers. A chessboard occupied a table between the cushioned window seats in the embrasure and there was an illuminated book of psalms should he or his father wish to read. It was all very tasteful yet opulent at the same time, and not what Henry had expected of Louis of France, but then in all likelihood this guest chamber was of the Queen's design and thus interesting when it came to assessing her personality.

Geoffrey sat on the bed rubbing his bad foot. "Remember, not a word of the other matter to anyone. It has to be handled with the greatest delicacy."

Henry picked up the harp and coaxed a ripple of notes from the strings. "And you think me indelicate?"

"I was reminding you what is at stake, that is all," Geoffrey replied irritably.

"I know what is at stake, sire. I am no more a child in need of correction than you are an old man in his dotage."

Geoffrey flushed and for a moment his eyes were dangerous. However, he chose to be amused and gave a short laugh. "But you are still an insolent whelp. I do not want you pushing yourself forward here. We need Louis's compliance."

"I shall be as meek as a lamb," Henry replied with a sardonic bow.

His father snorted with disbelieving amusement.

Louis sat on a magnificent carved chair in his chamber with a length of tapestry spread before it to cushion the knees of those who knelt in obeisance. Henry looked at the man whose place he would take in the Duchess of Aquitaine's bed if their plans came to fruition. In his early thirties, Louis of France was handsome with striking pale fair hair and dark blue eyes. His expression was open and pleasant on the surface, but with inscrutable undercurrents. Anything could have been going on his mind — or nothing. His cheeks were gaunt from his recent illness and he looked tired and pale, but not without presence. His right hand rested on a scepter with a decorated knob of rock crystal and gold, and a matching reliquary ring of rock crystal adorned the middle finger of his right hand.

Henry knelt to Louis because it was a formality to one's overlord and because kingship was an estate to be respected, but he did not feel at a disadvantage and he was not intimidated. Louis might be the anointed King of France, but he was still a man, governed by the limit of his abilities.

Louis rose to his feet and bestowed the kiss of peace on Geoffrey and Henry. Henry concentrated on guarding his own response from Louis's perception. As Louis's lips lightly touched his cheek, Henry tried not to shudder. There was something fascinating but unpleasant about the moment. He knew he was playing false in a way that went much deeper than diplomatic dissembling. He didn't want to be put in a position where he got so close that he gave something away.

"I hope you are recovering from your illness," Geoffrey said to Louis with concern in his voice, as if he had not been earlier speculating to Henry about what would happen should Louis succumb to *la rougeole* and die as inevitably some did.

"Thank you, my lord," Louis replied. "With God's help I am well."

"I am glad for that, sire," Geoffrey replied, "but at least your indisposition has given us the opportunity to negotiate rather than fight."

"Indeed," Louis said. "It is better to have the harvest in the barns than burned in the fields."

Henry struggled to keep still and not fidget while platitudes were exchanged. In England the harvests of his supporters were constantly being burned in the fields. He needed to go there and deal with the matter but had to resolve difficulties with Louis first.

One of the irritants to their dispute, Giraud de Berlai of Montreuil, was brought forward from the antechamber, still in his fetters. The iron had chafed his wrists raw, and he stank of the dungeon at Angers where his family still languished.

Louis sat up straight, the diplomatic smile leaving his lips. "What is this?" he demanded. "Why have you brought this man to me in chains?"

Geoffrey shrugged. "He is my vassal but he has plotted to subvert me and he has plundered the monks of my patronage at Saint-Aubin. I bring him to you because he is one of the causes of our dispute."

Bernard of Clairvaux had been standing behind Louis, listening and observing, and now he stepped forward and struck his staff on the ground. "What does it say of a lord when he is vindictive beyond all charity? You are abasing this man out of your own pride

553

and anger."

Geoffrey sent the Abbot of Clairvaux a scornful look. "If I was vindictive beyond all charity, this man would be dead — hewed and hanged on a gibbet long since and his family cast out to starve. Do not seek to lecture me, my lord abbot."

Giraud de Montreuil stumbled over to Bernard and knelt at his feet, head bowed. "I throw myself on your mercy," he said, almost weeping. "If you and my lord king do not intercede, I shall die in fetters as will my wife and children."

"I promise you such a thing will not happen," Abbot Bernard said, his gaunt features set and grim. "God is not mocked."

"Tell that to the monks of Saint-Aubin," Geoffrey retorted. "If you want him, then bargain for him; otherwise he returns with me to rot in Angers."

Bernard set one hand to the shoulder of Giraud de Berlai in reassurance and fixed his burning stare on Geoffrey. "You shall return him nowhere, my lord, because your days on this earth are numbered unless you repent."

Geoffrey narrowed his eyes. "You speak neither for God nor for the King, old man," he retorted. "Number your own days before you count the time of others. I will discuss no further with you. You have no authority over me." Turning on his heel, he stalked from the chamber, leaving a stunned silence.

Henry bowed to Louis, ignored the Abbot of Clairvaux and the miserable chain-bound former castellan of Montreuil, and hastened after his father.

In the stables, Geoffrey waited tight-lipped for his groom to saddle his horse.

"That went well," Henry said sarcastically.

"I will not have that Cistercian vulture hanging his black prophecies over my head and meddling in my business," Geoffrey snapped. "I came here to negotiate with Louis, not the Abbot of Cîteaux."

"But Louis must have done it deliberately."

Geoffrey took the bridle from the groom. "As deliberately as I am riding out now," he said. "Let them stew in their own broth. We are here to negotiate, not to let them take control. This gives them time to retire 'Saint' Bernard from the fray and now we both know where we stand."

The Angevin guests, father and son, had arrived back from their ride. Alienor concealed her impatience and stood with outward calm while her women finished dressing her. Clothes and appearance were important tools of diplomacy, especially when facing the Count of Anjou. She had never met his son, the upstart young Duke of Normandy, and she was curious.

They had ridden in earlier in the day, but already there had been trouble. Although she was yet to greet them, she had heard that father and son had walked out following a sharp exchange with Bernard of Clairvaux. Alienor had taken small notice. Such dramatic gestures were a frequent ploy of political negotiations. By all accounts, the Abbot had retired to pray, taking the castellan of Montreuil with him, the fetters struck off, and Geoffrey and his son had returned from their ride and reconvened talks.

Marchisa held up a mirror so that Alienor could see herself in the tinned glass. A beautiful, poised woman returned her gaze and Alienor added an alluring half smile to that weaponry. She had become an expert at wearing masks, so much so that sometimes it was difficult to find her true self beneath the layers: the laughing child in Poitiers, her future a golden, untrodden road, glittering with possibilities. "Well," she said to Marchisa, and her smile hardened like glass. "To battle."

Negotiations had ended for the day with both sides wary as the dust settled from the morning's outburst but satisfied that progress had been made and understandings reached. As the courtiers mingled in the aftermath of discussion, a fanfare announced the arrival of Louis's Queen. Henry's heart began to pound, although he remained outwardly calm. It didn't matter what she looked like or how old she was, he told himself. She was only a means to an end and he could still have his mistresses as long as he didn't flaunt them in her household.

She was tall and willowy, the length of her legs hinted at with subtlety by the way her gown flowed around her as she walked. Her shoes caught his eye, for they were embroidered with tiny flowers and exquisite. As she passed Henry and he bowed, he inhaled a glorious scent that was as fresh and intoxicating as a garden in the rain. His concerns about her being a hag vanished in a single bound. Indeed, she looked eminently beddable.

She bent her knee to Louis in a businesslike fashion that acknowledged his kingship as a matter of duty, then she rose and turned to greet Henry's father, extending a slender hand decorated with a single large sapphire ring. Her gesture emphasized the sweep of her sleeve and bared just a little of her wrist, further stirring the delicious scent of her perfume. "It is so good to see you again, my lord," she said, her smile warm but regal. "You are very welcome."

"It is always a pleasure to be in the presence of such poise and beauty," Geoffrey replied with a courtly bow. He turned to Henry. "You have not met my son before. Madam, may I present Henry, Duke of Normandy, son of an empress, grandson of the King of Jerusalem, and future King of

England."

She turned her smile on Henry now, the curve of her lips slightly less warm than for his father, but nonetheless without strain. There was curiosity and sharp intelligence in her gaze. "Your father sets great store by you," she said. "I am pleased to welcome you to Paris."

Henry bowed. "I hope I may justify his faith in me," he replied.

"I am sure you will."

"He does so even now," Geoffrey said. "Mark me, he is destined for greatness."

She smiled again and gave a small lift of her brow to show that she acknowledged a father's pride while not being taken in by superlatives. "I do mark you, sire, but as you know, I always make up my own mind." She turned again to Henry. "You must take the opportunity to visit Saint-Denis. I am sure the building and the late Abbot's collection of gems and relics will interest you."

"Indeed, madam, I intend to," Henry replied with a formal bow. Close up, she was very beautiful. Her skin was dewy and flawless, albeit that she was no virginal girl. Everything about her was tasteful, judged to exquisite perfection. He wondered how much it would cost to keep a wife like that in the style to which she was clearly accustomed — even if the revenues were hers.

He could tell that she was assessing him

too, although not in the same way that he was assessing her. He wondered how her body would feel under his in the marriage bed and how experienced she was. What would she look like with her hair down? He lowered his gaze so that she would not see the intent in his expression. He was under explicit instructions from his father to do nothing to jeopardize their chance at Aquitaine, and that meant not alienating Alienor and not giving away by so much as a look or a word out of place what their intentions were beyond negotiating their truce.

She moved on to talk to others in the gathering, playing her role with consummate ease, knowing what to say and how to behave toward each person, although it was noticeable that she and Louis avoided each other beyond the most formal of exchanges.

Henry admired her poise, but was wary. A woman of such dazzling accomplishment might be a great asset to his future, but she might create difficulties too if she proved mettlesome. From the rumors he had heard, Louis of France had not been particularly successful in taming her, so it behooved him to think well on the matter.

"Your foot is troubling you, I can see," Alienor said as she and Geoffrey partnered each other for a moment in the dancing that had followed the afternoon's banquet. He was favoring the left side and she could see the pain reflected in the tension in his face.

"It is nothing." Geoffrey dismissed it with a wave of his hand. "An old wound from a spear. It will settle down presently — it always does — but if it pleases you to sit with me a little while, I shall be glad of your company."

Alienor sent servants for a comfortable chair, cushions, and a footstool and had her own chair placed beside it.

"Perhaps a game of chess?" Geoffrey suggested.

Alienor gave him an astute look. He was up to something. His foot might indeed be sore, but he had deliberately manipulated this situation. "If it pleases you, my lord," she said and sent a servant for a board and playing pieces.

"I hear all goes well now with your discussions," she said.

Geoffrey half smiled. "Now we have laid the ground rules and ceased the meddling of that cadaver from Clairvaux, yes. I am sure we can bring matters to an amicable resolution for all."

Alienor returned his look. Anything that discommoded Bernard of Clairvaux pleased her. She wondered if Geoffrey wanted her to intercede over some part of the negotiation in her role of queen as peacemaker. Geoffrey shifted position in the chair and moved his foot until he was comfortable.

"My son dances well, does he not?" he said, indicating Henry, who was in the midst of the next set, moving with energy and grace. His smooth young face was alight and his smile dazzled each partner in the change and turn.

"I am sure he does all things well, my lord," Alienor replied with composure. The chess set arrived and she occupied herself in setting up the pieces on the board.

Geoffrey said quietly, "You think me a fond father for singing his praises, and to an extent that is true, because all men desire to be proud of their sons and to know their line will continue in strength. But I also see the man he will become. He governs Normandy well."

"With his mother's help and yours," Alienor qualified.

Geoffrey hesitated as if he was about to argue the point, but then shrugged. "Henry is more than competent and he learns very quickly indeed."

"What is all this to me?" Alienor asked. "You approached me about a match between your son and my daughter before Louis and I traveled to Jerusalem and Louis refused. He is certainly not about to change his mind now."

Geoffrey studied the board and picked up a pawn. "I was not thinking of your daughter," he said and fixed her with his sharp, crystal gaze.

Alienor's stomach tightened, but she refused to show him how much he had disconcerted her. "That is interesting." She resisted the urge to glance in Henry's direction. "It would be a good move for Anjou, but what would I gain?"

"You would be Duchess of Normandy and you would wear the crown of England."

"You are walking ahead of yourself, my lord. Normandy, perhaps, but England lies in the balance, and why should I want to be queen there when I know neither the country nor the people?"

"Because it would be a fresh start among those who would not judge you," Geoffrey replied smoothly. "Make no mistake, he will be king. He has greatness in him. It would not disparage you to accept such a match."

"Perhaps not, but I say again it would not benefit me either." She moved her own pawn to match his and leaned back. "The Archbishop of Bordeaux once told me you sought to marry your son to me when he was still in swaddling."

Geoffrey's lips twitched. "He is not in swaddling now." He gave her a forceful look. "The moment your annulment is sealed, you become fair game to be seized and forced into another marriage. There are many wolves out there, and surely it is better to be in the company of those you know and who have come to you respectfully. You may think you are able to protect yourself, but you still need the weight of a mail shirt behind you, and he needs to be more than just a hired man or a loyal vassal. Even my termagant of a wife would tell you that."

"You are bold coming to me with such a proposal."

"There is no point in not being bold, but I am not rash, and neither is Henry. All we ask is that you consider the matter."

"I will say neither yes nor no," Alienor replied, maintaining a neutral expression, and set out to defeat him at chess. When she did, he accepted it with a rueful smile.

"Perhaps you would like to play Henry," he said.

"Does he often beat you?" She glanced at the young man as he left the dancing at his father's beckon.

"Let us say we are evenly matched."

"Then I would expect the same outcome."

Geoffrey looked amused. "Sometimes things are not as you expect," he replied and vacated his chair so that Henry could take his place. Then he limped off to speak with a French baron who held lands on the Angevin border.

Alienor appraised with fresh eyes the young man who took his father's place at the other side of the checkered squares. What would it be like to be the wife of this supposedly accomplished young man, who had been such a model of modest propriety thus far? She was only nine years older than him, which might either be a gulf or no distance at all. In terms of experience, however, he could not begin to compete. He was a blank page; a very young man whom she might be able to manipulate into whatever she wanted him to be. She needed to know more about him first before she even began to consider such an enormous leap.

His eyes were bright and intelligent, and he already knew how to guard his thoughts. His lips were tender with youth but set in a straight line, and his jaw was determined. How would it be to lie with him in the marriage bed? To perhaps bear red-haired, gray-eyed sons and daughters? To have Geoffrey of Anjou for a father-in-law? That notion almost made her recoil. To wear a northern crown should his ambition and luck bring him to England's throne? She knew little of that country; it had always lain in the periphery of her vision, misty, green, and cold. If she felt far from home in Paris, England was a step farther still.

With an open hand and a sunny smile Henry gestured her to begin. "Please, madam," he said. "It is your turn to make the first move."

■ ■ ■ ■

"Well," said Geoffrey when he and Henry retired to their chamber for the night, "that was not so difficult, was it?"

Henry shook his head and gave his father a rueful smile. He had been steeled to encounter a used-up woman going past her prime, but the reality was one still young and beautiful with poise and charisma, who would make a fitting consort for any sovereign. He was used to women with strong personalities, his own mother being one such, but while his mother was abrasive in her opinions and like harsh steel, Alienor was liquid gold. She still wasn't the innocent young virgin with whom he would have been most comfortable, but it was no disaster. "She is very beautiful," he admitted. They had reached a stalemate in their game of chess. He had told himself he could have won but had held back in order to be diplomatic, but at the back of his mind he had the worrying suspicion that she had been doing likewise.

"Louis is a fool to release her and let Aquitaine go, but that is his concern to deal with, not ours," Geoffrey said. "The Duchess is the kind of woman to make up her own mind and do as she chooses. We do not have to work at pleasing a labyrinth of advisers and I doubt she will take anyone here into her confidence."

"So our success stands or falls on her decision?"

"Precisely," Geoffrey said. "You did well today. I think you have made a good impression on her but without putting yourself so far forward as to seem brazen, and without calling yourself to the attention of Louis and his courtiers. I am confident that no one has any idea of the plans afoot. All they can talk about is me bringing Giraud de Berlai here in fetters."

Henry went to the window and looked out. "She will consent," he said softly, more to himself than his father, and his mind was on the great wealth of Aquitaine and what lay open to him as its consort duke. In the space of a few hours he had gone from a state of reluctance to being very keen indeed.

Geoffrey poured wine into the rock-crystal goblets and brought one to the embrasure. "To success," he said.

Henry took the cup and toasted his father in return. "To dynasty," he replied.

Alienor sat in bed, her knees raised under the coverlet to form a lectern on which she had placed the sealed letter that had arrived from Poitiers as dusk fell. She wound a twist of her loose hair around her index finger. For all her reputation as a temptress, the only man who had ever seen her hair unbound in the bedchamber was Louis. Contemplating the strand between her fingers she imagined the young Angevin's stare should she choose to accept his offer and give him a husband's privilege. It was an interesting proposal and one that had merit, but she needed to think the matter through carefully, because it was her choice this time even if that choice was constrained by who and what she was.

Letting the twist of hair spring free, she smoothed the letter on her upraised knees and bit her lip. Her heart's desire and her longing lay at Taillebourg with the man who had dictated this letter, but political necessity and the welfare of Aquitaine made their bond untenable. As a girl of thirteen she had believed anything was possible, but time had wrought wisdom and tempered rashness. Her father and his advisers had been right. If she had married Geoffrey, Aquitaine would have tumbled into chaos as factions fought each other for the right to rule.

In the Holy Land she had dreamed of annulling her marriage to Louis and doing as she pleased, but even that had been no more than a fevered dream. Whatever she had with Geoffrey would always have to be kept secret and circumspect. It was her sacred duty to protect Aquitaine and increase its luster. Whether marrying Henry, Duke of Normandy, would help her achieve her goal was another matter. The chess game had told her nothing about him save that he was fiercely intelligent and keen to please her without being obsequious. In some ways he reminded her of the squires she had raised to good service in her household. If she could raise him to good service too, then all might be well.

She heaved a pensive sigh and broke the seal on Geoffrey's letter. The glow from the oil lamp shone on the ink, but the muted light made the words hazy. Ostensibly it was a report of the current situation in Aquitaine. Louis's French castellans were preparing to leave the fortresses they had occupied and the country was being made ready for the final accounting before the annulment. However, the letter was coded too, and as always there was a private note written in the lines, with the relevant letters made that little bit larger or smaller. Geoffrey wrote that he longed for her return. He had been unwell with a malaise he had picked up in the Holy Land, but he was recovering and the sight of her would be enough to restore him to health.

"God keep you, my love," she whispered and kissed her fingers to the parchment before she put it away in her coffer. "We shall be together soon."

40

Anjou, September 4, 1151

The early September sun beat a hard yellow light on the cavalcade of the Count of Anjou and the recently confirmed young Duke of Normandy. The road was dusty under the bleached sky and the horses plodded with lowered heads, sweat darkening their hides. Banners hung limp on their staves without a breath of breeze to stir the silks. The knights rode without armor, having consigned their hauberks and thick padded tunics to the panniers of the pack beasts. Broad-brimmed straw hats emerged from the packs instead and men wiped their faces and the backs of their necks with cloths moistened from their water containers.

Being red-haired and fair-skinned, Henry was suffering, albeit stoically. The sojourn in Paris had been highly satisfactory. In exchange for a strip of land and a few moments of obeisance, Louis of France had officially recognized him as Duke of Normandy. He and his father had their truce, which meant he could continue his plans to invade England, and even if he had to make a marriage with the Duchess of Aquitaine, at least she was beddable and would bring him great wealth and prestige. He could still have his mistresses on the side if he chose. When he thought of the lands that might be his, all strung like jewels on a necklace, it made him smile.

Last night they had stayed at Le Mans; tonight they would sleep at Le Lude, and then ride on to Angers to confer with their barons and household.

"Christ, it's too hot," his father said. "I feel as if my bones are burning inside my skin."

Henry glanced at him. They had been riding in silence for a while, each given to his own thoughts. His father's face was flushed and his eyes very bright. "There's a good bathing spot about a mile farther on," he suggested. "We could stop to eat and cool off."

Geoffrey nodded. "I am not hungry," he said, "but a moment out of the saddle would be welcome."

Henry was ravenous. Even the oppressive heat had not stifled his appetite and the thought of bread and cheese had been at the back of his mind for the past several miles.

They arrived at a sandy bank where the river pooled in blue-green shallows and there was some willowy shade to set out a simple picnic. Henry stripped to his braies and ran across the warm grit into the water with a joyful shout. His face and hands were tanned red-brown from a summer spent on campaign outdoors, but the rest of him was milk-white in contrast. The water was deliciously cool once he was thigh deep, and he threw himself backward to float, arms and legs outspread. His father joined him, also stripped to his linens, but when Henry wanted to horseplay and dunk him, Geoffrey fought him off and snarled that he wished to cool off and to be left in peace.

Shrugging, Henry did as asked and went to drown Hamelin instead.

Geoffrey eventually emerged from the river with chattering teeth and refused the food his squire presented to him in a folded napkin. "Good God," he said. "Why would I want to eat any of that? It smells as if you've been storing it down your braies."

Someone made a quip about a big sausage, which caused a belly laugh, but Geoffrey did not join in. Instead he went to hunch in a blanket by himself, a cup of wine in his hand, from which he barely drank.

"What is wrong with him?" Hamelin asked.

Henry shook his head. "Too much sun probably. His foot has been troubling him these last few days and you know how he sulks when he is in pain. Let him be and he will be all right by and by."

Refreshed and rested, the troop dressed and moved on. Geoffrey struggled to mount his horse and he was still shivering. A short while later, he drew rein to vomit over the side of his saddle.

"Sire?" Disconcerted, Henry drew rein. His father's face was still flushed and his eyes were as opaque as scratched blue stones.

"Don't look at me like that," his father snapped. "It is nothing. Press on, or we'll not reach Le Lude before nightfall."

Henry exchanged glances with Hamelin but said nothing other than to order the cavalcade to pick up the pace.

They reached Le Lude upon the hour of sunset, the sky the color of a bruised rose in the west. The soldiers opened the gates to admit them and they trotted into the courtyard. Geoffrey sat on his stallion for a moment, gathering himself. He had been sick twice more on their journey and his whole body was shaking. When he eventually moved to dismount, his knees buckled, and only the grip of Henry and Hamelin, who had been standing close by, saved him from falling. Feeling the fire in his father's flesh, Henry knew a terrible sense of foreboding.

Over the next three days, Geoffrey's condition deteriorated. His lungs became congested and a violent red rash flushed his body, mute evidence that he had picked up the *rougeole* contagion while in Paris. The physician shook his head and the chaplain took the Count of Anjou's confession. Unable to believe this was happening, Henry paced the sickroom like a caged lion. His father had been a constant in his life, always there, always a support even when Henry no longer needed a prop to lean on. They had often irritated each other and there was the constant friction of masculine rivalry, but nevertheless their bond was strong and affectionate. Father to son, son to father, and man to man. Henry wanted to be independent of his sire, but he did not want to let him go.

"You will wear a hole in the floor," Geoffrey said, his voice weak and querulous with irritation. He was propped up in the bed, supported by numerous bolsters and pillows. The fever had lessened over the last couple of hours, but his breathing was labored and his extremities were blue.

Henry came to the bedside and took his father's hand. "There is nothing else I can do," he replied.

"Hah, you never could sit still," Geoffrey said. "That is a lesson you could learn from Hamelin." He nodded at his bastard son, who sat on a chair by the hearth in the bedchamber, his head bent over his clasped hands, his despair almost palpable.

"I can be still when I am dead."

Geoffrey gave a snort of bleak amusement. "You are a great comfort to me."

"You would not want me to be still."

"Sometimes it would be an advantage. Sit. I want to talk to you while I still have breath and reason."

Reluctantly, Henry took his place at the bedside. It was his duty to keep vigil, but all he wanted to do was saddle his horse and ride like the wind to outstrip death.

Geoffrey summoned his reserves and spoke with sucking pauses for breath. "You are my heir. Anjou will be yours as well as Normandy."

Henry flushed. So much for his younger brother's constant demands that Anjou should be his. He was glad his father saw eye to eye with him on that score. "I will govern and exalt them well," he said.

"See that you do. Do not let me down in this." Geoffrey was silent for a time and closed his eyes while he mustered the energy to speak again. "But your brothers must have something. I leave William's gift to your discretion, but I want you to give Geoffrey his due."

Henry stiffened. That was not so good. The only due that Geoffrey deserved was a kick in the braies. "His due, sire?"

"He is to have the castles of Chinon, Loudun, and Mirebeau. These are the traditional heritage of a younger son."

Henry tightened his lips. He had no intention of letting his younger brother have control of those castles. They were too strategic and important. He knew full well that the upstart desired all of Anjou. He would not be content with such an inheritance and would only use it to foment rebellion.

"Do you hear me?" Geoffrey demanded hoarsely.

"Yes, sire," Henry muttered.

"Then swear to me you will do this thing."

Henry swallowed. "I do so swear," he said through his teeth. There were no chaplains around at this moment to hear the oath. A dying man should not try to impose his will on the living.

Geoffrey bared his teeth. "I hold you to your oath on pain of my curse," he gasped. "You will also care for Hamelin and advance him. He is your right hand and sired of the same seed. I expect you always to acknowledge that. He will be your greatest ally."

Henry nodded with more readiness to this command. "I shall look after Hamelin, sire," he said with a glance over his shoulder. "When England is mine, I shall find him a suitable heiress and lands of standing."

"And your half sister at Fontevraud. Make sure Emma is cared for also."

"Yes, sire. I shall do all that is necessary."

"Good." Once more Geoffrey paused to

575

replenish his reserves. For a moment Henry thought he had fallen asleep, but as he began to disengage his hand, Geoffrey tightened his grip. "Your marriage." He fixed Henry with a bloodshot stare. "Do what you must to secure your marriage to the Duchess of Aquitaine."

"Sire, I shall."

"Women are fickle and will lead you down twisted paths if you allow them to. Always be on top of your wife in every sense of the word, because she will try to ride you as women do with all men."

Henry almost smiled at the analogy, but concealed his humor as he saw his father was in complete and grim earnest.

"Do not trust women. Their weapons are not the blade and the fist, but the glance, the soft word in the bedchamber, and the lie. Put your own men in her household whenever you can, and watch her carefully, for if you do not, you will never be master of your own domain." Geoffrey's chest heaved as he strove to articulate the words. "Keep her with child, and make sure your seed overcomes hers so that she bears you sons; otherwise she is no wife. It is for you to rule and for her to provide what you rule." His grip tightened on Henry's hand with a sudden surge of strength. "That is the way of God, and do not forget it, my son. I leave this in trust to you, as it was left in trust to me."

Henry realized these were the last words of

wisdom and advice he would ever receive from his father. He would no longer have that standard in his life, that solidity that his father had provided, and thus he focused on them with increased intensity. "I shall not fail you, I promise, sire."

"I know you will not. You are a good son; you have been a joy to me from the moment you were born. Remember me when you have sons of your own . . . and name one for me."

"Sire, I shall be honored to do so."

Geoffrey let out a breath that shook his body. "I am very tired," he whispered. "I will sleep now."

Henry's urge to stride about and do things had vanished somewhere during the final efforts of speech from his father. These were taut moments before the final stillness. The time between each labored breath and the next. He had never been good at waiting. The world was too full of opportunities and promises, bursting like juice from a ripe fruit, ready to be devoured. And yet what did he have to give his father now but his word and his time?

Hamelin drew near to the bedside. "I heard what he said." He gave Henry a keen look. "And what you said; all of it."

"I meant it about an heiress and lands," Henry said. "But only if you swear fealty to me alone."

Hamelin's jaw tightened. "I will not swear

you fealty while our father still lives, but when you become Count of Anjou, you will have my allegiance. I do not love you; there are times when I hate you, but that has nothing to do with putting my hands between yours and swearing to be your man in exchange for what you can offer."

"I do not love you either," Henry retorted, "but I would trust you with my life and I will reward your service well."

A look of mutual understanding passed between the brothers, and they knelt, shoulder to shoulder, to keep watch.

41

Raoul de Vermandois had spent an enjoyable evening playing dice with Robert de Dreux and a few other courtiers. Some folk, Louis included, had retired early to bed because on the morrow the court was setting out for Aquitaine as soon as dawn lit the sky. The carts were loaded; the packs for the sumpters were piled up in a corner of the great hall near the door with an usher guarding the heap like a dragon sitting on a pile of treasure. It was a journey to begin the end of Louis and Alienor's marriage. Once the tour of Aquitaine was complete, Louis would withdraw to France, and all that would remain was the formality of the decrees and the seal of the Church.

"You'll be a free man too, eh, cousin, with the Queen's mad sister out of your life," Robert said to Raoul. His face was wine-flushed. "I warrant you regret ever laying eyes on her."

"I do not regret that, only what came to

pass afterward." Raoul scooped up his winnings from the game.

"Admit it, you seduced her because she was the Queen's sister and you thought to gain influence through the back door of the bedchamber."

Raoul shrugged. "If I did, I would not be the only man at court." He rose to his feet and trickled a handful of coins into the cleavage of the courtesan who had risen with him. He did not want to be alone tonight. Felice was buxom and good-natured and exactly what he needed. "I'm for my bed," he said.

Robert raised his brows. "I can see you are, and with a nice soft mattress."

"That's where I store my treasures." Raoul dipped his fingers between the courtesan's breasts making her squeal again. "In my mattress."

He left the dice table and took her to his chamber, kissing and fondling her along the way. His sexual appetite was voracious, although not in the ways Petronella had been demanding of late. To her, the act affirmed her desirability and convinced her she was loved. But the effect was always fleeting and the more he gave, the more she wanted and was still not satisfied. If he refused her she grew angry and accused him of wasting himself on other women. Well, now he was, and it wasn't a waste, it was a pleasure. Knowing that Petronella was leaving with

Alienor gave him a feeling of having been sprung from a trap.

He swung open his chamber door and pulled Felice into the room with him. She laughed as he pressed her against the wall, kissing her neck, rubbing between her legs. Suddenly she screamed and began pushing him away, her eyes wide in horror. Raoul turned and saw Petronella advancing on them, his hunting knife raised in her hand, poised to strike.

The sharp instincts of a fighting man saved Raoul from being ripped open. He ducked sideways and seized Petronella's wrist, wrenching it until she was forced to drop the dagger and he was able to kick it away.

"You son of a whore!" she shrieked. "You son of a whore! I knew it was true. Everyone told me it was my imagination, but I knew it wasn't!" She struggled in his grip, trying to claw him. "You spurn me in favor of a whore! You disparage me with a slut!"

"Fetch my chamberlain," Raoul shouted at Felice as he struggled to hold Petronella. "Rouse my squires and send Jean to summon the Queen."

Felice fled.

"I hate you, I hate you!" Petronella sobbed, kicking and flailing.

"That is why we must part," he panted, his face contorted with effort and shock. "There is naught left in you but destruction. You would have murdered me."

She bared her teeth. "Yes, and I would have danced in your blood!"

For an instant he felt a horrible dark thread of arousal, but knew that to act on it would be vile, mutual assault and he was sickened by his own response. "You are not well." He gripped her hard, holding her away from him. "I will have no part in this. You must be looked after by those more able to deal with you."

The chamberlain and squires arrived with Alienor close behind. For an instant Petronella became a wild thing, redoubling her efforts to get at Raoul, but then suddenly, as if she had taken a mortal blow, the fight went out of her and she flopped like a slaughtered doe.

"Bring her to my chamber," Alienor said brusquely. "Marchisa will tend to her."

Raoul hefted her in his arms and followed Alienor, with the squires leading the way by torchlight up the winding stairs to Alienor's rooms. Alienor directed him to place Petronella on her bed, and Marchisa hastened to her side.

"She tried to kill me," Raoul said with a mingling of pity and revulsion. "She was waiting for me with a knife."

Alienor sent him a contemptuous look. "You were with one of the courtesans, were you not?"

Raoul spread his hands. "What if I was? My union with Petronella has long been impossible. I dare not lie with her because I fear for my life — that she might have a blade under the pillow and stab me to the heart. She constantly accuses me of bedding other women even when I have been chaste." His lip curled. "I decided I might as well hang for a sheep as a lamb."

"You knew she was volatile from the first."

He puffed out his cheeks. "I thought she was a lively handful, but, God's eyes, not this."

"You also knew she was the sister of the Queen and thought her worth the risk. You plucked the fruit and enjoyed the taste, and now you say it is poisonous."

"Because it is! There is no reasoning with her." He made a wide gesture with his arm. "All that remains are these black moods and despair. She no longer knows what is imagined and what is real."

"I will deal with her. Just leave; I cannot bear your presence here."

"If I were you, I would make sure she does not have access to any kind of weapon."

Alienor closed her eyes. "Just go, Raoul."

"I will pray for her, but it is finished." He left the chamber, his step heavy and his shoulders hunched.

Felice was waiting for him in his chamber, wrapped in his fur-lined cloak and nothing else, but he dismissed her. That appetite had become as cold as yesterday's pottage.

Kneeling at the small prayer table in the corner of his chamber, he lit a candle and bowed his head. When he rose from his prayers, his knees were so stiff they felt as if they had turned to stone and the unscarred side of his face was slippery with tears.

Biting her lip, Alienor looked at Petronella, who had turned her face to the wall and closed her eyes.

Marchisa said softly, "I can do nothing for her. She is in God's hands, madam."

"She is exposed to too much upheaval at court; yet if she retires to Raoul's estates, she only broods and grows worse. I have been wondering whether to send her to my aunt Agnes at Saintes. She might not find comfort in a nunnery, but she would be supervised and better protected."

"Madam, I believe a routine of structure and prayer would help her greatly," Marchisa agreed.

Alienor sighed. "Then I shall consult with Raoul and write to my aunt and see if she will give her sanctuary. We used to go there often when we were children." Her expression grew sad as she remembered running with Petronella in the sun-filled cloisters when their father had visited Saintes. The giggles and laughter, weaving in and out between the pillars, stretching to tag each other, their dresses hoisted to their knees and their braids flying, blond and brown, adorned with colored ribbons. And then in the church, kneeling to pray but still sending mischievous glances to each other. Perhaps at Saintes, God would remove this darkness from Petronella's soul and cast out her demons.

"Oh, Petra," she said softly and stroked her sister's tangled cloud of hair with a loving, troubled hand.

Standing in the palace gardens, Alienor watched the children at play in the golden September morning. They were an assortment of ages, ranging from toddlers only just finding their feet to long-limbed youngsters on the verge of puberty. Among them were Petronella's three, Isabelle, Raoul, and little Alienor. Being without their mother would demand an adjustment but since of late Petronella had been unable to care for them, the parting was going to be less intense. They had been told their mother was unwell and was being taken to the convent at Saintes for rest and healing.

Busy with a piece of sewing, a golden-haired little girl sat beside her nurse. Fair wisps had escaped her braid and made a sunlit halo around her head. She was intent on her task, her soft lower lip caught between her teeth. Another woman held the hand of a toddler with the same blond hair, helping her to balance as she took determined but unsteady steps across the turf.

Alienor remained where she was, feeling marginalized, a part of the tableau yet removed from it like a border on a manuscript. She had bidden farewell to her daughters last night, feeling nothing beyond a regretful sadness as she kissed their cool, rose petal cheeks. She did not know these children of her womb. The intimacy had been in their carrying, not their lives after the parting of the cord. In all likelihood she would never see them again.

Alienor filled her gaze with a final look at her children, fixing the scene in her mind because it was all she would have for the rest of her life, and then turned away to join the entourage preparing to leave Paris and take the road to Poitou.

On the third day of their journey, Alienor and Louis spent the night at the castle of Beaugency, ninety miles from Paris and one hundred and ten from Poitiers. Sitting side by side in formal state for the meal provided by its lord, Eudes de Sully, they presented a united front as King and Queen of France, yet a vast chasm yawned between them, and it was not a calm space. They were desperate to be rid of each other, yet still tied by the process of the law. Louis considered it Alienor's fault that God had penalized them by denying them a son: she was responsible but he was paying the price. He chewed his food in dour silence and responded to comments in curt syllables.

Alienor was silent too as she concentrated on enduring the moment. Each day brought her closer to freedom from this travesty of a marriage, yet annulment would bring its own crowd of dilemmas. Raising her cup to drink, she noticed a messenger working his way up the hall toward the dais, and immediately she was concerned because only very important news would disturb a meal in this way. The messenger doffed his cap, knelt, and held out a sealed parchment, which the usher took and handed to Louis.

"From Anjou," Louis said, breaking the letter open. As he read the lines, his expression grew somber. "Geoffrey le Bel is dead," he said. Handing the note to Alienor, he started to quiz the messenger.

Alienor read the parchment. It had been dictated by Henry and, although courteous, gave the barest details. The messenger was relaying the meat of the story: that Geoffrey had been taken ill on his way home after bathing in the Loire and was to be buried in the cathedral at Le Mans.

"I cannot believe it." Alienor shook her head. "I know he was not altogether well in Paris, but I did not think he was sick unto death." She felt a welling of deep sorrow, and tears filled her eyes. She and Geoffrey had been rivals, but allies at the same time. She had enjoyed matching wits with him and had basked in the glow of his admiration. Flirting with him had been one of her pleasures and he had been so beautiful to look upon. "The world will be less rich for his passing," she said, wiping her eyes. "God rest his soul."

Louis dismissed the messenger and murmured the obligatory platitudes, but there was a glint in his eye. "Well," he said, "we shall have to see about the new young Count of Anjou and whether the boy has the mettle to cope with his responsibilities. I thought him an ordinary youth when he came to court with his sire."

Alienor said nothing, partly because she was struggling to absorb the shocking news and partly because this changed everything. She was also wondering how ordinary a youth Henry actually was.

"It can only be good for France to have an inexperienced youngster to deal with."

"He loved his father dearly," Alienor said. "That much was clear when they came to Paris. He must be sorely grieving."

"As well he should." Louis turned away to talk to his nobles. Alienor made her excuses and retired to her allotted chamber. Calling for writing materials, she sat down to pen a letter to Henry, telling him how sorry she was and that she would pray for his father. She commended Henry's fortitude and hoped to express her condolences to him in person on a future occasion. The tone of the letter was courteous and conveyed nothing that could be misconstrued as inappropriate, even by the likes of Thierry de Galeran, whom she had no doubt would read her correspondence if he got the chance. She sealed the letter and bade her chamberlain give it to the messenger from Anjou. Pouring herself a cup of wine, she sat down before the hearth and gazed into the red embers, thinking that if she did marry Henry, she would be facing Louis squarely across a political chessboard and would need every iota of skill and good fortune to survive.

Alienor entered Poitiers riding a palfrey with a coat dappled like pale ring mail. La Reina perched on her gauntleted wrist, white feathers gleaming. The sky was as blue as an illumination and the sun, despite encroaching autumn, was strong enough to be hot. Alienor felt a wonderful sense of freedom, of coming home, as her vassals flocked to greet her. At first there was no sign of Geoffrey de Rancon, but she could see several Taillebourg and Gençay barons among the gathering. And then she glimpsed him in the throng, recognizing immediately the dark wavy hair and tall, straight posture. He turned and her rising heart sank again as she saw it wasn't Geoffrey at all, but a much younger man — a youth almost.

He approached her and knelt with bowed head. "Madam, my lord father sends his apologies for his absence and hopes to meet with you shortly. A slight illness has kept him from riding out to greet you, and I have come as his namesake and in his stead."

Alienor knew Geoffrey would not have stayed away for a "slight" illness. Nothing short of catastrophe would have prevented him from being here today and she felt a frisson of anxiety. There was nothing she could do here though, trapped in a public situation with a young man who had no notion of the depth of the bond between herself and his father. "Then I wish him a swift recovery and I hope to see him soon," she said and bade him rise.

He inclined his head but she saw the doubt in his eyes. They were both speaking in platitudes and knew it.

Once again Alienor held court in her great hall in Poitiers. A silk hanging powdered with gold stars canopied the thrones where she and Louis sat side by side. La Reina perched on a tall stand at Alienor's side, symbolizing her authority. Alienor had not been to Poitiers since before the long journey to Jerusalem, and although the decoration in the hall was rich, the entire place needed refurbishment. Some of the mortar had seen better days and after the wonders of Constantinople and Jerusalem, it seemed parochial and small. Once she was free of the marriage, she vowed to herself she would build a new one to better represent the standing of Aquitaine among the courts of the world.

Louis retired early to his prayers, his mood sour. Alienor suspected it was because her vassals had greeted her with cheers and snubbed him. The joy with which the talk of an annulment was being received was a blow to Louis's pride. His jealousy filled Alienor with amused contempt and she held court with relish. The more Louis scowled, the more she flirted and exercised her wit and power. She knew her vassals were pondering what would happen once the marriage was annulled. Already men were vying to be castellans of the fortresses that Louis's French garrisons were giving up. Alienor was entertained by the overtures made to her by barons eager for their share, but she neither hinted at nor promised anything she was unprepared to give and she remained cautious. If Geoffrey was as indisposed as the hints suggested, she could not rely on him as she had hoped. She decided to make a visit to Taillebourg her next priority.

Alienor and Louis arrived at Taillebourg on a

wet morning in early October. The great fortress guarding the Charente crossing shone as if it were clad in mail, and the river was a sheet of beaten steel, reflecting the heavy sky. The rain was fine and felt like moist cobwebs on Alienor's face as they rode under the entrance arch and into the courtyard. Geoffrey's son had ridden ahead the day before to make all ready, and he hastened to welcome them and bid them enter out of the rain. His sisters Burgundia and Bertha were present too with their husbands. Burgundia was tall like their father with his dark hazel eyes. Bertha was plump and merry with dimples in her cheeks, although her customary sparkle was subdued as she knelt to Alienor.

The great hall was spruce and cared for. A lively fire burned in the hearth; the floor rushes had a sweet, clean aroma. Fresh candles burned in the sconces to augment the weak gray light from outdoors. Alienor gazed around the room and felt memories pressing in on her, demanding acknowledgment. She had played chess with Geoffrey in this hall and joyed in music and dance with him and his family. She had seen his children lying in the cradle and wept for them all when Geoffrey's wife had died in childbirth. Later, she had looked at Geoffrey with a young woman's first awareness in the spring, and he had taken her hand. Then her father had died and her world had crumbled. Last time she had come to Taillebourg was as Louis's bride.

She and Louis were shown to separate chambers this time. There was not even the pretense of unity. Alienor was relieved that her allotted room was not the one of her wedding night but a smaller chamber with warm red hangings and a brazier to keep out the chill from the river. Soft lamplight gave the room a welcoming feel. A selection of books stood on a hinged chest seat, arranged to catch the best of what light there was should she wish to read. As Marchisa was helping her to remove her cloak, the eldest daughter Burgundia brought a brass bowl of warm scented water for washing.

"I was sorry to hear your father has been unwell," Alienor said. "Dare I hope he is any better?"

Burgundia looked down, concentrating on not spilling the contents of the bowl. "Your visit will much improve his spirits, madam," she replied. "He has talked about it often and it heartens him."

Alienor washed her face and hands and dressed very carefully. She donned an undergown of the finest linen, delicately embroidered, then a dress of green silk with hanging sleeves stitched with pearls and emeralds, and a gold belt decorated the same. She had Marchisa coil her hair in a net of gold mesh and perfumed her wrists, throat, and temple with some scented oil that Melisande had given her in Jerusalem. Lastly, she pinned to her gown the eagle brooch Geoffrey had sent her. Toilet complete, she drew a deep breath, steadied herself, and went to see him.

Geoffrey's son was present in the chamber, together with various officers of the household. Geoffrey himself sat in a chair by the clear light of the window embrasure. He too had dressed for the occasion and wore an embellished tunic of deep red wool. As Alienor entered the room, he rested his hands on the chair arms and pushed himself to his feet.

She strove to conceal her shock at the sight of this skeleton clad in a parchment-thin covering of yellow flesh. He trembled with the effort of standing upright.

"Madam," he said weakly. "Forgive me that I cannot kneel to you."

Alienor stretched out her hand to him. "There will be no talk of forgiveness between us," she said. "We have known each other too long for that to be necessary. Please — sit."

Gripping the table at the side of the chair for support, Geoffrey eased himself down and gasped. His son produced a cushioned chair for Alienor, facing his father. "Why did you not tell me you were so sick?" Alienor demanded.

Geoffrey gave a languid wave of his hand. "Because I hoped I would improve. I still hope with God's blessing to do so because there comes a time when there is nothing left but hope, whether for recovery or salvation. If that is gone, what remains but a void? I knew you would come, and I prayed to be given the grace to see you again."

Alienor's throat closed. This was unbearable. She wanted to throw her arms around him and could not because of the public situation. "I am here now." She covered his hand with her own, the gesture appearing concerned and compassionate to the eyes of witnesses, but meaning so much more.

"My son will serve you well. I have had him in harness ever since my return from Antioch and he is both skilled and diligent."

Alienor glanced at the young man and he bowed to her, his complexion ruddy. "I am sure you will be a credit to both your father and to Aquitaine," she said, and then, turning back to Geoffrey, lowered her voice a note. "There are things I would say to you of a private nature between friends."

Geoffrey gestured to his son. "Leave us," he said. "I will summon you if it becomes necessary."

Since the lord's chamber was public during the daytime, the young man's "leaving" meant withdrawing out of earshot but not quitting the room.

"I do not know what to say." She continued to pitch her voice low, dreadfully aware that they might be overheard. "I am filled with great sadness. I hoped to have you for many more years to come."

He gave a wan smile. "You will always have me," he said. "Nothing has changed. We have always spent more time apart than together, have we not?"

"Not from choice."

"But it is the way of the world."

She noticed how cold his hands were and the effort he was making to breathe. "It does not make it easier to bear." She looked down and bit her lip. "I have received an offer of a second marriage when this one is annulled." She paused to steady herself, then raised her head and said, "Henry, Duke of Normandy, has asked me to accept his suit."

Geoffrey gazed at her with yellow-shot eyes and his expression did not change. "And what did you say?"

"I gave no answer. I wanted to discuss it with you, but I can see you need to rest."

Geoffrey gathered himself. "I have enough strength to talk with you even if my light is dwindling," he said with dignity and leaned back in his chair. "He is much younger than you."

"Yes," she replied. "Not long into manhood, although already in the thick of the fray. He came to Paris with his father." Knowing that Henry's father was so recently in his grave brought the specter of mortality farther into the room. "I did not know what to make of him. He was circumspect and quiet much of the time, but I think it was a deliberate ploy. It does not accord with what I hear of him from others who say he is brisk and confident in all things. I am not sure of him, and that makes me hesitate." *And I thought I would have you at my side, to advise me, but it is not going to be.* "His father was eager to have the match agreed, but he has always wanted to unite Anjou and Aquitaine — and he was careful, as you would expect. If Louis had caught even the edge of a notion about their plan, he would have had them skinned alive."

Geoffrey drew a labored breath. "If you do marry the young man, Louis will not forgive either of you for as long as he lives."

Alienor raised her chin. "I do not care for Louis's opinion in this. As his wife I have often feared his moods and been disgusted by the way he has treated me, but as a political opponent, he does not frighten me. He is not my equal."

"Indeed not." Geoffrey gave a wry smile. "You have time to think on the matter and to observe the Duke's progress."

She nodded. The word "time" was another that filled her with grieving.

"You will have to make a match with someone," he said. "And there are few enough of worthy status."

She swallowed. "You know my thoughts on that."

"Indeed I do, but we both know it would not be the right road for Aquitaine, and it is a path that cannot be taken now anyway." His head drooped as if it was too heavy for his neck to support, and there was a gray tinge to the sallow hue of his skin.

"I will make sure your son is given the attention and support he needs," she said, striving to keep her voice steady. "I will do my best for him as I know he will do his best for me and for his father." She removed her hand gently from his. "I think you should rest awhile."

Geoffrey forced his head up. "You will visit me again before you leave?"

"Of course; you do not need to ask." She stood up and lightly touched the side of his face in a gesture that to others was the affection of the Duchess toward a loyal vassal in difficult circumstances, but in her heart it was a deep cut. This was not a good place to bid farewell.

He took her hand and held it there. "If I could buy back a spring morning from my young manhood and take you there forever, I would do so," he said in a hoarse whisper.

"Don't . . ." Her voice wobbled.

"I want you to hold that thought and make it into a memory. It never was, but it will always be."

Her heart was bleeding freely now. "Yes," she said. "Always."

He paused to gather his breath. "Go on. I will catch you up presently. I am well now I have seen you." He released her hand and Alienor left the room as if she were on an ordinary errand, but once outside the door, she leaned against the wall and let the tears come, and they were like acid.

Geoffrey did not have the strength to hide his own grief as he watched her walk away. It was as if there were a cord stretching from his heart to her hand. He did not care who saw him weep, knowing that to observers it would only seem the folly of a sick man, grieving because he no longer had the power to serve his lady and Aquitaine. The truth would go with him to the grave, and the truth would be his private consolation.

42

Beaugency, March 1152

Alienor gripped the arms of her chair and, drawing a deep breath, raised her chin. She was back at Beaugency, seated on the dais in the great hall, waiting for the gathered bishops to declare her marriage to Louis null and void. The document of annulment was prepared. All it needed now was for the ink to dry on the final parchment and the seal to be attached.

She had arrived yesterday from Poitiers to hear the judgment of the Church and receive the decree of annulment. These were her final hours as Queen of France and the end of a fifteen-year marriage that should never have been. Louis sat enthroned beside her, his expression impassive. The shy, silver-haired youth had become a petulant, God-obsessed man of thirty-two with permanent frown lines between his eyes. Yet he was still handsome in shadowed light, and he was in a position of power. Alienor knew men with daughters would be casting eager eyes over him, keen to clamber up the spokes of Fortune's Wheel, but God help the poor girl who won that race.

The Bishop of Langres rose from his seat among the gathered clergy. His chest was puffed out like a peacock's and his eyes were razor bright. Just now they were concentrated on the sheet of parchment in his hand, the seal dangling from it on a plaited cord. Alienor suspected it was just his notes, but he wanted everyone to think it an important document.

"I wonder," he said, scratching the side of his jaw, "if I might raise the issue of the Queen's infidelity." As the words emerged, he raised his head to look around the gathering. "This has been documented on several occasions and we have witnesses who can attest to it."

There was a rapt, anticipatory silence. Alienor felt as if her stomach had clamped to her spine. She concentrated on keeping her face a blank mask, but her mind was racing. What did he know? What was he going to say?

The Bishop turned to the table and produced one of the golden clasps with which she was wont to cuff her gowns. "This was found in the bedchamber of the Queen's uncle at Antioch — not only in his bedchamber, but in his very bed!" He raised his brows to emphasize his point. "I have witness statements here to prove it!"

Alienor's mask slipped and revulsion twisted her mouth. The cuff had been a personal gift from her to Raymond's Countess. What a surprise that it should be seen in Raymond's bedchamber. The comment about the cuff being found in his bed was idiotic, because no one would indulge in bed sport wearing such jewelry, and if they took it off, they would not leave it between the sheets. However, she could see where this was leading. If he could pin adultery on her and make it solid, then she stood to lose everything.

At the table, Gofrid of Bordeaux rose to his feet and loudly cleared his throat. "My lord bishop, the case for annulment is being judged on the consanguinity of the King and Queen and no other matter. You know this."

Langres turned to face Gofrid. "I also know we should have the truth laid before us, not concealed by connivance and distractions."

"Connivance?" Gofrid drew himself up to his full height. "This lady is much maligned." His voice was powerful with indignation. He made a sweeping gesture toward Alienor, who immediately put her head down and looked modestly at her hands, which were folded around the prayer beads in her lap. "She has had to suffer the slur of these ridiculous and unsubstantiated claims, none of which can be proven, no matter how much you bluster.

"You see before you a pious lady who holds to God's laws and respects the way of the

Church. I have been her friend and tutor since her childhood and I vouch for her virtue every bit as much as you malign it. To have this vile calumny thrown at her by a supposed man of God is not only unfair, it goes against the teachings of Christ Our Lord. The truth will out. It will be known at the last in God's court where all of us must answer to our own consciences, for who is it, God asked, that would throw the first stone? We are not in a position to judge on this matter, but should remain with the one at hand where we can decide. Consanguinity is the business before us here today — that and none other." His voice became thunder. "This lady is not on trial!"

Behind him there were murmurs of approbation. Alienor raised her hand and surreptitiously wiped her eyes. She did not have to pretend.

Louis raised his hand. "You speak eloquently, Archbishop," he said. "Let us decide on the one matter, as you say." He inclined his head to Alienor. There was no kindness in his gaze and Alienor did not expect any as she reciprocated with a nod of her own. It was not in Louis's interests to have the whole rotten corpse of Antioch rolled over to expose the maggots, because he too had things that were better kept hidden.

Standing by the window embrasure in her

chamber, Alienor handed a packet of correspondence to young Geoffrey de Rancon. The new lord of Taillebourg and Gençay was present at Beaugency as part of her entourage, charged with escorting her safely back to Poitiers when all was settled. "Will you see these given to Saldebreuil?" she said. "He will know which messenger to send them by."

"Madam." He bowed and straightened, a deep frown creasing his brow. "I did not believe a word of what the Bishop of Langres said."

"I hope you did not."

He flushed scarlet and stammered a negation until she took pity on him. "The Bishop of Langres was bound to speak. The charge of adultery would sit so much better with him. We have never seen eye to eye. If he can do me a disservice, he will. It is of no consequence. I shall have no more dealings with him soon."

The young man bowed again and made his escape. A sad smile curled her lips. He reminded her so much of his sire in the way he stood and the expressions that crossed his face, but there was a vast world of difference. He was still a boy learning to tread in a mature man's footsteps. Nevertheless, his presence had helped her deal with his father's death. Together with Bertha and Burgundia he was a part of Geoffrey that remained in the world, a part she could help along the way, and it made her grief bearable.

Scarcely had Geoffrey departed than Archbishop Gofrid arrived. He was clad in his episcopal robes but had replaced his miter with a small skullcap. His tall posture had developed a weary stoop and his face drooped with fatigue.

Alienor kissed his ring and he set his hand on her head in blessing. She bade a squire pour him wine and directed him to a table set with a meal of succulent poached salmon and fresh bread. Gofrid gave her a grateful look and sat down. Having washed his hands in the finger bowl held by another squire, he blessed the food and set to with a will.

After a diplomatic interval Alienor turned to her guest with an expectant look.

"Matters are progressing much as I expected." Gofrid paused to rinse his mouth with wine and swallow. "The French were trying to keep a grip on Aquitaine by having the Bishop of Langres use those tricks today, but it will not work."

"How could Langres begin to suggest that there was any impropriety between me and my uncle?" she said with angry contempt. "We arrived in Antioch after a rough sea voyage and we were there for less than two weeks. I sought my uncle's protection because even then I desired an annulment, as you know." She curled her lip. "I also hear vile rumors that I am supposed to have bedded with the former Count of Anjou. Is that likely? It is all foulsome gossip intended to dispossess me of my lands by darkening my name."

"There are always those who dip their quills in venom," Gofrid replied. "Rest assured, the Bishop of Langres shall not prevail. He has an unsavory reputation himself — he only holds his position because Bernard of Clairvaux is his cousin and was persuaded to discredit the rival candidate. The grounds for annulment of this marriage stand or fall on the matter of consanguinity, nothing else."

"Let us hope they do." Alienor shuddered. "If I have to remain wed to Louis, I swear that instead of accusing me of adultery, I will be hauled to trial for his murder."

Gofrid gave a sour smile. "I do not think that will be necessary. This has come too far to fall down now. Louis desires this annulment as much as you do." Finished eating, he dipped his hands in the rose water and washed them again.

Alienor replenished their cups. "I want to talk to you about the future — about a decision I have to make."

Gofrid wiped his hands on a napkin and fixed her with a steady blue gaze that made her feel as if she were his pupil again, under his strict but benevolent scrutiny.

"I know I cannot remain unwed." She toyed with the base of her goblet. "I have a duty to

Aquitaine to rule and beget heirs of my body to follow in my stead."

"Indeed, daughter, you do," Gofrid replied cautiously.

"You should know that I have received an offer of marriage — from Henry, Duke of Normandy."

His brows rose. "When was this?"

"In Paris, when he and his father came to negotiate a truce. It has its merits, I think."

"Duke Henry mentioned this to you himself?"

She shook her head. "I believe it was at his father's prompting. I barely spoke with the young Duke and he was being very careful because of the situation. Aquitaine would be an enormous prize for him, but is he worth the prize to me? You can understand my wariness."

Gofrid took a drink of wine to give himself a moment to think. It would be unwise for Alienor to take a husband from among her own barons. Better she should wed a man outside of Aquitaine. Henry FitzEmpress would certainly fulfill that criterion. Fifteen years ago Gofrid had told her she must marry Louis of France. He could still see that frightened girl superimposed on the accomplished young woman in front of him now and it pained his heart. She trusted him and he wanted to do his best for her, and for Aquitaine. "I do not know the young man in question, but his reputation is growing daily and his breeding is illustrious. It is fitting you should marry someone who has the potential to become a king."

"I thought that too," Alienor said, "but I hesitate to make the leap. He is young, and perhaps I can influence him, but if so, then like Louis he will be open to the influence of others too. I had to fight Louis's mother when I wed him. By all accounts the Empress Matilda is a formidable woman who has her son's ear. How shall I fare on that battleground?"

Gofrid stroked his beard. "You are wise to be cautious, but I do not believe you will have the same difficulties. You are a grown woman in your full bloom. Empress Matilda is aging and dwells at the abbey of Bec. She may rule Normandy, but she will not stir her finger in other stews. Henry did not spend his childhood training to be a monk, although he is well educated, so that path may be easier for you also."

"You speak as I think." Alienor's tension eased at the Archbishop's approval. A pensive, almost sad look crossed her face. "But if I accept the offer it seems in many ways like a choice borne out of no choice."

Their discussion was interrupted by the arrival of Saldebreuil de Sanzay. "Madam." He approached the table, breathing hard from his run up the stairs, and bent his knee.

Alienor gestured him to rise. "What news?"

He grimaced, dark curls bouncing against his jaw. "I have heard there are moves afoot to have you seized once you leave here with the annulment granted."

"Seized?" She felt cold. "By whom?"

"My informants tell me you should beware of Theobald of Blois. You should be on your guard when you travel through his territory and avoid all invitations to spend the night at any of his castles."

Alienor's breath shortened. So it had begun already, the scramble to seize her and force her into marriage by imprisonment and rape, so that the man concerned could appropriate her land for himself, impregnate her, and have his offspring, should they be male, claim Aquitaine. Theobald, Count of Blois and Châtres, was older than Henry of Normandy and Anjou, but by so little that it made no difference. He was just another ambitious young hunter chasing down his doe by whatever means lay to hand.

"Then we must take appropriate precautions," she said. "Saldebreuil, I trust you to see me safe and I give you leave to do whatever you must. If there is one 'suitor' there will be others. See that our horses are well shod and swift and that all the weapons are honed . . . and pay your informant well."

"Madam." He bowed and left. The Archbishop also rose to leave.

"You see what a prize I am," she said grimly. "Even before the annulment is sealed and lodged with the Church, ambitious men are already planning my future."

Gofrid kissed her forehead. "God watches over you and protects you," he said.

"Aided by an alert constable and men who are well paid to keep their ears and eyes open," she replied tartly. "God tends to help those who help themselves."

43

Beaugency, April 1152

It was done and Alienor was free, whatever freedom meant in this new context. The annulment had been pronounced by Gofrid de Louroux, and she was at liberty to return to Poitiers. Standing by the open window in the chamber that had been hers for the duration of the conference, she fastened her cloak and looked out on the fresh April morning.

From where she stood, she could see people leaving: the entourages of various bishops accompanied by laden baggage trains. Bernard of Clairvaux rode a white mule, his belongings borne in a plain bundle strapped to his crupper. Alienor shuddered. At least she would not have to suffer involvement with him ever again. She strongly suspected he had been behind the Bishop of Langres's attack. For a man who professed to love God, he was filled with the vinegar of hatred and self-righteousness.

She felt bereft rather than elated by her

freedom because of all the wasted years with nothing to show but acrimony and loss. The best to be said was that the business was finished and cut off like a piece of fabric from a loom and could be rolled up and stored away, never to be looked at again.

"Madam, the horses are saddled," announced young Geoffrey de Rancon, looking around the door. "If we make haste now, we can bypass Blois by moonlight."

Alienor turned from the window. "I am ready," she said. "Let us go home."

She was waiting in the courtyard for her palfrey to be brought to her when Louis arrived, cloaked and booted for his return to Paris. On seeing her, he froze.

"It is finished," Alienor said to bridge the awkwardness, her tone bereft of emotion. "I wish you Godspeed on your journey, sire."

"And I you," he replied stiffly.

"We shall not meet again." She would make sure of it. There were moments in their marriage when she had loved Louis and many more when she had reviled and hated him, but just now she felt numb. It was as dust. She would ride away and not look back.

Thierry de Galeran emerged from the hall, his hand on his sword hilt. He stared at Alienor as if she were a stain on his tunic. She returned his look with equal revulsion. Without this man to poison Louis's life and bed, without Bernard of Clairvaux and his noxious sermons, without all the petty, power-hungry men of Church and State fighting for influence over Louis, their marriage might have stood a chance of survival.

"Madam." De Galeran gave her a bow that managed to be of the utmost courtesy while mocking her at the same time.

Saldebreuil arrived with her palfrey: a chestnut gelding with a gliding gait that would eat up the miles effortlessly. The horse was lightly laden and glossy with condition. Saldebreuil's courtly flourish as he boosted her into the saddle wiped out de Galeran's insult. Since the journey was a long one, Alienor was riding astride as she would do for the hunt rather than with a lady's platform saddle. Her skirts were full to cover her dignity, and beneath them she wore leather hose tucked into strong boots. There was no impropriety as Saldebreuil helped her into the saddle, but still she was aware of Louis's disapproval and her impatience flared. His next wife would have to be a nun to please him.

Young Geoffrey de Rancon unfurled her eagle banner. The morning breeze caught the silks and they rippled in a bold dance. She gave the gelding a dig with her heels, clicked her tongue, and swept out of Beaugency at a trot. A hundred and thirteen miles lay between here and Poitiers: more than three days of hard riding. On an ordinary progress that time might extend to almost a week, but Alienor wanted to be safe behind her own walls as swiftly as possible, because when this journey ended, a new one could begin.

The chestnut covered the miles at a steady pace. Alienor and her troop stopped at the roadside at noon, spreading a white cloth on the grass to eat a simple meal of bread and cured beef washed down with slightly sour red wine. Then they were on their way again, riding steadily until dusk fell and the Loire rippled like dark gray silk in the evening breeze. Clouds were encroaching from the north and it started to spit with rain. Alienor drew up her hood, but nevertheless enjoyed the fresh green scents awoken by the moisture. A blackbird was singing its heart out and others answered, claiming their territories in the dusk. The spatters grew heavier, dimpling the river.

"Listen," said Saldebreuil suddenly.

Alienor tilted her head. The birdsong turned to chips of alarm as four men rode out of the dusk toward them. Their clothes were ordinary, but their mounts were strong and glossy.

Alienor's escort reached for their swords, and she prepared to flee. The leading rider raised his hand and put down his hood, revealing a thatch of rumpled golden-brown hair. "Peace to all. I mean you no harm," he said. "I am here to help you. My name is Hamelin FitzCount, half brother to Henry, Duke of Normandy and Count of Anjou. I have come to see you safely past Blois."

Alienor stared at him, more than a little taken aback. He was handsome with a look of Henry, although his coloring was softer. The straight mouth was the same though and the set of the shoulders. "That is most laudable," she replied, "but why should I trust you?"

He spread his hands. "There are but four of us. We are scarcely going to overpower you, and it is against our interests to lead you into a trap with Blois. I serve my brother and I am loyal to him." He dismounted and bowed deeply to her, although he did not go so far as to kneel. "There is a welcome party waiting for you at Blois, one I suspect you do not wish to attend. They have patrols out searching for you too, and you will not win past them. They intend taking you by force and wedding you to Count Theobald this very night."

Alienor did not doubt his information, but was still wary of trusting him. "What are you going to do? Lead us by another road in the dark?" She gestured to his men. "You are hardly equipped to fight."

"Not the road," Hamelin swiftly replied, "but the river as far as Tours. I have arranged with a pair of bargemen to take a party tonight, but they do not know your identity. You must disguise yourself, madam, or stay well in the background. It is best they do not associate you with the Queen of France." He glanced around. "We should make haste."

"What about the horses?"

"A few chosen men can take them down to Tours by a different route and rendezvous there."

"You mean split the group?" Saldebreuil shook his head.

Hamelin nodded. "It is the best way."

Alienor looked at the four men. Her instinct was to trust Hamelin because he had nothing to gain and everything to lose if he betrayed her to Blois. Coming to a decision, she turned to Saldebreuil. "Lend me a tunic and your spare gambeson."

Saldebreuil's dark brows rose. "Suppose this is a trap?" he muttered.

She shook her head. "It is not in the interests of Henry of Anjou's half brother to play false. He is bastard-born without the affinity or resources to fight the war he would cause. You take the majority of the troop and act as a decoy. If Theobald of Blois is after us, then let him chase you, not me."

Still looking dubious, Saldebreuil nevertheless reached to his saddle pack and handed over the requested garments.

Alienor dismounted. With her escort forming a circle around her, facing outward, she removed her dress and, with Marchisa's help, donned the tunic and gambeson. The bulk of the latter concealed her curves. A leather belt with a sheathed knife, a short gray cloak, and a separate woolen hood, pulled up to conceal her hair and hide her face, completed the disguise. She removed her rings and put them in a pouch at her waist and crouched to rub dirt into her hands. Her gown was stuffed into a coarse woolen bundle tied to a spear haft. Alienor grimaced. "It will pass at a distance, but I doubt it will fool anyone who looks closely," she said.

"A distance is all we need and it is dark," said Hamelin.

The bulk of her troop together with her maids prepared to go with Saldebreuil. The latter was still not happy, but held his tongue. He stayed with her as Hamelin led them down a muddy path to the riverbank where two barges were moored, the last of the light gleaming on their wet strakes and the barge masters awaiting their passengers. Since it would have seemed odd if she didn't help, Alienor stowed some of the baggage on board, keeping her back to the barge master and hiding her face in her hood. She heard Hamelin speaking softly to the barge owners, hinting that this was a secret mission on the King's behalf, and she heard the clink of coin as silver changed hands.

She settled herself in the first barge on a

pile of fleeces, her knees drawn up to her chin and her cloak furled around her. The crew took up the oars and maneuvered the barges out into the channel. Saldebreuil and the bulk of the troop rode off in another direction with the spare horses and the maids to act as a decoy. Alienor bent her head into her knees and tried not to feel afraid. Hamelin Fitz-Count joined her, sitting down on a heap of sacks and exhaling hard. "I will see you safely to your borders, madam," he said, his voice pitched low and his face turned toward her so that only she could hear. "My brother sets great store by you."

"Your brother sets great store by Aquitaine," Alienor said sharply, but then relented. "He must also set great store by you to send you."

Hamelin shrugged his broad shoulders. "There is little love lost between us, but we are practical men. He knows he can count on my skills and I know that of the three legitimate sons of my father, he is the only one worth following."

"Why is that?"

"Because he sees horizons when the others can barely see as far as the end of their own noses. I see horizons too, and if I keep faith with him, I will have a secure future."

"At least you are honest," Alienor said.

"A bastard son has little else in his pocket to trade," Hamelin said with a pragmatic shrug and a wry smile.

The crew hauled up a large canvas sail to aid their efforts, and with the wind behind them, the barges, cumbersome though they were, left a silver ripple of speed.

Moments later they heard shouts, the thud of hooves and jingle of harness from the riverbank. Alienor shrank against the side of the barge and pulled her hood forward, her heart in her throat, but the riders paid no heed to the barges and trotted on past, lanterns swinging.

"They'll be on the trail of your troop," Hamelin warned. "They won't think to look on the river. Even if they do realize what has happened, we shall be long gone."

Alienor strained her ears for the sound of combat, but the hoofbeats faded and there was nothing. Saldebreuil would have had the good sense to keep everyone moving at a strong pace and they had a decent head start. She closed her eyes and shivered but did not allow herself to be overwhelmed by her anxiety. Instead, she released it in laughter.

Hamelin gave her a look askance.

"Less than half a day since I was sitting in the hall at Beaugency, still the Queen of France and gowned as befitted my station. Now I am sailing down the Loire in the middle of a rainy night, wearing my seneschal's spare tunic, dirt on my face, and being hunted like a felon."

His mouth quirked. "In which position would you rather be, madam?"

"I do not think the reply is in doubt," she said, but did not elaborate.

The rain continued and the drops were like cold daggers in her face because of the wind direction. She found another sheepskin to huddle beneath and dozed, her arms folded tightly across her body.

They reached Tours at dawn and were reunited with Saldebreuil and the rest of the troop. Alienor was stiff and cold from the boat journey, tired too because she had barely slept, but she felt exhilarated. She had decided to remain clad as a youth until she was over her own borders because it was easier to travel that way. Their story was that Marchisa and Mamile were being escorted to a convent where Marchisa was to retire in respectable widowhood with her maid.

"Thank God you are safe, madam," Saldebreuil muttered as the company ate, drank, and rested their horses at a pilgrim hostel before setting out again.

"The journey was cold and wet, but no trouble," she replied. "But I was worried for your sake. We heard and saw a patrol riding after you."

Saldebreuil smiled darkly. "It would take more than those fools from Blois to outwit my experience, madam. They chased us half

620

the night, but gave up eventually."

"I shall be glad when we reach Poitiers," she said with a shiver. "All I want to do is sleep secure in my own bed and do as I please."

They approached the crossing of the River Creuse at Port-de-Piles shortly after noon. Alienor was wary because this ford was an obvious spot to ambush anyone heading south into Poitou. A scouting party, including Hamelin FitzCount, had ridden ahead to reconnoiter the ford while the main party stopped a little off the roadside to snatch a swift meal of bread and cheese.

The party soon returned at a swift trot. "We were right to be wary, madam," young Geoffrey de Rancon said grimly. "There are armed men waiting at the ford. The moment we arrive they will be upon us."

One of her escort shouted, pointing down the road. Their own troop had not been alone in sending scouts, and she saw two horsemen wheeling around and galloping back toward the ford to raise the pursuit. Saldebreuil swore. "Go back, madam. Take the left fork in the road!" He slapped her horse's rump.

Alienor clung on as the gelding broke into a canter. Dear God, was there no end to this? She was almost within her own territory and still she was not safe.

Alienor and her troop rode hard for the next

several hours, alternating between trot and canter. She kept looking over her shoulder but even when she saw an empty road, her imagination filled it with spear-brandishing pursuers, mounted upon tireless horses twice as fast as her gelding.

"Who were they?" she asked during a moment when they slowed their horses to a brisk walk to give them respite. The space between her shoulder blades tingled.

Saldebreuil shook his head. "I do not know, madam."

"I will tell you," Hamelin said grimly. "They were led by my half brother Geoffrey. We are less than a day's ride from Chinon, which is his by the terms of our father's will. Henry knew he would try something like this."

Alienor's mouth twisted. "Younger sons may see me as fair game for their ambition," she said with contempt, "but I put a far greater value on myself than a stepping stone to raise their place in the world. It is a vile disgrace that I cannot ride in safety to and from business with my overlord."

These attempted abductions made her realize that she could not remain unwed. Every time she ventured forth from one of her strongholds, determined suitors would be lying in wait to seize her and bring her before a priest. In truth she had no choice.

44

Poitiers, April 1152

Alienor gripped the sealed packet in her hand, knowing this was her last moment to change her mind. Waiting for the messenger to come to her, she stood by the window, looking out on the beautiful spring day. Everything was in leaf and bud and glorious blossom. It was a few days past the anniversary of her father's death and he had been in her thoughts. Geoffrey de Rancon too, although his grave had been made in bleak autumn. All that remained were poignant memories, and she must face reality, not live on dreams. Truly it was time to make a new beginning — and what could be better than wedding a young man in the April time of his life?

Her chamberlain announced the messenger and, with a sigh, she turned from the window. The man, whose name was Sancho, doffed his cap and knelt to her. She had selected him to bear this message because he was reliable, discreet, and intelligent. The letter itself was worded in such a way that if he was apprehended, the news he carried would not be obvious to the casual reader, although Henry would understand. After a final hesitation, she bade him stand and gave him the packet.

"Deliver this to Henry, Count of Anjou, and make sure he and no other receives it," she said.

"Madam." Sancho bowed his head.

"And give him this." She handed him a soft suede hawking gauntlet. "Tell him I hope he will find it useful in the future. Here is silver for your expenses during your journey. Ride swiftly, but do not take risks. Go now."

From her window she watched him leave, swinging into the saddle of a fiery bay courser, its hooves already in motion. He would change horses along the way and only stop to sleep when he had to. Depending on Henry's whereabouts, she estimated he should receive the letter within ten days at most, which meant she had a little less than three weeks to prepare her wedding feast.

Henry was at Lisieux overseeing preparations to invade England. The sound of axes chipping wood and the pungent scent of hot pine pitch filled the spring morning. Ships, soldiers, and supplies were all being stockpiled, ready for a full summer campaign across the Narrow Sea.

Henry had been just two years old when his grandfather King Henry I had died and Stephen of Blois had stolen the throne. He was nineteen now, Duke of Normandy, Count of Anjou, and ready to remedy the situation. He knew his supporters in England were desperate after seventeen exhausting years of unrest, but he also knew Stephen was aging and his barons were looking to the future. Several had already made cautious approaches to Henry, eyeing him up as a potential leader instead of Stephen's son Eustace, who was unpopular. Henry was prepared to do everything in his power to bring these men over to his side.

He looked up from a tally listing the latest arrival of horses to see his chamberlain approaching with a messenger in his wake. The latter's face was weather-burned and wore lines of exhaustion, but there was a gleam in his eyes.

"Sire," he said in the accent of Poitou and bent his knee. "My mistress the Duchess of Aquitaine bids you greeting."

"And you are?" Henry demanded. It was always useful to fix faces and names in one's mind.

"Sancho of Poitiers, sire."

Henry gestured him to stand. "Well, Sancho, I assume you are here to bring me more than just your mistress's greeting?"

The man produced a letter and a hawking

gauntlet from his battered satchel. "Sire, the Duchess bade me say that if you care to visit her at Whitsuntide, she will be pleased to take you hunting and discuss matters of mutual interest."

Henry gave the messenger a sharp glance before lowering his gaze to the seal attached to the document by a plaited silk cord. The imprinted wax bore the image of a slender woman in a dress with hanging sleeves. A falcon perched on her left wrist and she held a lily in her right hand.

Henry read what she had written and then raised his head to glance around the bustle of the camp. This would put an anchor on his immediate plans, but he had to act on the contents in Alienor's letter. He might not have an emotional investment in a match with her, but this was about dynasty and power. He felt a glimmer of satisfaction as he reread the message. He had been almost certain she would ask him, but he had still harbored a shred of doubt because women were fickle. Hamelin had told him about Geoffrey's stupid and pathetic attempt to abduct her on the way to Poitiers. He intended to put his younger brother in his place the moment he had dealt with more pressing matters.

There was no need to cease his preparations to invade England. He could go and marry Alienor while his officers continued to work. Thoughtfully he donned the hawking gauntlet and stretched and clenched his fist inside it. The smell of new leather tingled in his nose, rich and slightly metallic, and for some reason it made him feel hungry, as if he had not eaten in a week.

He sent across the camp for Hamelin and, when his brother arrived from supervising the testing of a new siege machine, told him to make ready to ride to Poitiers. "I am going to be a bridegroom and I need a second to stand with me," he said.

Hamelin folded his arms. "What about England?"

"Having the wealth of Aquitaine to support us is all to the good. England will benefit greatly."

"Louis won't be pleased," Hamelin said.

Henry waved his hand as if swatting a fly. "I can deal with Louis; I have his measure, but he does not have mine."

"In law you should ask his permission as your overlord," Hamelin persisted.

"You are jesting!" Henry punched his half brother on the arm with his gauntleted fist. "Presented as a fait accompli, Louis will give it, but I would have to be out of my mind to make such a request beforehand. To seize the moment, you must be ahead of it." He cast his gaze to the position of the sun. "It's too late to ride today, but we can make ready to move at first light — and travel hard."

■ ■ ■ ■

That evening in his chamber, Henry checked over the small baggage pack he intended taking to Poitiers. He needed to ride fast and light, but had made room for fitting clothes for his wedding and a gift for his bride. He looked at the two jeweled cuff clasps shining in their leather case. Set with sapphires, emeralds, and rock crystals, they were part of the German treasure belonging to his mother. She had given them as funds for his campaign, but he judged they would do better service as a gift to his bride.

Aelburgh entered the room, her thick ash-blond hair tied back from her face in a red silk ribbon. She was cradling a small baby in her arms. She sat down on a stool, unfastened her dress and chemise, and put the infant to nurse.

Henry eyed her full white breast and rosy-brown nipple before the baby covered the areola and began to suckle vigorously.

"The child is a drunkard," he said with amusement and a pang of tenderness, for this was his firstborn son and proof that his seed was sufficiently strong to beget healthy male children. The baby, christened Geoffrey, had been born seven weeks ago. The Church said a man should not have intercourse with a woman when she was feeding an infant but

Henry had little time for such persnickety rules, considering them the work of stifled priests, not God, and he had brought Aelburgh and the baby with him on campaign for comfort and company.

Aelburgh smiled. She had beautiful white teeth and full lips. "He is greedy like all men," she said and, looking down, she gently stroked the baby's fine sandy-gold hair.

Henry laughed. "I am feeling rather greedy now, I admit," he said, "but for a different kind of sustenance."

As soon as Aelburgh had finished feeding the child and put him in his cradle, Henry took her to the bed and buried his face in her wonderful hair. The energetic bout of love-making and the pleasure of his climax dimmed his energy and soothed him for a moment and he was content to lie beside her, his arms folded behind his head. She laid her hand on his stomach and lightly tugged on the fuzzy stripe of hair running from his navel to his groin.

"I have to leave you for a while," he said. "But keep the bed warm for me."

She lifted her head. "I thought I was coming with you?"

"Sweetheart, I am not talking about England. I have business in Poitiers first. I will visit you and the child when I can, but it may not be for a while. Do not worry, you will be well provided for in my absence."

"But I thought . . ." She sat up and looked at him, her gray eyes wide.

Henry said wryly, "I am getting married, my love — to the former Queen of France and Duchess of Aquitaine. When a lady of such rank and wealth sends you a proposal, you do not turn it down."

Twin notes of caution and dismay entered her voice. "Married?"

Henry grimaced. He did not understand the foibles of women over such matters and it made him impatient. "I have told you I will look after you. Don't worry."

Aelburgh bit her lip and looked away. "Is she beautiful?"

He gave a small shrug. "Her looks matter little. It is what she is and the lands she has that make her needful to me. I chose you for yourself." In its own way, Henry's gallant remark was true, but he used it in a calculating way to placate her. Now that his sexual appetite had been sated, his mind was already on the journey to Poitiers. He was fond of Aelburgh and loved the child, but they were peripheral when set against the drive of his ambition. "Sleep now," he said, setting his hand to her waist. "I may be taking a wife, but you should not confuse business with pleasure."

"And I am the mother of your firstborn son," she said with defensive pride.

"Yes, you are." He stroked her hair, but his

630

mind was on the future and all the golden possibilities that the Duchess of Aquitaine's letter had opened up.

"Well?" Alienor turned to Marchisa, spreading her arms to show off the magnificent red damask gown woven with an eagle pattern in thread of gold. She had just received news that Henry had arrived with a small, fast-traveling entourage and he had been shown to the chamber prepared for him.

Marchisa curtsied. "You may no longer be a queen, but you look every inch of one — not of France, but of Aquitaine."

Alienor's smile was brittle. "And perhaps of England one day. Let us go and see what this prospective husband of mine has to say for himself."

Alienor's vassals and servants knelt as she made her entrance. Raoul de Faye and Hugh de Châtellerault escorted her to her chair on the high dais where she was joined by Gilbert, the elderly Bishop of Poitiers, and Archbishop Gofrid of Bordeaux. The scene set, she commanded Henry and his entourage to be brought into the great hall and announced.

Henry's complexion was ruddy from recent scrubbing. He had washed his hair and its wet color was almost as dark as cinnamon. He wore a tunic of dark blue wool with scarlet edging dotted with gems. Standing at his side, she recognized Hamelin FitzCount, today clad in the garb of a courtier.

Henry stepped forward and, kneeling to her, bowed his head. "Madam," he said. "I came as swiftly as I could."

"For which I thank you," she answered formally. "Welcome to Poitiers, sire."

He sent her an upward glance and for the first time she met his gaze in full daylight. His eyes were crystal-gray with a flash of green in the depths and filled with piercing intelligence. His lashes looked as if they had been swept with gold dust. He had smooth, fair skin, a square jaw, and a young, soft beard of warm red gold. He possessed the handsomeness of youth and, although not a boy, he was still only a very young man and that gave her a tug of fear. "I hope to make you not only Duchess of Normandy and Countess of Anjou, but Queen of England in due course," he said with bold assertion.

Alienor raised her eyebrows. "I do more than hope in my intention to make you my consort duke of Aquitaine."

They appraised each other keenly. Still kneeling, Henry took her hand and pressed it to his lips and, while he held her captive, placed on her wrists the gem-studded cuff clasps he had brought with him. "This is the first of many gifts I shall bring to you. Not just of jewels and gold, but of empire and prestige." He raised his voice as he spoke so that it carried around the hall. Alienor listened to the rumbles of approbation from her vassals. This was what they desired to hear. She was pleased, but wary too. She did not want a husband taking over her domain, yet she needed a man who would be strong and keep his word by practical deed. She also did not want a boastful boy who promised all and delivered nothing. But Henry's eyes were not those of a boastful boy. They were knowing and steely far beyond his physical years.

She eyed the clasps. Jewels to adorn a queen, or a new set of fetters? Leaning over, she gave him the kiss of peace. "I hold you to your word," she said and, as she raised him to his feet, the hall erupted with cheers of acclaim.

The rest of the day was taken up in formal feasting. Alienor noticed how much Henry fidgeted, as if his body was unable to contain his bursting energy, but he managed to be charming and urbane too. He found the right words to say to each person while absorbing everything about them. He was like a spinster with a basket full of raw fleece, drawing out and twisting threads of policy from the basic material. How could he be only nineteen? She looked at his hands as he broke bread. The left one was enhanced by a magnificent sapphire ring. His right bore a long scratch across the back and a black mark on a fingernail where he had suffered some sort of blow. These were the hands of someone accustomed to grabbing the reins and forcing his horse in any direction he chose.

"You were a great deal more circumspect when you were in Paris with your father," she said.

Henry reached for his cup. "I had good reason to be. I did not want to arouse suspicion because we were there to negotiate a truce, and that was difficult enough without Louis getting the scent of anything else."

"A wolf in sheep's clothing then?"

"Rather call it a lion being a lamb."

The remark made Alienor laugh. He might be young, but he had an instinct for the right word in the right place, a skill Louis had never possessed.

He leaned back in his chair, the cup resting on his gold belt buckle. "My only regret is that I cannot stay in Poitiers and be a proper bridegroom. I still have urgent business in Normandy and a throne to acquire in England."

"That is indeed a pity," Alienor said, but she was thinking she could rule her own domain and be safe because she would be a married woman. She would indeed have her freedom.

"I shall return when I have done what I must and we can become better acquainted." He smiled at her. "I wasn't going to give this up for a more convenient moment."

"If you had not come, there would not have

been a more convenient moment," she replied with asperity.

"I realize that." He sent her a bright glance. "But I did answer your summons and I do recognize the importance of this union — for both of us."

Later there was dancing and as Alienor clasped hands with Henry, a spark jolted through her and was reciprocated. He was a good dancer, energetic and lithe at the same time. He was taller than her but only by a little, and they moved in harmony, but the looks they sent each other were like sparks, adding frissons of desire and challenge.

Alienor's vassals, well-oiled with wine by now, demonstrated some of the more robust masculine dances of the region. Henry mastered the different steps with nimble dexterity. Alienor observed the pleasure he took in the movements and how unselfconscious he was. He could laugh at himself when he tangled a move and take sweeping bows at the applause when he succeeded. Louis would not even have attempted to join in such sport. Henry's enjoyment was infectious and at one point she laughed so much she had to hold her sides. It had been so long since she had felt such emotion that it almost frightened her. It was difficult to stop and she could feel the edge of tears. As the dance finished, she took the decision to retire.

Henry bowed. "Until the morning,

madam." A gleam lit in his eye. "And tomorrow, we shall not have to bid each other good night at all."

Alienor's face grew warm. "No," she said and departed with her women, feeling flustered. His touch tonight had roused her more than she had expected, but then she had been sleeping alone for a long, long time, and he seemed to be genuinely interested in her beyond just the need for an alliance. Unless he was a complete boor in the bedchamber, it would not be difficult to make a pleasure of their wedding night.

While her women turned down the covers and freed the bed curtains from their hooks, she knelt at her little devotional altar and prayed that she had done the right thing to please God and the best for Aquitaine. She wanted to settle into a partnership of equals where she and Henry could blend their skills. She wanted unity in her household and support. She wanted children: sons and daughters who would eventually inherit her role.

Before she rose from her knees, she vowed to make this marriage as good as it could be. This time she would succeed.

Henry, who needed little sleep, did not retire until much later. He continued to socialize with the Poitevan barons, finding common ground and deciding whom he could trust and whom to watch, deliberately impressing his personality on them and issuing a warning that he was not to be trifled with despite his youth.

When Henry eventually retired, his own prayers were swiftly said, but heartfelt nevertheless. He thanked God for His goodness in dropping this plum into his lap. Alienor was attractive, even if she was nine years older than him, and she intrigued him. She was very different to Aelburgh, but then one was a mistress and one a wife and their relationships with him were on a different scale.

Thinking back to his initial reluctance to the match, he smiled ruefully. Being married to Alienor, being Duke of Aquitaine, might just turn out to be very rewarding indeed — in every way.

45

Poitiers, May 1152

Alienor and Henry solemnized their marriage
in the cathedral of Saint-Pierre in Poitiers.
The pillars of the nave were twined with all
the flowers of a full southern spring. Lilies,
roses, and honeysuckle added their scent to
the perfume of incense, rising in veils of
smoke to heaven. Once more Alienor received
a wedding ring on her heart finger; once more
she took the vows. For better or for worse . . .

Outside the cathedral, Henry faced her and
brought her hands to his lips. "My wife," he
said. "Now we have an empire to rule and a
dynasty to raise."

His words could so easily have sounded like
the overblown bragging of an immature boy,
but they didn't. It was a serious statement of
intent and she shivered with excitement,
because standing on the cathedral porch in
this moment, all things seemed possible.

She beckoned and a servant stepped forward and set a hawking gauntlet on her wrist.

Her chief falconer presented her with one of the snowy Talmont gyrfalcons. "You have your glove?" she asked Henry.

He looked around and Hamelin handed him the one Alienor had sent with the letter of proposal. Henry drew it on and Alienor transferred the gyrfalcon carefully to his wrist.

"This is Isabella," she said. "I gift her to you as a symbol of our marriage. Only the rulers of Aquitaine have the right to fly these birds."

Henry stroked the gyrfalcon's pale breast with a gentle forefinger. "Isabella," he said and gazed at the bird with delight and desire. Those emotions were still in his eyes as he turned to Alienor.

"The females are more powerful than the males," she said, not showing him how much his look moved her.

"Is that so? It is a good thing that I have a way with such noble creatures then," he said with a half smile.

She raised her brows. "I shall be interested to see your way."

Henry bowed. "I hope not to disappoint, madam."

She tilted her head. "I hope not too."

Henry was attentive to Alienor throughout the wedding feast. Sharing his trencher with her, he displayed competent carving skills and sound table manners. He was full of smiles and amiable words for everyone, but with the controlled dignity of a magnate. He also drank in moderation and Alienor was glad. She had seen what happened to young men in their cups and did not want to deal with the consequences on her wedding night.

"What is England like?" she asked him. "I have always thought of it as a cold land steeped in fog."

"It can be," he replied. "When you get the sea mist they call haar rolling in, then it is like being at the end of the world, but all the moisture and rainfall makes it green and lush."

"And that is supposed to recommend it to me?"

He laughed and shook his head. "It is the land of King Arthur too. There is a legend that Christ himself walked there in his young manhood. The smell of England is fresh and coastal. Its people are hardy but it is no colder than here in the winter. The English have a strong administration and judicial system and it has much wealth in wool. When my grandsire Henry was king, it was a prosperous nation. Stephen of Blois has squandered it all, but if it was husbanded properly, it could once again become a great asset." His expression hardened. "My parents strove throughout my childhood to keep alive my claim to England and Normandy. I shall not negate all their toil and I shall prevail over the usurpers."

Alienor had not seen him so vehement before; he had guarded his emotions up to now, and this new side to him intrigued her. "It is a great undertaking," she said.

"Indeed." He drew back a little, once more becoming the courtier. "That is why I need an exceptional wife to stand at my side and bear sons who will take the dynasty forward."

"I gave Louis only daughters."

He shook his head. "The giving of daughters was all his. I shall give you sons — there is no question of that — and our empire shall stretch from the borders of Scotland all the way to the Pyrenees, and our influence shall be felt far beyond that, for my kin sit on many thrones, including that of Jerusalem."

She noted his arrogance, but she believed him too, and anticipation flowed through her veins like warm wine.

The bedding ceremony was formal and dignified without boisterous jests. This was a duke and duchess being escorted to their chamber and dynastically and politically a serious matter. One or two people were rowdy with drink but were contained by the others. Pale pink rose petals strewed the bedsheets and green garlands festooned the canopy posts. Wine and light refreshments stood on a cloth-covered small table near the bedside, and the room was well lit by candles and lamps burning scented oil.

Alienor and Henry were each undressed

behind screens by their attendants before being brought to each other clad in chemise and nightshirt. The Bishop bound their hands again with a stole as he had done at their marriage to symbolize their union and blessed them, signing the Cross between their brows with holy water. The bed was liberally sprinkled with the same and Alienor and Henry placed together in the bed. Then the guests left and they were alone.

Henry faced Alienor and touched her hair. "It is the color of a Roman coin," he said, bringing a handful to his face to breathe in the scent. "It smells like a flower garden strewn with spices. I have wanted to do this all day."

Alienor leaned toward him. "You will not find this perfume anywhere else," she whispered. "It comes all the way from Jerusalem."

Their lips were almost touching. His hand left her hair and lightly brushed her throat. "It intoxicates me," he said. "You are so beautiful."

It was balm to her soul to hear him say that. She slowly unfastened the ties on his shirt. "And you are a young lion," she said softly.

He drew away to pull off his shirt and for the first time she saw his body. He was lithe with youth but now she realized where he got the strength to command a powerful warhorse to his will and to hold his own with his men. He was indeed a young golden lion with broad shoulders and a toned flat belly. A light fuzz of red-gold hair formed a pectoral cross from his chest, running in a soft stripe into the rolled-over waistband of the braies he was wearing under the shirt. Suddenly Alienor's mouth was parched while other parts of her body were soft and ready with need. It was lust, not love, and yet it was more than lust because it was sanctified by the Church and they both had a duty to see their union successfully consummated.

He took her face in his calloused palms and kissed her. His beard was soft and his lips were softer still. She returned the kiss and wrapped her arms around his neck. He reached down to the hem of her chemise and drew it over her head. Through his braies, she could feel the heat and strength of his arousal.

She made a move of her own because she had had enough of passivity with Louis and needed to exert her will as an equal. She kissed Henry's upper chest and then lightly bit the tight stub of his nipple. Henry gasped and thrust against her. The buck of his hips was wildly erotic with only that layer of light linen fabric between skin and skin. She moved to his other nipple and then back up to his throat. He kissed her again, harder this time, more assertively. She reached to the drawstring of his braies, unfastened them, and rolled them down over his hips, and then she gasped because he was magnificent and far bolder than Louis's half-mast efforts.

Henry gave a congested laugh. "I am ready and willing to do my duty if you are ready to do yours." He nuzzled his beard against her throat. Now it was his turn to nip and suckle and Alienor felt as if she were drowning in lust. He rolled on top of her and she took him in her hand, to feel all that wild young vigor. Henry shuddered and closed his eyes, and she looked at him, trying to judge how close he was, and if he would last. Without more ado she guided him into her body and welcomed him.

He gasped as she closed around him, and she could feel him trembling. He raised himself on his forearms for a moment, holding very still, and then he lowered his head and kissed her face, her throat, her neck. She ran her hands over his sides, feeling the curve of his ribs and the muscular arch of his buttocks.

He began to move. Alienor had expected him to be swift to the finish, but he exhibited both restraint and stamina. When he finally claimed her mouth and thrust hard and strongly, he took her over the edge and she clung to him, nails digging into his biceps, legs clasped around his as he gave her his seed.

Panting, he withdrew from her and kissed her gently. "I do not think we shall have any difficulties in the matter of the bedchamber," he said with a chuckle.

Rising on her elbow, she leaned over to kiss his shoulder. "No," she agreed. He was sensual and comfortable with his body — totally unlike Louis. Making love with Henry she had become a woman again, and she knew if she thought about it too hard, she might cry, which would not be a good thing to do in front of him. She had to be an equal partner.

Leaving the bed, Henry prowled the chamber like a dog examining new territory. His hair gleamed in the candlelight as he picked a date off a silver tray and ate it while studying a wall hanging that depicted a hawking scene.

"This chamber belonged to my grandmother," she said, stretching. "I remember her holding court here when I was a small child."

"I have heard tell of her and your grandsire." He looked around with an amused glint in his eyes. "Was she really named Dangereuse?"

"Who has not heard of them?" Alienor shrugged. "Scandal followed them both as closely as their shadows. She left her husband for him, and they lived for their passion, but it was so strong it was almost a sickness."

She slipped a blanket around her shoulders and went to pour wine into a single cup.

Mention of her grandmother made her think of Petronella, who was just like Dangereuse. It wasn't good to feel that obsessively about anything.

"It was my grandsire's name for her, and she always used it when I knew her, but her real name was Amaberge."

"Why the nickname?"

"Because she was unpredictable and wild. She and my grandsire were passionate about each other beyond reason — truly it was a kind of madness. But as girls we loved the music and dancing in her chamber. We loved to hear her stories and to be swept along when she was in a good mood, but we were afraid of her too — of the darkness inside her."

Henry looked thoughtful but said nothing.

"My grandsire built this tower as a range of domestic apartments, but this room was always hers. My other grandmother retired to the abbey at Fontevraud."

"My aunt is abbess there," he said. "My father's sister, Mathilde. And my sister Emma lives there in the secular house of women."

"Your sister?"

"Half sister. She and Hamelin share the same mother and my aunt has mostly had the raising of her."

"Is she going to take vows?"

Henry shook his head. "Not unless she has developed a sudden vocation. I would ask you the favor of visiting Fontevraud while I am in England."

"Of course."

"And I would also ask you to consider taking Emma into your household as one of your ladies. She is amenable and her stitchwork is superb. I think you and she will do well together."

"As you wish," Alienor said, feeling intrigued. It would be interesting to meet Henry's aunt and half sister, and it was one of her duties as Henry's wife to foster ties with his kin and sponsor positions for them as appropriate.

"I do wish, thank you." He drank the wine and taking another stuffed date, fed it to her. She licked his fingers with a delicate tongue to remove the stickiness. He put his hands in her hair and kissed her, and once more he was hard with arousal. Picking her up, he carried her back to bed.

The second time was slower than the first, but more intense. Henry was almost sobbing as he reached completion and Alienor gripped him for dear life, feeling as if she were being drawn through the heart of a thunderstorm. This time when their bodies parted, he pulled her close and set his arm across her and in moments was asleep.

The warmth of his body and his strong arms around her made her feel secure and protected for the first time since her girlhood.

In the early days, Louis had clung to her out of his own need and with Geoffrey she had never had a chance to lie like this, but Henry was confident in his own body, they were man and wife, and she no longer had to be afraid.

Henry woke up in the early morning feeling pleased and full in the heart. The shutters were open and white southern light streamed through the window. The bed curtains were open as they had left them last night and he was lying curled up close to his bride. She was breathing quietly, her golden hair spread on the pillow. He lifted himself up to look at her. The deed was done. Aquitaine was his and so was its beautiful duchess. Their union was better than he had expected it to be. She had known how to pleasure him and had derived great pleasure herself. Despite not being a virgin, she had still felt as tight as one. And the smoothness of her arms and those long, cool fingers . . . He loved the delicate pale skin of her throat, the little place just under her ear, the perfect angles of her brow and cheek and jaw. There was nothing he would change. He ran his hand lightly along her arm from shoulder to hand, admiring the pale silkiness of her skin, and remembered what his father had said about her — that he should beware of her and always make sure he had the upper hand. Well and good. He would make sure by whatever means at his disposal that he kept her full cooperation and loyalty.

Alienor sleepily opened her eyes and smiled at him. Henry withdrew, slightly uneasy to be caught looking. Even with what they had shared, they were still strangers, and she was not one of the regular women of the camp with whom he could josh and tumble in the daylight. Sitting up, he began to dress.

She watched him while gathering her hair in a golden sheaf over one shoulder. "There is no hurry today."

Henry shook his head. "I have matters to sort out with my men and much to do. I will see you later — we will ride out together." He kissed her on the lips and on the cheek and was gone.

Frowning, Alienor leaned back against the pillows. Henry was clearly not a man for leisurely bed talk. If he was awake, he had to be in motion, and she would have to adapt herself because in this case it would certainly be easier than training him to slow down. She admired all that vigor and energy, but she did wish he had lingered a little. She had woken in the night and enjoyed the feel of him next to her. All that golden strength. She had to get to know him properly now, and he her, but acknowledged it would not happen until he had dealt with the matter of England.

Later in the day they went riding as he had

said, and Henry carried his new gyrfalcon Isabella on his wrist. Alienor kept La Reina in the mews so that Henry could concentrate on the pleasure of his hawk without competition. He proved an adept handler of the bird and she flew for him in strength and beauty and fierceness. He laughed with joy as he watched her soar and dip. She caught several rock doves, and then a plump cock pheasant. Grinning broadly, Henry tucked one of the tail feathers in his cap. Watching him sent a pang through Alienor's heart. He was so alive. A man full of himself to the point of brimming over, but in confidence, not conceit.

They stopped to picnic by a stream and Henry gave Isabella to an attendant, who fastened her to a perch.

Alienor handed her new husband a cup of wine to wash down the bread and cheese he was devouring with appetite. "So now that we have helped ourselves to a marriage," she said, "what are we going to do about Louis?"

He swallowed and looked at her, his gray eyes bright with question. "Why should we do anything?"

"By rights as vassals in chief we should have asked his permission before we wed."

He snorted. "That was never likely."

"No, but now he has the right to turn on us and bring sanctions — perhaps even military ones."

Henry shrugged. "If he does, he will not catch me sleeping, because I never sleep."

"You cannot be in three places at once."

"You think not?" He looked amused. "A Roman tactician Vegetius said that courage is worth more than numbers and speed is worth more than courage. My army stands at Barfleur, but I can mobilize fast if I have to and change my direction. I have better men around me than Louis does, and I can control mine. In my camp, the rider is on the horse, not the other way around. I knew the risks," he said, "and I still took them, because the rewards far outweighed the perils." He gave her a look, his gaze smoldering and predatory. "Would you not agree, madam?"

She toasted him with her cup. "I am still deciding," she replied.

Henry set his cup down and drew her close to kiss her. "But you are open to persuasion?"

Alienor laughed. "I am always open to persuasion."

Henry was ready to leave. In the courtyard his entourage waited for him as dawn pearled the sky. He fastened his cloak and with impatient vigor cast it back over his shoulder, a mannerism with which Alienor was already becoming familiar.

"God speed you, my husband," she said. "I will pray for your success and your early return."

"I will pray for that too," Henry said with a grin. "This is like being invited to a feast where one is only allowed to snatch a taste of the first course before being dragged away."

Alienor raised her brows. "It will keep your hunger sharp," she said.

"There are no doubts on that score." He embraced her, his touch possessive now. He had gained confidence even in two days, but she enjoyed this assertion of his masculinity. It felt so good to be thought of as desirable rather than reviled as a creature of temptation.

She watched him lithely mount his horse: a fresh one from her stables. His own hard-ridden bay was resting up. This one was an iron-gray dapple with a raven mane and tail. She had provided horses for the rest of his entourage too.

Henry reined the horse about and rode over to her. "Until I come back to you with a crown." He made the horse rear and paw the air in a final salute, and then dropped him to all fours and rode out at a gallop, raising a cloud of dust.

Alienor felt a sense of emptiness when he had gone. She returned to her chamber. The maids had not yet tidied it and the bedclothes were rumpled. Henry's pillow still bore the indentation of his head. A strand of red-gold hair sparkled there and gave her a sudden catch of breath. More evidence of his arrival in her life lingered in the sight of yesterday's shirt and braies crumpled on the floor at the bedside. Henry was certainly not tidy and persnickety like Louis. She stooped to pick up the garments, pressing them to her nose to inhale the acrid, masculine scent.

After a moment she told herself off for behaving like a day-dreaming girl and put the clothes with the other linens to be washed by the laundry maid.

46

Paris, Summer 1152

Louis looked at his seven-year-old eldest daughter, kneeling to pray with her eyes squeezed tightly shut. Her braided hair was pale flaxen like his and, kneeling in her blue dress with her head bowed, she looked angelic. Noticing a hint of her mother in the line of her cheek and her posture, he was stirred by a pang of regret and unease.

He felt nothing as strong as love for her but he did possess a kind of tepid affection. She was a good girl who said her prayers, sewed accomplished seams, and only spoke when addressed. However, she was rarely in his eye line. His visits to the nursery reminded him of Alienor's failure to give him a son, and his two daughters were tangible proof of God's disfavor. But for now, they were the heirs of Aquitaine and he still had a claim through them.

"Amen," Marie said. She crossed herself and stood up, her eyes downcast. At her side stood Henri, lord of Champagne, to whom she had just been betrothed. His brother Theobald, who had made an abortive attempt to abduct Alienor on her way to Poitiers, had been betrothed to little Alix. She was only just walking and beginning to talk in single word imperatives and had been carried to church in the arms of her nurse.

From Notre Dame, the royal company processed solemnly back to the palace where a formal feast had been arranged to celebrate the betrothals. Henri treated Marie kindly, kissing her cheek and bidding her be a good girl and grow up swiftly so he could welcome her into his household as Countess of Champagne, after which she was taken away to the nursery with her little sister. In the great hall, the future husbands relaxed and basked in the knowledge that they were betrothed to princesses of France and that Aquitaine was now firmly in their sphere.

"My daughters will leave for the convent of Aveney on the morrow," Louis told the future bridegrooms. "They will be raised properly, uncorrupted, to make them fitting consorts."

Sage nods of agreement followed his pronouncement. Convents were safe and suitable places to raise gently bred girls and keep them pure in thought and body.

"How is my lord de Vermandois?" asked Henri. "I was sorry to hear of his illness."

"He is recovering," Louis said shortly. "I

have no doubt he will return to court soon." Raoul had been suffering from a general malaise ever since the annulment of his union with Petronella last autumn and his swift remarriage to Lauretta, sister of the Count of Flanders. There had been numerous risqué comments about the new bride wearing out her elderly husband, all of which Louis was trying to ignore.

An usher sidled toward him, a scroll in his hand. Louis beckoned to him with a sinking heart. A message delivered at the table was always important news — usually not good. He took the letter, broke the seal, and, as he read what was written, grew white around the mouth.

"What is it?" Robert de Dreux leaned toward him in concern.

Louis's expression contorted. "My former wife has married Henry of Anjou."

A taut silence gripped the dais table.

"But he's in Normandy!" Robert spluttered. "He's at Barfleur!"

"Not according to this letter." Louis swallowed, feeling sick. "He is in Poitiers and my wife — my former wife — has married him."

"Good God."

Louis could not believe what he had just read. He felt sick remembering how the young man had come to court. The lowered eyes, the wary but respectful deference, and all a front for secret negotiations. The thought

of Alienor and the red-haired whelp from Anjou in bed together curdled his stomach. How
could she, only two months after their annulment, and with a youth of nineteen? And
behind his back. The bitch, the whore!

"They cannot do this," Robert said furiously. "They are vassals in chief; they must
have your permission to wed. Since neither
of them has sought it, they must be brought
to account."

Henri of Champagne and his brother nodded vigorous agreement, for the development
was a massive threat to what they stood to
gain from betrothals to Louis's daughters.

"I shall summon them to answer," Louis
ground out.

"You think they will come?" Robert gave a
disbelieving snort. "You'll have to go further
than that. Their marriage is consanguineous.
You must write to Rome and bring the full
force of the law down upon them."

Louis nodded, although he was still reeling.
Why had she done this? Out of lust because
she was a corrupt woman? Because she
believed she could manipulate a youth of
nineteen into doing what she wanted as she
had once manipulated him? Henry himself
clearly had delusions of grandeur. "If they do
not answer the summons, I shall indeed take
it further."

"Believe me, they won't," Robert said. "Act
sooner rather than later."

657

"I will act when I decide," Louis snapped. He stamped off to be alone with his anger and humiliation that Alienor had seen fit to cavort with Henry of Anjou. Louis's only consolation was that if she could not give him sons, she was never going to bear them to Henry, because God would punish the couple and render them barren. His own situation with recourse to his heirs was all her fault.

He was kneeling at the portable altar by his bed when his chamberlain craved admittance.

"What now?" Louis demanded furiously. "Did I not say I wished to be left in peace?"

"Sire, I am sorry to disturb you, indeed I would not do so, but news has arrived that my lord Raoul de Vermandois is dead." The man held out a letter.

It was not unexpected but it still hit Louis like another body blow. Raoul had been a constant in his life ever since Louis had emerged from the cloister as a frightened child to become the heir to the throne. At times they had been at odds, but mostly Raoul had served him well; he had been steadfast in policy even if a fool with women and unable to control his impulses. He left three children all under age who would now become wards of court. They could not possibly go to their mad mother and Louis would have to decide where to bestow them.

He dismissed his chamberlain and knelt once more to pray for the dead man. Tomorrow he would have masses said and bells rung for Raoul's passing. He felt like a tree in the forest, where all the trees either side that had given him support, shelter, and camouflage were being cut down one by one, leaving him to bear the brunt of the storms alone.

"How did de Vermandois die?" Alienor's aunt Agnes, Abbess of Notre Dame de Saintes, fixed her niece with a compassionate but inquisitive gaze. Her eyes were so light a brown as to be almost pale gold, and they missed nothing.

Alienor had been furnished with a cup of wine and a platter of the abbey's delicious chestnuts candied in honey, which usually she loved, but for now was too preoccupied to enjoy. She was here to see Petronella, attend on her aunt, and tell her about her new marriage. "He had been unwell for a while and retired from court, but suffered a seizure while in bed with his new wife, having been warned to abstain." Alienor grimaced. "He was ever ruled by that part of him, although Petronella's jealousy always imagined it to be more than it was."

Agnes shook her head. "May God have mercy on his soul."

"The manner of his death is not something my sister needs to know," Alienor said quietly.

"Of course not," Agnes agreed. "Such news would do more harm than good."

"How is she?"

Agnes took a moment to ponder. "Much improved in her mind. The services and daily prayers have been of great benefit. I cannot say she is happy, but she is no longer distraught. I do not believe she is ready to leave us — may never be, but neither do I believe she will take vows. I shall take you to her in a moment."

Alienor knew what was coming. Agnes would want to know everything about Alienor's marriage to Henry as just exchange for looking after Petronella. She gave her aunt an edited but fair telling of the tale.

"And are you content?"

Alienor smoothed her dress over her knees and looked at her wedding ring. "I have no complaint, but then I barely know him. He left for Normandy almost immediately."

"From what I hear he is intelligent and well educated."

Alienor smiled. "He soaks up knowledge like moss soaks up water and is thirsty for more. He is never still, except when he sleeps, and then he is so still that his breathing barely stirs the covers." Her face grew warm. When he slept he looked so young and vulnerable that she felt a great welling of tenderness toward him, some of it maternal, some of it the pangs of a lover for her mate.

"You have much to deal with between you. It is a great gamble you have taken."

"But more attractive than the alternatives. He has the capacity to rule an empire." She raised her chin. "We both do."

"Yes, niece, you do. I have always thought that, ever since you were a small child. You ran rings around us all."

The wine and chestnuts finished, Agnes took Alienor to a quiet, sunlit cloister where two women sat embroidering, one a nun, the other Petronella, robed in a dark blue gown, her head covered by a plain white wimple.

"Petra?" Alienor went to her with hands outstretched.

Petronella lifted her head from her sewing and looked at Alienor. Her face was finedrawn, but her eyes were clear and knowing.

"It is so good to see you!" Alienor kissed her sister on both cheeks and embraced her warmly. "I hear you are faring well!"

Petronella returned the hug. "So they tell me." As they parted, she gestured around. "With all this light, there is little room for the darkness, and when it comes I pray to the Holy Virgin to help me — and she does."

"I am glad."

Petronella picked up her sewing again and began to work steadily and neatly. "I did not want to come here," she said. "But I know now you were right. If I returned to court, everything would fall to pieces around me. Here I am safe."

Agnes and the nun quietly departed, leaving the sisters alone. Alienor hesitated and then drew a deep breath. "I have so much to tell you that I hardly know where to start. Two weeks ago I married again, to Henry, Count of Anjou."

Petronella stopped sewing and looked at her in her old, knowing way. "You were planning that, weren't you? When they came to court in Paris. I knew it! I knew you were up to something!"

"I had it in mind but didn't make the decision until the annulment was actually pronounced," Alienor said defensively. "It is a good political decision, and I had no choice but to remarry because the moment the marriage was dissolved I became a magnet for every unwed man of ambition."

Petronella took up her needle again. "No," she agreed. "I do not suppose a nunnery would be a choice for you." A note that was almost accusation entered her voice.

"I would not be safe even if I retired to one — some power-hungry fool would abduct me and force me into marriage, and then what would happen to Aquitaine? Perhaps one day I shall find peace in one, but not now." She bit her lip. "Petra . . . I have to tell you something about Raoul."

Petronella set her jaw. "I do not want to hear it," she said. "I have cast him out from me like a devil. He was the cause of my sickness. I loved him beyond bearing and then I hated him. Now he is nothing."

"Petra, he . . . I . . . he is dead. He had been unwell for a little while." She looked at her sister with trepidation.

Petronella pricked herself and a bright drop of blood welled onto the delicate white linen. She watched it soak in. "You always come to tell me people are dead," she said in a trembling voice. "First our father, and now my husband. I should run away when I see you coming."

Alienor felt grief-stricken for her sister. "I wish I was not the bearer of these tidings, but someone had to tell you, and the responsibility falls to me. I could have sent you a letter and asked Aunt Agnes to read it, but it would have been the coward's way."

Petronella looked away down the cloister. "I do not care," she said. "I will not care." She looked at her pricked finger. "He has made me bleed for the last time." Leaving her sewing on the bench, she rose to her feet and walked a few paces before suddenly crumpling to the ground and beating her fists in the dust and howling. Alienor rushed to pick her up and their aunt and the nun came running from the other side of the cloister.

"Yes," Alienor said as she held and rocked Petronella. "He has hurt you for the last time. Hush now, sister, hush. You can be at peace now."

■ ■ ■ ■

A week later, Alienor arrived at the abbey of Fontevraud to visit Henry's aunt this time and collect her new chamber lady.

Fontevraud lay within Angevin territory, close to the Poitevan border. It had been founded on land donated by her maternal grandfather, William, the ninth duke of Aquitaine. His two cast-off wives had retired to the secular house and Alienor's grandmother Philippa had died here well before Alienor was born. The abbey was Benedictine, the complex housing both monks and nuns in separate buildings, and was ruled overall by an abbess, currently Henry's aunt Mathilde.

Mathilde was a handsome woman of middle years with clear, youthful skin and keen gray eyes like Henry's. Her brows and eyelashes were sandy gold, hinting that beneath her wimple, her hair, if allowed to grow instead of being shaven three times a year, would be Angevin gold. She had been a nun at Fontevraud ever since the death of her young husband on the White Ship more than thirty years ago.

"I am pleased to greet you and offer felicitations on your marriage to my nephew," she said with cordial formality.

Alienor curtsied. "And I am pleased to call

you kin, madam abbess." She gazed at the pale stones gleaming in the sunlight. "This place is truly beautiful."

"Indeed it is," Mathilde replied. "It has a special tranquility, and I hope all within its walls benefit. I certainly did when I came here as a young widow."

She brought Alienor to the church and as the women entered the pale-columned nave Alienor felt a sense of wonder and rightness. High windows blazed early summer light onto the tomb of the founder, Robert of Arbrissel, and the entire space glowed as if it were an antechamber to the great hall of heaven. The walls were painted with scenes from the life of the Virgin, but they did not detract from the clarity, but rather upheld and enhanced it. Here was no reliquary of a church like Saint-Denis, but one of pure and living light. Alienor felt as if she could stand at its center, open her arms, and feel God's love pouring into her like sunshine. Drawing a deep breath, she inhaled a lingering scent of incense, and with it came a feeling of serenity and spiritual grounding.

"You sense it?" Mathilde smiled with approval. "This place gives me sustenance every day."

From the church, Mathilde took Alienor to the secular guesthouse set aside for women who did not wish to take vows, but for one reason or another needed a safe haven away from the world. Many were widows who had retired to spend a peaceful old age, but younger women stayed too, sent by their families for education and safekeeping.

"Emma?" Mathilde called softly to one of the latter, who had been sitting sewing near the window. She was swift to set aside her needlework and join them and clearly had been expecting the summons.

"My lady aunt," she said and "Madam" to Alienor as she curtsied. Mathilde made the introduction. Emma was slender and not as tall as Alienor, but well made. There was a resemblance to her father in the shape of her face and the grace with which she bore herself. Her hair, glimpsed under her gauze veil, was a thick golden brown with a hint of red, and she had lovely hazel eyes.

"Your brother desires you to join my household as one of my ladies," Alienor said. "Now he has a wife, there is a fitting place for you outside of the cloister — if you wish to leave it, of course. You have a choice."

Emma swept her a look that Alienor thought at first was shy, but then realized she was being appraised just as much as she was appraising Henry's half sister.

"I mean what I say," Alienor said. "Having a choice is a gift more valuable than gold. You do not need to give me an answer now."

"Madam, I shall be glad to join you." Emma's voice was quiet but firm. "I am happy here, but I am also pleased to serve my kin and I thank you for asking whereas my brother would have commanded."

Alienor approved of the reply. Emma Fitz-Count had both grace and backbone. "You may be my lord's sister and subject to his will," she said, "but it is my business how I select the ladies of my household. I hope we shall quickly come to know each other and be friends." She gave Emma a conspiratorial smile, and Emma returned it in kind.

Abbess Mathilde took Alienor to the nun's cemetery behind the church and showed her a simple stone slab, the grass around it well tended and clipped short. The delicate scent of dog roses from a nearby trellis perfumed the air. "This is the resting place of Countess Philippa, your grandmother," she said. "She died before I came, but some of the nuns knew her well and will tell you about her."

Alienor knelt at the graveside to pray, setting her hand to the sun-warmed stone. "I am glad she found peace here." It would indeed be easy to live in tranquility in this place. The birds were singing and the sun was a benediction on her spine. One day, she thought . . . but not now.

She dined with Emma and Mathilde in the Abbess's lodging, the women sharing a simple dish of trout and fresh bread.

"Last time I saw Henry was at his father's

funeral, God rest my brother's soul." Mathilde made the sign of the Cross. "He had matured so much from the reckless imp I remembered, but then he has had to. There is so much expectation and responsibility resting on his shoulders."

"Indeed," Alienor murmured. Emma said nothing and kept her eyes downcast, making Alienor wonder at the relationship between Henry and his half sister.

"He still fidgets though," Mathilde added, lightening the moment. "He is never still — even in church."

Alienor laughed and agreed. "It is a pity he does not spin because if he was given a distaff full of wool and a spindle, he would have enough for a tunic in no time." She looked thoughtful. "But his mind is always focused. He is like the hub of a wheel with many different spokes of purpose going out, and all of them direct and clear. I believe he is capable of ruling everything that comes under his hand."

"You see it well," Mathilde said. "My nephew is a rarity indeed, although I admit my bias. He is the nearest I shall ever have to a son." She leaned across to squeeze Emma's wrist. "And you are the closest I shall ever have to a daughter. It is time you went out into the world, but I shall miss you."

The women were interrupted by the Abbess's chamberlain, Sister Margaret, bearing a message for Alienor on a travel-stained scroll.

Alienor broke the seal and swiftly read the contents.

"Trouble, my dear?" Mathilde looked concerned.

"The French have struck at Normandy," Alienor said, glancing up from the letter. "They have attacked and seized Neufmarché — Louis and Robert de Dreux and the Blois brothers. Henry could not get there in time from Barfleur." She bit her lip. "Also Eustace of Boulogne and Henry's brother Geoffrey." The whole world, it seemed, was determined to quash them before they could succeed. She felt an initial jolt of fear, but her anger and contempt were stronger. "The rats were bound to come crawling out of the corners. It does not surprise me, so I know it will not surprise Henry."

Mathilde looked dismayed but resolute. "I am sorry to hear it, but it does not surprise me either."

Alienor rolled up the parchment. "I will conclude my business here and return to Poitiers to wait for Henry — as we were going to do before. This is reason to be wary, not alarmed, because our enemies are inept and Henry is not." Despite her bold words, she hoped her young husband had not bitten off more than he could chew.

"They will try to bring him down because

if they do not succeed now, they never will," Mathilde said with a partisan gleam in her eyes. "That brother of his is a vain, silly boy. He will not rest until Henry makes him Count of Anjou and Maine, and that will never happen, no matter how much he rebels." She shook her head. "The men of Anjou are not good at sharing. My brother Elias was always being locked up for raising rebellion because he refused to accept his lot. It is in the blood, my dear, as you will doubtless discover once you bear Henry sons."

Alienor grimaced and Mathilde responded with a humorless smile. "Forewarned is forearmed. You have the strength to deal with what is given to you."

That was hardly a comfort, Alienor thought. "It is too late tonight to set out for Poitiers," she said. "A few hours more will make no difference." At least he had not yet sailed for England and had troops in readiness.

That night she dreamed of dark crimson roses dripping with blood and in the morning awoke to discover that her flux had begun and Henry's seed had not taken root. She had not really expected it to for the sake of one night, but still, it heightened her anxiety. Before she took leave of Fontevraud, she prayed again in the church and knelt to Mathilde to receive her blessing. And then, with Emma at her side, she joined the rest of her entourage and rode south toward the safety of Aquitaine.

47

Poitiers, August 1152

Alienor had spent the morning occupied with the business of government. The hall and courtyard in Poitiers was in a state of constant activity with the comings and goings of messengers, petitioners, scribes, and servants. She had heard from Henry in the field. He had chosen not to take on his enemies in direct combat, but had attacked them in vulnerable areas they were not expecting and with such speed that he left them baffled and reeling. She had ensured her own borders were secure because Henry's rebellious brother Geoffrey controlled several castles too close to Poitou for comfort.

She gazed at the new silver seal sitting by her right hand. She had commissioned it immediately after her marriage and the legend around the rim declared her Alienor, Countess of Poitou, Duchess of the Normans, and Countess of the Angevins. This was hers, this was her power, and she was never going to give it up to usurpers. Every document that went out from her court bore that authority, and it gave her deep feelings of pride and satisfaction.

Deciding to clear her head before the dinner hour, she called for her horse to be saddled. It was a fine late summer day and her palfrey was eager to trot. Alienor gave the horse its head and as the trot became a canter and then a gallop, she relaxed into the speed, enjoying the sensation of freedom and the illusion of outrunning her cares. Some of her courtiers considered her reckless but that was not what her race against the wind was about. She well knew the difference between being reckless and taking a calculated risk.

Eventually Alienor slowed the gelding to a walk and patted his sweating neck. They had reached the lichened Roman soldier, who looked little different from that time fifteen years ago when she had ridden out with Archbishop Gofrid and he had told her she was to marry Louis of France. The wide, white stare remained the same, although perhaps his cladding of lichen had spread a little. She gave him a wry smile of acknowledgment. He would be here long after she was dust.

Looking up, she became aware of a horseman cantering toward her in a cloud of pale dust. A handful of men rode behind him, but he had outstripped them by a hundred yards.

Alienor's escort put hands to their weapons, but she gestured them to stand down. "It is my lord husband," she said. Suddenly her heart was pounding. What was his urgency? Had there been a disaster? Was he fleeing and preparing to defend Poitiers?

Henry slewed to a halt before her. His black courser was blowing hard, the linings of its nostrils as red as expensive cloth. Sweat dripped from its hide, and from Henry too. He was scarlet in the face and his eyes shone like gray crystals, fierce and bright.

"Lady wife." He swept her a bow in the saddle. "I left you in haste, and in haste I return." His smile dazzled. His beard was fuller than at their marriage, and his hair needed cutting. Alienor was overjoyed to see him, and delighted too that he wore a smile, but she was still anxious.

"I am glad to see you whole and un-harmed," she replied, "and I am flattered by your haste, but where are the rest of your men?"

"Following. I outrode them," he said cheer-fully.

"For any reason?"

"Only that they were too slow and I was most eager to greet you." He gave her a plain-tive look. "And now I am very thirsty and I need to wash and change and eat and drink."

"All at once?" Alienor gave him a teasing look.

"Why waste time?" he said.

Alienor turned her palfrey and they trotted back to the city together with their entourages falling in behind. "I take it you do not bring bad news?"

"Well, not for us," Henry said with a gleam, "but Louis has turned tail to Paris claiming a recurrence of his fever and the brothers of Blois have retreated with him." A triumphant note entered his voice. "I told you that speed counted for more than courage and numbers."

As they rode, Alienor learned that Louis had tried to take Pacy, but Henry had ridden hard through the night, foundering horses but reaching strategic areas almost two days before he was expected. He had drawn them off by burning the Vexin, seizing Bonmoulins, and harrying the land like a demon. "They could not stand my pace and fury," he said with a smug and savage grin. "They were expecting a rash boy who had overstepped his mark, but they got me instead."

Alienor gave the servants orders concerning Henry's men and had a bathtub prepared for her young husband in the private chamber at the top of the Maubergeonne Tower. An attendant placed fresh bread and chicken on a board set across the bathtub so that Henry could eat and soak at the same time.

"What of your brother?"

"Geoffrey?" Henry made a face. "He's

always wanted what is mine and will do anything to get it, even conniving with the French. Much good it has done him, the fool. He shut his castles against me so I took them from him. He has no idea how to keep men loyal and has neither the wit nor the talent for warfare. I besieged him at Montsoreau — if you can call it a siege; he didn't stand. He does not have a backbone either."

"What have you done with him?"

"Accepted his submission for now and put my men in charge of his castles. I have sent him to my mother in Rouen. I would have kept him with me but I do not want to spoil my time here with the sight of his sulky face." He paused to drink some wine and bite into the bread and chicken.

"Your aunt Mathilde said there was no love lost between you."

"Hah, she's right. Geoffrey's always been a brat and resented me."

"And your other brother?"

"Will?" Henry swallowed. "He's a brat too. He was always whining and telling tales when he was a child — still has that inclination now, but he's no threat. He will be happy to take whatever Geoffrey drops through stupidity. Like Hamelin he has his uses."

Chewing another mouthful he began to wash. The bathwater had changed color from clear to milky gray. The sight of his wet, dark copper hair curling on his nape against his pale skin filled her with tenderness and a spark of lust. "And what do your brothers think of you?"

He gave a snort of amusement. "Hamelin would like to see me fall from a personal point of view, but he also considers I have the most to offer him and that it's better to be faithful and not bite the hand that feeds. He likes Geoffrey and William even less, and they have only scraps to offer. Geoffrey wants me dead and that's the end of the matter. If I had not promised my father on my soul I would not harm him, the feeling would be mutual. William is still becoming his own man. He won't run with Geoffrey for the same reasons as Hamelin — it's not a safe bet, so he regards me as the devil he knows."

She pursed her lips. "So brotherly love is no part of the mix?"

"God no!"

Alienor took the dining board away and Henry stood up. Attendants sluiced him down with jugs of warm water and he stepped from the bath onto a fleece rug where attendants toweled him dry and dressed him in clean, soft garments.

"I learned long ago," he said, "that to get the best from anything you have to be entirely familiar with its workings, be it a water mill, a ship, a horse, or a man."

Alienor gave him a teasing look. "And what about me?"

Henry lifted one eyebrow. "I am going to enjoy finding out."

Alienor dismissed the servants with a peremptory gesture and sat on the bed. "That will take you a lifetime. Water mills, ships, horses, and men — they are simple to understand and deal with, but you will find me more of a challenge."

"Ah, so you think men simple to deal with?" The atmosphere was charged with erotic tension. Alienor stroked her throat, drew her hand down over her braids, and halted at her waist, with her fingers pointing downward. "Men are governed by their appetites," she said.

"As are women," he retorted. "Indeed the Church teaches us that women are insatiable."

"The Church is governed by men, who have their own appetite for control. Do you believe everything the Church tells you?"

Laughing, he joined her. "I am not gullible." He unpinned her veil and unwound her hair, running his fingers through the strands and breathing in their scent. "So, if I am governed by my appetites, and you are insatiable, perhaps we shall never leave this chamber."

She laughed in return. "My grandfather wrote a poem about that very thing."

"About two women, their ginger tom cat, and a traveling knight?"

"You know it?"

"Hah, I have heard it recited around more campfires than I can remember. One hundred and ninety-nine times over the course of eight days, was it not?" He unfastened the brooch pinning the neck of her dress. "Your grandfather was prey to poetic exaggeration, I suspect. I am not about to die trying to emulate his imagination. I always say that quality is better than quantity!"

Alienor leaned over Henry. His chest was still heaving from their most recent bout of lovemaking and there was a beatific smile on his face. "Well, sire," she said, "it seems to me you are indeed trying to match the record in my grandfather's poem."

Henry chuckled. "No one could blame me if I did. Is there any wine? I'm parched."

Alienor left the bed and went to see to his request. Henry sat up, dried himself with his shirt, and took the cup she gave him.

"Why are you smiling?" he asked after he had drunk.

"I was thinking that last time we shared a bed, you could not wait to be out of it and away."

Henry grinned. "That was because it was morning and I had things to do. I did not need the sleep, and both duty and pleasure had been successfully accomplished." He sobered. "Do not expect me to keep regular hours."

"I don't, but I should know how long you are staying for this time. Do not tell me you have to rush off to Barfleur again?"

Henry shook his head. "I have decided to wait until after Christmas. I have plenty to occupy me here." He gave her a playful look. "I know little of Aquitaine and Poitou save that they are lands of vast resources and changing landscapes. I want to see them; I want to know about them — and about you and your vassals. And you have never been to Normandy. In turn you must familiarize yourself . . . and meet my mother."

Alienor's heart sank at the notion of meeting the formidable Empress Matilda. She intended to find out everything she could about her in order to be prepared. She had learned how to deal with Henry's father, but a woman of the experience and temperament of the Empress Matilda was another matter entirely. She still bore the scars of her clashes with Louis's mother, who had made her position as a new wife very difficult. How much of a mother's son was Henry? "Indeed," she said guardedly.

"And to beget heirs, we must be together. I desire sons and daughters of you, as you must desire them of me."

"We are certainly doing our best to succeed," she said with a smile, but she was thoughtful. She would have to guard against him becoming too familiar with her people even while he would be her sword should she need to curb them.

Henry drank his wine, kissed her once again, and left the bed to dress.

"Your sister is proving a great help among my women," she remarked. "She is skilled with a needle as you said she would be, and I enjoy her company."

"Good." Henry nodded. "My father wanted me to do well by her, and she can be put to better use than sewing altar cloths in Fontevraud."

Alienor eyed him. "I would have thought you might have more tender sentiments for an only sister," she said.

He shrugged. "We sometimes played together as children and she was always at my father's court for the great feasts of the year, but mostly we lived different lives. She is kin and I acknowledge my duty to her. Doubtless we shall become better acquainted now she is attending on you." He raised his glance to her. "What of your own sister? She is young enough to leave the cloister and remarry. Do you not wish to accommodate her among your women?"

Alienor shook her head. "I do not think that would be wise," she said, a pang arrowing through her at the thought of Petronella.

He gave her a questioning look.

"She is . . ." She hesitated. The earlier scandal concerning her sister's marriage was common knowledge, but Petronella's fragility of mind was less well known outside the French court and Henry did not have to be told. "She is best left in the cloister for now," she said. "Life at court would be difficult for her. She does not wish to take another husband, and I shall not force her."

Henry shrugged. "As you wish," he said, plainly considering the matter of small consequence amidst his own plans. He sat down before the fire and began reading from a pile of correspondence on the trestle. "Where to first? Talmont?" A spark lit in his eyes. "I very much want to do some hunting."

Alienor managed to smile even though her sadness for her sister was a lingering emotion. "So do I," she said and, donning her chemise, joined him at the trestle.

48

Rouen, Normandy, Christmas 1152

Bleak but intense winter light fingered through the high windows of the abbey of Bec. The air was cold and pure, almost icy. Gold and gems sparkled on crosses and the choir sang the *Te Deum* as Alienor knelt at the foot of the steps leading to the dais that had been set up in the nave. Above her on a cushioned marble chair sat Henry's mother, the Empress Matilda. The gown beneath her ermine-lined cloak glittered with dark jewels, and a gold diadem that would not have looked out of place at the palace of Constantinople shone on her brow. It almost seemed to Alienor as if the jewels were wearing the woman. The Empress's face was lined with the years of strife she had endured in her fight for her heritage, but her bones were hard and strong and her expression imperious. Having greeted Henry, she directed him to a chair on her right.

Head bowed, Alienor mounted the steps

and knelt again to present the Empress with the gift of a gold reliquary in the shape of a scepter, set with rubies and sapphires. Inside the rod, concealed behind a rock-crystal door, was a sliver of the finger bone of Saint Martial. Alienor said in a respectful but not obsequious tone, "My lady, my mother, my queen, my empress. I honor you."

The Empress accepted the gift graciously, with a look of genuine pleasure and approval. Taking Alienor's hands between hers, she kissed her, making a formal pledge in return. "Daughter," she said. "You are mine now, and I will do my utmost to protect you and your rightful estate." She indicated Alienor to sit in the left-hand chair and the service resumed. Henry sent Alienor a smiling look filled with pride, and Alienor returned it, feeling buoyed up and optimistic.

At the formal meal to acknowledge and welcome Alienor as Duchess of Normandy, the women continued to take each other's measure. Alienor thought her mother-in-law stiff and formal, but not the harsh termagant she had been prepared to encounter. The Empress was plainly very proud of Henry. There was a particular light in her eyes when she looked at him, but she did not try to oust Alienor from her position — rather she seemed to accept her role as a fitting consort for her eldest son.

"It is a difficult world for women born to

great estate," she said to Alienor as they dined on tender beef in pepper and cumin sauce. "As you must have cause to know."

"Yes, madam," Alienor said wryly.

The lines around Matilda's lips grew more pronounced. "I fought with everything I had to keep my claim to England and Normandy alive. Now it is Henry's task to continue that fight and take the crown that is rightfully his as it was rightfully mine." She looked at Henry with intensity. "And it is ours to help him in that endeavor."

Alienor was not intimidated by the Empress's autocratic tone. Providing Matilda did not meddle in the affairs of Aquitaine or come between her and Henry, she was prepared to keep a diplomatic peace. "I will give him all the help he needs," she replied.

Following the meal, the family retired to the Empress's personal chamber for a less formal family gathering. Alienor was reminded a little of Louis's apartments in Paris because much of the decor took the form of crosses, prayer books, and religious objects. Her mother-in-law was devout and paid more than just lip service to God.

She was aware of Henry's brothers in her periphery. Geoffrey had made his peace and everyone was being civil, but it did not mean Alienor had forgiven him for his attempt on her, or that she could bring herself to like him. If a dog bit you once, you didn't give it a second opportunity. No one mentioned his bid to abduct her, but the awareness created tension and the atmosphere between Geoffrey and Henry bristled with hostility. William, the youngest, was pleasant enough toward her, but was overshadowed by Henry's vibrant charisma. It was as if all the parental fires had gone into forging the first bright child, and only the tail end of the comet and the detritus had been left to flesh out the others.

"You say you did not spend much time with your half brothers?" Alienor said to Emma. She was becoming increasingly fond of the young woman, who, despite her quiet demeanor, had a playful side and a keen perception.

Emma shook her head. "Only at some of the Easter and Christmas gatherings, and mostly they had no time for me, and — and when they did, I tried to avoid them."

Alienor raised her brows.

"I was our father's only daughter and even if baseborn, I could claim his attention in ways they could not. They would pull my hair and taunt me when they thought Papa wasn't looking." She gave a small grimace. "But sometimes he was looking, and then they would be in trouble, and I would have to avoid them even more."

"They will tease you at their peril now you

are part of my household," Alienor said firmly.

Emma flushed. "I would not have you think that I am a complainer or a teller of tales — nor that I cannot stand up for myself."

"I think none of these things. I am glad of your company, but I protect those who serve me."

"I do not want to cause trouble between you and my brother," Emma said swiftly. "He has been as kind to me as often as he has been unkind."

"One does not cancel out the other," Alienor replied, but smiled to give Emma reassurance. "You have not caused trouble. I well know the ways of men, even if I do not have brothers."

"The ways of men?" Henry arrived at her side and lightly took her elbow. "What is this?" His tone was jocular, but there was a wary look in his eyes.

"I was asking your sister how it felt to be the only girl amid a passel of brothers."

Henry grinned. "Privileged," he said. "In all senses of the word."

"You used to pull my hair," Emma said. "And throw frogs at me."

"And give you rides on my pony and take you around the stalls in Angers to buy ribbons and pastries."

"Yes," she said. "As I told my lady duchess, you were kind to me too."

"And as I told Emma, now she is in my household," Alienor said, "she may anticipate ribbons and pastries and never again have to worry about the hair-pulling and frogs."

Henry gave her an amused look. "Do I consider myself warned?"

Alienor arched her brows. "That is for you to decide, husband."

He started to reply, but then his gaze fixed upon a travel-worn man in early middle age who had followed an usher into the room. His fur-lined cloak was draggled with rain.

"Who is that?" Alienor asked.

"My uncle Reginald, Earl of Cornwall." Henry's good humor vanished and he became as alert as a terrier. "What is he doing here?"

Alienor had heard Henry speak with affection of his uncle, who was a mainstay of his support in England. He was bastard-born to one of old King Henry's numerous concubines and staunch to the Empress's cause. The weather was vile and for the Earl to have made the hazardous sea crossing meant there must be serious news.

The Earl went straight to his half sister the Empress and knelt to her. Alienor immediately noticed the strong resemblance to each other in the sharp gray eyes and the jut of the chin.

Matilda kissed him and raised him to his feet. He turned then to greet his nephews and Alienor. She felt the rasp of his beard as he kissed her cheek in formal greeting. His touch was icy.

"What has happened?" Henry demanded, cutting to the meat of the matter.

Taking a cup of spiced wine from a servant, Reginald went to stand near the fire. "The defenders of Wallingford are desperate," he said. "If you do not come now, we shall lose our foothold in England. We have nothing left to give and if you leave it until the spring, it will be too late. Even stalwarts such as John the Marshal are finding it difficult to hold on. We are close to victory, but we stand in peril of losing all we have fought for. Stephen is isolated and vulnerable because of the death of his wife, who was his backbone, but her death also means he has thrown himself into a final effort to bring us down. We need you. I would not have crossed the sea at this time of year unless the summons was beyond urgent. You know how much I hate water."

Without hesitation, Henry nodded. "I will come," he said. "I will begin preparations immediately and sail the moment I am ready."

Alienor felt a glimmer of pride for her young husband. He saw a difficulty and addressed it head-on. She also noticed how older men deferred to him. He had their confidence and it came not just from attitude but from deed.

Color was gradually returning to Reginald of Cornwall's complexion and his strained expression had relaxed a little. "The Earl of Leicester is eager to talk with you and may be brought to either keep away from the dispute or change allegiance. The same with Arundel, but they will not make a move unless you come in person. There is much concern over the notion of accepting Stephen's heir as the future king."

"No surprise there," Henry said, curling his lip.

"You need to prove yourself a viable alternative once and for all," said his uncle. "This is the point at which you succeed or you fail."

"I have not failed yet," Henry replied, "and I do not intend to now. That is not the future I have planned for my dynasty."

Henry stayed up late, planning with his knights and retainers. Alienor went to bed and fell into a heavy sleep, but woke up when he returned in the early hours. She immediately felt nauseous and had to rush to the latrine where she stood over the hole, heaving, retching, and bringing up bile.

Clad in shirt and braies, Henry hastened over to her and held back her hair from her face. "What is wrong?" he demanded. "Shall I fetch your women?"

"Nothing is wrong," Alienor gasped when she could speak. "Indeed, I suspect everything is very right." Her stomach was still quivering, but she managed to stand up.

"Will you bring me a cup of wine?"

He did so, pouring one for himself too by the light of the single lamp. She sipped slowly, taking her time. Henry watched her with anticipation in his eyes, waiting for her to speak, although she suspected he must know the reply.

"It is early days yet, but I think I am with child," she said. "I have missed two fluxes and have been feeling unwell for a few days now. It would seem on the eve of your going that our prayers for an heir have been answered. I certainly hope I am not being sick for any lesser reason."

Henry put his wine down, did the same with hers, and pulled her gently into his arms. "That is wonderful news. Do you know when?"

"The end of the summer or early autumn. I am not entirely sure."

"You have done me proud." He kissed her tenderly. "And you have done well in telling me now."

"I would rather that than send word by letter once you were in England."

"It is a great gift." His smile lit up his face. "I shall have even more reason to make a success of this for my son."

Alienor bit her lip. Not every child was a son, but every man expected of his wife the duty of bearing one.

"Is there anything to be done to alleviate

the sickness?"

"Food," she said. "Plain food. A little dry bread and honey."

Henry strode to the door and bellowed. A bleary squire staggered off and returned with a loaf on a platter and a crock of honey, which Henry snatched from him and brought to her. Sitting cross-legged on the bed, he fed her small morsels and watched her chew and swallow. Between one mouthful and the next, Alienor went from queasy to ravenous and ended up devouring every last morsel.

"Lie down." He patted the bed, a gleam of excitement in his gaze.

Alienor looked at him askance but did as he asked.

He reached up behind his neck and unclasped the chain from which hung his gold cross. Holding it between finger and thumb, he dangled it over her abdomen. "The cross goes up and down for a boy, and side to side for a girl," he said.

Alienor laughed. "Where did you learn such women's lore?"

"My mother showed me when she was having William. I was very small, but I remember her letting me do this — although she was farther along than you are."

"Did it work?" She looked at the chain glistening in his hand, hovering just above her womb.

"Yes," he said and gave a pained smile. "I

would have preferred both my brothers to be girls, of course, but this only predicts; it doesn't alter the sex of the child."

The chain slowly started to move up and down in pendulum sweeps, becoming more and more vigorous. "A boy," Henry said with laughing satisfaction. "A strong and healthy boy. I did not doubt it for one minute."

Alienor raised her brows. "Did you not?"

He shook his head. "Louis did not have it in his loins to beget sons on you, but I do — a whole dynasty of them!"

"But what if it had gone the other way?" she asked. "What if it had said a girl?"

He shrugged. "It would only be a matter of time before we had a boy. Daughters are valuable too. Only a man insecure in himself would fret over such a thing at this stage." He fastened the cross around her neck. "Wear this and think of me," he said, then he lay down at her side, pulled the covers over them both, and settled down to sleep, his hand over her belly in a protective, proprietorial gesture.

Alienor remained awake for a short time, stroking Henry's arm where it lay across her womb, and thought of the family they would become. And then she reached to the cross he had placed around her neck and smiled.

49

Poitiers, August 1153

A burning August sun bleached the blue from the sky and gripped Poitiers in the fierce talons of a heat wave. High in the Maubergeonne Tower, the confinement chamber was insulated by thick stone walls. Linen curtains hung across the shutters, letting in air, but maintaining shade. A baby's wail filled the room where moments ago there had only been Alienor's voice, raised in a final cry of effort.

Hair drenched with sweat, chemise bunched around her hips, she raised herself on her elbows to watch the child being lifted from between her blood-dabbled thighs. The little body was streaked with blood and mucus, and the pulsating cord obstructed its genitals so Alienor could not tell the gender. And then the midwife pushed the cord to one side and beamed.

"A son, my lady. You have a fine boy, praise God, praise God!"

The wails became lusty roars as the midwife wiped out the baby's mouth and laid him upon Alienor's belly. He screwed up his face and thrashed his limbs, but as he felt the warmth of Alienor's flesh, he grew quieter. She reached down to touch and feel him. Alive, squirming, perfect.

The midwife gently lifted him off Alienor, snicked the cord with a small, sharp knife while intoning a prayer, and then removed him to a table where a bowl of scented warm water had been prepared for his first bath.

"Do not swaddle him," Alienor commanded. "I would see him first."

The woman gently washed the baby's tender limbs and then returned him to his mother, wrapped in a soft towel. Alienor held him close and checked his fingers and toes, his little ears, his puckered face. His hair gleamed like new gold, so did the tips of his eyelashes. He was going to be red like his father. And between his legs, the very obvious proof of his gender. Alienor swallowed. Her throat was tight and she knew she was going to weep a flood of tears, some of joy, some of grief, but all of healing. She held the baby to her breast and kissed his face again and again. "He is to be named William," she said. "For the Dukes of Aquitaine and Normandy and the Conqueror King of England."

The bells of Saint-Pierre pealed out the news that an heir to Aquitaine was born and every church in Poitiers took up the joyous clamor and from there rang the tidings to all the towns and villages beyond. Scribes frantically copied out the news and messengers galloped from the city, heading far and wide with the announcement.

Sitting up in bed sipping wine, Alienor watched the baby snuffle in his sleep and smiled with triumph. Now let Louis eat his words that she was a useless bearer of girls. How right this marriage must be that God had shown His approval and she had borne Henry a son on the first try. She only wished he were here to share this moment with her, but he would know soon enough, and even without him, the savoring was sweet indeed.

Henry eyed the white stallion recently purchased by his groom. The horse was intended for parade and ceremony rather than everyday riding. Being so full of energy, Henry was always hard on his mounts and wore them out swiftly, but this one was to be coddled for occasional use.

"Lame," he said, his nostrils flaring with temper. "I have paid five pounds of silver for a lame horse that has only been a waste of stable space thus far. How is that a good purchase?"

The groom flushed. "It was not lame when I bought it, sire."

"Hah, it wouldn't be, but you were duped

all the same." Henry walked around the horse again, looking at its trembling flank and the white of its eye. "No good for breeding either. Nothing but dog meat. Get it out of my sight." He dismissed both horse and groom with angry impatience. He expected good service in all parts of his life as a matter of course, and when it did not live up to expectations, it made him angry.

He had been in England since the winter and during that time had undertaken two serious campaigns, both of which had ended in stalemate because the barons on either side would not commit to a pitched battle. Everyone was weary of war; everyone wanted peace and, even through the skirmishing and posturing, negotiations were going forth. It all took time and effort, and Henry was having to school himself to a patience he was far from feeling, and it exacerbated his irritation when he could not trust his groom to do a small thing such as selecting a sound palfrey.

Henry retired inside the keep at Wallingford to read the day's messages and give further orders. A scout had arrived to report that Stephen was in Norfolk, striving to bring the troublemaker and renegade baron Hugh Bigod to heel. Henry had no intention of pursuing him there. Indeed, in some ways it was all to the good that he was chasing Bigod. Henry found the baron useful as an ally, but it did not mean he trusted or liked him.

The man had proven himself a cunning, self-serving bastard.

He paused to ruminate and his gaze crossed the chamber to rest casually on Aelburgh and little Geoffrey. He watched her play with the child who was just beginning to walk and he smiled a little at the infant's determination. It was good to have a domestic presence even at the heart of a battle camp — something to offer comfort but not important enough to require attention until he chose to give it.

As he reached to take a cup of wine from an attendant, another messenger was ushered into his presence in haste by Hamelin, his expression bright with suppressed excitement. "Tell the Duke what you have just told me," he commanded.

"Sire." The man knelt to Henry. "Eustace, Count of Boulogne, is dead."

Henry put his cup down and stared at the man and then at Hamelin. "What?"

"Sire, he choked on his food while claiming hospitality at the abbey of Bury St. Edmunds. Men are saying it was the wrath of the saint coming down on him because he had raided the monastery lands. He is being borne to Faversham for burial."

Henry leaned back in his chair and absorbed the news. This must be God's intention — His way of making everything right by clearing a way that had been blocked. Eustace had been the boulder in the path to peace and now he was suddenly gone. In Stephen's camp, and with Stephen himself, everything would be unraveling thread by thread. Even those who had stayed with him would be looking for a new allegiance and now there could only be one. He possessed all the youth and vigor Stephen lacked. All he had to do was continue undermining the older man's plinth until he toppled him. And now Stephen's eldest son was dead, that plinth was precarious indeed. Suddenly the matter of the lame white horse became a trivial thing. "God rest his soul, and God bless Saint Edmund," Henry said with a serious face and levity in his eyes.

"Stephen has other sons," Hamelin said. "There's still William."

"But he will not challenge us as Eustace has done," Henry replied. "He is malleable, for which everyone will be thanking Christ. I doubt he will stand in our way. Even if he does . . ." He let a shrug speak for the rest.

A week later another messenger arrived in Henry's camp on a lathered horse, this time from Aquitaine with the news that Alienor had been safely delivered of a fine, healthy baby boy, christened William, the name they had agreed before Henry left for England.

If Henry's cup had been full before, now it ran over. He had known she would bear a boy, but the proof in the letter confirmed that

God was smiling upon him, especially when he realized his son had been born on the same day, perhaps taking his first breath at the very moment that Eustace was choking to death. If that was not God's will in the matter, he did not know what was.

Louis broke the seal on the letter that had arrived from Henry, Duke of Normandy and Count of Anjou. He did it slowly, glancing around at the courtiers in the chamber as a matter of course to see who was watching him. He was feeling sour and unwell today. His physician said there was too much melancholy within him and had bled him to balance his humors, but that had only given him a sore arm and a headache. The news of Eustace of Boulogne's death had done nothing to improve his dark mood. It meant that another obstacle had been removed from Henry FitzEmpress's path to the English throne. It also meant his sister Constance was now a widow and he would have to go about extracting her dower from Stephen and finding her another husband.

Slowly he unfurled the scroll and, with a feeling of mild dyspepsia, read the customary flourishes of salutation. Then he came to the place where Henry was pleased to inform his overlord that God had seen fit to bestow the joy and blessing of a strong, healthy son on him and the Duchess of Aquitaine. The words burned themselves into Louis's brain while he sat and stared at them. How could such a thing be? Why had God not favored him instead of that Angevin upstart? What had he done to make God turn His face against him in such a way?

"Bad news?" asked his brother Robert, raising his brows and holding out his hand for the letter.

Louis drew back and, rolling it up, tucked it inside his sleeve. Everyone would know soon enough, but it was a wound he wanted to keep to himself for as long as possible. "I shall tell you later," he said. "It little concerns you."

Robert gave him a look askance.

"It is between me and God," Louis said and left the room. He wished the messenger had foundered on his way to Paris and fallen into a bog so that he did not have to carry this letter, this knowledge against his breast.

Arriving at his chamber, he dismissed everyone and lay down on his bed. He was filled with grief for the son he did not have — for the son that Alienor had miscarried long ago when she was his young, fresh bride. For the fact she had borne the heir that should have been his to Henry of Anjou, while giving him only daughters. Feeling desolate, abandoned, and full of self-pity, he covered his head with a pillow and wept, wishing he had never been drawn from the cloister to become a king.

50

Angers, March 1154

"Madam, your husband the Duke is here," announced Alienor's chamberlain.

Alienor stared at him in dismay. "What, already?"

He looked wry. "Yes, madam."

"But he was not due until . . . Ah, never mind. Delay him as long as you can."

He gave her a dubious look but bowed out.

"Oh, that man!" Alienor cried, torn between infuriation and joy. His heralds had arrived this morning, announcing he would be here toward nightfall, but the daylight was still strong and there were several hours until sunset. "I do not see him for more than a year, and then he springs himself upon me and I am not prepared."

"It will not take a moment to finish," Marchisa said, practical and optimistic as always. "Your lord may notice you, but he will not care if your hair is plaited in six braids or two."

"But I will care," Alienor complained, but only because she was annoyed. In truth it did not really matter. "Make haste then," she said. "They will not be able to hold him back for long."

Her women coiled her hair in a gold net and tightened the laces on her tawny silk gown to emphasize her once-more trim figure. The nurse busied herself with baby William who at seven months old was a vigorous bundle; no longer bound in swaddling, but clad in an embroidered white smock. The nurse put a bonnet on his head, and Alienor told her to draw out a quiff of his hair so that the glittery red-gold color was plain to see.

Not entirely satisfied, but knowing it would have to do, Alienor hurried to the hall and settled herself on the ducal chair on the dais with the baby in her lap. Emma and Marchisa arranged her skirts in a graceful swirl and Alienor drew a deep breath.

Moments later she heard Henry's voice protesting that no, he did not need to change his clothes, and no, he did not want to don his coronet, take refreshment, comb his hair, or anything else anyone might concoct to delay him. He flung open the door and stalked into the room, his cloak flying like a banner and his stride hard and fast. His complexion was flushed and there was a gray glitter in his eyes that verged on anger. Then he stopped abruptly and stared at Alienor, his chest heaving.

She met his gaze with pride, revealing none of her trepidation, and then she lowered her eyes to their son, who wanted to stand up and bounce in her lap. "This is your papa," she said to the child, pitching her voice so that Henry could hear. "Your papa is home to see you." And she looked at Henry again, directly and with triumph.

Henry took a deep breath and walked forward. His gaze was no longer angry, but bright with pleasure and eager anticipation. "You look like a madonna," he said hoarsely.

Alienor gave a demure smile. "This is your son," she said. "William, Count of Poitiers, future Duke of Normandy and King of England."

Henry took the infant from her arms to have a good look at him. He held him above his head and little William shouted with laughter and dribbled on his father.

"Well, that's a fine start; my heir spits on me." Henry grinned, lowering his son, transferring him to one arm and wiping his forehead with the cuff of his tunic.

"He has your eyes and your hair," Alienor said. Affection and happiness bubbled up within her. Louis had never made any attempt to be playful or engage with their daughters but Henry was fearless and natural holding the child.

"But your features," Henry replied. "What

a fine little man."

The baby squirmed in his arms and seized hold of Henry's cloak brooch, which had caught his eye. Henry carefully prized his heir's chubby fingers from the object and handed him to the waiting nurse.

"Like you he is never still," Alienor said. "He makes his wishes known to everyone — and they had better obey or else."

He raised his brows and looked amused. "Certainly like me then."

Alienor rose to greet him with a formal curtsy now that he had seen his son, but he met her halfway and kissed her.

"I missed you," he said.

They straightened together and he set his hand to her waist.

"I missed you too. It has been a long time." She was intensely aware of his touch. "We have a great deal to talk about. Letters say much, but they are not flesh and blood."

"No, more is the pity. You wrote often that you were well, and I am glad to see it is the truth."

Alienor thought that he was bound to be glad, for had she died in childbirth it would have left him with a claim impossible to pursue and all her vast resources would have been lost to him. Given that their son was seven months old, she suspected that he was also inquiring if she was sufficiently recovered to conceive another child. "Yes," she said, smiling, "I am quite well."

Formal greetings over, Alienor and Henry retired to the greater privacy of the lord's chamber in the castle tower. Henry's squires had put his baggage in the chamber during the greetings in the hall, and wine and food had been set out on cloth-covered trestles.

Alienor glanced at his baggage, which was only what Henry had carried on his horse. The rest would arrive later on the slower traveling carts. There were a couple of sacks and a long piece of rolled-up leather.

He saw her look. "I have not come home to you empty-handed," he said. "I have gifts for you fit for a queen."

"I should hope so after so long a parting." She indicated the baby now in the nurse's arms. "My gift to you is a son."

Color came up in his face. "Mine to you, and to him, is a kingdom," he replied. "As I promised when we wed."

Alienor's breath shortened. She had received news from England but it was haphazard and patchy. "A kingdom?"

Henry dismissed the remaining servants with a flick of his wrist, including the nurse with little William. "Stephen has agreed I should inherit the crown when he dies, but I had to consent to the formality of becoming his adopted son and heir." He looked wry. "So now I have three fathers. The man who sired me, my Father in heaven, and Stephen the usurper — God help me. It was a way out of the morass. Everyone views me as the heir to the throne, but they are unwilling to fight any more to set me upon it. Stephen's lords acknowledge my claim, but will not see me crowned while Stephen lives. My own lords will not chance a pitched battle when they know it is only a matter of time. It took many hours of negotiation, but it is done. I am Stephen's heir, acknowledged by treaty, and all men are sworn to uphold my claim." He took her around the waist and pulled her close, nuzzling her throat with his beard. "And that means I can give my attention to our domains here, and spend time with you and our son." He deftly unlaced the side of her gown and slipped his hand inside to cup her breast through her chemise.

Alienor shivered with lust. It had been so long. There was so much she wanted to ask him, but it could wait. She would not receive an answer from him if she asked now. The suggestive surge and retreat of his hips against hers, the feel of his hands on her body, the smell and touch of him was creating an overriding need. Her own hands became very busy and Henry muttered an expletive. With his braies around his knees, he heaved her onto the bed.

"Now," he gasped as he knelt over her, poised. "Speak now if you are not ready to conceive another child because I am ripe to bursting!"

Alienor laughed breathlessly. "Is this one of your fitting gifts?"

"Oh yes," he said, his jaw tense and his stomach sucked in. "What could be more fitting than this?"

He thrust into her full measure and she clasped herself around him, glorying in his vigor and energy, his frank sexual need and pleasure, so different from Louis. Delighting too that he welcomed her responses and did not expect her to be passive in the exchange. He was a young golden lion and she was his mate and his match.

Henry lightly stroked Alienor's belly in the aftermath of their mating. "I would fill you again and again for the pleasure of the begetting," he said. "We shall make a fine dynasty of sons and daughters between us."

Alienor turned in his arms to face him. "Your part is simple," she said. "You would find the constant bearing harder toil."

"I concede that I would, but each to our duty and our role."

Alienor arched her brows. "Indeed, but being the bearer of my heirs and yours does not mean I cease to be a duchess. I am more than just a brood mare, I warn you."

He looked a trifle taken aback. "Of course you are more; that is taken for granted."

"As long as you do not take *me* for

granted," she said, determined to push her point home. "I may carry and bear the children, but I will receive my due in every part."

He kissed her again. "You will be honored as is your right, I promise."

Alienor returned the kiss, but felt a slight misgiving at the tone of his voice. She was swiftly learning that her young husband was a force of nature carrying all before him. People had to bend to his needs; he did not bow to theirs. He would only keep his word if it suited him to do so. She had to make herself matter to him in every way, not just as the key that opened the door to Aquitaine and the provider of heirs. "Do not give your promise lightly," she said to him, "because I will hold you to it down all the days of our marriage."

"Then hold me to it; I shall not prove wanting." He continued to nuzzle and kiss her. He had been going to tell her about Aelburgh and little Geoffrey, but since they were far away in England, he decided for the moment she need not know.

As their lovemaking progressed, Alienor straddled him, taking control of the moment.

"Then let us seal your promise," she said, moving upon him lightly, the tips of her hair trailing over his chest and belly. "I am your wife, your lover, the mother of your children." She tossed her head and rose and fell and saw his fists clench on the sheets. "I am a duchess with lands and vassals; I am of ancient lineage. I have been a queen, I shall be so again, and I will have all that is my due."

Henry swallowed and gritted his teeth. "Christ, woman . . ."

"Swear it." She rose and settled.

"You already have my promise," he gasped, "but I do so swear again."

"And you must swear again," she said, "because three times is binding." She leaned over and bit him lightly on each nipple, enough to cause a sharp sensation verging on pain, but exquisite.

His face contorted. "I swear it!" He seized her hips to hold her still and arrowed into her, climaxing harder than he had ever done in his life, and she took her pleasure from seeing his and knowing in that moment the power was all hers.

"What will your mother say about Stephen adopting you?" she asked when they had both recovered and were refreshing themselves with wine and curd tarts from the platters on the trestle.

Henry gave a grunt of amusement. "She will be incensed, I have no doubt. It was bad enough that Geoffrey of Anjou was my sire, and to have me adopted by the man who stole her crown will disgust her." He shrugged and took a bite from the tart Alienor was feeding him. "She will accept it, though; she is pragmatic and she has no choice. I just won't refer to Stephen as my 'stepfather' in her company."

"What of Stephen's other son? What does he think of his father making you the heir and cutting him from the inheritance?"

"He was not best pleased at first, but not prepared to take it further. No one would support him, including his own father. We had a long discussion before the tomb of my grandsire at Reading and William agreed to step down. Those who began the fight are growing old and do not want to see their own sons caught up in the conflict when there's a sensible solution under their noses."

Henry went to pick up the long leather roll from his baggage. "We must arrange a ceremony to display this before everyone." Within the roll, wrapped in a purple silk cloth, was a scabbard of embossed leather over a wooden core. The sword hilt within was of Nordic style, beautifully crafted and engraved. The grip was bound with red silk cord and the hilt ends were fashioned into the shape of beasts with open mouths.

"This is the sword of my great-great-grandfather, Duke Robert of Normandy," he said. "He left it to his son, William, who then bore it into battle when he came to conquer England. It has hung at the tomb of my grandsire in Reading Abbey for almost twenty years and it is mine now. William of Boulogne will not contest my right to wield it. It was given to me as a token of my future kingship by the consent of all the barons in England." His eyes shone as gray as the light on the steel and as sharp as the blade. "Stephen will live out the rest of his life as king, and when he dies, the crown will be mine."

Alienor felt the power in him and her heart filled with pride and exultation, but it did not blind her to practicality. "What of your enemies, those who have built castles and made themselves little kingdoms throughout this war?"

"The order has already gone out that all adulterine castles are to be demolished and everything restored to what it was on the day when my grandsire was alive and dead. This sword symbolizes a return to the peace and justice we had before — and shall have again. That is my priority."

She nodded with approval. It was a future vision made of practicality, not golden dreams. Something worthwhile, steady, and solid, which, in due course, would be built to last. For the moment they had Normandy, Anjou, and Aquitaine to govern — and each other to enjoy.

51

Drawing rein, Henry gazed at the walls of Fontevraud Abbey and began to smile. "It's good to be back," he said. "My father often brought me and my brothers here to visit our aunt Mathilde and sometimes left us in her custody while he went about his duties."

Alienor looked amused. "I expect you disrupted the life of the nuns?"

"We were not allowed to — our aunt saw to that; but we were indulged by the ladies of the Magdalene house who had not taken vows." A look that was almost yearning crossed his face. "If I were to call somewhere home, this would be it."

His words gave Alienor food for thought. This, then, for Henry was a place of the heart. Not Rouen, not Angers, nor even Le Mans, but Fontevraud. And that must be because of the feelings it evoked.

Abbess Mathilde abandoned all formality in greeting Henry and hugged him to her bosom with all the fondness of an aunt for her favorite nephew. "It has been so long!" she cried. "Look at you, a grown man!" She turned from a grinning Henry to Alienor and embraced her fondly. "And your beautiful wife. Welcome, welcome. And where is my great-nephew? Let me see him!"

Alienor took little William from his nurse and handed him to Mathilde.

"Just like his father as a baby! Look at that hair. He's a proper Angevin." She gave the baby a smacking kiss on the cheek.

"I should hope he is, madam my aunt," Henry said. "Lions breed true."

She took them to their lodging in the guesthouse where she had refreshment brought, and then sat down before the hearth to dandle the baby in her lap. "So," she said to Henry, "you are now officially England's heir."

"God has willed it so," Henry replied.

Mathilde bounced William up and down, making him crow with laughter. "Strange to think had my husband not drowned, I would have been Queen of England and my son heir to the throne." She kissed her great-nephew's soft cheek. "Motherhood was not my path, but my nieces and nephews have brought me great pleasure — as has my work here — and I have contentment that I would not have found in the world. Everything happens for a reason."

Alienor felt a brief moment of envy for Mathilde's lot. "To have power and contentment at the same time, that is a rare thing indeed."

"Yes, but hard won." Mathilde gave her a shrewd look. "When I came to Fontevraud, my heart was full of grieving and bitterness. It took many years of prayer and searching to discover joy beyond sorrow and to accept what had happened instead of railing against the dish fate had served to me. I found healing here and I rediscovered my pleasure in life. If not for Fontevraud and God, I would still be lost."

During their time at Fontevraud, Alienor witnessed a very different side to Henry. He was still exuberant and full of restless energy, but in church he found the patience to be quiet, and the sharper edges of his character smoothed out and became more relaxed. He slept for longer at night and was not in a tearing hurry the moment he rose in the morning. Fontevraud's spirituality was a grounded, practical one that well suited his personality, and the place had been that kind of haven for him since childhood.

"When it is my time to leave the world, I have a mind to lie here," he said as he walked hand in hand with Alienor in the early morning through the cool, wet grass of the cemetery.

"Not in Angers or Le Mans?" she asked.

He shook his head. "Nor Reading or Westminster. All of those places will be open to my hand in the days to come and I can walk there as I choose. But here . . ." He sent her a self-conscious glance as if admitting to something untoward that made him vulnerable. "Here is a place that I can carry in my heart like a sacred fragment within a reliquary. Even if I do not visit, I know it is here for me."

Alienor's throat and chest tightened. "That is a wonderful certainty to have."

"Yes," he said, "because I can carry it with me and at the same time set it aside and focus on the business in hand."

It was eminently practical, she thought, and so fitting to Henry's character. To live in the world and walk through it with power and vigor, and then have a place of personal, tranquil repose when all was done.

She felt the hard grip of his hand and the cold brush of the grass under her feet — solid, tactile reality, weaving a fabric of memory she would keep until she too was laid in her tomb, wherever that might be — perhaps here at his side.

Empress Matilda held her wriggling grandson in her arms. "You have done well, daughter," she said. "A fine healthy boy to carry the line, and more in the fullness of time, one hopes."

"If God wills it, madam," Alienor replied with courtesy. From Fontevraud, she and Henry had traveled into Normandy and had spent the past three weeks in Rouen with the Empress. Alienor was feeling the strain of being constantly polite and deferential to her mother-in-law.

The Empress meant well in her advice, but Alienor did not always agree with her notions and attitudes and was often infuriated by Matilda's patronizing air. The Empress was of the opinion that Alienor had much to learn from an older and wiser mentor, and she did not shirk the duty one whit. Alienor was rapidly coming to understand why Geoffrey of Anjou had mostly chosen to live apart from his wife. Even toward Henry, who was her golden child, her firstborn who had achieved every goal set before him, she was no doting mother. Even a much-loved son could benefit from the vast bounty of her maternal wisdom.

"When you are a king, you should not be too familiar with your subjects," she lectured Henry as they sat before the fire. "You must preserve the dignity and the distance that exists between you and them."

Henry nodded. He was playing chess with his knight Manasser Bisset. "But I need to know about them too. A distant king is one who may be duped or surprised because he is not paying attention."

"There are ways of finding out. Never be

overfamiliar is what I am telling you."

"You are wise, Mama," he said without looking up.

"Demand respect and respect shall be given. Do not let any of them dictate to you. That is not the rule of a true king." She warmed to her theme. "You should rule them, not the other way around. They are like squabbling children. Divide them and you will conquer them, and after that you must keep them divided. Promise much and give little. Keep them hungry as you would your hawk. That is the way of an accomplished prince. Do not let them sit at ease with their muddy boots under your table."

Alienor clenched her teeth to prevent herself speaking out of turn. Her mother-in-law had lost her one chance at being crowned queen precisely because of her haughty behavior. She had incensed the citizens of London and been forced to flee from her own precoronation feast when the mob had turned on her. She had been high-handed and insulting to men who came to tender their allegiance and had made more enemies than friends. Stephen with his garrulous, easy ways had held on to the crown for nineteen years and even now his barons would not desert him. For the rest of his life he would be King of England. There was a message in that too.

"Mama, rest assured, I shall think on your advice when I treat with the English barons,"

Henry said smoothly. "I value your counsel, you know that."

The Empress gave him a hard, slightly suspicious look. "I am pleased to hear it," she said.

"Your mother is a lady of great wisdom and experience," Alienor said that night when she and Henry retired. "But is she right about England?" She studied a cross on a chain that Matilda had given to her. It was an ostentatious and rather hideous thing set with numerous gemstones of assorted shapes and sizes. Alienor knew Matilda would expect her to wear it. She had been most insistent when pressing it on her, calling her the daughter she never had.

"I always listen to my mother's advice," Henry replied, "but that doesn't mean I take it." He was standing before a table and by the light of a freshly lit candle was examining correspondence that had arrived earlier. "She often has useful things to contribute, but it is six years since she left England and much has changed. Besides, she has no notion of how to bend. She would rather snap herself in two."

Alienor put the necklace in her coffer and closed the lid so she did not have to look at it. "Yes, I receive that impression." She kept her tone neutral. She had great respect for her mother-in-law even while her patience was wearing thin, and she was still cautious about Henry's reaction to his mother, because she did not know yet how fond or influenced a son he truly was.

"She has kept the fight alive and her contacts with the Church and the German Empire are invaluable." He gave Alienor a penetrating look as if he could read her thoughts. "I may be her son, but I am my own man."

"That is good to know," she said steadily.

Without reply, he picked up the next piece of correspondence, read it, and suddenly he was tense and alert.

"What is it?"

"Hah. Your former husband desires a meeting to settle the future so that there may be peace and amity between us."

Alienor took the letter from him. The language was that of Louis's scribes, but it was as Henry said. Louis desired to settle the matter of Aquitaine and was willing to relinquish his claim. "We have been asking him to do that ever since William was born, and he has always refused," she said. "Why now?"

"He says he desires to visit Compostela and worship at the tomb of Saint James and wants a truce so he can do this."

"That sounds like Louis," Alienor said with a grimace. "If he had his way, he would spend his days traveling between shrines playing the pilgrim king. Suger pleaded and pleaded for him to come home from Outremer, but he refused to heed him until forced because he was too busy adding this tomb or that shrine of miracles to his tally."

Henry shrugged. "I am sure he will receive all he deserves from his pious wanderings, and in the meantime his obsession does us no harm and might even be to our advantage."

Alienor pursed her lips. "Perhaps, but we should be cautious. Louis may be superficial, but he is devious."

"So am I," Henry said with a glint in his eyes.

Taking shelter from the burning August sun under the awning of a painted canvas pavilion, Henry met with Louis at Vernon, midway between Paris and Rouen.

Alienor had been feeling unwell for several days and suspected that once again she was with child. She had told Henry yesterday as they approached their rendezvous. He had been highly delighted and almost smug. Not only was it further proof of his virility, it was also a barb with which to bait his French rival. They had, however, left their infant son in Rouen with his grandmother. It would have been a jibe too far to bring him, and a political meeting was no place for an infant. To make matters less awkward, Alienor was not attending the face-to-face gathering but was remaining close by to ratify documents and put her seal to them.

Among the French courtiers attending the assembly was Louis's sister Constance, widow of King Stephen's son Eustace, and she came to visit Alienor while the men conducted their negotiations elsewhere. Now fully grown, she had a strong look of her mother in the line of her jaw and the way she carried herself. She had the same pale hair as Louis and a long, thin nose. She greeted Alienor with cautious civility.

"I was sorry to hear your mother had died," Alienor said. "She was a noble and determined lady, may she rest in peace."

"I hope I can be a credit to her," Constance replied. Her voice was quiet, but it had an underlying steeliness, and that too reminded Alienor of Adelaide.

"You do her justice." Alienor tried to sound sincere.

Constance inclined her head, accepting the compliment. "I am soon to be married again," she said.

Alienor was immediately alert, knowing that the groom would be significant to French interests. "I congratulate you. May I ask to whom?"

Constance gave Alienor a calculating look. "To the Count of Toulouse."

Alienor went very still. So that was why Louis was open to negotiation. He might have relinquished his claim to Aquitaine, but by allying with Toulouse he could pressurize her borders from two directions and retain his influence in the south. He knew full well that Alienor's goal was to add Toulouse to her territories. In marrying his sister to the Count, he would give his own descendants a presence there, should Constance bear off-spring. "I wish you well," Alienor said, managing to keep her tone neutral. Indeed she meant Constance no harm, because after all she was only a pawn, and Alienor had known enough hardship caused by the will of others in her own life. Nevertheless, she was heartsick.

"Toulouse belongs to Aquitaine," Alienor told Henry when they were alone in their tent. A heavy dusk had bruised the sky with purple and blue. She slapped at a mosquito whining close to her ear. "I will not have Louis laying hands on it through his sister."

"You cannot stop the match," Henry said. "I agree it is an irritation, but as a ruler it is his duty to find a way to compensate for the loss of Aquitaine."

Alienor scowled. It was the truth, but that made it no more palatable.

Henry lay back on their traveling bed and pillowed his hands behind his head. "He is doing more on his 'pilgrimage' to Compos-tela than worshipping Saint James and marrying off Constance. He is also planning a marriage with the house of Castile for himself — to the eldest daughter of King Alphonse."

She stared at him. "He told you that?"

"With a smile on his lips." Henry said, making a face but at the same time unperturbed. "The bride is thirteen years old. He will be fortunate to get a living child out of her if he takes her now. Whatever happens, we still have time before he has an heir. Even if he does father a living baby, what chance is there of it being a boy?"

"And Constance?"

Henry shrugged. "There is time there too. We could always wed our own dynasty into that one and take Toulouse by marriage alliance in the next generation."

Alienor wondered if Henry was being flippant. Something must have shown on her face because he added: "I am not just planning for tomorrow, but for ten years' hence and more. I agree we should watch the situation, but what matters is that he has relinquished his claim to Aquitaine. As far as Toulouse is concerned, I will put my mind to a campaign in the near future." He gave her a sleepy smile and changed the subject. "I told him you were with child again. I have never seen a man try to smile while swallowing vinegar." He patted the bed and beckoned to her. "Whatever his schemes, we still have every advantage, my love, and he has none."

"We must make sure it stays that way," she said as she joined him. "Louis often suffers ill luck in what happens to him from day to day, but he always survives."

"I have his measure," Henry said confidently. "Have no fear of that. And he does not have mine." He unfastened the pendant cross from around his neck and dangled it over her flat belly. Together they watched it swing gently up and down and begin to gather momentum. "Another boy," he said and smiled.

On their first night back in Rouen, Henry was quieter than usual and heavy-eyed when they visited his mother at the abbey of Bec to tell her about the meeting at Vernon and give her the news of Alienor's pregnancy. Alienor was tired herself after their long ride and thought little of it. The Empress more than compensated for the gaps in the conversation by holding forth on everything from the right way to wear an ermine cloak to the usual complaint about how inept Stephen was as a king. She was also complaining that Emperor Heinrich of Germany had asked her to return the relics, jewels, and regalia that she had brought home to Normandy from her widow-hood.

"They are mine," she said with an angry gleam in her eyes. "And they shall pass to my sons." She turned to Henry. "He even demands the crown you are going to wear at your coronation, but he shall not have it. Not one piece of gold, not a single gem from its setting."

"Indeed not," Henry said, but without his usual spark of irony or relish. He rose to his feet and stooped to kiss her cheek. "Mama, I will speak to you more in the morning."

She looked surprised, and then concerned. "What is wrong?"

"Nothing, Mama." Henry gave a dismissive wave as if brushing aside a fly. "I have told you, I am tired, that is all. Even I need to sleep sometimes."

That brought a severe smile to her lips but did not banish the anxiety from her eyes. "Rest well then," she said. "And God bless your slumber."

"Are you sure you are well?" Alienor asked him as they arrived at the palace.

"Of course I am," he snapped. "God on the Cross, why do women always make so much fuss? I'm tired, that is all, and my mother would try the patience of a saint. Do not you follow her example!"

Alienor raised her chin. "If women make a fuss it is because we are the ones who always have to clear up afterward and deal with the debris, but you have made yourself clear. I shall not ask again."

They retired to bed, irritated with each

other. Henry fell asleep almost immediately, but it was a restless slumber in which he moaned and tossed and turned like a demon.

In the early hours of the morning he woke up complaining of a sore throat, saying he was frozen, although his skin was as hot as a coal to the touch. The night candle had burned down to the stub and Alienor felt her way into her chemise and stumbled to the door to summon the servants. Behind her she heard the sound of Henry vomiting. "The Duke is sick," she said. "Bring fresh bedclothes and warm water."

She hastily dressed while servants stripped and replaced the stained bedclothes. Henry huddled before the embers of the hearth, a cloak draped around his shoulders and his body shuddering. Kneeling at his side, Alienor took his hands in hers and felt the scalding beat of his blood against her skin. Even by the shadowy light of candles she could see that his eyes were glazed.

"Ask me again why women make so much fuss," she said.

"It's nothing," he replied, his voice thick and hoarse. "A chill. I will be all right by morning."

But by morning he was delirious and struggling to breathe. His throat was so swollen and raw that he could barely swallow the potions the physicians gave him. They bled him to cool the excess heat of his blood, but it had no effect.

Alienor sat at the bedside, insisting on bathing his body herself and dribbling honey and water into his open mouth. He was propped up on pillows to help him breathe, but every rise and fall of his chest was an effort. She could see his diaphragm sucking in and out, making hollows under his rib cage that echoed the shape of Christ's image upon the crucifix hanging on the wall.

The Empress flurried in from Bec soon after dawn. The weather had turned autumnal and she entered the room bearing the smell of rain and wood smoke on her clothes.

"Henry?" She hastened to the bedside and, as she looked at her eldest son, her expression filled with shock. "How can this be? How can this have happened?" She flicked an almost accusatory look at Alienor.

"He must have picked up some bad air at the French court," Alienor said, and then bit her lip. The air of the French court had been very bad for his father too. She was terrified lest he die. There would be more conflict and war, and she and her children would be at its center. She would be forced to make another marriage or else find herself constantly under siege from ambitious suitors.

"Not my golden boy," Matilda said. "Not after all this." She gazed around at the servants with sharp eyes, marking who was present and what was being done. "He is not going to die." She pushed an attendant out of the way and pressed her hand to Henry's forehead. He groaned and struck out. "Burning up," she said. "He needs to be purged and his blood cooled."

"That has already been done, madam my mother," Alienor replied.

"Then do it again until it works. He must have fresh spring water to drink, and gruel, and make sure it is tasted first by someone else." She clucked her tongue as if at the incompetence of everyone else, and Alienor clung to her own civility by the tips of her fingers, because she and Matilda were allies in this, and if they argued, they would weaken each other when they needed to be united.

For the next hour the Empress stamped around the chamber issuing orders, flinging blame about indiscriminately and behaving like the termagant of her worst reputation. But then she stopped for a moment and passed a trembling hand across her eyes, and Alienor's angry resentment melted, for underneath all the bluster and rage, she glimpsed and recognized desolate terror.

Alienor and the Empress took turns at Henry's bedside, wiping down his fevered body, changing his shirts and linens, spooning liquid into his mouth. The fever stripped the flesh from his bones and his body shook as if his pounding heart was going to break out of his body. Chaplains and priests came and went, but always stayed close to hand. Throughout Rouen prayers were said for Normandy's desperately sick young duke. When the Empress was not at his bedside, she was kneeling before the altar at Bec, entreating God to spare her son's life. She ruined her knees on the hard stone flags, and neither noticed nor cared.

Alienor sat beside him in vigil as the evening of the third day fell. He still lived, but it was more of a status quo than an improvement. She took his hand, tanned from the summer sun, but paler farther up his wrist and covered in faint golden freckles overlaid by a shimmer of fine gilt hair. "How will you build your empire and leave your mark lying here like this?" she asked him. "How will you see your sons grow tall and strong? How will you beget daughters if you leave now?"

She could not tell if he heard her, but his chest gave a spasmodic heave. "You will be an almost king," she said bitterly, "and that is worse than none at all. Even Stephen has bettered that . . . even Louis." Her voice shook. After a moment she unclasped her hand from his and went to the coffer at the foot of the bed. She unlocked it and lifted out the purple silk wrapping containing his great-great-grandfather's sword. Carefully she unrolled the delicate cloth, took the scabbard, and unsheathed the blade. The steel had a dull glitter, cold as a winter morning. She brought it to him and put it in his hand, curling his fingers around the silk binding on the hilt. "This is yours," she said. "Take it and use it, for if you do not, then it will rust away in the hands of others less able."

Gripping his other hand, she pressed it to her womb where new life was growing. And then she bowed her head and prayed.

She woke several hours later with the dawn filtering through the shutters, its gray light touching the sword and lighting a steely gleam along the blade. Her mouth was parched and her eyes felt hot and gummy. Henry's hand was cold and for one terrible moment she thought his soul had flown his body in the night. His eyes were open, staring at her.

"An almost king," he croaked. "What kind of insult is that?"

Alienor gasped, her breath leaving her as if snatched from her chest by an unseen force. She touched his cheek and it was gently warm under her palm. "The worst kind," she said shakily once she had drawn another breath. "I hope I never have to apply it to you." She held a cup of watered wine to his lips. "Will you drink?"

He took a clumsy sip, spilling the liquid down his chest. She dabbed it away with a napkin. His heartbeat no longer thundered against his rib cage and his skin was cool to the touch where it was exposed to the air. She pulled up the bedclothes.

"Christ's bones," he wheezed. "My chest feels as if it is full of rusty nails."

"You terrified us," she said. "We thought you were going to die."

"I dreamed I was drowning, but the sea was made of fire," he said. "And I dreamed I was being ripped apart by an eagle and fed to its young, but they were my young too." He drank again, this time more steadily, and then he looked at the sword down by his right hand. "What is this doing here?"

"I brought it to you last night to help you fight because nothing else seemed to be helping — not all the prayers and supplication and entreaty. I could see you leaving my reach and I did not want to lose you. The sword drew you back." Her chin wobbled. "You came so very close, my love. You do not know, but those who watch over you did."

She knew the fight was not over. One moment of lucid awakening did not signal a full recovery. They would have to be very careful with him in the days to come, and she knew he would not be an easy patient.

Henry was sleeping again when the Empress arrived, but Alienor was able to report that he had eaten some sops of bread in milk and his fever had abated. The sword had been locked in its chest and the bedclothes neatly folded over Henry's torso.

"Thank God!" Matilda made the sign of the Cross on her breast and eased onto a stool at the bedside. "I prayed all night to the Virgin that his fever would break, and she took pity and listened to a mother's entreaties!"

Alienor bit her tongue and did not tell her about the sword.

"How frail we are." The Empress used the long sleeve of her gown to wipe her eyes, and then she straightened her spine and she rallied, her expression becoming proud and autocratic. "I will watch over him now. You go and sleep, my daughter."

Alienor looked at the Empress's dark-circled eyes and pale, dry lips. "You have not slept either," she said.

"That does not matter; I have often gone for days without sleep in my life. You are with child and you must take care for both your sakes. It is my turn now."

While Henry recuperated, Alienor spent her time at his bedside. For one who was usually so exuberant and brimming with energy, he was content to let time and rest render their cure. She fed him meals in bed, tempting him with tasty morsels of meat on skewers, little marrow tarts, and custards. She told him amusing tales and brought musicians to play for him, especially his favorite harpist. She read to him from all manner of books, both serious tomes involving the law and judiciary, and lighter tales from history and myth. Being widely read, he already knew many of them, but was content to hear them again, saying he loved the sound of her voice and the exotic accent of Poitou in her Norman French. She played chess with him, and they tallied even scores. She told him what was happening at court and they discussed a future campaign against Toulouse, planning strategies like an extension of their games of chess.

Day by day Henry improved. His appetite returned and he took up business again, summoning his barons and knights to his chamber and dealing with them for as long as his energy lasted. There came a morning when Alienor arrived to find him absent and his attendants making up the bed and clearing the crumbs of a meal from the table by the embrasure.

"My lord said he was going out for a ride," said Henry's chamberlain, "and that if you asked for him, he would see you and the Empress at the dinner hour."

She knew then that all was back to normal, and although she was relieved and delighted that Henry was back to full health, a part of her regretted the loss of the moments spent together in this chamber enjoying mutual pursuits, because once again he would be too busy throwing himself at the life he had so nearly lost to find the time for his wife.

52

Rouen, October 1154

In the cold October morning, Alienor sipped the ginger tisane Marchisa had made for her while her women dressed her in warm robes. It was the first morning in several months that she had not felt sick on rising. Her belly, still flat a week since, now showed a soft curve, and her new gown of bright brown wool was gathered at the front around a red braid belt to emphasize that area.

Henry had come to bed late and risen early, his energy so abundant that it was impossible to believe six weeks ago he had almost died. Today he was setting out to deal with the matter of a rebellious vassal at Torigny, and although she would have liked to keep him by her for at least another week, she knew the limits of what was possible.

She sent Emma to fetch little William and his nurse, but the woman arrived minus her charge. "Madam, the Duke has taken him," she said. "He said something about the stables."

Alienor called for her cloak and went down to the yard where she found Henry trotting his palfrey, Grisel, around the area, with William perched in front of him. The baby's squeals of delight rang out as he grabbed for the reins and his father's face was bright with laughter and pride. Henry was dressed to leave, his tunic topped by the padded garment usually worn under his mail, but used now as protection against the sharp wind. Little William was wrapped in his father's cloak. Seeing Alienor, Henry reined about and trotted over to her.

"I was giving our heir an early riding lesson," he said. "He learns fast."

"Of course he does," Alienor said. "He will be on a destrier by the time you return . . . unless of course you want to take him with you?"

"Not until he can fasten his braies to his hose, put up a tent, and learn to be silent at the appropriate time," he chuckled, handing the baby down into her arms. William began yelling and strained himself toward Henry and the horse. Alienor kissed him, but swiftly bundled him over to his nurse.

Henry dismounted and took Alienor's hands. "I hope to be back in Rouen before the Feast of Saint Martin," he said.

"Have a care to yourself." She stroked the back of his hand where he had snagged himself on a thorn bush during a hunt two days ago. "I will hold you in my prayers."

"And I will keep you and our sons in mine." He touched her belly and then, cupping her face, kissed her. The gesture was sincere, but she could see his mind was on the open road and that he had already left her.

Alienor's visits to the Empress at the abbey of Bec-Hellouin were a thing of duty rather than a desire to spend time in the company of her mother by marriage, but today had been bearable thus far. Little William had recently taken his first steps and Matilda had been encouraging him in his newly acquired skill, brimming with pride as he toddled between herself and Alienor.

Alienor was taking a soothing footbath, the water imbued with herbs and scented oil. Little William wanted to splash in the water, but the Empress enticed him away with a piece of bread and honey.

Alienor put her hand to her belly. "The new babe keeps the same hours as his father," she said wryly. "I thought William was active, but this one is never still."

The Empress smiled and lifted her grandson onto her knee to eat the food. "I wondered when you made this marriage with my son whether the advantage was worth the risk," she said. "You had a certain reputation, even if it was unwarranted gossip, and only two daughters from a marriage of fifteen years, but you have done well — thus far."

Alienor felt a surge of irritation. The woman's sensibilities were a strange paradox. She was thoughtful enough to offer the pleasure of a relaxing footbath, but then destroyed the gesture by her blunt and patronizing attitude. "I wondered too whether the advantage was worth the risk," she replied. "Whether I was looking at a boy trying to fill a man's shoes, but thankfully my doubts have been assuaged, just as yours have."

The Empress started to look offended, but suddenly a glint of wintry humor softened her expression. "I think we have both come to an understanding, daughter," she said.

Which was not the same as liking, Alienor thought, but it would suffice.

There was a sudden commotion at the door where Emma had opened it to a panting messenger, who gasped out that he brought news of great import.

Alienor and the Empress exchanged fearful glances. The Empress gave her grandson to his nurse and Alienor hastily dried her feet and donned a pair of soft shoes. Dear God, what if Henry had been taken ill again? What if he had been injured — or worse?

The messenger, windblown from his journey and splattered with mud, came forward and knelt to the women. "Mesdames," he said, addressing both of them, "I bring news from my lord the Archbishop of Canterbury." He swallowed and gathered himself. "King Stephen died of a bloody flux at Dover four nights since . . ." He held out a packet bearing the seal of Theobald of Canterbury.

The Empress grabbed it from him and broke it open. The parchment shook in her hand as she read what was written. "I have waited so long for this," she said, covering her mouth. "So very long. I knew the day would come, but now . . ." Her chin trembled. "Henry was little older than my grandson when I began the fight. All these years . . . all these long, long years." Silent tears spilled down her face.

Alienor was stunned. She had expected Stephen to live for several more years yet — enough time to deal with Toulouse and raise her children in the warmth and joy of the south. Instead, she must turn and face a different prospect. She did not know the English. She did not know their ways or their tongue beyond a few words. She had thought she would come to it when she was Matilda's age, and that by then she would be ready. She swallowed hard and set her jaw. Within her the quickening child turned and somersaulted. The messenger was still kneeling and she bade him stand. "Does my lord know?" she asked. "Have messages gone out to him?"

"Yes, madam, at the same time I came to you."

"Go and find food and refreshment. Take some rest and be ready to ride again when you are summoned."

"Madam." He bowed and left the room.

The women gazed at each other in the still moments of irrevocable change. The tears were still wet on Matilda's face, highlighting the broken veins and ravages of advancing years. "I have been pushing against this for so long," she said. "It is like having your shoulder to a wheel and then suddenly the cart draws free, and you stumble into thin air." She went to the window, throwing the shutters wide on the gray October afternoon. "My son is a king," she said. "At last, he will wear the crown that was stolen when he was two years old."

Alienor struggled to absorb the immensity of the news. Once more she would be a queen. When she married Henry they had talked of empires on their wedding night, but his coming into his birthright meant that now it was real.

Alienor accompanied the Empress to give thanks to God in the cathedral at Rouen. Gleaming on the altar was the imperial crown that Matilda had brought from Germany almost thirty years ago — a heavy object of burnished gold set with a mosaic of gemstones of differing colors and dimensions, from emeralds no bigger than a baby's fingernail to a sapphire the size of a small clenched fist.

"I would have worn this at my own coronation," Matilda said, "but now it belongs to my son, and to William in due course."

Such was the aura of weight and power emanating from the crown that Alienor shivered. It would take a strong man to wear this, and a stronger woman to stand at his side.

As the women left the cathedral, the bells began to peal and were answered by all the churches across Rouen until the sky rang with joyous clamor.

53

Barfleur, December 7, 1154

Standing in a fisherman's shelter on the harborside Alienor drew her fur-lined cloak closely around her body and stared out across a sea the color of a dull hauberk. There was sleet in the wind and the waves were brisk, crested with white foam. Henry's small fleet rocked at anchor amid a steady traffic of barrels and boxes, chests and sacks that were being borne from hand to hand up the gangplanks and stored on board the vessels. One ship longer than the others, an *esnecca* with sixty oars, flew a red-and-gold banner from her mast. Servants were putting the final touches to a pavilion to provide shelter on the crossing. She watched Henry bustling about on deck, checking this, poking into that, making sure that all was to his satisfaction.

They had been stranded in Barfleur for six weeks while the wind blew in the wrong direction and winter storms made the crossing more of a risk than leaving England to its own devices. Now the wind had changed and the seas, while still vigorous, had settled enough to embark. To catch the tide, they needed to be gone within the hour.

A flurry on the quayside announced the arrival of the Empress. She was dressed in full regal splendor as if for the highest court occasion, and the effect was both magnificent and incongruous against the wide seashore and battering weather. The wind flapped her veil and blew her jewel-encrusted gown against her spare, upright body.

"Madam." Alienor curtsied to her.

The Empress inclined her head. "So," she said. "It is finally time." Her jaw was rigid with tension.

Alienor nodded but said nothing. In the weeks that they had been waiting for the weather to turn, Matilda had made it clear she would never set foot in England again. It was a place too full of hard and bitter experience. "You have no memories of England," she had said to Alienor. "It is your turn to go and make them — and may they all be good ones." She had not smiled. "The people want a new young king and his fecund wife. They want summer out of winter. I am wise enough to know that, and to send the new green shoots into England with my blessing but without my presence."

Henry returned from the ship, dusting his

hands. The wind blustered through his cop-
pery curls and his eyes were narrowed against
the sleety wind, showing the creases where
one day lines of age would develop. The
energy emanating from him was as vigorous
and exuberant as the sea. This was his moment and he was seizing it with every fiber of
his being.

"Are you ready?" he asked Alienor. "The
tide will not wait much longer."

"Yes," she said and raised her chin. "I am."

Henry turned to the Empress. "My lady
mother." Kneeling to her, he bowed his head.

She set her hand to his ruffled curls in a
tender gesture of benediction and stooped to
kiss him on both cheeks before raising him
up. "Go with my blessing," she said, "and
return to me an anointed king."

Alienor knelt too and received the same.
"God be with you and the child in your
womb," Matilda said, and her kiss was maternal and warm.

Henry and Alienor joined the *esnecca,*
Henry going first and handing Alienor down
into the ship from the gangplank. The fresh
smell of the sea was powerful in her nose and
the slap of the tide rocked the ship, making it
difficult to balance. The horizon was a misty
haze.

On the shore, standing at the Empress's
side, Hugh de Boves, Archbishop of Rouen,
raised his hands to bless the ship and the

endeavor of its passengers, and the last mooring rope was cast off. The rowers took up the oars, wind surged into the sail, and the gap between land and sea widened to a yard of choppy gray water, then ten yards, then a hundred.

Alienor let out a long, cloudy breath as the coast of Normandy grew smaller and the figure of the Empress became a small dark finger on the shore.

Henry drew her against him. "Are you well?" He stroked the curve of her belly, now six months round.

"Yes." She smiled to dispel the anxiety in his gaze. "I am not afraid of sea crossings."

"But something is troubling you?"

She drew back to look up at him. "When you set foot on England's shore it will be as her rightful king. It is your destiny. You know the land, you know the people; you have lived there and fought for your birthright. England only belongs to me because it belongs to you and I have yet to make it mine in my heart." She looked around. They had cleared the harbor and there was nothing in sight now but rough gray water. "But I am going into the unknown, and I do it out of the faith I have in you, and for our children, both the born and the unborn."

He gazed at her, his eyes matching the wintry hue of the sea. She could feel the energy vibrating through him almost like the waves surging at the prow of the ship. "I will not break that faith," he said. "I swear to you. What is unknown is not yet written, and it is our chance to write as we choose — God willing."

He kissed her and Alienor tasted cold salt on his lips and felt the firm grip of his hands either side of her womb. He was right. The unknown was unwritten, and together they faced the greatest opportunity of their lives.

AUTHOR'S NOTE

Alienor (Eleanor) of Aquitaine is one of the most famous queens in Western history and the subject of numerous biographies, plays, and historical novels. More than eight hundred years after her death, she still exerts a magnetic fascination that continues to draw in each new generation. It could be said that she is one of the longest established examples of the cult of celebrity!

I have wanted to add my own Alienor novel to the oeuvre for some time, because although she has been the subject of a wide variety of works before, I feel a great deal has lain undiscovered or unsaid.

Alienor's story has been constantly reinvented to suit each generation and I find the different versions fascinating. I was particularly interested in an article by historian Rá-Gena C. DeAragon titled "Do We Know What We Think We Know? Making Assumptions about Eleanor of Aquitaine." The piece is widely available online for anyone who wishes to look it up. The basic premise is that for all that has been written, we actually know very little and assume an awful lot about Alienor — and that includes the historians.

While writing *The Summer Queen,* I was constantly told that Alienor was a "woman ahead of her time." But my own take is that she was a woman of her time doing her best within the boundaries of what society would permit. Any attempt to go outside those boundaries was immediately and sometimes brutally quashed, but she was nothing if not resilient.

I have called her Alienor in the body of the novel and not Eleanor because Alienor is what she would have called herself and it is how her name appears in her charters and in the Anglo-Norman texts when she is mentioned. I felt it was fitting to give her that recognition.

Alienor's birth date in the past has been given as 1122, but historians now accept the more likely date of 1124 and that her marriage to Louis VII took place when she was thirteen — the age of consent for a girl then being twelve years old. I suspect her father knew he was not going to return from Compostela and arranged a secure future for his daughter (so he thought!) and Aquitaine before he left on his pilgrimage. Alienor is sometimes seen as a political player at this stage in the game, but when one looks at the hard facts, it becomes very clear that the power lay in the hands of the high barons and clergy of France and Aquitaine, and they were the ones brokering the deals.

We know Alienor's father was on battle campaign with Geoffrey of Anjou the year before he died and I wonder (this is pure speculation) if he broached the subject of a betrothal between Alienor and his infant son Henry at that point. We do know from the historical record that the Counts of Anjou had long sought to unite their lands with those of Aquitaine. Geoffrey, keen to continue that pursuit, hoped to betroth little Henry to Alienor's daughter Marie, and that match was considered for a while, before finally being turned down on the grounds of consanguinity (the all-purpose twelfth-century get-out clause should it need to be invoked). Geoffrey was still pursuing a link with Aquitaine though. I strongly believe that as the head of the family, the initial driving force behind the marriage arrangements that took place between Alienor and his then eighteen-year-old son Henry in Paris in 1151 were of his design. That Geoffrey did not live to see the marriage is a pity. It would have been interesting to observe the family dynamic.

I work hard at the historical research and do my best not to defame the dead, and I try to portray my characters within the realms of historical likelihood and to stay true to their characters, inasmuch as we know them from primary sources. However, this is a work of historical fiction and, within the parameters of integrity I set for myself, I have had the leeway to explore paths where historians might not choose to tread.

One of the great speculations of Alienor's life is whether she committed adultery and incest with her uncle Raymond during her stay at Antioch during the Second Crusade. Several chroniclers accused her of improper behavior while on the journey and there are dark hints about certain goings-on in Antioch, but when one reads the texts, none go so far as to accuse her of having sexual intercourse with her uncle. Some biographers have taken the bit between their teeth and decided Alienor probably did have an affair with Raymond anyway, but to me the evidence fails to stack up. Alienor and Raymond were both astute players who had been through the political mill. They were together for around nine days, and while I am certain that plotting and maneuvering went on, I can't see either of them kicking over the traces and going mad with lust for each other in that short space of time, especially as Raymond was known to be a devoted and faithful husband. It doesn't ring true.

I do suspect — but cannot prove through conventional research — that Alienor had a long-term affair with her vassal Geoffrey de

Rancon. Finding Geoffrey at all in the historical record is difficult. There are numerous different and contradictory genealogies, not to say some far-fetched longevity in some of Alienor's biographies that have the same Geoffrey around in the reign of Richard the Lionheart, when, given his earlier career, he would have been pushing a hundred! The Geoffrey de Rancon mentioned in Richard's reign was obviously a son or grandson of the man known to Alienor.

Walter Map, one of the less reliable chroniclers with a tabloid journalist mentality, suggested that Alienor had an affair with Geoffrey of Anjou when he was seneschal of Poitou. Whether Geoffrey ever held this title is dubious, and whether he would have found the time, place, and suicidal bravado to romp with his overlord's wife is also open to doubt. I had an epiphanic moment while researching when I came across Sidney Painter's article "Castellans of the Plains of Poitou in the Eleventh and Twelfth Centuries" published in *Speculum* in 1956, where he discusses the career of various de Rancons in their position as important ducal castellans. I have a suspicion that this is the smoke that started the chroniclers' fires and they attached the scandal to the wrong Geoffrey. I also suspect that Alienor's closeness to Geoffrey de Rancon was the cause of some of the scandal hinted at in Antioch. It certainly makes far more sense to me than Alienor and her uncle leaping into bed together at the drop of a hat. De Rancon up until that point had been a mainstay of the crusading army, but at Antioch was sent back home. Historians debate whether this is because he was in disgrace having nearly gotten the King killed during the crossing of Mount Cadmos (now called Mount Honaz in northern Turkey), or whether he had completed his stint and was needed back in Aquitaine. Perhaps there was another reason. It's a point still open to conjecture — as is Alienor's relationship with her uncle. My own take on the proceedings based on all aspects of my research and filtered through reasoning and imagination is that Alienor and Geoffrey de Rancon conducted a clandestine affair that has escaped the history books but might just be seen as a flicker in the shadows in the comments of certain chroniclers. Alienor and her uncle may have spent a lot of time together, but my belief is that they were formulating policy and even plotting against Louis rather than enjoying each other's bodies. Certainly Alienor asked for an annulment and Louis was worried enough to leave Antioch at night, abducting his wife by force when she refused to leave of her own accord.

Alienor's sister Petronella proved a conundrum. In the records she is sometimes referred to as Aelith and sometimes Petronella.

I have used the latter as it is a name of southern France and perhaps linked to the cathedral of Saint-Pierre in Bordeaux. Petronella did indeed marry a man decades older than herself, and it appeared at the outset to be a love match. Chronicler John of Salisbury tells us she died circa 1151, but then she just may appear in a later pipe roll of Henry II in connection with Alienor. I have steered a middle course in the novel to explain her exit from the stage. I suspect that she may have had a lot in common with her maternal grandmother, the notorious "Dangerosa" or "Dangereuse." The latter was a nickname, and one has to wonder how she came by it!

Readers will not find Henry's mistress Aelburgh in the historical record under that name. However, he did have a mistress called "Hikenai" of whom the chroniclers were disparaging and who was the likely mother of his son Geoffrey. I take it that Hikenai was probably a garbling of "Hackney," the term for a common riding horse and derogatory, so I gave her the name that turned up in my Akashic Records research.

In *The Summer Queen,* I have given Alienor dark blond hair and blue eyes. This is based on my alternative research method of the Akashic Records, which I use to fill in the blanks and explore what happened in the past from a psychic perspective. You can find out more about them on my website. Using conventional resources, it is a fact that we don't know what Alienor looked like. One modern historian tells us she had black hair, an olive complexion, and a curvaceous figure that didn't run to fat in old age! However, there is not a shred of evidence to prove this and is, I suspect, modern male wish fulfillment! Another historian gives her "sparkling black eyes." Again, it's pure fabrication. There has been the suggestion that a mural at Chinon depicts a crowned, auburn-haired Alienor riding a horse, but this is now thought to be unlikely; it probably depicts Henry's children, including the Young King as the crowned figure. However, we do know Alienor had blond hair in her ancestry as one of the Dukes of Aquitaine was called William the Towhead, suggesting his hair was the color of straw.

It has been quite a journey researching Alienor's young womanhood from 1137 to 1154 and bringing her story to life. By turns I have been fascinated, frustrated, enlightened, and uplifted. I have come to admire Alienor's grit, dignity, and endurance in often distressing and trying times. Also her wit, intelligence, and determination. On occasions I have been very angry on her behalf for what was done to her, and for all the lies and damned lies told about her down the centuries. However, drawing Alienor out from the shadows has been ultimately one of the most rewarding experiences of my writing career.

She was a woman of her time, but what a woman.

I am so looking forward to continuing the story of her marriage to Henry II and her life as Queen of England in *The Winter Crown* and *The Autumn Throne*.

SELECT BIBLIOGRAPHY

In my opinion the most useful biographies are Ralph V. Turner's and Jean Flori's, and the Wheeler and Parsons series of articles provide an excellent summary of aspects of Alienor's life.

Panofsky-Soergel, Gerda. *Abbot Suger on the Abbey Church of St. Denis and Its Art Treasures,* second edition. Edited, translated, and annotated by Erwin Panofsky. Princeton, NJ: Princeton University Press, 1979.

Baldwin, John. *Paris, 1200.* Redwood City, CA: Stanford University Press, 2010.

Boyd, Douglas. *Eleanor: April Queen of Aquitaine.* Stroud, Gloucestershire, UK: Sutton Publishing Ltd, 2005.

Eleanor of Aquitaine: Lord and Lady. Edited by Bonnie Wheeler and John C. Parsons. Hampshire, UK: Palgrave Macmillan, 2002.

Flori, Jean. *Eleanor of Aquitaine: Queen and Rebel.* Edinburgh, Midlothian, UK: Edinburgh University Press, 2008.

Gobry, Ivan. *Histoire des Rois de France: Louis VII, pere de Philippe II August, 1137–1180* [in French]. Paris: Pygmalion, 2002.

Grant, Lindy, and David Bates. *Abbot Suger of St-Denis: Church and State in Early Twelfth-Century France.* New York: Routledge, 1998.

John of Salisbury's Memoirs of the Papal Court [Historia Pontificalis]. Translated by Marjorie Chibnall. Nashville: Thomas Nelson & Sons, 1956.

Kelly, Amy. *Eleanor of Aquitaine and the Four Kings.* Cambridge, MA: Harvard University Press, 1991.

King, Alison. Akashic Records Consultant.

Meade, Marion. *Eleanor of Aquitaine: A Biography.* London: Frederick Muller Ltd, 1978.

Odo of Deuil. *De Profectione Ludovici VII in Orientem — The Journey of Louis VII to the East.* Edited and translated by Virginia Gingerick Berry. New York: Columbia University Press, 1948.

Owen, D. D. R. *Eleanor of Aquitaine: Queen and Legend.* Oxford: Blackwell Publishers Ltd, 1993.

Painter, Sidney. "Castellans of the Plains of Poitou in the Eleventh and Twelfth Centuries." *Speculum* 31, no 2 (1956).

Pernoud, Regine. *Eleanor of Aquitaine.* New York: Collins, 1967.

Sassier, Yves. *Louis VII.* Paris: Fayard, 1991.

Seward, Desmond. *Eleanor of Aquitaine: The Mother Queen.* Newton Abbot, UK: David & Charles Publishers, 1978.

Turner, Ralph V. *Eleanor of Aquitaine: Queen of France, Queen of England.* New Haven, CT: Yale University Press, 2009.

Weir, Alison. *Eleanor of Aquitaine: By the Wrath of God, Queen of England.* London: Pimlico, 2000.

The World of Eleanor of Aquitaine: Literature and Society in Southern France between the Eleventh and Thirteenth Centuries. Edited by Marcus Bull and Catherine Léglu. Suffolk, UK: Boydell Press, 2005.

ACKNOWLEDGMENTS

I would like to thank the lovely people who have been involved in the process of bringing *The Summer Queen* from first idea to finished novel. Obviously the writing and crafting is mostly my input, but no author is ever an island and so many have helped me along the way.

I would like to thank the team at Little, Brown UK, especially my editor, Rebecca Saunders, who is always there for me and braced for my "enthusiasms." Also my copy editors, Richenda Todd and Hannah Green; their eagle eyes and advice have been so helpful. Any errors that remain are mine. Thank you also to the team at Sourcebooks: Shana Drehs, my editor, and Heather Hall, whose painstaking work is much appreciated.

My agent Carole Blake and everyone at Blake Friedmann are without compare. I have the best agent in the world — it's official.

I owe a big thank-you to Thea Vincent at Phoenix Web Designs for putting together my marvelous website, which is a constant work in progress.

My thanks to the regular bunch of readers and writers at Facebook and Twitter for daily discussions on all things historical, medieval, and especially the Marshal family! I can't name you all individually but you know who you are.

Another thank-you goes to my dear writer friend Sharon Kay Penman, who is an example to every author of historical fiction.

I couldn't have written *The Summer Queen* without the insight and rare talent of my very good friend and colleague Alison King.

And last but never least, a special thank-you to my husband Roger who has a knighthood for services rendered, with a special mention for a constant replenishment of my tea mug and cookie plate!

The employees of Thorndike Press hope you have enjoyed this Large Print book. All our Thorndike, Wheeler, and Kennebec Large Print titles are designed for easy reading, and all our books are made to last. Other Thorndike Press Large Print books are available at your library, through selected bookstores, or directly from us.

For information about titles, please call:
(800) 223-1244

or visit our Web site at:
http://gale.cengage.com/thorndike

To share your comments, please write:
Publisher
Thorndike Press
10 Water St., Suite 310
Waterville, ME 04901